The Girls Who Broke The World

Andrew S. French

Neonoir Books

Chapter 1

Stoker: The Farm

Before he'd been awake an hour, Charles knew his father would hurt him.

'Get up, boy; today you become a man.'

There was a low grumble in Jack Stoker's voice, rising on the last word to mock his only child. Charles was under the bedcovers, dreaming of magical lands and unicorns, when his father bellowed at him from the kitchen.

His daily routine of suffering had begun.

He slipped away from his protection, stumbling into the cracked sink next to the stack of wood masquerading as his bed. He glanced towards his only friends slumped in the corner, those toy animals stolen from school, which were as dirty and dishevelled as he was. They wouldn't save him today.

No one could save Charles.

The water on his face froze his skin with an icy caress. He tried not to look at his body in the mirror, closing his pale blue eyes to the scars crisscrossing his fragile frame. In the dark and arctic temperature, he ran his fingers through his wounds, a reminder of his father's cold embrace. He touched his cheeks and nose, smelling dirt and blood under his fingernails.

'Don't make me beat more sense into you, boy.' The usual spiteful viciousness dripped from every word of the old man's crooked mouth. Charles stared into the mirror and hoped he wouldn't end up looking like his father, with those tortured eyes and cheeks too big for his face.

'I want to look like you, mother,' he said as he placed his fingers on the glass and wondered if the dead observed the living. Tiny, delicate breaths drifted from his brittle lungs and settled over his reflection. He closed his eyes and his mind in readiness for the day. Charles stuck the whole of his head into the sink, submerging his face into oblivion, the liquid swimming over his face. He imagined his mother's voice trying to calm his beating heart, but such a thing was impossible: she was dead, and it was his fault.

The water crawled up his nose, sticky wetness which irritated him and made breathing difficult. His instinct was to thrust his head up, but part of him wanted to stay there forever, to leave his life and join her. Only he didn't believe in another world beyond this one, no matter how often his father tried to beat his beliefs into his son.

The icy water warmed his heart when a hand grabbed him by the neck, pulled him upwards, and threw him against the wall. He hit it hard, grimacing as he slid to the floor and curled into a ball. He squeezed his body as small as possible, waiting for the next blow.

'No time for slacking, boy. We've got work to do.'

His father seized him by the shoulder, his thick fingers digging into his son's bones and creating new bruises. It was a familiar pain to Charles.

'Breakfast?' he asked through trembling lips.

'Get dressed and downstairs before I throw you into the shit pen with the pigs.'

Jack Stoker glared at his son before opening the bedroom window and allowing the fragrance of the countryside to rush into the room. As winter approached, manure covered most of the Stoker farm, piled up on carts, ready to be transported throughout the country, a sea of shit to bring growth across the land and money into Jack Stoker's impoverished life.

Charles scrambled into his dirty clothes as his father stomped down the stairs, ignoring the stink wafting off them and dreaming about a mother he never met. He tied a piece of string around his waist to keep the trousers from dropping off his skinny frame, his father's hatred echoing inside his head.

'You killed her,' were the first words Charles remembered understanding. 'You murdered her, so you must pay for your sins.'

His father took the strap to him daily to cleanse his son of things Charles knew nothing about. He recognised the look in the old man's eyes as he fell into the living room, hitting the corner of the table with his shoulder, electric pain shooting through his body. He rested there for a second, wanting relief but finding none as his father sharpened the giant axe in his hand. Every neuron in his brain screamed at him to get up and run. He crept to his feet, favouring his throbbing leg as soreness shot through his knee and staggered back towards the door. His father's cruel whistle assaulted his ears as he stumbled outside.

The early morning sun was struggling to climb over the horizon, battered by the torrent of rain engulfing it. A large bundle of wetness slapped Charles across the face, the embrace of the elements shaking his body. He liked this weather, its constant misery matching his own. If it was okay for nature to shed so many tears, then it was no shame for him to do the same.

His father's heavy boots splashed through the puddles behind him, kicking dirt and shit onto the back of the boy's legs. Gorilla-type hands grabbed his tattered shirt and pulled him off the ground so he hung in the air inches away from the puddles.

'You've made God cry, boy; you and your many sins.' His father dragged him across the mud to the barn he wasn't allowed inside. 'Everything was fine until you came along. Then God punished us.' His mother was dead, the farm was struggling, and he believed his father was evil, but Charles still didn't believe in God. For what God could be so cruel?

His feet sloshed through the mud as they strode past the pigs in the sty. He loved to play with the little pigs when his father wasn't around. Along with the dogs, they were his favourite animals on the farm. The hens made too much noise, and the cattle scared him.

'You're in for a treat today, boy.'

Charles shivered, the cold matching the rainwater oozing across his back. His father unlocked the barn door and shoved him inside. The first thing to hit him was the stink of rotting flesh, the unmistakable stench of death.

'What's this place?' His words were drowned out by the sounds of the cattle and his father's laughter.

'It's our bank, boy; it keeps us alive.'

His father took Charles to the far end of the slaughter-house. All the animals were squashed together in the shadows. The old man's hand was on his back, caressing the fresh welts, before pushing him onto his knees and his face towards the mud, so he stared at the feet of the cattle.

Do you call them feet or hooves? I can't remember.

He swept the water from his eyes. Down on the ground, Charles heard it, the other voices in the charnel house. At first, he thought some neighbours were also there, but that made little sense. The closest farm to them was three miles away, and they hated Jack Stoker as much as his son did.

'Let us out,' he heard. It was a slow, individual murmur, building into a roar. As Charles pulled his nose from the dirt, he understood who was speaking, what was talking: it was the cattle.

'We don't want to die!' they shouted.

He couldn't believe his ears and glanced around in a frenzy to see if somebody was playing tricks on him. Sometimes, the kids at school would mock him about his poor clothes, throw him down and call him the "Mother Killer." Maybe they were all working together with his father to further torment him.

Charles rested his head against the dirt, an aroma of shit and rotting meat creeping up his shivering body before crawling into his nose and between his lips. Tears hugged his eyes as yesterday's mouldy bread and cheese shot out of his mouth. He dragged his trembling fingers across his cold lips, wiping his cheeks and scanning the whole building in search of anybody else.

But nobody was there besides him and his father. And those talking cows. Only now, they were screaming as the old man walked towards them, swinging the big axe around in the air as if he were swatting flies. The grin on his father's face was the same one he had when dishing out his parental beatings.

'We don't want to die,' they howled in unison as Charles

buried his head in the mud and thrust his fingers into his ears, thinking he'd gone mad.

'Pick yourself up, boy, or I'll use this on you,' his father said.

The scars on his chest and back throbbed into life, burning new pain in his mind. He tried to shut out the screaming he shouldn't be hearing, lifting himself from the sanctuary of the ground. There was no choice but to stare at what was coming next. Closing his eyes would only aggravate his father's fury even more.

He forced himself to watch the old man's barbarity reach its full horrific rage as he turned the barn red. The blood streamed into Charles' eyes and swam through his veins, matched by flesh and liquid scattered all over the walls and the ground. It was like one of those sprinklers they used on the dry earth that consumed their land yearly, spraying the ruby liquid over his father's manic face and splashing Charles. The place stank of blood and death. His hair was matted with the stuff as he stumbled outside.

'Get yourself cleaned up, boy; you've work to do.'

The old man wiped his muscular arm across his cheek, but not hard enough to remove the cruel grin etched into his flesh. Charles pulled the last of his strength from deep inside him, waiting until his father returned to the house before staggering into the pigsty fence and spilling his guts again. The pain in his stomach cut like a knife into every one of his internal organs. His eyes were pinned to the dirt when the pigs spoke to him.

'You should let us out, Charles, or we'll be next in the slaughterhouse.'

'Is this a nightmare?' he said to the sky. A few bigger pigs walked over to the fence and stared at him through the gaps.

'You can understand us, Charles? It's a sign you should set us free.'

He wiped the drool and vomit from his mouth, looking straight into the eyes of the largest pig. 'A sign from who?'

The pigs looked at each other. 'It's a sign from your God. He's given you the gift of understanding so you can set us free; set all the animals free.'

Charles stood straight and tall, the rain falling and washing away his tears and shame. It continued to drop like it intended to rinse him clean, melting into the earth like the rainbow colours of paint he splashed onto the paper in his art class at school. The same paint the other kids poured into his hair and dabbed into his eyes while the teachers did nothing.

Is it God's tears telling me to give these animals their freedom?

'Let us go, Charles; you know it's the right thing to do,' the largest pig said.

'Let us go, Charles,' they all chanted together.

'Let us go.'

'Let us go.'

The pig's chanting mixed with the noise of the rain swimming inside his ears as he strode towards the front gate, reaching down for the lock which separated them all from freedom. He used one hand to wipe the wetness from his eyes before placing the other on the latch.

'What's all this racket?' his father shouted as he swung his clenched fist into the side of his son's head, the boy hitting the ground again. As his nose met the hard surface, breaking the bone in two pieces and creating a scar he'd carry for the rest of his life, the pigs stopped their chanting, and all he heard was their sorrow washing over him.

'All is lost,' they said. 'All is lost.'

'A nice bit of bacon for tea tonight, boy; what do you think?'

It would be the last time Charles Arthur Stoker would let any animal flesh pass between his lips. Twenty years later, he met the most magnificent creature he'd ever seen. His father was long gone, but now there was something else for him to look up to.

Chapter 2

Emma: The Con

The bruise on Emma's cheek had turned a vibrant shade of purple.

Shit! Shit! Shit!

'You have an appointment in one hour with Fiery Dragon Publishing.'

'Yes, Alexa. Thank you.'

Emma searched the bathroom cabinet, hoping Jane might have left some makeup when she stayed last week. But it was a fruitless quest, and she cursed her sister while peering into the mirror, avoiding the bruise and scrutinising the other marks on her face.

'How does an eighteen-year-old get so many shadows under her eyes?'

She knew the answer but was unwilling to confess it to herself – numerous late nights, neglecting the right food, and consuming alcohol when she shouldn't.

'Alexa, do I have any notifications?'

'You have one new message from Jamie. Shall I read it to you?'

'Yes, please.' She was more polite to machines than people, which amused her sister.

'I'll meet you in the usual spot in the centre,' Alexa said without sounding like Emma's boss at the comic shop. 'Don't forget your portfolio.'

As if she could. She'd worked hard for two years for this opportunity and wouldn't blow it now. The bruise acquired at the morning Fight Club session couldn't dissuade her.

Maybe it hadn't been such a good idea to go for her daily workout when she had such an important meeting only a few hours later. Apart from her art, her weekend work at the vets was Emma's favourite thing in the world, but her sessions at the Fight Club always put her in a happy mood. The exercise made her feel better about herself despite the sporadic bruises, and it was the perfect way to let off steam. Her body ached, and there was still the smell of sweat in her nostrils and the taste of blood at the back of her throat, but she felt great.

And it was the most exciting thing she did in her life.

Monday to Friday, with the occasional Saturday, was working in the comic shop. She loved it most of the time, and Jamie was a decent boss, even though he was only a few years older than her, but sometimes the customers got right up her nose. Most were okay, but there was always one who thought because she was a "girl" she couldn't know anything about comics, movies, science fiction, or whatever blokes believed was their natural domain.

She still remembered yesterday's argument with the guy wearing the Winnie the Pooh t-shirt where the little bear had an *Alien* facehugger attached to its head. The customer smirked at Emma, with a face that launched a thousand shits and an intellect to match.

He pointed at her Yoda t-shirt. 'Why are robots such

crap sharpshooters only apparently able to fire single rounds? I get the same ick when I watch anything *Star Wars* - you can build a craft capable of interstellar travel, but you can't build an AI-aiming laser gun. Then I'm all about the plot holes - mightily did I laugh when I first clapped eyes on AT-AT walkers - has there ever been a more stupid armament design? Might as well strap a machine gun onto a giraffe.'

'Are you buying that copy of *Power Girl?*' she asked him.

His cheeks bulged as he stared at the cover. 'Of course. I have every issue she's ever appeared in.'

Emma grabbed the book and scanned the bar code. 'I always thought she got dressed in the dark.'

He took the comic from her as if it was an important Egyptian artefact. 'What do you mean?'

'Well,' she said, 'her costume looks like it had a fight in a boob shop and she lost.'

His grin unnerved her. 'Nah, it's great. Everybody likes it.' He laughed at his mates giggling near the cardboard cut-out of Batman. 'Maybe you should cosplay her at the Comic Con this weekend. You'll need to dye that white hair, though. You look like a Targaryen from *Game of Thrones.*'

Emma was about to punch him when Jamie appeared, slapping the bloke on the back.

The customer is always wrong.

She shook the memory from her head and gazed at her reflection again. Her mouth was so dry she could light a match on it, and the rumbling in her stomach sounded like the train company building a line from her brain to her gut.

Emma rubbed her belly, knowing she was too nervous to eat anything. Perhaps there was time to fashion a costume for the meeting – it was at a comic convention, and hundreds of people would be there dressed up in cosplay.

No, there wasn't enough time. And she didn't have what she needed for her Harley Quinn outfit, anyway. Well, she had the baseball bat – that always came in handy in her neighbourhood.

Emma grabbed her portfolio and rushed out of the flat, ensuring she'd left food for the cat before leaving. She hadn't seen the ginger moggie in a few days but wasn't worried, knowing he could look after himself. He'd wandered into her kitchen two months before with blood dripping off his ears and a pocket watch tied around his neck.

'What the...?' she said as she approached him, expecting the cat to scoot off or bare its claws at her. But it didn't, letting her patch up the wound and peer at the back of the watch, assuming the owner's name to be on it, yet it wasn't.

'Meow,' the cat said as she stroked that ginger fur.

Now, it would come and go as it pleased, which was okay with her because she hated the idea of having pets and people "owning" animals. She called it Cat and left the watch around its neck as she always found it amusing, and it didn't appear to impact the moggie's movement.

Emma double-checked that the bedroom window was open for him to enter, then ran for the bus. She caught it just before it departed the stop, staggering to the back and having to stand since there were no empty seats. The stench was overpowering, a pungent mix of body odour, stale cigarette smoke, and the sickly sweet aroma of cheap air freshener. Emma's nose wrinkled in disgust as she grasped the handrail, her palms slick with grime. The bus juddered along the pot-holed streets, and she swayed unsteadily, bumping into the other passengers crammed around her like cattle.

She glanced at her fellow travellers, an unsavoury bunch resembling extras from a zombie movie - bloodshot eyes, pallid skin, rotting teeth. The man beside her was wheezing like a broken accordion, foul breath blowing in her face each time he exhaled. She spied an insect crawling through the greasy hair of a girl clinging to a pole. Lovely.

The roar of the engine vibrated through Emma and made her teeth chatter. The windows were opaque with filth, filtering the morning light into a dreary gloom. Somewhere nearby, a baby wailed, its cries mingling with the squeals of brakes and the driver's creative cursing whenever traffic slowed their progress.

Over the toxic funk of the bus, Emma detected whiffs of onions and curry from a takeaway box perched on someone's lap. Her empty stomach clenched in longing, but she gritted her teeth and ignored it. No time for food now. She had to get her portfolio to the publisher if she wanted her big break as a comic artist.

Feeling a tickle on her neck, Emma slapped at it, her fingers crushing a plump fly. She hated hurting any living thing but shuddered in revulsion, skin crawling with imaginary insects. Only two more stops until her destination. She could make it.

The bus finally wheezed to a stop, and she rushed through the crowd, emerging into the crisp autumn air with relief. The trials of public transport were worth it. Her dreams were close if she could just ace the meeting. Chin up, portfolio clutched tight, she strode towards the convention centre, nerves and excitement warring within.

Emma stepped into the pulsing chaos of the Comic Con, instantly assaulted by a haze of stale sweat, cloying perfumes, and the tang of desperation. Cosplayers swarmed around her, a human rainbow of spandex, foam rubber, and fraying hobby store wigs. She spotted no less than three iterations of Harley Quinn posing provocatively, pale beer guts peeking between cropped tops and low-slung shorts. A paunchy Batman stood behind a crop-top Catwoman, pawing at her tail as she batted her spidery false lashes and chewed gum.

Jamie emerged from the crowd, his Joker makeup smudged and running from the heat. 'Holy skin-tight onesies, Batman, it's a body odour crisis!' he exclaimed, waving a gloved hand before his nose. 'Have these guys never heard of soap and water? I'm choking on Eau de Desperate Geek.'

Emma smiled, anxiety churning in her empty stomach. 'No kidding. I need a gas mask just walking through these hormones and regret stew.'

Jamie laughed and threw an arm around her shoulders. 'Don't worry, Emma, you'll knock them dead. Your stuff is incredible. Everybody in the shop loves your art. You know that, right?'

She nodded, trying to silence her inner doubts. She smoothed her simple top and trousers, hoping to look professional. Her portfolio felt slippery in her sweat-damp hands. This had to work. It was her only shot to escape her dead-end life and do what she loved.

Her phone vibrated with a message, and she checked it. It was from Jane.

Don't miss your meeting. I hope it goes well. I told Mum all about it, but she's in one of her more confused states. Can you visit when you're finished?

Emma didn't think her heart could beat faster, but the news that her mother's dementia was worsening created invisible fingers clawing at every internal organ. She replied immediately to her sister.

Should I come over now? I can always get another appointment later.

She waited for the reply. In the spandex and foam rubber sea, Emma spotted a trio of Avengers looking like they'd escaped from the clearance bin at a party supply store. A scrawny Captain America waved a plastic shield attached to his forearm with dusty tape. His star-spangled onesie was two sizes too big and sagging at the crotch. Nearby, a pot-bellied Thor tried vainly to pull his too-tight leotard over his hairy gut bulge. He swung his hammer dangerously, oblivious to the Black Widow he nearly decapitated. The Widow looked no better, scarlet yarn wig askew over a blotchy face caked in bargain bin makeup.

Her phone pinged again.

Don't you dare! You've waited a long time for this. Come see us after. Mum will be fine.

Emma took a deep breath and put the mobile away. The booth for Fiery Dragon Publishing was nearby. The meeting should only be a formality as they'd assessed the samples she'd sent them electronically, and she'd scanned the contract they emailed her.

'How are you feeling?' Jamie asked her.

She gripped the portfolio. 'It's now or never.'

He nodded. 'Remember me when you're rich and famous.'

Emma laughed, her attention caught by the cosplayers dressed as police officers approaching them.

She thought something might be wrong only when they started shouting her name.

Chapter 3

Crowley: The AA

C rowley, the cat, scampered across the rooftops, his legs stiff from too much sleep, annoyed at himself for being late. The evening drew in, its dark embrace sending chills through his fur. The weather was about to turn, a massive fragrance of oppression ready to drop at any second. He dodged the obstacles littering the way, discarded cigarette packets and empty beer bottles the rat packs had scattered everywhere after another boozy session on the tiles. Spots of rain filtered down onto his untidy ginger-flecked hair, making him regret forgetting his umbrella. The watch hanging around his neck, acquired from the back room of a bankrupt toy shop last year, told him he was five minutes late, motivating him to pick up speed as his destination appeared on the horizon.

The creatures of the night were creating sweet music. The Mice Musical Combo and Choir, decked out in pink fluorescent rodent zoot suits, serenaded the audience with their version of "Shoplifters of the World Unite" as the entrance of the building loomed up ahead. As he reached the entrance, Crowley leapt from the high wall, landing to tumble across the courtyard and towards the startled group of guards. The impact of the concrete sent shockwaves through his toes and chest, causing his heart to beat even faster. His body, speeding on the wet ground, knocked down the security snakes at the door and sent a couple of pompous ducks scrambling for safety, their squawking hurting his sensitive ears.

When he came to a stop, the hostile audience cast their eyes at him in a fury. He thought, not for the first time, what a crime it had been to pass a law that members of Anthropomorphic Anonymous couldn't eat each other.

Crowley gazed around his surroundings, ready for a long night, the adrenaline vanishing from his veins as his heart returned to normal. He didn't recognise any of the animals. There were two mean feral cats, a nervous guinea pig, a pigeon that appeared high, and a hyperactive Chihuahua who struggled to keep her energy under control. A group of magpies peered at him with suspicion-laden eyes.

'Put Crowley in the corner with the other latecomers.' The Master of Ceremonies, a gruff-looking bullfrog, shouted the orders to the startled security snakes. They righted themselves up, fangs bared, with alcohol-drenched expressions devouring Crowley as he entered, ushering him into the shadows.

Crowley winked at them. 'Have you been slithering into the wine vats again, boys?'

Their aroma was as ripe as a school of fish who had missed their lessons on personal hygiene. He made a show of putting a paw on his nose. Two guards stepped away from the door and hissed at him, forked tongues flickering like whips searching for flesh to burn. One of them poked him with a dessert fork until he was pushed up against a damp wall with the others who'd turned up late.

'Ouch!' The tiny metal cut into his skin.

'Do we have to be here?' The guinea pig's voice was so quiet it was difficult to hear. The poor animal's nervousness was because somebody had placed a 'Go Back Home' sticker on its backside, and he couldn't get rid of it. There were a couple of water voles opposite, snorting and pointing, and Crowley hoped they'd miss the last cart back to the river.

'AA meetings are compulsory.' He slyly removed the sticker from the guinea pig's back, crushed it into a small circular shape, and flicked it towards the water vole with his large eyes and an even bigger nose. The vole was in the middle of an exaggerated giggle, and the paper dropped into his mouth like the sun sinking below the horizon. It fell to the ground, choking on the foreign body working its way down his throat.

Crowley grinned while the vole's companions slapped their colleague hard on the back until he spat the intruder across the room. The water voles glared at Crowley with hate-filled eyes, but he didn't care. As he turned away from them, he noticed they weren't the only ones staring at him; so was the little Chihuahua with the large moon-shaped eyes.

'Did your human name you?' the pooch said.

The petite dog's voice ran ahead of itself so fast Crowley didn't understand what she was saying. She bounced up and down on her tiny feet and repeated the question. He stared at the hound and wondered why humans loved dogs like this so much; all nervous energy she could hardly contain.

'She didn't give me a name, but the AA registered me with her surname.'

He'd always found humans to be a strange breed, but Emma Crowley had been his favourite of a long bunch he'd allowed to stroke and feed him. And she was the one with the coolest name. He wouldn't admit it to anybody else, but he liked the title Crowley. It was so much better than what his parents had given him.

The sizeable Alsatian working as the bullfrog's body-guard was bored and restless, stooping to scratch his chin on a wooden signpost with the words 'Keep your dog on a lead' stamped onto it. The bats overhead acted as high security, keeping their eyes on the groups of rabbits chasing each other in the centre of the room.

'No hanky panky in public,' the Alsatian barked at them, but they ignored the warning, haring around as if their lives depended upon it.

'My name is Chirpy!'

Crowley had forgotten about the pup, worrying about Emma's fate. The little dog levitated six inches off the floor between each word, bouncing with enough energy to power the lights across half the city. Her enthusiasm was endless, but not for everything.

'I want to leave here,' Chirpy said.

Crowley was sympathetic, but the weekly AA meetings where the local animals aired their concerns were unavoidable unless you wanted to be ostracised from the civilised community. Not that he thought it was civilised that night, seeing the large group of mice wearing tiny shirts with the logo 'Rodent's First!' agitating against a colony of rats trying to ignore their smaller brethren. A couple of grumpy Badgers stood behind them, shaking their heads in disgust.

'Give it an hour for the important bods to remind us

why they're so important and why we should thank them for keeping order. Then we can scuttle off,' Crowley said.

'No, I want to leave this neighbourhood. Everybody's mean to me.' Tears formed in Chirpy's eyes as she spoke. Even an old cynic like Crowley felt sorry for the canine. As a cat, his instinct was to cross the road if a dog came towards him, but over the years, he'd learnt to assimilate and knew as many friendly dogs as he did unpleasant cats.

'Integration is the only way forward for us as a community,' was the AA mantra, but some animals wanted to return to their hives. And they would do anything to achieve it.

'How long you have been here, kid?' Crowley asked the little dog.

Before Chirpy replied, the intoxicated pigeon fell over before them, mumbling something about secret messages and spies before getting its beak stuck in the dirt. Chirpy peered at the bird as it lay on its side, its legs running but going nowhere, with its eyes glazed over.

'Don't mind him,' Crowley said. 'He's too partial to some of the samples he delivers. Are you new around here?' The little pooch was nervous, squatting her backside close to the pigeon's quivering face in anticipation of an imminent expulsion. 'You can't do that here, kid; the big dog will punish you if you do.'

'But...but...somebody always picks up my poop.'

Crowley grinned at the nervous pooch. 'That's a human's job. We won't do it for you. The only time an animal would touch your mess is when they're going to shove it in your face.'

AA rules stated animals should always be cordial to each other, but those rules were broken regularly. He had the scars to prove it.

Chirpy controlled herself by bouncing even higher. Crowley worried she might get stuck in the ceiling. He checked the time on his watch as the meeting began. As the MC picked a live locust from between his teeth, Crowley pulled up on his haunches and settled down for the formalities.

The hamsters were complaining again about the lack of housing and relying too much on handouts from food banks. The sheep nodded, agreeing with everything, even if one thing contradicted another. The red squirrels and grey squirrels were staring at each other across the room as if they'd start a war at any second. Cornelius, the envoy of the horses, reported all was well down at the stables. As usual, some wag shouted 'Neigh' when Cornelius finished.

At this point, Crowley closed his eyes, deciding to nap and recharge his batteries. He was skilled at shutting out the other animals' noises, but he couldn't stop the images of Emma crawling into his head. The first time he saw her, she was handing out food to the birds in the park, and he followed her to the dingy squat where she lived, joining her there before she moved out to somewhere better. He thought of Emma as he tried to move to one side, but found something weighing him down. He opened his eyes to see Chirpy lying across his tail and grinning at him.

'Do we have to come to these meetings?' The dog was as curious as she was excitable.

Crowley yawned before replying. 'The world isn't a big enough place for us to escape from the tentacles of the AA.'

'You got that right, my old friend,' a gruff voice said from the middle of the shadows.

Chirpy leapt high in the air, hitting the ground with a bump and falling onto her side. She yelped in pain as they stared into the oncoming darkness. The shadow strode towards them in slow motion, Chirpy cowering backwards as the shape got closer. Crowley moved his body in front of the little dog, his mind a ball of confusion containing a disagreeable tasting cocktail of surprise, anger and hate.

He'd promised not to think about Emma again that night, but it was impossible not to, as the real architect of her current plight was before him. He should have been fearful, not only for his own life but for the little dog's as well.

Yet he could only focus on Emma as he stared at the dark creator of all his problems striding towards him.

Chapter 4

Pandora: The Project

Pandora had put her father in the ground and her mother in a straightjacket. For once, the thought of her parents made her smile.

'Good morning, Ms Halcyon,' the guard said as she scanned her ID through security. It was undoubtedly morning, but she doubted any good would come of it.

She dropped off the newest report on the way to her latest reprimand. The other agents whispered in the corner and shook their heads. Pandora's reputation preceded her and hung around like a giant blanket, ready to smother those who got too close.

The bravest of her colleagues threw fake smiles at her and fashioned small talk about reality TV shows and football games she wasn't interested in. She wondered where her boss recruited these people before remembering how she fell into the organisation in the first place. Two years at the Project, and she'd only made one friend, and she'd nearly got Lulu killed. That's what they told Pandora. That's why she was about to receive another lecture.

'Boredom will kill me before anything else.'

Pandora grabbed the small plastic toy from the desk next to hers. She was puzzled by its appearance of a yellow rectangle with arms, legs, and manic eyes, guessing it had something to do with ingesting psychedelic substances. It squeaked in her hands as she threw it against the wall and made her way to her assessment.

The organisation Pandora worked for was not one recognised by the public. They didn't advertise their services, promote their wares in the media or over the internet, recruit through job centres, newspapers, or scour the country's finest educational establishments. They searched for society's outcasts and throwaways. That's how they recruited Pandora.

Her colleagues pushed their faces into computer screens as she strode past them. Tossing back her long, red locks and daring anyone to look at her, Pandora headed for the stairs. The small, cramped stairwell reminded her of the dark shadows they'd acquired her from. The stink of bleach resurrected depressing memories of her mother's obsessive need to keep everything clean, even her only child. She forced the door open and stared at the man behind the desk. His grunt was the signal for her to wait. She detested waiting for anything.

Pandora's working hours were weird, like the job itself, or at least until she made a mistake. Well, they termed it a mistake, but she couldn't see what the problem was. Nobody died, and she completed the mission. They should have given her a bonus. Instead, she waited in the damp office with its haggard wallpaper and out-of-date celebrity magazines for a so-called superior to reassign her.

She needed something to read, her mind creeping into

tedium while kicking her heels. Pandora fell in love with books when she was seven, using fictional worlds to hide from the real one. She devoured novels at a phenomenal rate, five or six a week. Old people, anyone over the age of twenty-five, were fixated on paper, but a digital screen was a boon to her, so she could read wherever she was.

Pandora loved the smell and feel of an actual book, but nothing compared to the millions of words stored on her phone. Only, she wasn't allowed to bring it into the building. They claimed security reasons, so all she had were the gaudy magazines on the table before her. She had her memories, but dipping into those was too dangerous. There was no telling what she might fish out if she stumbled into the wrong parts of her brain. And her brain was prodigious. They'd told her that at school.

Precocious is what they also called her. Pandora took it as a compliment, even though her mates used it to mock her, not that they were really friends. They were like ants; okay to study behind a piece of glass, but not worth too much effort. Apart from the practical jokes she played on some of them. Those humorous episodes entertained her until the last one broke a kid's arm. She smiled every time she remembered it.

But she enjoyed reading and learning until her parents decided she needed to be home-schooled. She got used to it and didn't miss any of the kids or the teachers until she realised why her mother and father wanted to keep her there, and it wasn't for her benefit – quite the opposite.

The monotony of the office dredged up too many unwanted thoughts, forcing Pandora to look for something to occupy her mind. She grabbed a magazine, stared at the semi-nude women on the cover and ran through the headlines about how to lose weight, eating only fish sticks and recommendations on what to do to satisfy your lover. Sitting before her superior, she considered composing an article about those two things.

'You could've got both of you killed.' He snorted the words out like some fat hog.

'I would agree with you, but then we'd both be wrong.'

He ignored the jab. 'Your partner is undergoing therapy. How do you feel about that?'

She gazed right through him. 'When you're barely clinging to sanity by your ragged fingernails as your feelings thrash inside you like a sack of feral cats, nothing brings more joy than getting slapped in the face with someone else's messy emotions too. It's pure bliss trying to soothe their anxiety and mop up their tears when you're already soaked in the blood from your own gaping emotional wounds. You'd give anything for them just to keep their feelings contained while you quietly go mad. But no, they insist on opening the floodgates in your face, then expect you to dam it up and divert the flow, even as you're drowning in it. It's okay though, really. I love excavating other people's emotional trauma when I can barely bury my own. It fills me with serenity and light. Please, everyone, projectile vomit your feelings directly into my mouth forever. I want to marinate in them.'

'Okay,' he said. 'I'm reading your latest psych evaluation.'

He must have cultivated the smugness in the darkness of his solitary life. Pandora diagnosed his dishevelled appearance to indicate a man with very few social interactions outside his place of work. The top of his shirt was stained yellow from fresh eggs, its pungent aroma creeping up her nose.

'Would you like me to decipher the longer words for you?' she said.

He ignored her to squint at the screen. It wouldn't take much for Pandora to accidentally fall into the computer and shove it into his face. She imagined swapping out one of his flash drives for something she'd been working on with a self-replicating virus which would swamp his machine with pornography.

The stink of old paper drifted through the room, but it wasn't enough to disguise his poor hygiene. He smelt like two pigs having lousy sex, with a face to match. A pair of thick glasses rested on his prominent nose, which he continually pushed back into place as they slid down his ski slope of a conk. He coughed loud and long, gasping for air like a demented town crier.

'There are some anomalies in your chart,' he said.

Pandora didn't like the idea of having a chart. Her father had been obsessed with plans and diagrams, mapping out her daily routine to the last second. For years, she thought it was because the two of them, her mother as well, wanted her as some social engineering experiment. As terrible as that sounded, it would have been better than what really happened.

'What type of anomalies?'

She had a sudden urge for a piece of chewing gum. Not the modern tasteless stuff, but the strawberry-flavoured chud some kids used to have at school. She imagined rolling it through her fingers before stuffing it up his nose.

Suffocation by chewing gum. That would be a new one.

Her mind invented fresh ways to kill using only sweets. Clubbed to death with a Toblerone, blinded by a Twix. Throat sliced with an After Eight Mint, conked on the head with a Terry's Chocolate Orange. Pandora's stomach rumbled with hunger.

He struggled to speak while fighting a losing battle to keep those giant specs on his face. They clattered onto the table, knocking over pills he hastily fumbled into his pocket. Boredom ate at her. A hyperactive mind is what the doctors told Pandora before her parents stopped trusting in experts and decided the best advice was their own. Her father threw the prescription drugs in the bin when they left the surgery. Not that she wanted to take them. She always remembered the day her mother nearly choked on one of the dog's anxiety pills.

What a shame she didn't.

'Some of your responses show unusual activity in your brain,' he said in his best clinical voice, even though he wasn't a doctor. Not to her knowledge, anyway. He could have been a doctor of comic books, an expert in surfing, a professor of UFO studies, or one of those other useless university courses on offer these days. A glorified pen pusher, that's all he was. While she risked her life in the outside world, he sat behind that desk and vegetated.

'What?' she said.

'This might be why you did what you did.' He pushed the monitor to one side to look at her. There was nothing good about it.

She smiled at him. 'I can explain it to you, but I can't understand it for you.'

Her guts churned, and she craved a cigarette, desperate for the smoke to fill her lungs. It was another addiction Pandora had to thank her parents for.

'You can explain why you nearly got your partner killed?' He leant back into his seat, self-satisfaction painted over his wretched face.

Pandora couldn't explain it.

So, the Project sent her to babysit one of their clients, and she hated babysitting. She didn't know it then, but the assignment would change the world forever.

And provide her with the opportunity for mass revenge in one fell swoop.

Chapter 5

Emma: The Prisoner

'They said I burnt down my school, but that's a lie. I only stood and watched it go up in flames.' Raya showed Emma her hands. 'Because I had these from the other fires, they said I must be guilty. It was all a fix-up, I tell ya.' Raya laughed. 'But everybody in here says they're innocent. What about you?'

Emma stretched out on the uncomfortable bed, staring at the grey clothes the guards had given her. 'The police charged me with theft – jewellery from a museum.'

'Wow!' Raya said. 'A jewel thief. You're the first I've ever met. Usually, it's drug dealers, thugs, gang members, or murderers.'

'I didn't do it,' Emma replied. 'I don't know how those jewels got into my flat.'

Raya laughed. 'Yeah, like I said, everybody's innocent in here.'

Emma slammed her hand on the bed, pain shooting through her fingers. 'No, I am innocent. Somebody must have planted that stuff in my flat. Someone who hates me.'

Raya reached into her top and pulled out a cigarette and a match. 'Keep a lookout on the door, Em, will ya?'

'Sure.' Emma slid off the bed and went to the doorway, peering along the corridor of the detention centre. 'Won't the guards smell the smoke?'

'Na,' Raya said. 'Most of them are too busy sniffing drugs themselves to notice anything else. This is the slackest pokey I've been in for security.'

After the police dragged Emma from the Comic Con, they told her there was overwhelming evidence to convict her of the recent theft of jewellery from the museum. She was too stunned to speak initially, but a few minutes in a custody cell at the cop shop soon shook her vocal cords into action.

'Are you mad? I've never visited that museum. It's full of stuffed animals. I wouldn't be seen dead in there.'

An hour later, they sent her to the Larchwood Detention Centre after a brief conversation with a court-appointed lawyer.

'The government fast tracks juvenile criminals now,' a uniformed man informed her. 'Back to Victorian values.'

Emma shuffled into the intake room, harsh fluorescent lights assaulting her eyes. The dingy walls were bare except for a few faded motivational posters warning against violence. A gloomy, neglected potted plant drooped in the corner. The only decor was a grimy fish tank burbling against the far wall, its lone inhabitant drifting listlessly.

The stale air smelled of fried food, turning Emma's stomach. She heard the steel doors clang down the hall, muffling the cries of new arrivals. A matronly guard entered, her smile not reaching her narrow eyes.

'Empty your pockets and hand over your things, dear.

Then we'll get you into some proper clothes.' Her tone was sweet but left no room for argument.

She surrendered her wallet, her throat tightening, wondering what had happened to her portfolio. The guard rifled through the items before handing Emma a rough uniform that hung shapelessly on her thin frame.

That was twenty-four hours ago. Now, she shared a cell with Raya, waiting for Jane to get her out.

Raya puffed on the cigarette. 'So, your sister's a lawyer?'

Emma nodded. 'She's ten years older than me, and well, we've never been the closest, but she won't let me down with this.'

Raya sighed. 'I wish I had family to help me.'

'What happened to you?'

Raya took a long drag, blowing out smoke that mingled with the cell's stale air. 'Let's just say I got dealt a bad hand. I grew up bouncing around foster homes. Ran with a rough crowd. Never could catch a break.' She rubbed the scars on her palms. 'Maybe I made some mistakes, fell in with the wrong folks. But the arson charge was bogus. Just because I was there didn't mean I lit the match.'

Emma leaned against the wall, arms folded. 'I believe you. The system's so quick to judge people like us.'

Raya nodded, flicking ash onto the floor. 'What about your sister? She going to be able to clear your name?'

Emma chewed her lip. 'I hope so. Jane's a great lawyer, but she's got her hands full with a big case right now.'

And she needs to look after Mum.

'You've got to stay tough in here, Em. You can't show any weakness, or the predators will pounce.' She grinned. 'But if you stick with me, you'll be okay.'

Emma picked at a thread on her uniform. 'I just have to be patient, I guess. At least I've got you for company.'

Raya laughed. 'Yeah, us wrongfully accused girls gotta stick together. We'll get through this, trust me.'

'Shit!' Emma said. 'I forgot about my cat. He's all alone now.'

'You like animals?' Raya said. 'I wasn't allowed pets.'

Emma shook her head. 'I don't treat Cat as a pet. Owning animals is unethical. They can never really have a good life in a human home.'

'Yeah, I know what you mean. I went to a party once where a woman was wearing a snake like a necklace. It was sick.'

Emma nodded. 'We claim to be animal lovers, yet how we relate to them is often self-serving. Rather than meaningful bonds, we pursue easy relationships on our terms. We want pets that are low maintenance, who won't disrupt our lifestyle or impinge on our comfort.'

'My stepdad kept a tarantula in the kitchen,' Raya said. 'He'd feed it greasy slugs and worms while I had breakfast.'

Emma tried not to picture that as she continued. 'Our interactions centre around what emotional value they can provide us, not what's best for the animal. We hire dog walkers and board them at kennels to avoid being inconvenienced.'

Raya agreed. 'Most kids at my school got cats or dogs as presents, then half of them ended up tossed out of the house a few months later.'

'If people really cared about animals,' Emma said, 'we'd only engage in rescues and helping animal sanctuaries' wildlife rehabilitation – things we find fulfilling but also help the animal. It's dirty, difficult work fuelled by compassion, not selfishness. We should examine our motives and ask ourselves if we want pets for them or for us.'

Raya puffed smoke into the cell. 'It's a shame we can't ask them what they want.'

'If we truly valued animals intrinsically, more of us would dedicate our time and resources to improving their lives and protecting their interests above our own. We need a more ethical approach of humane stewardship rather than treating them as commodities for our enjoyment.'

Raya stubbed out the cigarette as footsteps echoed down the hall. 'Guard's coming. Here's hoping your sis works some legal magic for you soon.'

Emma hoped so, too.

Chapter 6

Pandora: The Box

The man sitting opposite Pandora in the café bookshop wore a shirt with the inscription "Cleanliness is next to godliness" scrawled on the front, the top obscured by the large crucifix hanging from his neck. He'd spilt half a cup of coffee over his trousers and was busy pulling some living creature from the larger of his nostrils. His teeth were brilliantly white, as if he'd washed them in vanilla paint. He reminded her of someone from her past. She wanted to take the teaspoon from her table and scoop out his eyes. But he wasn't one of those she pursued, and she turned her attention to why she was there.

Pandora stared across the road at her target. He slipped money into his pocket and shook hands with two blokes in pressed suits and cheap shirts. They wore braces and were obviously criminal types.

'Don't make it so obvious, Wyatt. You'll get us both into trouble.'

She peered around the combined café and second-hand bookshop, staring at her coffee beside a copy of *No Longer*

Human by Osamu Dazai. It would make light reading for her later once her assignment was over.

I'm just a damn babysitter.

Pandora loved bookshops, but she wanted to be somewhere dirty and brash and loud; the louder, the better. Somewhere with crashing explosions jumping from the speakers, where the music shuddered through the floor, and her skin stood on end, a place where strange people with terrible haircuts and worse clothes were the norm.

Outside, a sea of rainbow balloons crisscrossed the road high in the sky, coloured spots floating across her eyes against the blue background. Pedestrians peered up and cooed at the adorability above them while she chastised herself for not having any darts to hand. She hated childish things.

Pandora took another sip of the sweet drink, the liquid warming the sides of her mouth and swimming down towards the cold parts deep inside her. She was desperate for a cigarette, staring out the window at the man she was following. He'd moved away from the two suspicious-looking blokes and sat with a woman she didn't recognise, smiling and laughing together as if they were enjoying a casual summer afternoon. Pandora disliked the sun as much as she did seeing other people having a good time.

'Why have you stopped working, Wyatt? You promised us something that would change the world.'

It was annoying having to look after this man, waiting for him to perfect the chemical experiments her employers were paying for. Frustration grew inside her, a ball of energy pushing against her chest like the creature from *Alien*. And the longer Wyatt took to complete his work, the longer she'd be stuck with him unless she gave it all up and started another new life elsewhere. It would be her fourth life in eighteen years, and the contingency plans were already in place.

But the Project wouldn't let her go without a fight. They didn't spend all that time and effort training Pandora to wave her goodbye with a smile. Not that any of them knew how to smile. And there was no golden handshake with the Project. Yes, it would be a fight, but she liked a fight. All her life had been a battle, from the first time her dear mama had slapped her across the head until now.

'Would you like a refill? It's free.'

The young woman had a smile she wanted to sink into. She was about the same age as Pandora, with cerulean blue eyes resting on perfect skin. They'd been flirting with each other since Pandora walked in. It was a lovely distraction, but she couldn't let it interfere with her focus. Not that Wyatt Wells was much to focus on.

Pandora stared at the woman, noticing something about her face, how the sparkle in her eyes twinkled like stars running across the night sky, depositing some of their radiance into Pandora's heart. She had a smile that made a person feel more human and happy to be alive. It was unusual for Pandora since she hadn't felt human for a long time, not with what she'd seen and done. And the things she'd experienced.

'Well, since it's free,' she said and beamed at the woman, seeing it achieve its aim as the other girl's legs buckled a little as she poured the coffee.

Nothing good in life is free.

That's what her mama had taught her. Pandora kept smiling; one glance at the pretty woman, then one across the road at Wyatt, but all she thought about was her mother and her State-paid habitation inside the inappropriately named rest home.

You're getting free accommodation, free food and drink, and your arse wiped at least twice a day, Mama. What do you think of that?

'Is your boyfriend cheating on you?'

It was a pretty voice, sounding like a weeping angel. She flashed the attractive young woman her comeliest smile, touching her hand as she took the new drink.

'He's not my type; I prefer cute smiles, brown hair and blue eyes,' she said to the cutie with brown hair and blue eyes. The woman blushed again while Pandora returned her scrutiny to Wyatt. If he didn't get his serum right soon, the Project would move on to other experts and cut him off at the knees. Literally cut him off at the knees. One of the few things she liked about her employers was how ruthless they would be when they didn't get what they wanted. They could have been a surrogate family for her if she didn't despise most of them.

Like my real family, then.

She reached into her jacket and removed the box containing her cigarettes. She opened the small container, her other hand rolling the lighter between her fingers.

'You can't have that here,' the woman said, her face turning pink. Pandora thought she was embarrassed at having to issue the warning.

'Maybe we can share one later,' Pandora replied with a glint in her eyes.

'I ... I ... don't know how to smoke,' the woman stuttered. Pandora was amused at her nervousness, seeing her eyelids flicker at a hundred miles an hour.

'It's simple; you just put your lips together and blow.' She forgot all about the man she was watching. 'I promised myself I'd quit smoking when I fell in love.'

It was enough to make the woman blush again. Pandora

only foresaw a future where she smoked twenty a day, every day until she slipped away from her mortal coil.

'What's your name?' she asked as the woman turned to leave.

'Amelia,' she replied. The colour in her cheeks could have lit a darkened room.

'Pleased to meet you, Amelia – I'm Pandora,' she said, standing to greet her as the French did, stopping at the horrified look on Amelia's face, wondering how she might have misread all those signals.

Amelia slipped in closer and put her hand on Pandora's. 'We're not allowed to fraternise with the customers.'

Pandora grinned and moved her head to one side, exposing the artwork on the back of her neck, enjoying how the word 'fraternise' sounded. Amelia's eyes were drawn to the magnificent phoenix rising from the top of Pandora's shoulders.

'Does it signify something important to you?' There was a slight tremor in her voice as she spoke.

'All art of the flesh should signify something for its wearer. Otherwise, there's no point in having it.' She ran her fingers across the red ink inside the dark bird, catching a glimpse of its reflection in the window. 'It's a symbol of my resurrection.' She was amused to see Amelia's eyes widen. 'Don't worry, it's not literal – I didn't die.'

Amelia laughed and moved closer to her. She'd wanted to die many times. Now, she wanted to escape into a new life. And to punish those who'd made her desire death.

'I want to get something on my neck or legs, but I can't while working here. It's not allowed,' Amelia said.

'Maybe you should think about finding different employment,' Pandora said to the other woman while pondering on her advice.

Amelia kept on smiling as she returned to her duties. Pandora's gaze followed her to the other side of the room, forgetting what she was doing there, dreaming of those lips glued to hers, imagining her hands undressing that uniform.

A large man got up to pay as Amelia approached, knocking her arm to one side and forcing her to drop a cup. It exploded in a blast of noise as it hit the floor. The sounds shook Pandora back into the world, and she remembered what she was supposed to do. She left the cigarette on the table and peered out the window again.

'Damn!' she said.

Wyatt was nowhere. She'd be in even more trouble with the Project if she lost him. She grabbed the book and threw money onto the table, leaving an impressive tip. She headed for the door, one part of her brain concentrating on finding her target, the other side staring at Amelia near the exit. Pandora took her hand as she left, taking Amelia's pen and writing her phone number in Amelia's palm.

'Call me tonight,' she said as she stepped outside.

The pavement was smooth grey stones, with the occasional crack to show where the elements had assaulted humanity's infringement into nature. As she left, a scruffy ginger cat ran across her foot. Pandora's flinch was an automatic response, her eyes closing as she fell backwards into the window, her hand steadying her body against the glass as she dropped the book.

Her breathing was slow, and the darkness behind her eyes transported her back to childhood. She was trapped in that box again, claustrophobia pressing down on her in the gloom. Blackness consumed her, her lungs shrivelling in the search for air, her mind losing all control and descending into anxiety.

The sounds of scratching came, and tiny feet crawled

over her, feral cats spitting and digging into her flesh. Her father's laughter mixed in with feline shrieking. She dug her fingernails into her skin, returning her to the present. She opened her eyes and saw the ginger cat leap onto the wall and run across the rooftops. The sun was on her face, but she could have sworn the animal had a watch hanging around its neck.

Pandora pushed all thoughts of cats and her childhood from her head and retrieved *No Longer Human* from the pavement. Then she went looking for Professor Wyatt Wells and the chemical concoction he was creating for her employers.

Chapter 7

Crowley: Cool for Cats

'How good to see you again, my old friend,' the darkness said to Crowley. Splinters of moonlight slipped into the room through the shattered roof above their heads, allowing them to gaze upon the full majesty of the cat called Darkstar. Even the insides of his eyes were devoid of colour until he blinked, and a deceptive slither of white gazed into the soul.

'We've never been friends,' Crowley replied.

'Somebody wants to see you, Crowley. You and your little friend,' the dark cat said. Chirpy whimpered. Crowley peered at the ticking hands on the watch around his neck and mustered his best apology.

'I'm sorry, Darkstar, I need to be somewhere else. Come on, Chirpy, I'll walk you home.' He resisted the overwhelming temptation to whistle, instead turning away from the darkness and heading towards the exit.

'The Bullfather wants to see you.'

Crowley froze, closing his eyes as a shiver ran through him, hoping he could escape his looming fate by shutting out all the remaining light. This was just like the last time, and that ended in disaster.

'What's a Bullfather?' Chirpy said, rediscovering some of her chirpiness.

'Follow me,' the ebony cat said, scowling at Crowley and ignoring the little dog.

Before Crowley could tell him it would be impossible, a pale piece of cloth moved from side to side in front of his eyes. Somebody with a modicum of common sense had tied a white handkerchief around Darkstar's tail so they could follow him in the dark.

'C'mon, Chirpy, you'll be okay.' Crowley didn't enjoy lying to the pup, but he had no choice. Not if they wanted to stay breathing. 'How long have you been in the city, kid?' He kept looking at the dog's big eyes to forget about the white cloth they followed and what it signified.

'About six months, I think.' The excitement left her voice, replaced with a sad resignation that whatever was happening now was beyond her control.

'You don't like it here?'

Crowley loved the city much more than the country-side. The human constructs were perfect for slipping through and hiding inside, creating shadows across most of the environment, and shadows were precisely what he needed in his line of work.

'I get lonely,' Chirpy said, tears forming. Crowley wanted to put his paw on the little dog's head, but the idea made him uncomfortable.

'What does your human do with you, Chirpy?'

The pooch perked up again. 'He takes me for long walks, and we play ball, and he lets me run after the rabbits and the squirrels.' Her voice rose even higher.

Oh, oh.

'That's a no, no. You can't chase other animals without permission from the AA.'

The kid was miserable, and her mouth hung low. Crowley hoped she was okay, staring at the blackness they followed as the pit of his stomach shrank into a painful knot. Meeting Darkstar was not good. The black cat was ruthless if he didn't get his way. To refuse him meant a lot of pain, as Crowley was aware from bitter experience.

I need to think of a way out of whatever mess this is.

The joy returned to Chirpy's face as she spoke. 'But I like bath time the best.'

Crowley froze, staring at the little dog in amazement: no animal enjoyed getting a bath. Fish didn't count. They followed the Dark One again before they got into more trouble.

'Doesn't your human let you watch TV?'

Some animals were as fascinated by television as much as humans were, though he'd never understood the attraction. Chirpy's tail wagged enthusiastically, and Crowley pictured her hovering away like a furry helicopter.

'Oh yes, sometimes. We watch many moving pictures, but I don't understand most of them.' She was disappointed, her eyes on the verge of crying.

'You won't,' Crowley said. 'Humans are incapable, or at least most of them are, of any real understanding of life. So they fill their minds with dull, pointless things to try to forget how stupid they are.' The bitterness in his own voice surprised him.

Guilt. It's guilt for what I did to Emma.

Chirpy bounced up and down on her little feet. 'Didn't you like your human, the one called Crowley?'

He ignored the question and kept on following Darkstar. Now was not the time for him to wax nostalgic about the unfortunate Emma Crowley. The image of her behind bars because of his mistake depressed him immensely, his heart sinking into the pit of his stomach. She should be his priority, not the dark cat and his devious schemes.

'Best not to get too close to any human,' he said regretfully.

The whiteness ahead of them swayed from side to side like a swing, and all it did was fill him with dread. The last time he'd seen Darkstar, the other cat had tried to kill him. As he dwelt upon his complicated past, he recollected their previous five or six meetings being to the death.

'It's been six times, if you're wondering, my old friend.'

Darkstar's uncanny knack for guessing what Crowley thought was as worrying as it was creepy. That was bad enough, but being summoned by the Don was disturbing. He stared at the tiny dog scampering to keep up with him, hoping she wouldn't poop herself in the presence of the Bullfather.

As he contemplated the dire consequences of such an action, the shimmering white beacon stopped, and the dark voice spoke again.

'You're granted permission to gaze upon the magnificence of the Bullfather.'

It was over six months since he'd been in the great one's presence, but you never forgot meeting the giant bull. Nothing had changed much – the Bullfather was the biggest, meanest-looking animal Crowley had ever seen and still bore the weirdest resemblance to Marlon Brando. The raven perched on his head was new.

'We want you to acquire something for us,' the bird said.

Crowley raised his eyebrows towards where he assumed Darkstar was standing, almost seeing his fur flickering in the wind.

'You're not worthy of the Bullfather's voice. He speaks through Evermore,' Darkstar said.

He didn't know what to say, thinking of an answer as Chirpy piped up.

'I want to go home.'

The poor pooch was on the verge of tears. Crowley knew why the Don required his special services, but was curious why the kid was there.

Evermore spoke to the dog. 'We want you to go home and take Crowley to meet your human.'

'Poppepper Widget?' Chirpy said.

Before Crowley could ask the kid what he meant, Darkstar's great teeth reappeared to enlighten him.

'The stupid mutt can't say the full name of her human. Professor Wyatt Wells has something the Bullfather needs, and you will get it for us.'

'You mean steal it?' It was inevitable as soon as the black cat delivered the summons. Crowley was only good at one thing but was the best at it.

'Once a thief, always a thief,' cried Evermore.

'What do you need me to pinch?'

The raven looked at the black cat, which looked at the colossal bull. The bull stared at Crowley as if preparing to eat him whole.

'It's called Doolittle.' Darkstar's voice made Crowley's flesh creep.

'What is it?' Something not too heavy, he hoped. The last thing he'd stolen for them had given him a bad neck for days.

And it had put Emma in prison.

'You'll know when you find it,' squawked the bird.

Crowley gazed at the bull's unmoving face, contemplating how far he'd get if he leapt towards that bovine throat with his claws extended. It wasn't just because of this latest demand; he owed the Don for what happened last time.

Emma.

Ultimately, he was responsible for Emma's fate, but the Bullfather had gotten them into the mess in the first place. Emma would still be free if they hadn't forced Crowley into the museum.

As he visualised tearing through that flesh, there was movement behind the Don, a flash of fierce red eyes and sharp yellow teeth. There were at least five sets of them: foxes, the Bullfather's favourite method of violence. The bird spoke again, but Crowley missed it while he was dreaming.

'The dog will get you inside,' said Darkstar.

Moonlight shimmered around them. 'How long do I have?'

The raven and black cat spoke in unison. 'Three days.'

'And what do I get in return?' Crowley asked, knowing full well the answer he'd receive.

'You get to live,' Darkstar replied.

They turned away together, leaving the little dog and grumpy cat staring at each other in confusion.

'What's a Bullfather?' Chirpy asked as Crowley peered at his watch to see it had stopped.

'Our doom if we don't follow their orders.'

I'll steal this Doolittle, whatever it is, and then I'll do everything I can to get Emma out of prison.

The ginger cat and hyperactive dog scampered towards a destiny that would change animals and humans forever.

Chapter 8

Emma: Orange Crush

'Why is Bambi in prison?' Seven-year-old Emma had asked when her mother took her to the zoo for the first time. Her sister, Jane, was seventeen and obsessed with the penguins, but Emma couldn't take her eyes off the deer looking depressed and bored in their enclosure.

She'd watched the Disney movie the week before and had difficulty separating reality from fiction. She was doing the same thing ten years later, but that afternoon at the zoo as a child was never far from Emma's mind.

Some screams in prison during the night were from girls who'd seen rats scuttling through their cells. Many other cries were because of the human vermin sharing their space with Emma. She smiled at Jane across the table and decided not to tell her about that. She stared at her sister, who wore a smart suit and blouse and considered how different they were.

'They haven't set a court date yet, but I'm hopeful they'll allow bail.'

She was proud of Jane's career as a lawyer, but she

never imagined her big sister would be the one trying to get her out of jail. As Emma peered at the walls, all she could think about were her responsibilities.

'Are you looking after George?'

Jane shuffled her papers, sighing at the mention of the hamster she'd picked up from Emma's place.

'I'm keeping him at the office. I thought you didn't like putting animals in cages?'

'It's just while I find him a safe place to live. Couldn't you take him to your flat? I hate to think of him all alone in that terrible building.' She nibbled at her nails, a nervous habit she hoped to kick.

'He'll be fine. Don't you have a cat as well?' Jane could never keep up with Emma's revolving-door collection of pets. Not that Emma classed them as pets.

'He comes and goes as he pleases.' Emma played with the ends of her hair.

'Let's concentrate on you for now. You're still clueless about the circumstances surrounding your DNA's presence at the crime scene?'

She detected the frustration in her sister's voice, no matter how hard she tried to conceal it. 'I've never set foot in that museum in my life, Jane. I swear.'

'And the jewellery discovered in your flat?'

'I don't know how it ended up at the back of the cat box. It's a mystery to me.'

Emma's story had never changed since the police arrested her at the Comic Con, no matter who questioned her. She had nothing to offer on the theft and found the whole thing ridiculous. Why would she want to steal some jewels from a museum? And who would be stupid enough to keep them in their flat?

If Dad were still alive, I'd have been out of here in a flash.

Her father's long membership in the Freemasons had brought the Crowley family many benefits over the years.

'Do you have any enemies?' Jane asked.

Emma narrowed her eyes and stared at her sister, surprised by the question. 'What do you mean enemies?'

'Someone who hates you enough to steal jewellery worth half a million and then plant it in your flat, not to mention they had your DNA and left it at the crime scene.'

'What type of DNA?' Emma said while going through a list of enemies in her mind.

Jane searched through the papers the prosecution had provided as part of their case. With the right story, Emma believed Jane could explain to a jury that the jewellery in the flat could have been put there by anybody. The DNA evidence was harder to explain.

'According to the forensic report, the DNA is from your hair and saliva. Did you go to the museum and spit on something? You always had the most disgusting of habits.'

Emma scowled at Jane, her eyes fluctuating between stretching upwards in amazement before shrinking into annoyance.

'I've told you, sis, I've never stepped foot in that place. It has a section full of stuffed animals on display, and that's barbaric.' Revulsion dripped from Emma, her lips curling into an unpleasant shape reminiscent of a cracked half-moon.

'Then how did your DNA get there?'

A wild idea popped into Emma's head. 'Could it have come from a kiss?'

'I suppose so,' Jane replied.

'I read a piece in a newspaper a few years ago about a famous tennis player who failed a drugs test, and they discovered cocaine in his system. His defence was he'd kissed a woman in a nightclub the night before, and that's where the drug came from. He got his ban overturned with that excuse.'

She sat back in her chair, feeling happy for the first time since the boys and girls in blue had placed their cold fingers on her shoulders.

'Have you been kissing famous tennis players?' Jane asked.

Emma laughed. 'No, I wish! But I've kissed a few ordinary people.'

'Who in particular?'

Emma's smile vanished as she thought about her recent painful breakup. The tears had all been on one side, and it wasn't Emma's makeup swimming like a liquid rainbow down the face.

'It could be Heather, my ex-girlfriend.'

'Okay. Why would Heather keep saliva from your kiss and then go to all this trouble of framing you?' Jane made notes as she spoke.

'My kissing is quite memorable.'

'Can you be serious for once?'

'It was a nasty breakup.'

'It must've been.' Jane put the pen down to check her phone. 'Do you have contact details for her?'

'Heather Halep. If you go to my flat, you'll find photos of her on my laptop. Some are a bit risqué, so don't be a prude.'

Emma let her mind drift back to the better times she'd had with Heather, the delicate taste of her lips, that enchanting smile and the cheeky gleam in her eye when they got up to no good.

'I wish I had such luxury, dear sister, but the police have your computer and plenty more of your belongings.'

'Damn!' Emma hated other people getting hold of her stuff.

'Do you have an address for her?'

She regained her composure. 'She was living in a commune on Broad Street.'

Jane sighed. 'You certainly can pick them.'

'Don't be a snob, Jane.'

Broad Street was in the city's more downtrodden areas, full of squats, alternative communities and homeless shelters. It was a far cry from the peaceful family cottage they'd grown up in. Emma liked it there because nobody questioned anybody about being different.

Her sister lived at the other end of the spectrum, the perfect representative of 'normal' society in her flawless suit and blouse, with immaculate hair and face groomed to within an inch of its life. As Emma stared at her, she wondered, not for the first time, how different they were. She trusted Jane but had little hope she'd be released soon.

'What's it been like in here?'

Emma laughed at the question: 'It's been brilliant. Three meals a day made for me, no washing up, loads of free time, and I didn't need to pass an interview to get a job. What's there to moan about?'

As she finished speaking, she regretted the sarcasm; her sister didn't deserve it. But it was better than telling her what happened inside the Larchwood Juvenile Detention Centre.

The pure whiteness of every room, with nothing on the walls apart from placards and posters displaying the rules of behaviour, drove Emma stir-crazy. She would have sworn a rat was staring at her from the shadows only last night. At first, she thought it might have been looking at the chocolate she was eating, but it continued to sit in the corner, peering at her after she finished.

'*Red-eyed rat is glaring at me,*' she wrote in giant letters across one full page of her diary and then left the book open on the floor so the creature could see what she'd done. It was at this point she feared for her sanity. She decided not to tell Jane about the rat.

'What's the news with Mum?' Emma had tried to forget about the illness, aware she could do nothing about it, but it was impossible.

'She hasn't been well the last few days.'

Emma noticed how her sister's speech dropped a tone, and her eyes narrowed as her guilt increased. 'Has her dementia worsened?'

It was the guilt of a child who'd been too busy with their own life to consider what others were doing with theirs. Jane had always been the strongest in the family, stronger even than their father, who'd completed two tours with the military in the Middle East. Still, she observed the sudden paleness in Jane's face and how her shoulders slumped, giving her the look of a much older woman.

'She told me not to tell you.'

'Tell me now,' Emma said, forgetting all her troubles.

'I don't want you to be worried, but the doctors have seen no improvement.'

Jane touched Emma's hand as she spoke, even though she wasn't supposed to touch the 'prisoner', and their eyes locked in sisterly love. Emma knew there wasn't a cure for dementia, but she hoped.

'I can't be here then, not when she needs me.' She raised trembling fingers and pushed the tears from her cheeks.

The guard outside the door knocked on the window: their time together had run out. Jane got up to leave.

'Which is why I'm hoping to get you to an open prison where they'll let you out unsupervised on day releases.'

'Thank you,' Emma said, even though it was unnecessary.

'I will try to find Heather; at least it's something to consider.' She grabbed her things and stood. 'I'll be back tomorrow.'

There was one last smile between them as the guard let Jane out, and Emma returned to her cell, her thoughts a jumble of confusion and worry. Not since her incarceration did she even think about how her DNA ended up at the museum or how the jewellery found its way into her flat. She assumed it was all a terrible mistake and somebody would realise it sooner rather than later.

Now, she feared that wouldn't happen.

'I have to get out before Mum forgets who I am.'

Chapter 9

Pandora: Winter of Discontent

Pandora lost Professor Wyatt Wells down one of the capital's busiest streets.

Darkness had descended upon the city, and a fine drizzle murmured in the air as she slipped into an empty booth in her favourite bar, the back of her throat turning into sandpaper. She grabbed a beer from the bartender and ignored his crooked grin. It was the zenith of low-life drinking establishments full of celebrity wannabes, failed Hollywood princesses, kings and queens of the night. Wrinkled posters plastered the walls advertising faded musical groups, gaudy strip shows and outrageous acts of magic. It was a dump, and she loved it. The strong alcohol aroma battered Pandora's nostrils, forcing her nose to wrinkle slightly to avoid the stink.

Some terrible music created by a hundred monkeys sitting in front of a hundred sets of drums boomed from the speakers. The plastic of the booth squeaked against her legs as she slipped inside it, nipping her flesh as she settled into its discomfort.

The bar was half-empty, a few committed alcoholics

together in the corner, seeing who would gag on their own sick first. There was an antique pool table on one side of the room where a man with greased back hair contemplated a problematic-looking shot. On the wall behind him was a painting of a garish yellow-snaked Medusa screaming silently at everybody.

Pandora's thoughts returned to Lulu and their last assignment together, that night in the dark with a blanket of whiteness around them. The cold of the beer bottle transported her back to that bitter evening.

'Why didn't you let me pick you up?' Lulu said as she handed Pandora a lit cigarette and exited the car to stand beside her partner.

'I don't like cars,' Pandora replied, sucking on the ciggie, eager to get warmth into her body. It was a cold night, with the ice cutting into her skin. The snow drifting around the car was heavy in the air and even heavier on the ground.

Pandora's lips cracked against the shivering wind, a slither of ice covering her heart. Stakeouts were cemented at the top of her not-to-do list. For some reason, her partner appeared to enjoy the long periods of doing nothing. Lulu was physically imposing, tall as a tree, thick of muscle and bright of intellect. Personal space was as mythical as Thor and Hercules when Lulu was around. Pandora discovered this when the Project took her to one of their safe houses, and Lulu stood in the kitchen cooking eggs. She put the pan down and threw her large arms around Pandora's trembling fifteen-year-old body. Three years had passed, and the older woman was the closest thing to a friend Pandora had.

'Your mother is being moved to a new facility.' Lulu was more concerned about Pandora's family than she was. Her intentions were good but misguided. 'Do you want to see her latest reports?'

Pandora's heart matched the elements swirling around her. 'Do I need to tell you again what she did to me?'

What both of them did to me.

At least he was six feet under, rotting inside a box similar to the one he'd forced her into on so many occasions.

'I'm not excusing what she did, Pandora, but family is family.'

Pandora didn't want the conversation, and the sub-zero temperature didn't help her fractured mood. She focussed on why they were outside on such a terrible night, ignoring the hammering at the back of her head.

'Forget about her, Lulu. If we don't get him tonight, we might not have another chance.'

The person in question was Shoeless Joe Star. Pandora never asked why her employers tasked her to find a particular individual, but she knew from gossip that Star had a specific reputation.

'He won't escape again,' Lulu replied.

'Why's he called Shoeless?'

Lulu switched off her scowl and changed into full-on nostalgia mode: ancient cases and old criminals were her favourite hobbies. She'd been in the business for two decades, and her work was legendary.

'Joseph Star, career criminal since the age of fourteen, when, according to him, he killed the next-door neighbour's son who'd tried to stab him in the face. They were out in the fields when the fight occurred. Joseph had nothing to defend himself with, so in creative desperation, he removed one of his shoes and struck the other boy in the head with it.'

'That must have been some shoe.' The image created an imaginary itch in Pandora's foot.

'Young Joseph happened to be a dedicated follower of

fashion. The footwear style at the time for boys was to stick small pieces of metal to the bottom of their shoes, like the horses of old, and it was a piece of this decoration which struck the other boy dead. The corner of the metal pierced his skull and into the front of his brain.'

'Lovely.'

'He claimed that first one as self-defence, but it gave him a taste for it, and the urban legend is that he always beats his victims into bloody pulps with his pumps.'

Pandora had visions of Star throwing loafers and brogues at her when they apprehended him. The snow got so thick it was hard to see clearly, her breath turning to ice as it slipped from her mouth and into the gloom.

She was eager to do something physical, to blow away the memories of her hated parents. 'I'm not staying out here all night.'

'You won't have to. Here's our target.'

Lulu dropped the car keys into her pocket, ready to grab him. He walked up the steps, shopping bag in hand, not a care in the world. They strode towards him in the shadows, but Pandora shivered in the cold as she released a horrendous sneeze.

He shot them one look, dumped the bag, and ran. Lulu swore, cutting the cascading snowflakes apart. She didn't have to say anything else; the grimace creeping across her face was enough. Star sprinted like an athlete in the thick snow. They chased him down the side of the building, across the road, and through another row of street houses. She enjoyed the thrill of the chase, the muscles in her legs flexing as she bounded over the ground.

They moved as fast as they could in the drifting terrain, running past abandoned buildings and the rusted skeletons of long-dead motor vehicles. Pandora hurdled over sleeping, tattered torsos and whiny dogs. They chased him for ten minutes, sprinting through broken-down playgrounds where the swings teetered in the winter wind, crossing a shit-stained bridge strewn with discarded baby clothes and crushed glass, before catching sight of him as he plummeted down a hill and landed in front of an ominous-looking structure.

Lulu pointed towards the abandoned school. 'He went in there.'

Pandora rushed forward, moving through the slush and following his trail. Electricity coursed through every inch of her, chemicals of excitement sparking energy in her brain.

'Wait!' Lulu shouted, but Pandora threw caution to the wind, body flowing with adrenaline. She left her partner behind, something she'd been taught never to do, running through the gloom of the corridors. The cabinets hanging off the walls were full of ancient triumphs of faded bronze and gold statues of a bygone time.

Pandora scanned the room, but not quick enough to stop the cricket ball smacking her in the face, knocking her into a glass cabinet at the side, her body slumping to the ground. Lulu ran past her and after their target.

Pandora clutched the side of her skull and scrambled to her feet. She ignored the radiating pain and rushed after her partner. She turned the corner, the moonlight hovering above the damaged lockers and splintered benches creeping inside the broken windows. Her head swirled as moonbeams danced through the puddles.

She checked the place, seeing nobody. Snow fell all around her, adding to the wetness on the ground. Pandora stared at her reflection in the cold liquid, her skin shivering in the dark. She didn't recognise herself, the mania in her eyes reflecting heat in the puddle. She was transfixed by what she saw, her face vibrating from where the ball hit her.

Then, there was an intruder next to her mirrored image, and her reflexes sprang back to life at the sight of the wooden bat swinging towards her head. Pandora moved to one side, but it hit her arm, forcing her to scream. The momentum took her into an open locker door, the jagged edge slicing across her cheek.

He grabbed her head and pushed hard against her skull. She jerked back, shoving him away from her. He shouted something she couldn't understand as he got ready to strike again. Pandora gazed into his crazed eyes as Lulu ran at him. The bat crashed into her nose like a meteor hitting the moon. She crumpled to the floor, still conscious but bleeding.

He pulled a knife from his pocket and grinned, the sharp end heading towards Lulu's throat. Shattered glass was all around Pandora, bits of her face shimmering in its shiny pieces. She grabbed the largest bit and thrust it into his thigh. He hit the floor near her like a great Redwood tumbling to its death, screaming in misery. She lay next to him in perfect symmetry, resembling two halves of a broken chocolate bar.

She dragged herself from the ground as Lulu stood and tied Star's hands behind his back. The bruise on her head was the size of a small nectarine, the throbbing in her skull increasing rapidly.

'That was foolish of you, Pandora. You know I'll have to report this.'

Lulu removed her phone and called headquarters as Star regained consciousness. Pandora grabbed his arm and helped him up.

'Why does the Project want you?'

'You should ask them, kid,' he said as Lulu dragged him towards the entrance. Pandora followed them, knowing she'd be reprimanded when they returned, chastising herself for being so foolish.

That was six months ago, and her punishment was babysitting Professor Wyatt Wells and his science experiment. She finished the beer and went for another, her mind a whirl of plans and ideas.

I need to get away, somewhere they'll never find me.

It was inevitable they'd come after her. The Project had invested too much time and money into Pandora to let her leave. She was an investment.

'I just need the right opportunity,' she said, smiling at the young woman leaning on the bar.

Chapter 10

Crowley: Stars

Crowley observed the little dog scurrying before him, jumping between shadows at things only she could see. He'd been given a deadline but was in no rush to get the kid to their destination. They'd left the shadier side of town and were a few hundred feet from the park.

'Your human left you in the park on your own?' Crowley asked her.

It was always dangerous for animals to be alone where the humans gathered. One of the first things the AA taught its members was how to stick together when moving through human locations. Chirpy regained some of her chirpiness when they moved away from the trio of animal weirdness back at the warehouse. The sight of Darkstar and the Bullfather was unnerving even for Crowley, so it was no wonder the dog was unsure of herself. He hoped the familiarity of her human might make her feel better.

'We go there every night. He lets me run around and swim in the lake.'

It sounded idyllic, apart from the swimming bit.

'And what's he doing while you're having a good time?'

Crowley had long ago given up trying to fathom the motivations of humans, but he was curious about the esteemed Professor Wyatt Wells. It couldn't be for a good reason if Darkstar and the Bullfather were interested in him.

'He talks to other humans. I don't understand many of the words they use.'

Crowley speculated what the late-night meetings in the park could be about, thinking about how humans deceived each other, from criminal activities to plain old adultery.

'And he gives them things,' she added.

Now, that wasn't suspicious at all. He wondered if it was related to the mysterious Doolittle he'd been tasked to steal.

'Do you know what a professor is, Chirpy?'

'Poppepper?'

'Professor.'

'Poppepper?'

'Okay, we'll work on that later. Do you know what a professor does?'

'Is he a teacher?'

'Something like that.'

A shiver crawled down the ginger hairs on his back as they continued walking and talking. There was an unsettling presence in the air, and it made him uneasy. He had a sensation of eyes following them, an unseen presence which was as cruel as it was invisible. His reunion with Darkstar had put all his mental faculties on edge. He tried to shake his concerns away and concentrated on the little dog again.

'They can also be scientists; do you know what they are?' He was determined to get to the heart of the Doolittle mystery before they went anywhere near Wyatt Wells's house.

'A signtiss?'

He tried not to smile at Chirpy's inability to pronounce certain words. The poor dog was either hyper-excitable or super nervous. He'd met plenty of canines over the years, including quite a few Chihuahuas, but none had ever been as strange as this one.

'Yes, a scientist. I think your human is a scientist.'

Why else would the Gruesome Twosome send him there to steal something? They kept moving, dodging the empty fast food cartons and discarded plastic bottles. Chirpy was distracted by the insects crawling through the green, snapping at them as they buzzed around. The entrance to the park was getting closer as the new friends picked up their legs and speed.

'There's an upstairs room in the house where he spends most of the day. I've only been inside twice. There are funny smells there, so I don't like it very much.'

Right on cue, the dog let out a massive fart resembling a volcanic explosion, sending Crowley into a coughing fit.

'Sorry,' Chirpy said, blushing.

Crowley tried to catch his breath, guessing what she'd said could only mean one thing: Professor Wells was a chemist. So, he'd been sent there to steal either a formula or something chemical. It tweaked his interest but didn't distract his focus as he carefully watched the homeless man sleeping inside the gates, making sure Chirpy didn't go too near the unfortunate human. You could never be sure what the two-legged creatures would do when you got close to their orbit.

They moved into the park, noticing a pungent aroma

from the rough sleeper, but it wasn't as bad as what Chirpy had just expelled from her backside.

'He smells like a run-down farm,' Chirpy said, surprising Crowley with her knowledge of one of those great animal prisons.

'Where will your human be now?' he asked the little dog.

'Near the lake, sitting on a bench,' she replied, getting agitated again and running around in circles, chasing something only her frazzled mind could see.

Crowley hadn't been in the park for a while, but remembered the lake was at the far end. It would take them another five minutes to reach at their current speed.

'Do you like coming here?' he said.

'Oh yes,' Chirpy replied, still running in circles. 'There are some wonderful things here.' She was panting so hard that Crowley worried she might collapse at any second.

'What type of things?'

The last time he visited the park, it had needed a complete facelift. Fires and vandals had destroyed huge chunks of grass and ruined most of the attractions and play areas. Drug addicts and other humans of the night were everywhere when he sprinted through its grounds.

'Here, I'll show you,' she said, darting off to the right and through some yellow and purple bushes.

He scowled at the distraction, with no choice but to follow the dog. He thrust his head between those blossoms and was stopped dead by what he saw on the other side.

'Wow,' was all he could say.

Chirpy jumped onto a colossal statue. 'I like to run across this and chase the squirrels.'

Crowley stared in appreciation at the massive piece of

concrete shaped like a giant human. Its arms were held out on either side while the head peered into the sky, waiting for something to fall from the clouds. At first, he thought it had collapsed to be in this position until, on further inspection, he understood somebody had designed it like that. Even though he wanted to get back on track, he jumped onto the beast and followed Chirpy into the middle, wondering what the statue's purpose was.

'There are a few things humans do better than us,' he said.

She'd stopped running, looking as solemn as he'd seen her in their short time together. 'I feel tall when I'm up here.' She lay on her stomach. 'I hate being so small.'

Tears were in her eyes, and he forgot all about trying to fathom the workings of the human mind and went to his new friend. He put his paw around Chirpy's neck and smiled at the little dog.

'Being small has its advantages, my friend.' Not so long ago, he wouldn't have consoled her like this, but now it was something he needed to do.

'Am I your friend?' she asked. Her tears were of joy, not sadness.

'Of course,' Crowley replied. There was a sensation in his chest he hadn't experienced for a while: warmth for a fellow animal. It made him think of Emma again as guilt exploded behind his eyes. 'But we must keep going and find your human before he misses you.'

The little dog grinned before jumping from the concrete edifice and dashing into the bushes, with Crowley struggling to keep up. As they returned to their original path, the tiny legs of the pooch appeared ahead of him.

'Wait!' Crowley shouted.

'C'mon then,' Chirpy yelled behind her.

He sprinted as fast as he could, his watch swinging from side to side and reminding him how late it was. They ran past great swathes of manicured trees and colourful rows of flowers. He glanced into the sky and marvelled at the shining stars, remembering his first night in the litter and how his mother had explained that all cats were descended from the stars.

He watched the little dog, joy on her face since escaping the orbit of the ebony cat and the great bull. In Chirpy's delight, he remembered that moment with his mother long ago before the humans separated them.

'My dear child,' his mother had purred as they nestled together in the straw. 'Do you see those twinkling lights up above? Those are the stars, where we cats originally came from long ago.'

His eyes widened as he gazed up at the glittering sky. 'We're from the stars?' he asked in wonder.

His mother nodded. 'Oh yes. Once upon a time, the stars grew lonely in the heavens. They wanted to explore the earth and make friends with the creatures below. So the stars gathered up bundles of light and formed them into the shape of cats. With a leap, the first cats jumped from the night sky to the world below. And those first cats were our ancestors.'

He snuggled against his mother's soft fur as she went on. 'We still carry that starlight within us, which is why our eyes glow in the dark. When you look at the stars, remember that we have stardust in our fur and the heavens' light in our hearts.'

The chill of the night couldn't remove the warmth he had for his mother, her and all the others he lost long ago.

Crowley peered at the glittering prizes in the sky, wondering how much trouble this quest for Darkstar might present him.

And he continued to question how he'd get Emma out of prison.

Chapter 11

Emma: Fire and Ice

'If you'd gone to college, this never would have happened,' Jane said.

'You believe I'm guilty?' Ever since they were kids, their relationship had fluctuated between fire and ice, with the occasional tepid moments.

'Of course not,' Jane replied. 'However, had you continued your studies, you wouldn't have had the time to get involved in whatever this is.'

Emma stared at her older sister, seeing the dark rings circling her eyes and the poor condition of her skin. There may have been a ten-year difference between them, but she noticed how much Jane looked like their mother.

'Will that be my defence when it goes to court?' Emma laughed. 'That staying on the fine path of education would have kept me on the straight and narrow?'

'Perhaps it would have guaranteed you were in better company.'

Emma raised her eyebrows in mock horror. 'I've been working two jobs, you know.'

'Two jobs? You're still at the comic shop?'

She noticed the disdain in her sister's voice. 'Of course.'

'So what's the other job?'

'I work as a vet's assistant on the weekend.'

Jane pushed her papers around as though looking for the information, ready to stand forward and bamboozle a hard-nosed jury with an astounding fact she'd just discovered.

'You see, your Honour and members of the jury, the heroine of our story couldn't be guilty because she was helping poor distressed animals.' Jane would take a bow, and everybody in the courtroom, even the prosecution, would give her a standing ovation.

That's how Emma imagined it would be. Instead, Jane said, 'A vet's assistant? How exactly did you get that job with no experience or qualifications?'

'Just luck, I suppose.'

'The prosecution will dig into your private life, so I need to know first.'

Emma leant back into the uncomfortable prison chair and puffed out her cheeks.

'I may have dated the owner once.' She grinned. 'It was possibly more than once.'

Jane took a pen and pushed it into the white of the paper. 'And what's her name?'

'Mrs Louise Temple.'

She'd met Louise in a club near the river. She was a little older than her usual 'type', but the breakup with Heather was still fresh in her heart – even though it was all Emma's doing – and she needed some fun to take her mind off other things. It was supposed to be only for a night, but one thing led to another, and then she had the job she'd always wanted.

And now she'd lost it again.

'Would your employer give a reference for you in court?'

'I don't see why not – I was the perfect employee.'

'Of course you were.' Jane scribbled down more notes. 'How did you find the time to work on your art, working two jobs and such a hectic social life?'

Emma shrugged. 'I have the vitality of youth.'

Jane pushed her pen away so it sat between them on the table like an accusing finger.

I'm not sure if she believes I'm innocent.

'You were always full of energy as a kid. It drove me crazy, you running around the house like an Olympic sprinter. And you couldn't stop scribbling and doodling over everything. Dad could never get that paint out of your bedroom wall.'

She ignored her sister's diversion down memory lane, turning to more important things. 'How's Mother?'

'No improvement, still waiting for the doctor's results.' There was a clinical detachment to Jane's voice that worried her. She knew Jane had grown more distant from all of them since their father's death, but she expected more from her sister where their mother's health was concerned. And she could tell when Jane was lying to her.

'Did you see her today?' Emma had lost all interest in her own predicament, needing to know everything would be okay with her mother.

The air was so brittle between them that Emma felt it would snap at any second. She watched the stress spread through her sister like water soaking into a sponge.

'She could go at any time. I've asked the authorities for a compassionate release for you, and I'm waiting for a response.'

The enormity of Jane's words punched her in the gut.

Their mother was dying, and she was stuck behind bars, unable to be by her side. 'Thank you for looking after her.'

Jane nodded, her eyes downcast. Emma studied her sister's face, noting the new lines etched around her mouth and cheeks.

'It's what daughters do,' Jane said.

'How are you holding up?' Emma asked.

Jane rubbed her temples, some of the hardness fading from her expression. 'Honestly? I'm exhausted. Taking care of Mum, dealing with this, it's a lot.'

She reached across the table, grasping Jane's fingers. 'Hey, you're not alone in this. We're sisters. I know I haven't been there for you or Mum recently, but I'm here now.'

Jane snatched her hand away. 'Yes, you're in *here* now.' Her expression was one of disappointment. 'And I need to do something about it.' She collected her things and stood.

'I know you'll get me out, Jane.'

She watched her sister leave, not knowing how she'd return to her dying mother.

Three hours later, Emma still pictured her sister in that room. She stood under a shower, its coldness cutting into the fog of depression and fear hanging over her. Some other girls were whispering behind her, but she ignored them, not wanting to get involved in prisoner politics. She closed her eyes as a river of pain seeped through her, the only release being an escape back into her childhood.

'Emma!' She could hear her mother shouting her name as she squeezed her eyes shut and listened to the sea. Their father instructed the girls not to go into the caves, which made Emma more determined.

'A family of dragons lives there,' Jane told her the first

time their parents took them to that hidden part of the coast. She didn't believe her sister; she was ten, not a child, but it still intrigued her.

'Emma,' she heard her mother shout again, never thinking how worried she might be. She knew Jane would be in the sea while their father went fishing.

Small crabs were running between the rocks, and she marvelled at how they crawled over everything in their way. She closed her eyes again and felt the wet sand seeping beneath her fingernails as her hands gripped the ground, her body hanging on as if the world was about to turn over and throw her away.

Emma let nature wash over her, literally and metaphorically, as water drifted in from an underground connection to the sea and touched her feet and legs. The thought of the place being untouched by human hands since time began gave her an incredible sense of euphoria. In the partial gloom, her senses were more heightened, the breeze from the water gliding over her skin and making it bristle as if caressed by electricity.

Her ears tuned into the noises the walls made, stone whispers flying through the ether. A noise from behind her, deep into the cave, startled her, and she sat up. Her gaze darted between the shadows, looking for her mother or Jane playing a trick on her, but she found nothing.

'Don't be silly,' she said aloud, hoping her voice would comfort her and still that beating heart thumping inside her chest. But it didn't help, sprinting back towards the light and away from her fears. She told herself everything would be okay and, just like the cats she loved so much, she had nine lives anyway.

She ran into her mother's open arms, expecting a

scolding for sneaking off, but instead, her mother swept Emma up with a smile brighter and warmer than any sun.

'How I missed you,' her mother said while fighting back tears and squeezing Emma just enough so they were glued together in familial love.

That was the face Emma saw as she stood underneath that cold prison shower. Her fate wasn't important now; she could only think about getting out and seeing her mother again. And she would do anything to make that happen.

Chapter 12

Darkstar: Bastet

T he stories of Darkstar's origins were many, legendary, and often unbelievable. Some said he landed on Earth in an alien spaceship and was the vanguard of a feline invasion. Others claimed he was grown in a laboratory so the humans could infiltrate the animal community and learn its secrets. But the one whispered the most, and Darkstar's personal favourite, was that he was the reincarnation of Bastet, the ancient Egyptian Cat Goddess. Darkstar encouraged and perpetuated this story, even naming his home Bubastis and littering the insides with small statues of the Sphinx he acquired from a broken-down gift shop storeroom.

Bubastis was his secret place, deep beneath the old underground, where no animal or human would ever find him. He spent less time there now, his duties as the Bullfather's lieutenant keeping him far too busy to relax. Soon, their plan would reach fruition, and there'd been no time to concentrate on anything else.

He lived mainly with the Bullfather and his acolytes in their safe place, with the Guardian to protect it and them.

However, Darkstar hated that land and its aroma of death, which spanned centuries and would never leave its ghostly, stone skeleton no matter how many times the Guardian tried to scrub it clean.

This was why he disappeared from there when he could. One of Darkstar's favourite spots was the train station. There was a time when he travelled up and down the country using the nation's railway network, hiding under seats and avoiding the humans when he could. He knew most of the stations intimately, where to find the best spots for discarded food and the warmest places.

He was on a train when he discovered he could hurt humans like they'd hurt him so many times. He was on the last service from Manchester to Leeds, underneath a seat in a deserted carriage. It was after midnight, and he was half-asleep in the shadows, knowing he had less than an hour before reaching his destination. It was the sound of drunken singing which brought him fully alert.

'Engerrrrlund, Engerrrlund,' they howled, swaying from side to side. He didn't see the hands coming from behind or know they were there until sweaty fingers pulled him from his hiding place by his fur.

'Here, Dave. You said you were 'ungry,' the ugly man holding Darkstar said to one of the others. 'This fat fecker will fill you up.'

He threw the cat at his friend and laughed. Darkstar twisted his body in the air, switching his head forward and pointing his claws towards the startled man before him. He landed on him with his paws pressed into the human's face, nails scratching down his skin and shredding flesh like paper. Then Darkstar sprinted into the next carriage with the man's screams ringing in his ears.

Darkstar spent the rest of the journey waiting for them

at the end of the train, but they never came. He was elated when he left the station, a new zest for life flowing through him. He was reminded of it every time he visited a station; it was one reason he loved returning to the place so much. There, he would watch the humans hurry back and forth with their pointless lives and meaningless journeys, oblivious to the real world happening around them.

It was late, so the station was close to empty, making him emboldened enough to sit proudly on one of the seats usually occupied by nervous travellers or desperate sleepers. Decade's old paint had fallen in chunks around the insides, leaving everywhere tattered and unkempt. A clock hung from the roof, its metal hands whining as time moved forward. Overgrown vegetation twisted through broken windows, tangling through the beams supporting the building. As he checked the surroundings, the encroaching gloom draped over the walls like a blanket. He smelt alcohol and saw the detritus of human existence creeping into every corner.

As the clock stole towards midnight, he was surprised to see a family of three enter: a weary-looking mother, a haggard father and a small female child who couldn't have been more than six or seven years old. They sat opposite him, slumped together like impoverished trees blown over in the wind.

As he studied his surroundings, the sight of the family sparked unwanted memories of his childhood. Unwelcome images floated through his mind: his younger brother caught in a trap set by humans, knives thrust into his kittenish flesh as Darkstar hid behind the bushes, his shame still over-whelming him. Bricks and stones assaulted his friends as he fled across the hills, following the rabbits leading him to safety, and the worst of all, his parents torn apart by dogs as the humans cheered.

'We can't help it,' the hounds cried, the scars on their flesh where they'd been tortured catching his gaze before those canine teeth ripped his mother's throat out. He didn't understand why the humans let him go that night. He allowed the darkness to creep behind his eyes and obscure all those hateful memories before returning to the nightlife in the station.

Plenty of other animals were there, but they were all keeping away from him; his reputation and who he worked for were significant deterrents to potential social interaction. He stared into the rafters, spotting the yellow eyes of the bats, contemplating the role they would play in the new world to come.

Rodents scurried around the station's edges, searching out leftover human food for survival. He looked forward to the day when no animal would have to do such a thing again. Other cats were there, paying their respects to him when he entered the station. However, that night, he wasn't interested in what other animals were doing because it was the people he came to observe, turning his focus back towards the family near him.

The parents wasted no time falling asleep on each other's shoulders. They had to be waiting for a train, which was hours away, going there because they had nowhere else to stay. It made him wonder again how humans could treat each other with such callous disregard. No animal would allow another animal to go without shelter if they could prevent it – even species which hated each other would still make sure none of their kind – animal kind – would suffer unnecessarily. The rules of the AA wouldn't allow it.

He'd been suspicious of the AA in its early days. The

gains it had made in making more animals safe from human cruelty had been significant and impressive, and now his and the Bullfather's plans were coming to fruition it wouldn't be long before the golden age of animals would replace humans as the dominant rulers of the planet. Everything would go as planned if Crowley did as ordered and brought the Doolittle to them.

As he thought about the future, he observed the child untangle herself from its sleeping parents and walk towards him, smiling at the giant mound of darkness before her. Not for the first time, he wondered how the humans perceived him in all his ebony glory. The kid said something in a language he didn't understand, but he recognised she meant no harm.

Darkstar had witnessed the degradation of human cruelty close up and had learnt how to recognise impending danger, but was confident the child was harmless. The girl got as close as she could, then reached out and stroked him under his chin. He purred his appreciation, knowing if the Bullfather saw him, the great bull would not be pleased.

The girl sat beside him and whispered into his ear in that strange tongue that sounded warm and comforting. They were immigrants or refugees; if they'd been native to the land, he would have known what she was saying. He'd learned several languages in his travels, but this was unknown to him.

She laughed a little, as quietly as possible, before singing something Darkstar assumed was a lullaby. It was sweet and lyrical, and the darkest cat in the world purred along with it. As the child continued to stroke and pet him, his thoughts turned all melancholic, feeling sad for the first time about what he and the others were about to do to humanity. And then his childhood memories rose from where he'd submerged them, and the pity vanished instantly with the images of his slain family.

'Does it have to be all of them?' he'd asked the Bullfather.

'Some won't be affected; they will be immune,' the bull replied, back when the annoying raven didn't speak for him. 'Everything's in place; nothing can be changed.'

'Not quite everything,' Darkstar said to himself.

The most critical part was missing, and it was up to his most hated enemy to get it. The irony of it made him smile. If he'd killed Crowley long ago, like he'd tried on numerous occasions, none of this would have been possible. No other animal could steal like the Thief could, especially from the humans. He and the Bullfather talked about using the Guardian to acquire the Doolittle, but even though he was human, the Guardian's intelligence was little more than average.

'Beaten out of him by his father,' the Bullfather would say when discussing which humans they could trust.

'Is he clever enough to gather more humans to our cause?' Darkstar had his doubts.

'I think he can. If we keep them all in the dark about our ultimate goal, then yes. There are enough animal sympathisers amongst them, so we'll receive all the support we require. Our contacts worldwide and distributors are in place; all we need is the product.'

Yes. All we need is for Crowley to follow his instructions.

He walked away from the smiling child, telling himself the world would be better off with fewer humans.

And better off without Crowley.

Once he did his job.

Chapter 13

Crowley: Birds Fly

Crowley returned to the job tasked by the Bullfather: the punishment for not following those orders would be swift and brutal. The giant bull's reputation for violence was known throughout the animal community, and all feared Darkstar.

What is the Doolittle?

He considered that as he followed the excitable dog deeper into the park. Crowley usually welcomed the darkness as a blanket to hide his true intentions, but at that moment, he wanted to be anywhere but there. Chirpy stopped running, standing in the shadow of the largest tree he'd ever seen. It resembled an enormous green mushroom, with shoots of multi-coloured leaves dangling from its branches. He crept towards it with tentative steps.

'It's scary, isn't it?' Chirpy whispered.

'That would be a good description.' There didn't appear to be any way around it, so wide was its reach. 'Do we have to go under it?'

'Yes,' Chirpy said. 'But don't worry. The crows who live there are friendly.'

'Great.' Crowley had never gotten along with crows.

'Then we must proceed through the dinosaurs, and we'll be there.'

'Dinosaurs?'

'They're gigantic carvings, just behind this tree.'

They were underneath the thin, low-hanging branches. An eerie silence made him think of Emma and her imprisonment. His contacts in the juvenile centre had been relaying information to him since she'd been inside. And none of it was pleasant.

Her skin and hair were on my paws as I stole those jewels from that museum. I can blame Darkstar and the Bullfather for sending me there, but I left bits of Emma behind.

But why did the police have Emma's DNA in the first place?

The question shattered in his mind as he heard shouting.

'It's the Thief!'

It came from above, thin and raspy, floating over his head like a promise of terrible things to come.

'It's the Thief,' more of them cried. It began as a slight hum before growing into a roar: a murder of crows yelling at him.

'It's the Thief.'

'What do they mean?' Chirpy asked.

'My reputation precedes me,' Crowley replied, picking up speed.

The further inside the belly of the great tree, the less illumination there was, his mind playing tricks on him. He expected his greatest enemy to appear and bare those dangerous teeth. Was this all some terrible trap set by Darkstar to make him pay for losing the jewellery the Bullfather had ordered him to steal? If only he'd taken the loot straight to them and not lingered at home first, panicking when the humans smashed into Emma's flat.

The noise fell from the leaves over his head, wings unfurling above him, delivering a chilling accompaniment to the words ringing in his ears.

'It's the Thief,' the birds shrieked as one.

'What have you come to steal from us?' they shouted.

Crowley considered closing his eyes and sprinting under the branches until he reached the light on the other side, shocked by how nervous he was. But he stopped, his legs transformed into stone, heart beating as if it wanted to explode. He was disappointed by his apparent weakness.

The birds were inches from him, their wings beating closer to his eyes. There was a smell of chalk just beyond his nose as something small landed on his head. Crowley's paw shot up and swatted whatever it was away, his feet moving forward in the moonlight. Feathers fluttered near his face as they shrieked again.

'It's the Thief.'

They were close, Crowley struggling to move, his paws sticking to the grass, his mind about to go into overload. He hated crows. He was about to drop to the ground and curl into a ball when the little dog's paw touched his shoulder.

'We're nearly there.' Her voice delivered calmness through him, his strength and confidence returning in waves. He opened his eyes and smiled at Chirpy.

'Let's get you to the Professor,' he said as they ran from the gloom into the fading illumination of the flickering park lights.

At the back of his mind was the faint whispering of the crows, reminding him of his vulnerabilities. He shut them out and moved forward until the dinosaurs appeared: enormous, long-necked, tiny-eyed beasts towered above them like gatekeepers protecting the secret world, while at their feet, smaller creatures sat and scowled.

'I don't like birds,' Crowley said, with the sound of the crows still ringing inside his ears.

'Why?' she asked as they left the giant tree behind them.

He stared ahead. 'Birds are descended from dinosaurs, so they have an inferiority complex. Imagine once being the planet's rulers, and now all they can do is flap their little wings and moan.'

They moved past the last of the dinosaurs and marvelled at what had come before them. A Stegosaurus with its colossal red spines stretching from its neck to the tip of its tail; the Tyrannosaurus Rex with its puny arms and powerful muscular legs; a Spinosaurus with a sail of skin protruding from its back; and the Theropod with its sharp serrated meat-eating teeth, ready to tear flesh from bones. Crowley stared at them all and wondered how long it would be before all the animals on the planet would be extinct.

They came into the clearing, and he spotted the humans nearby. Two bodies bowed in whispered conversation. He ran as fast as he could, desperate to get close enough to hear what they said, only to be foiled by the sight of the one on his right getting up and walking away. They were gone before he could move any closer.

He crept as near the ground as he could, pushing hard against the damp grass, the wet mud assaulting his senses. Chirpy kept on running and bounded towards her human.

'There you are, girl,' Professor Wyatt Wells said as the little dog sprang up and landed on Wells's chest with enough force to knock the wind from his lungs.

'Oooff,' Wells exclaimed. 'You must've missed me, girl.

Come on; it's time for us to get home.' He looked around him. 'I hope you had some grand adventures while I finished my business.'

'I did,' she said. All the human heard was a little bark.

Crowley stayed glued to the earth, ready to follow as soon as the man turned his back. Chirpy had told him Wells always had her sitting in the front as he drove home, which should work well for them if the kid remembered the plan they'd discussed.

The man and his dog strode from the benches and towards the exit, Crowley following behind at a safe distance, ready to put his plan into action, assuming Chirpy distracted Wells. The car park was only a couple of minutes away. He crept through the shadows, the words of the crows echoing in his head.

'*It's the Thief.*'

'*What have you come to steal?*'

'Just the Doolittle,' he whispered into the grass.

He saw the car as Wells, holding Chirpy, approached the passenger side. He heard the man breathing. Wells opened the door to throw the pup inside, arms bending like a Christmas tree overwhelmed by too many decorations.

Crowley waited for Chirpy to make her move, his fur standing on end. The distraction had to come now, Chirpy confusing Wells long enough for Crowley to slip into the back seat unnoticed. His claws dug further into the dirt, ready to push forward and pounce.

Then Wells took a stronger hold on the little dog, dropped her into the passenger seat and closed the door. As Wells walked to the other side of the car, Crowley watched his plan disintegrate in the darkness.

Chapter 14

Emma: Teenage Wasteland

Emma stared at the ceiling of her eight-by-ten cell, tracing the cracks in the dull grey paint. She'd counted every one several times over. One hundred and ninety-nine cracks crawled across the ceiling like crooked fingers, reaching to clutch her in their cruel grasp.

One hundred and ninety-nine. The number reminded Emma of the days her parents took her to Whitby, and they climbed that amount of steps up to the Abbey as she clutched a copy of *Dracula* under her arm. The memories shimmered in her vision as she pictured her mother now, sinking further into the darkness of her own mind.

I have to get out of here to be with her.

She heard the constant drip of the leaky tap in the corner, grating on her nerves. The thin mattress below her was lumpy and reeked of body odour - whether hers or someone else's, she wasn't sure. She shifted, the rough wool blanket scratching her skin.

She lay on the bottom bunk, gazing at the underside of

the top mattress. It was stained yellow with age and sagged heavily under the weight of its occupant.

'You awake up there?' Emma asked.

'No,' came the mumbled reply.

Emma snorted. 'Hilarious, Raya.'

There was a creak of rusty springs as Raya rolled over to peer at Emma. Her heavy eyeliner was smudged, her spiky pink hair poking out in all directions.

'I was trying to sleep until you so rudely interrupted.'

Emma sat up, smacking her head on the bottom of Raya's mattress. 'Ow! This stupid bunk is too low.'

Raya cackled. 'Maybe your head's too big.'

Emma sighed. 'How can you sleep in this dump, anyway? It smells like armpits, and the weird noises at night creep me out.'

'You get used to it.' Raya shrugged. 'I just pretend I'm somewhere else. I was on a beach with Chris Hemsworth when you disturbed me.'

'Well, I can't,' Emma said. 'I hate it here.'

Raya laughed. 'You've only been here a few days. You better hope your sister gets you out, or you'll never survive.'

Emma tried to smile through the doubts and fears swirling in her mind. 'At least I've got you to keep me company.'

'Yeah, we're like two peas in a pub.'

Emma's guts rumbled. 'I could do with a drink.'

Raya jumped down. 'I could get you something tomorrow if you want?'

'Booze? In here? How?'

Raya touched her nose. 'I know the right people. Nothing's out of bounds here – booze, fags, drugs, mobile phones. Anything you want.'

Emma's eyes narrowed. 'How would I pay for it?'

'Do you have any valuables – cash, ciggies, jewellery from that heist?'

Emma scowled at her. 'I told you I didn't steal those jewels. I don't understand how they got into my flat.'

Raya grinned. 'I'm only messing with you. When is your sister coming back?'

'Soon, I hope.' She felt terrible asking Jane to leave their mother, but it was the only way she'd escape her torment.

'Great. Get a message to her – tell her to bring you chocolate and cakes. The proper stuff is like gold dust in here. A packet of fig rolls is worth more than ten cigarettes. Pickled onion Monster Munch is even more valuable.'

'Stop yapping in there!' a guard shouted from the other side of the door.

Emma took the advice, slipping back into the bed and pulling the sheets close to her.

She put her head on the pillow and thought she heard rats scurrying across the cell.

The fluorescent lights buzzed overhead, assaulting Emma's ears as she lay on the thin mattress. She hadn't slept all night, kept awake by the constant noise. She stared at the ceiling, counting the cracks in the paint for the hundredth time.

The stink of industrial cleaners burned her nose, unable to mask the underlying stench of body odour and stale air. She took a deep breath and immediately regretted it, the chemical lemon scent making her eyes water.

She ached, the mattress offering little padding from the rigid metal frame underneath. Goosebumps prickled her arms in the chill. Hunger gnawed at her stomach. She thought of her mother's home-cooked meals, swallowing hard against the lump in her throat.

Emma sat with her head in her hands. She rubbed at the tension building in her temples, trying to massage away the pounding headache. She couldn't stop thinking about her mother. Did she even remember she had a daughter? Were people taking proper care of her? Was Jane doing it all on her own? Was she scared and confused without her youngest daughter?

Guilt churned in Emma's gut. She should be there, making sure her mum was okay. Instead, she was stuck inside, locked away like an animal.

However, that wasn't the only reason she felt guilty. She'd been so busy with her life, spending all her time in the comic shop and the vets, plus working on her art portfolio, that it had been ages since visiting her mother. She couldn't even remember when they last spoke on the phone.

I'm a terrible daughter and always have been.

Emma looked up, eyes on the photo taped to the concrete wall. Her mother's smiling face beamed at her. It was an old picture from before the dementia had stolen her memories and personality. Back when she was still Emma's vibrant, laughing mum, who would talk and joke with her for hours.

Tears pricked hot behind her eyes. She took a shaky breath, willing herself not to cry. Crying wouldn't help anything. She had to be strong, for her mother's sake.

She rose from the bed and walked to the photo, gently touching her fingers to her mom's face. 'I'm so sorry, Mum,' she whispered. 'I'll find a way back to you, I promise.'

Footsteps echoed down the hall, keys jangling on belts. Her body tensed, her heart pounding. The guards appeared outside the door, barking orders.

'Chow time, let's go.'

She shuffled out behind the other girls, shoulders hunched. She kept her eyes down, avoiding their curious stares. The clanging and chatter in the cafeteria overwhelmed her senses. She slid her tray along, not bothering to see what unidentifiable food landed on her plate.

'Emma, over here!' a voice called out.

Her head snapped up, relief flooding her as she saw Raya waving her over to a table. At least she had one friendly face in that hellhole. She sank onto the bench across from Raya, offering a weak smile.

'You must have had a long shower,' Emma said.

Raya shrugged. 'The longer the better to get the stain of this place from my skin.' She shovelled a heap of mashed potatoes into her mouth. 'So, how did you sleep?'

'Just peachy,' Emma replied, listlessly picking at her food. 'Nothing like sleeping on an old mattress under flickering lights all night, with the rats and the dripping tap doing my head in.'

Raya snorted. 'Yeah, it takes some getting used to. Better than a park bench, though.'

Emma gave a dark laugh. 'I guess so. But these clothes are really not my style.' She plucked at the baggy cotton pants of her prison uniform.

Raya grinned. 'Whoever designed these made a right nun's hoop out of them.'

Emma's chest hurt as she laughed. 'You say the strangest things, Raya.'

'Yeah, not as strange as this muck, though.' She picked at the grey mush on her tray. 'This grub will be the death nail for me in here.'

Emma studied the dining area, taking in the clumps of girls in matching uniforms. Some looked impossibly young to her, while others had hard, cold eyes that belied their age. Two were clearly pregnant.

What kind of people stick pregnant girls in prison?

A commotion across the room caught her attention. Two inmates were squaring off, voices raised. She watched as a girl threw a punch, catching the other square in the nose. Blood spurted as the prisoners grappled and flailed. Guards rushed in, dragging them apart. Emma winced as she saw blood dripping down the front of one girl's uniform.

'Jeez, that was brutal,' she muttered.

Raya shrugged. 'Happens all the time. You gotta have eyes in the back of your head in here.'

Emma thought of that as a guard approached her. 'Crowley, you're wanted.'

Emma's heart sank. Had her mother's health worsened? Was Jane there to get her out?

'What?' she said.

The guard glared at her. 'Stand up. You're off to see the governor.'

Chapter 15

Crowley: Chemicrazy

Wells slipped into the car as Crowley's plans slithered away. His mind was already working out how to track the vehicle when Chirpy surprised him with her skill. She leapt across the seats and glided through the small gap in the door and into the outside world, darting into the trees as Wells swore.

Crowley flexed his legs and pounced as the professor staggered after the dog, sneaking from the shadows and into the front of the car, then scrambling into the back and sinking into the darkness. As he pressed his fur as far down as possible, Chirpy shouted to him.

'Well done, my friend.'

'I hope you did that because you needed to shit,' Wells said as he put the car into gear and pulled out of the park, unaware of the other passenger.

It's the Thief.

Crowley heard the words inside his head.

'Are you okay?' Chirpy's high-pitched voice made him uneasy. Not because he had anything against the little dog, but because he didn't want anything to make Wells suspicious.

'What do you get up to when you scamper into the bushes?' Wells asked his pet.

And what are you doing with your mysterious friends?

Crowley wished they'd arrived earlier so he could have overheard their conversation.

'I have a new friend and I met the Bullfather and we're on a secret mission and I'm hungry and I saw the scariest cat in the world and I'm still hungry.'

Chirpy's stream-of-consciousness rambling was annoying even to Crowley.

'Are you hungry, girl?' Wells asked. 'I am, as well. We'll have something together when we get back.'

All the talk of food caused Crowley's stomach to rumble, making him thankful Wells had turned the radio on to listen to music. The noise drowned out the sounds coming from his gut. Some torturous song about the world ending blared from the speakers, forcing him to push his head further into the gap below the seat to escape it. Its only benefit was to distract him from the pain in his belly.

As he squeezed in as far as possible, his nose touched a scrunched-up piece of paper. Crowley twisted around until he got his paw on it, narrowing his eyes in the gloom to see the words: three things repeated until they filled the whole page.

'Pandora – The Project.'

His mind pondered what it meant as the professor acti-vated the electronic garage at his house. The vehicle moved forward as Crowley prepared for what came next.

'We'll be inside soon,' Chirpy said.

'Okay, girl, you'll get fed in a minute,' Wells said as he turned off the engine.

'I'm starving,' she replied, peering between the seats to glimpse her friend.

Wells got out and closed the door. Crowley's mind worked overtime, visions of being locked in the back all night crushing his plans. Then Chirpy helped him out. Wells opened the front passenger door, and the stink hit Crowley like a kick in the gut.

'Ohhh shit...'

The little dog had, all over the seat. She bounced past her human, running up the stairs, out of the garage and into the house.

'Follow me,' she shouted to Crowley.

'No food for you,' Wells screamed, turning away from the steaming poop festering under his nose, allowing Crowley the time to get out of the car – avoiding the dog shit – and sneaking behind the large pile of boxes near the stairs.

As the professor returned with a mop and some disinfectant, Crowley slipped from the shadows and crept upstairs. At the top, he found Chirpy waiting for him.

'You're very clever, my friend; very clever.' He was glad to be away from the smell.

'What?' the little dog said, surprise written all over her face.

'For the distraction, no matter how bad it stank.'

'Sorry, but I couldn't help myself. I've been holding that in since the AA meeting.'

'Shut your yapping,' Wells shouted from downstairs.

Crowley grinned. 'Where's the room you mentioned where he does his experiments?'

Chirpy didn't reply, running up another set of stairs and heading out of Crowley's sight so fast he wondered if the kid needed to empty her bowels again. He followed her as

Wells left the garage, the professor cursing at the top of his voice.

Sprinting upstairs, Crowley scanned the rest of the place: the house was very modern, with ornate mirrors hanging on the walls, several lights, and contemporary paintings of square-chinned men and women in floral dresses. The stairs led into a long corridor with a rug spread over a cold wooden floor.

Chirpy was sitting, waiting for him at the end. 'The door's closed.'

'Not a problem,' he replied, taking a run and jumping up to the handle, landing perfectly on it with his feet, his weight pushing down on the metal. The door clicked open as he dropped to the floor.

She stared at him in astonishment. 'That's impressive.'

He nodded. 'Stay here and keep guard. If Wells comes, shout out.'

The door opened enough for him to squeeze his fur against the wood and push inside. Everything was functional; there was no television, no bookshelf, no dining table, nothing there for leisure or pleasure, only the chair near the large bench adorned with beakers, tubes, phials, a centrifuge and a couple of laptops. There was a huge fridge freezer in one corner of the room, bits of paper and books stacked alongside it.

The floor was polished, dark, and free of either dust or clutter. The wood was cold on his paws as he crept in. He didn't know how to find this Doolittle, never mind getting it out of the house if it was too large to carry.

He jumped onto the chair and then the table, careful not to disturb anything, glancing everywhere in search of some clue but finding nothing but spotless, clinical neatness. It was as if no human or animal had ever set foot, or feet, inside this room.

But Crowley knew that to be untrue, still wondering how Darkstar and the Bullfather learned about Wells and this place. Something shining in the corner caught his attention. Six long phials of bright red liquid were sitting in the space between the computers, contained by a small wooden prison of individual columns. He sidestepped the beakers in his way, slipping past the centrifuge and sticking his head into the narrow space amidst the two digital screens. Each of the phials had a sticker on the bottom, displaying the words: The Project: X6.

The Project again, just like on the paper in the back of the car. He moved closer to the phials, poking his nose forward, trying to get a sniff of the ominous-looking red liquid.

'He's coming,' Chirpy barked.

Crowley snapped his head to one side, catching his cheek with a sharp whack on the edge of the laptop. He ignored the pain and jumped onto the cold floor, his eyes busy needing to find somewhere to hide, panic setting in until he ran to the pile of papers near the fridge and squeezed behind them. Wells shouted at the dog as he strode into the room.

'You do that again, and it'll be the pound for you,' he said without humour.

Crowley peered around the edge of his hiding spot, watching as the professor walked towards the table and eased into the chair, staring into the space Crowley had just occupied.

Chirpy followed him inside. 'Where are you?' the dog asked.

'Shut up,' Wells barked, hitting the power button on the

laptop closest to him as Chirpy's eyes darted around the room. The computer screen flashed awake, and the professor grabbed the mouse, moving it over the digital desktop until he found what he was looking for. Crowley noticed the mouse droppings beside his feet as a video sprang to life.

'Language processing in the brain. Experiment number six continued.' Wells stared at his digital self as his voice came from the computer screen. Crowley moved away from the dried rodent shit to get a better view of the video.

The professor picked up his dog and sat her opposite the laptop. 'Watch this, Chirpy; it's interesting.'

'Manipulating the cerebral cortex through chemical injection,' the digital Wells continued. 'Aural stimuli are received by the auditive organ and are changed to bioelectric signals on the organ of Corti. These electric impulses are transported through Scarpa's ganglion to the primary auditory cortex in both hemispheres. Each hemisphere treats it differently; the left side recognises distinctive parts such as phonemes, and the right takes over prosodic characteristics and melodic information.'

Wells grabbed the mouse and paused the video. 'I didn't realise I sounded so boring until I started watching these videos. Let's fast forward to the good bit.' He dragged the pointer across the screen until he reached the last few minutes of the clip. 'If it hadn't been for the Project, or Pandora, or whoever she is, demanding a chemical stimulus to increase brain power, I never would have made this fortuitous discovery.' He was scratching Chirpy's chin as the digital Wells continued.

'I can't give them this; it's far too important to fall into their devious hands.' The real Wells laughed at the screen. 'Which is why I've disabled all their spyware and hacking tools on the computers and removed the bugs and cameras they placed in this room, so it won't be long before Pandora comes to see me. And that means I've had to escalate my escape plans.'

The professor stopped the video again, getting up and walking to the refrigerator. Crowley edged backwards behind the stack of papers. 'But don't worry, Chirpy. You'll be coming with me.' He removed a water bottle from the fridge and took a large swig.

'And you, cat,' he said, peering into the shadows and Crowley's eyes. 'What will I do with you?'

Chapter 16

Pandora: Monday Morning

Just like the girl in the terrible pop song, Pandora hated Mondays. Memories she couldn't erase clawed at her from the pit she'd pushed them into, crawling their way up to remind her of the life she used to have. She removed the last cigarette from the box and pressed her face against the window, wanting the cold sheen of the glass to cut through her sickness. Lethargy had crept back into her bones before getting her latest assignment. A new existence was calling to her from somewhere.

I can't leave until I get access to the records. If it takes forever, I'll make those people pay for what they did to me.

Her reflection in the glass was a ghostly version of herself, pale eyes resting on tired lips. Her skin took on a translucent sheen reminiscent of those deep-sea fish you could peer inside. She stared out the window as she waited, examining the city and its concrete children. Anybody on the outside, looking up at her, would see another typical set of offices inhabited by anonymous worker bees going about their usual business.

'If anyone asks, say you work in financial services,' the Project had told her when she was recruited, which wasn't strictly untrue.

'I know nothing about that,' her fifteen-year-old self had replied.

'Don't worry,' they said through unemotional faces. 'It's part of your training.'

It was the most straightforward aspect of her training. First, they cleaned her up and dealt with her injuries, ensuring she was fit and healthy before the hard work began. During the day, she returned to her education and absorbed information. The evening was when her physical training happened, building up her strength, speed and stamina until she transformed from the skinny wraith the Project discovered living on the streets to a young woman with an athlete's physique.

Her favourite part of the training was the fighting skills they taught. It wasn't long before none of the others would enter the ring with her. She battered their egos as well as their bodies. It was just another reason why they hated her so much.

'What are you training me for?' she asked.

'To be better,' they said like a mantra.

When she turned sixteen, the Director explained her real purpose to her. The Project had wiped her past away, and she'd be a new person for them. It would be the beginning of her third life, but the traumatic parts of the earlier ones were always inside her.

She checked her phone, frowning as she questioned why the Director was late; it wasn't like her. She continued to look through the glass upon a fate she'd escaped, gazing at the ants as they hurried through the city.

There was misery in those streets, soaked through every slab of concrete, dripping from each building and saturating the dregs of humanity living there. The brightness of the neon adverts, the shiny billboards, and the constant noise of the shops, restaurants, and bars littered everywhere were all facades desperate to conceal the gloom of human existence.

They are only distractions to keep the masses compliant.

Sometimes, she pondered what her life would have been like if the Project hadn't discovered her shivering under that bridge.

Would my parents have found me, dragging me back to that life of torture and pain?

'Are you thinking about what you used to be?' Director Susan Adam had entered the room and got close to the window without Pandora hearing a thing.

That's sloppy.

She scrutinised the unassuming woman most would walk past, paying her no attention, which the Director wanted.

'If you're invisible, nobody will know what you're doing,' she'd told Pandora.

Pandora knew that to be a lie. She'd tried being invisible for most of her first life, desperate to hide from those who hurt her. None of it had worked. The Director badgered her to change her flame-red hair, a beacon to countless others. But Pandora didn't want to be invisible anymore. She needed the entire world to grasp who she was. She wanted people to know who was punishing them.

'I'm wondering what I'll do with the rest of my life,' Pandora said.

'I'm sure you'll have my job eventually.'

The thought didn't excite Pandora. She was grateful for what the Project had done for her, but she wanted more than that. Even though they'd helped her, it was just another prison.

They stood close to each other, their shoulders almost touching. The unlit cigarette nestled between Pandora's thumb and finger drew a scowl from the Director.

'When will you give up those poisonous things?'

Pandora stared across the smog that clung to the blue and white canvas. 'Only when I fall in love.'

Which will never happen. All the love was beaten out of me long ago.

'What's happening with our scientist?' Adam sat behind her desk and stared at the computer screen. Apart from two chairs, the desk and a laptop, the place was bare of anything else: no personal items anywhere and empty walls.

'No distractions,' the Director had said when Pandora asked about the room.

But Pandora loved distractions; they kept her mind from falling back into places she never wanted to visit again. She needed things to prevent her thoughts from wandering. Danger called out to her everywhere she went. Doing nothing drove her mad. Pandora's muscles ached from lack of activity as she sat opposite the Director. She stared at the cameras in the ceiling.

'Working on the latest batch, which he claims should be ready soon.'

When she'd caught up with Wyatt outside another dive bar, he promised her there would be a breakthrough shortly.

'I promise, Pandora. You'll have it soon.' He smiled, but she recognised the lie as it left his lips.

She pushed two pieces of paper across the desk. The weekly reports bored her, but she had no choice. She could have emailed the Director, but the Project was adamant they didn't want to leave an electronic trail.

Adam gazed at something on the screen as she spoke. 'And what is he doing outside his work?'

'Doing what normal folks do – searching for love and adventure.'

It was an interesting answer, one to draw the Director's focus away from the computer. Pandora wanted adventure. She craved it, but what about love? The idea was too strange for her to contemplate. Some people feared isolation and demanded human contact; they needed another mortal to cling to, to validate their life. She didn't need any of that. That was a weakness. Others were good for the occasional distraction, but real happiness could only come from within.

'Does that apply to you as well, Pandora?'

Pandora licked her lips and narrowed her eyes. 'I said normal.'

'You don't think of yourself as normal?'

She recognised the concern in the Director's voice. 'Is what we do normal?'

Adam's pale lips turned up slightly, an impression of a smile foreign to her face, her hands clasped together as if she were about to praise some imaginary god.

'Of course; we're a business like all the others. We collect knowledge and use it to make a profit.'

It wasn't a speech brimming with enthusiasm, but the Director believed what she was saying. However, if what Pandora was doing was just another ordinary job, she didn't know why she was still with them. She had no desire for an ordinary life. Who did?

'Yet, so far, we've profited very little from the scientist in your charge.' The Director's voice transformed from concern for her employee to irritation at not getting what she wanted. Pandora rose from the chair, wanting to leave as soon as possible.

'I'll speak to him again tomorrow and inform him of our concerns.' She stopped at the door. 'When can I return to proper work?'

The older woman gazed at the computer screen. 'Have you curtailed your impulsiveness?'

'Is this all part of my training?' For her, it was punishment.

'You finished your training six months ago. The Project does not send any of its staff into current assignments until their education is complete. We selected you for this job with Wells because your talents are best suited for the assignment.'

Pandora wondered what her specific talents were but didn't ask, having a different question instead.

'Who do I work for?'

The Director's grin resembled something from a 1940s horror film. 'You work for me, Pandora. You work for the Project.'

'Yeah, but who runs the Project? Who is the power behind it all?'

Adam crossed her arms. 'Why do you want to know?'

Pandora shrugged. 'Just curious, that's all.'

I need to know who to hide from when I escape this place.

The Director returned her focus to the computer screen. 'Don't worry, Pan – you've got years with us to discover all our secrets.'

She flinched, hating it when people shortened her name. And the thought of working for the Project for the rest of her life left a dark weight in her guts.

But it won't come to that.

She closed the door behind her, staring at the men and women in the corridor who appeared to be standard security types but who were all well-armed and highly skilled. She took the lift down to the exit and contemplated her impulsiveness.

And Pandora wondered how impulsive she was going to be.

Chapter 17

Emma: The Governor

Emma guessed from the look in the Governor's eyes that the woman was going to say no before she opened her mouth. That and the fact she had a mug on her desk with the words "You can't always get what you want" printed on it. The two Amazonian guards squeezing her arms were the only things stopping her from trashing the office.

'I'm afraid, Ms Crowley, I cannot grant your request for compassionate leave. I've informed your sister.' The Governor was a tiny woman of physique and empathy. Some god-awful wig sprang from her head, and Emma's nails trembled as she imagined her fingers tearing into the old woman's scalp.

'My mother is ill,' Emma croaked.

The Governor's muddy brown eyes and glare cut right through her. She closed the file by slamming her hand against the desk so hard that the small figurines of pink elephants and glitter-covered unicorns wobbled on their legs. She wondered which of her fellow inmates the Governor had confiscated them from.

'You should have thought of that before stealing from the museum. Theft is not a crime that the authorities or I take lightly. We have to make examples of people like you, or there's no telling what the rabble of this country will do.'

'She's losing her memory,' Emma half-whispered.

If I don't see her soon, she might not remember who I am.

'This is a prison, Ms Crowley, not a cheap bed-and-breakfast where you come as go as you please. You're here to be punished, not rehabilitated, no matter what the bleeding hearts say in the media.'

The strength vanished from Emma's legs as she flopped forward, only prevented from collapsing by the guard. She hung there like a drunken puppet, questioning how her world had turned upside down in such a short space of time.

'I'm innocent,' she claimed as the guards yanked her towards the door. They dragged her from the office and pushed her head against the wall.

'Get yourself cleaned up before going to your cell,' said the pig-headed one as she let Emma go. The chill grated against her skin, the drop in temperature not enough to cool the fire inside her eyes.

If only I'd spent more time with her. If only I hadn't argued so much with her.

Guilt swept through her like a waterfall. She'd ignored what was happening to her mother, fleeing from the consequences of that cruel condition, leaving her older sister to deal with it while swanning around the city on protest marches and activist meetings.

I wasted all that time on my portfolio when I could have been with Mum. And if I hadn't worked those weekends at the vet's, I could have taken Mum out.

'I swear you love animals more than you like people,'

Jane had said multiple times. And now her sister was the one who had to try to get her out of that damn detention centre.

'Everyone knows it's a prison!' she shouted at the wall plastered with the rules and regulations all his Majesty's guests had to follow. 'That stupid name won't fool anyone.'

STRICTLY NO DANCING ANYWHERE!!

Emma sighed at the words posted all along the corridor.

'They're sucking all the joy from this dump.'

And it was all because an impromptu rendition of *Thriller* had left the canteen with an unholy mess that morning. She found it funny to watch two dozen girls shake their plastic forks in the air and throw food everywhere. Considering what they were served looked like it had already been eaten before being slopped onto their plates, she was hardly surprised about the outcome. Maybe that's why the Governor was pissed off.

She trudged down the corridor for the showers, her mind rushing through how she could see her mother. Her only hope was an escape, and she had no idea how to do that.

She didn't see the arm that grabbed her by the neck as she stepped towards the cubicles. Rough fingers threw her at the taps. Her head hit something metallic. The whites of her eyes turned red between the cracks in the mirror as someone pushed her face against the glass.

'Don't worry, luv, you're gonna like this.'

The voice was like a crushed stone. The heat from the unknown girl's mouth seared the skin on Emma's neck. She spun Emma around and laughed. Emma flinched at the reek of nicotine, twisting her head to see her attacker flanked by two others.

'What do you want?'

The biggest one of the threesome pulled on that long white hair as if she was trying to shake Emma's skull from her shoulders. She stared at the worst-looking tattoo she'd ever seen, a squashed butterfly with a dog's face. Its owner was over six feet tall, with a head like a football blown up beyond its proper size. Even stranger was her face; her eyes were uneven to the point the right dropped closer to her swollen nose more than the left. The thuggish girl also suffered from an extreme case of alopecia, with huge clumps of hair missing from the top of her skull. She looked like the Bride of Frankenstein.

'We love the pretty ones, don't we girls?'

She grabbed the back of Emma's head, turning to her two friends. One grinned like a psychotic clown, while the other giggled non-stop.

'What do you want?' Emma demanded.

'We've seen you strutting around like a princess, preening yourself like you own the place. You posh ones always think you're better than the rest of us.' The strength of her bad breath matched the stupidity of her words. 'So, tonight, we have to teach you a lesson.'

'I hated school,' Emma said. 'And I'm not posh.'

The leader pushed Emma towards the giggling girl, who caught Emma in her skinny, needle-marked arms. She was so weak it was easy for Emma to shove her away and put her shoulders against the wall. She wouldn't let the Bride of Frankenstein grab her again.

'Gutsy; I like that. Do you kiss with the same energy?'

'Sure,' Emma replied. 'Here's a kiss with a fist.'

She punched the Bride, and the other girl's face exploded against her fingers. As blood splattered from her big nose, Emma twisted to the side. She expected the clown-faced teenager to jump at her, but the kid didn't move.

Emma punched her in the belly. She doubled over and spewed across the floor. The skinny kid ran away as fast as her scrawny legs could take her.

The fleeing girl distracted Emma from the immediate danger. It was long enough for the Bride to grab her around the waist. Her grip was like a pressure cooker. Emma tried to break away, but she was too strong.

'Don't struggle, lovely. I promise you'll enjoy this.'

Emma got the full force of her stink at that range, its strength shrivelling the hairs on the back of her head.

She wriggled in her arms. 'I'll beat you with toothpaste and deodorant when free.'

'Shall we dance?'

The Bride grabbed Emma's fingers and tried to snap them backwards. Emma pushed the other girl's hands down. The Bride whistled some awful pop tune before leaning closer to Emma's neck and whispering in her ear.

'Has your mother lost her mind yet?'

Emma's focus disappeared, replaced with visions of her mum all alone. The Bride took a firmer grip around her waist before hurling her against the wall. A sharp jab of pain stabbed her in the middle of her spine. She wasn't unaccustomed to physical agony, having spent every Tuesday night for five years preparing for this. This time, a better memory of her mum flickered inside her head.

'You need to be able to defend yourself,' her mother had said when she handed Emma her thirteenth birthday present: lessons at a local martial arts class. They were the only classes she ever liked, the only teacher she respected.

'Don't you ever speak about my mother again.'

She pressed her back against the wall, trembling. It wasn't because of the beast opposite her.

I have to get out of here and go to Mum.

Nothing would stop her, not even the terrible excuse for a human glaring at her.

'You could've been my pet for a while,' the Bride spat at her. 'But now I'm going to make you suffer every day and night.'

She lunged forward. Emma slipped to the side, putting her hand on the bigger girl's shoulder and pushing her down. The Bride rolled around like a slab of fat in a frying pan, her sour face suffering more damage as her jaw cracked against the tiles. Emma caught an aroma of sweat and desperation leaking from her.

Adrenaline surged through her, and she was happy in her skin for the first time since the arrest. Then she thought of her mother again, and the despair returned in waves.

The Bride leapt up with another grab at Emma, trying to punch her in the face, her arms floundering like a drunken windmill. Emma blocked each attack like she'd done a thousand times before against much tougher opponents.

'You won't last long in here.'

The Bride made it sound like a fatal promise, but Emma only grinned before kicking her in the gut. She hit the ground, wallowing in slow motion before her face smashed into the tiles.

Even though the other girl was bigger and heavier than Emma, she got her weight underneath her, tilting her to one side before rolling her across the floor and against the other wall. As the Bride groaned, Emma searched for the clown-faced teenager, but she'd disappeared, leaving her leader to her fate. She knelt near the Bride, Emma's long white hair falling over that ugly face like a veil of future pain.

Emma stood. 'You should pick on somebody your own size next time.'

'This isn't over,' the Bride shouted through broken teeth.

Emma let the words wash over her, wandering back to her cell and thinking about her mother, too busy to notice the pair of mice whispering to each other in the corner.

Chapter 18

Wells: The Scientist

Wyatt Wells never wanted to be a chemist. He desired a more comfortable life than years of constant study and the pressure to succeed. However, it was what his parents craved for their only child, and they always got their way, no matter how much he protested. He was six months into his second PhD when the strange woman visited him, though it was more of a case of breaking and entering than a visit.

'Your place is more of a mess than my love life,' she said as he entered his flat, dropping his books in shock at the sight of the redheaded teenager sitting on his sofa. There was a cigarette between her fingers and ash on the floor. She must have been there some time because she'd used the powder to draw an image of a giant bird on the ground with its wings spread like an angel. She blew smoke at him as he stood motionless. Pain shot through his chest, wondering if a disappointed buyer of one of his chemical creations was there to make him suffer.

'What?' he said.

'I didn't think I'd have to wait this long. Where have you been all this time?'

There was a tinge of irritation in her voice, her tone increasing as she stared at him. His mind was confused, thinking how young she looked to be a burglar. He regained his senses, ignored her question and reached into his pocket for his phone.

'Get out of my house.'

'Wyatt, if you're thinking about calling the police, that would be a mistake.'

She smiled as she spoke, her words a mixture of warning and advice. She was probably in her teens, unnervingly attractive and calmness personified. Yet, she scared him more than any criminals he'd met. Something lurked in her eyes, which were wild and uncontrollable, and Wyatt hated not being in control.

He set the phone down, his heart pounding. How did she get in? His home was supposed to be secure.

'Who are you?' he said, inwardly cursing how his voice trembled. 'What are you doing here?'

She glanced at his furniture. 'Do you have an interior designer? This place is fab.'

'What do you want?'

The intruder tilted her head, still smiling. 'What do any of us really want, Wyatt? Purpose. Meaning. I'm here to find mine. That and a good pair of shoes.'

She took a few steps forward, and he noticed a knife glinting in her hand.

'Look,' he said, backing away, 'I think you've got the wrong house. I'm nobody. Just a retired accountant.' That was a lie, but maybe it would throw her off.

She let out a chilling laugh. 'Oh Wyatt, you were never an accountant. I've been watching you. I know what you've done, the people you've hurt. And now, you're going to help me.'

Wyatt's back hit the wall. He was out of room and ideas. She kept advancing, a deranged excitement in her eyes. Desperately, he grabbed a lamp and swung it at her head. She dodged it easily and wagged a finger.

'Naughty, naughty. That wasn't very nice.' Her smile widened. 'But it's okay. I like it when they fight back.'

His hand shook. 'Who are you?'

She slipped the blade into her jacket and returned to the sofa. 'That's better. Do you want to sit with me?'

She pushed a pile of academic papers onto the floor and patted the space near her. Wyatt stared at her in the bright red trousers which matched her hair, glued to her body and looking impossible to get into.

'Who are you,' he asked again, trying to sound intimidating but knowing he failed miserably. His potential for violence in any situation was less than zero.

'I'm Pandora, here to present you with a proposition you can't turn down, Wyatt.'

There was steel in her voice. And she was right; he didn't refuse that offer.

Six months later, he was still confined to her clutches and the mysterious organisation she worked for. In all that time, he'd met nobody else from the Project, and he wondered if she was working independently and using it as a front.

However, it meant he could continue the work he'd started at university, supplying the criminal underworld with the various pills he created.

That annoying little dog was his perfect cover.

It was a simple task, made even easier when Pandora supplied him with his luxury home in one of the city's most secure gated communities. The Project provided the finances that allowed him to complete his latest doctorate, with an impressive monthly salary, and buy the house.

'What do you want in return?' he asked her during the first meeting as she dumped more ash on the floor.

'Nothing much, just the occasional favour. Between working with your criminal friends and your studies, you can do something for my employers and me.'

Her lips lifted upwards and pushed those immaculate cheeks out. Her perfect teeth shone at him, a warm glow simmering on her face. He gripped his hands as panic crept through him because she knew of his illegal activities.

'What criminal friends?'

'Don't worry, Wyatt, all your secrets are safe with me.' She shook her head and grinned at him. 'Retired accountant? That was a good one.'

Her smile was a ray of sunshine, so overpowering he needed sun protection to stop it from burning him. But in the end, he was going to burn them.

On that first night, she detailed his orders and outlined his benefits as an outside contractor for the Project. She also laid out the negatives if he failed them: if he failed her.

The more time he spent with her, the more terrifying she became.

However, Wyatt had invested most of his life doing what others told him to, and his breaking point had arrived a few days before the redhead appeared in his house. He'd already made plans for a new life before the Project entered his current one.

And a cat and dog were going to help him complete those plans.

'Hello, little cat,' he said as he peered at the ginger feline trying to hide from him.

Chapter 19

The Bullfather: Down on the Farm

The Guardian had made the room comfortable and pleasant, but the Bullfather couldn't sleep. Even though he was free, being on a farm, even a converted one, brought all the old memories flooding back. The dark speckling over his ribs and neck may have hidden his scars, but nothing could hide the pain that lingered in his mind.

Darkstar had gone out, Evermore was hunting, and the foxes, while great for security, were terrible for conversation. All they wanted to talk about was chasing humans and making them suffer. While he empathised with that, it made for tedious chat night after night.

He stared out the window, looking beyond the trees and towards the farm that had brought him to that part of the country, remembering what he'd escaped from. He was a purebred bull bought for breeding, the largest of his kind, purchased to service twenty-five to fifty cows during the breeding season. His life was difficult from the start, but he only discovered later that he was one of the "lucky" ones because the humans killed most male calves straight after birth. Nevertheless, the memories were still there of the knackerman wielding his shotgun and then burning the bodies.

Yes, he was lucky since he wasn't castrated or slaughtered. But he saw and heard those horrors inflicted on others around him.

They kept him with his mother for five months before they sold him. In his new "home", the humans inserted a copper ring through a small hole cut in the septum of his nose. Darkstar had it removed after the Bullfather's liberation, but the scars – and the memories – still lingered.

After the separation from his mother, the humans put him in a corral with sturdy fencing – no chance of escape, with plenty of feed and water available. He was there to breed. Initially, he was upset, refusing to settle down and perform his duties. He tried countless times to kick down the fence, but even with his great height and physique, the barriers were too strong for him. Many cows were there with him, but he either ignored them or repeatedly threw himself against the wood imprisoning him. He ached and bled, but it was useless; he was always trapped.

'Set me free,' he would shout at the humans, not understanding why they couldn't understand him, fighting against them as they tried to get him to mate.

'He's a gay breeder,' he heard them say, not knowing what it meant as they laughed.

After two weeks of unsuccessful attempts at bovine copulation, they chained him in a fetid barn. Twice a day, one would visit him with an electrical prod, sending pain surging through him as punishment or incentive. He put up with it all, seeing the burns on his flesh as marks of his strength. He refused everything they tried until the cows spoke to him.

'If you don't breed, they'll kill you.' The whites of the cow's eyes approached him in the fading light of the day. The sadness in her dispirited voice echoed in his heart.

'Why?' he said, confused by the world surrounding him.

'Because we're cattle. Do you know what that means?'

He shook his head and fought back the tears.

The cow was Clara, and she told him the truth. 'We're food for the humans, bred to provide sustenance for them, to exist and die so they can live. You're here to make more cattle, to breed with us. If you do that, we'll all stay alive longer.'

'But we'll all die eventually?'

'Everything dies eventually, even the humans.'

He did as Clara asked, even if he hated it, but his hatred of the humans grew every time he bred, dreaming of the time before his death when he could inflict pain on one of them, to kill one of them. It was all he lived for.

Then he met Darkstar, and his whole life changed.

'I know a place where we can go, somewhere safe, near here,' the ebony cat told him.

'Everybody can leave the farm?'

'No,' Darkstar said. 'Just you.'

'Why me?' he asked.

'Because you can lead. I see it in you.'

'What about all the others?'

'We can't save everyone,' Darkstar replied.

'But we should,' said the Bullfather.

Therefore, a plan was born as birds and mice helped him escape the coral. Then Darkstar stole him away and led him into the night, listening to the cries of the other animals, determined to change that infernal existence but not knowing how. He didn't know if fortune or fate had brought them together.

'Where are you taking me?' he asked his rescuer, trying to see the ebony cat but failing in the gloom. Only when Darkstar slipped into the moonlight could he be seen.

'There's another farm not far from here.'

'Why is that place any better than the one we've just escaped?' He trusted the cat, but didn't know why until he acknowledged his desperation. He left the land of his prison and stared towards the river separating the two farms.

'Because there's a human there who'll keep us safe.'

The Bullfather stopped, frozen under the moon's steely gaze. 'A human? Humans cannot be trusted.' He'd lost sight of the cat again, wondering if he was dreaming, only his fear stopping him from turning back.

'This one can,' was the reply from the shadows.

'Why?' he asked the darkness.

'Because he understands our language,' the cat said as the river approached. 'And because he feels our pain.'

The Bullfather continued walking, staring at the stars glistening in the night sky.

'Why me?'

'I need your help,' the cat said to the bull.

He stopped moving, motionless and contemplating how a human could help them. 'What help?' He stared into the cold waters separating them from their alleged sanctuary.

'I require your help to get me across this water. I need a ride on your back.'

The Bullfather didn't know he could laugh until it happened without warning. No occasions in his life had been happy or joyous enough to elicit such a response, so he was surprised at the sounds from his mouth upon hearing the dark cat's request.

'Of course, of course; how else could this night get any stranger?'

Darkstar didn't wait for a second invitation and jumped onto the great bull's back.

'I hate water,' the cat said to the bull.

'I've never walked through it before,' the bull replied, the river rising above his legs and settling into the middle of his torso. Its touch felt odd to his hide, a chill ripple flowing through him.

'Don't put your head under it,' Darkstar warned.

'What are these creatures I see under the water?'

He'd forgotten all about his escape and the ebony cat's bizarre tale of a life of safety with a human who understood them and would care for them. All he thought about was the cold liquid splashing against his body, the strange things below him and his unexpected freedom. It was a journey beyond his wildest dreams.

'They are fish,' the Darkstar answered. 'Not the brightest of creatures.'

'What's your name?' the bull asked the cat sitting on his back.

'They call me Darkstar. And you?'

The giant bull climbed from the river and set foot on the bank, the farmhouse lights shining ahead in the distance.

'I have no name,' he said, with no trace of emotion.

Darkstar jumped onto the wet ground. 'Well, we can't have that.' He stared into the great bull's face as they continued their journey. 'You remind me of Brando.'

'What's a Brando?' the bull asked the cat.

'He's a human, an actor in the movies. One of the humans I lived with would spend all day watching them, and his favourite was *The Godfather*, with Brando.'

The bull didn't know what a movie was, but he liked the sound of the name.

'You can call me the Bullfather,' he said as the lights got closer.

Darkstar smiled. 'Such an appropriate name for a leader.'

'Leader of what?'

'We'll think of something,' Darkstar replied as they marched into the farmhouse grounds, heading towards the back door.

'I've never been inside a human dwelling.' The Bullfather was nervous again.

'Don't be worried. Everyone is waiting for you.'

The dark cat strode through the door. The great bull wondered if his bulk would fit through the narrow space, hearing the wood scraping from the frame as his hide squeezed inside. A menagerie of animals and a lone human greeted him.

Darkstar broke the silence. 'My friends say hello to the Bullfather.'

A litter of kittens slept in the corner, their mother sitting beside them. Two large dogs were near the unlit fireplace; a group of foxes were breathing heavily at the exit to the kitchen, while a dozen or so piglets were rolling around at the feet of the human whose eyes had never left the bull since he entered the house.

Then he stood and bowed to the Bullfather. As he did so, the bull noticed the many scars covering the man's head and neck.

'My name is Stoker,' the man said. 'I will guard you with my life.'

Chapter 20

Crowley: Trapped

rowley sprinted from behind the stack of papers, his paws pounding on the floor as fast as the fear overtook his heart. All he had to do was get outside; he could always return later for Darkstar's stupid item.

He ran towards the door, eyes glazing over when he saw it was shut, but building up enough speed to jump into the air and land on the handle. He waited for it to drop, frustrated when it refused to budge. Crowley panicked, claws slipping on the door, and fell onto the floor. The blood rushed through him, the electricity in his veins threatening to explode.

No, no, no! This couldn't be happening.

Crowley's fur stood on end, back arching in fear. He was trapped.

In desperation, he searched for another escape route, seeing the window. He raced over, leaping onto the sill. To his dismay, it was also latched shut. Wells was right behind him, laughing.

'Is that how you got inside? That's brilliant. Anyway, let's return to what the other me was saying on the video.'

He turned his back on Crowley and slipped into his seat. Chirpy was still in the room, a little furball of confusion. Wells didn't bother with the clip, swinging the chair around to continue his narrative in the flesh.

'Some of the most important scientific discoveries were accidental: X-rays, the pacemaker, gunpowder, dynamite, anaesthesia, penicillin, and even Viagra. Now we can add Doolittle to the list – though we must create a better name than that. Which one of you little creatures thought of that label?'

He pulled Chirpy into his lap and grinned. Crowley trembled, searching for a way to get Chirpy and him out. He glared at the man and hoped the pooch would poop again.

'What's happening?' the dog said.

Wells beamed at his pet. 'I hate science, always have done. You wouldn't believe the amount of bullying I went through at school just because I was 'a science nerd'. I don't suppose the thick black glasses and terrible haircut helped.' He sighed as he stroked his dog's back. 'At first, it was my parents who pushed me into it and then, as I thought it would end with my PhD, Pandora and the Project forced their way into my life. I was going off on a world tour before she appeared.'

'How do we get out of here?' Crowley said.

Chirpy squirmed in her owner's grip. 'I don't know.'

Wyatt Wells stared into the tiny dog's eyes. 'Okay, that's enough confusion, my little animal friends. I got bored and tested the serum on myself, hoping that expanding my brainpower would allow me to think of a way out of the Project's grasp. Imagine my disappointment when all it gave me was a massive headache and zero increase in my intellect: I suppose it could have been worse. At least I was alive, and my brain wasn't frazzled into mush like the others.' He shook his head. 'I feel sorry about them, but the Project is to blame for what happened. I only follow their orders.' He smiled at Crowley. 'And the redhead – she has to take some of the responsibility.'

All this talking and Crowley still hadn't thought of a way out of the mess of his making. He stopped pondering his fate, thinking about Emma and his accountability for her imprisonment. Maybe this was his punishment for what he'd done to her.

He peered at the door. Wells must have locked it.

How do I get the key from him?

He let the professor ramble on. 'But there was one unforeseen side-effect; it sent me mad.' He appeared unstable to Crowley, those small human eyes shrinking even further into his face, the tremor of his voice rising with every syllable.

'We need to find the door key, Chirpy,' Crowley said.

Wells continued. 'I started hearing voices, but not just any old voices. My lovely little dog spoke to me, telling me many things. I ignored them, thinking it would wear off when the drug left my system. But that was three weeks ago, and it's still happening, so I guess the effect is permanent.'

He stared at Crowley as if he were the cat who got the cream.

'Everywhere I went, animals were speaking. Some were happy, but most were sad, grieving their lot at the hands of humans. I can't blame them, really, or blame you. I'm pissed at humanity most of the time, and I don't have somebody trying to eat me.' He stroked the little dog's head. 'The birds gossiping on the power lines, the mice in the subway, even the fish in the pet store – I heard them all, and it was a revelation once I realised I wasn't crazy and that the drug had changed me.'

'What's he saying?' Chirpy asked Crowley.

Wells seemed to love every minute of his rant, grinning like an insane clown at a psychotic circus. 'Did you see the mouse shit near the fridge? In the new world of strange, that might've been the most bizarre moment, hearing them talk about stealing the Doolittle and the fulfilment of some grand plan. I gathered they were talking about my serum. They'd overheard me proclaiming its potential for greatness and disaster and, for some reason, decided they must have it, which is why you're here now.'

Crowley was unmoving during the whole tirade. Wells laughed, dropped Chirpy onto the floor, and smiled at the ginger cat.

'What's the matter, friend? Cat got your tongue?'

Chapter 21

Emma: Raya

They don't care what 'appens to us when we're inside,' Raya said when Emma told her about her mother's illness. 'As long as there are no riots or they avoid ending up on the news for the wrong reasons, we're just money-making cogs for them.'

They'd entered the dining area under a multitude of staring eyes. Emma's reputation had grown since the incident at the showers. She was under the constant glare of the prison thugs, threats of violence manifesting in many voices and in every look she received. Raya was her only friend.

She stared at her fingers. 'They could have let me out to see her. I'm not violent.'

'When was the last time you saw your mum?' Raya asked. She ate strangely coloured peas as she spoke.

Emma ignored the plate in front of her, turning her nose away from the bizarre aroma wafting up from the table. A group of tattooed amazons passed them, sneering at her.

'A few days before my arrest, I took her for coffee,' she replied. In reality, it was the other way round, her mother paying as usual since Emma was always short of funds.

'The doctors say I'm getting better,' her mother said, looking at her youngest daughter through tired eyes. Emma cursed herself for not recognising the signs or paying more attention: being so selfish. For not realising her mother was lying to her.

'She hasn't been in touch while you've been here?' Raya asked as a hulking woman over six feet tall brushed past her, jabbing the corner of her tray into Raya's shoulder as she went. They were the only ones sitting there, ostracised from the rest of the inmates since Emma's violent dalliance with the Bride.

'She doesn't know I'm here,' Emma replied, her voice choking on something which was supposed to be roasted potatoes but tasted like small pebbles struggling to get down her throat. 'I told Jane to keep it from her. I don't want her worrying about me.'

Not when I'm worried about her. Knowing I'm in here might only make her worse.

'You could appeal the Governor's decision,' Raya said as she shovelled dingy-looking food into her mouth.

'Even if it worked, it would take too long. I have to get out soon.' Emma's voice was flat and grim, understanding her limited options. 'I need to escape.'

Raya nearly spat her peas all over the floor, a sizeable choking sound erupting from her throat until it transformed into a peculiar burp loud enough to make the table rattle. She followed it with a raucous laugh as the rest of the room scowled at her.

She moved closer to Emma and lowered her voice. 'How do you plan on doing that?'

'I'll start a fight; get myself transferred to a hospital. It should be easy. Nobody will think a teenage girl is going to run away.'

She'd thought about it all night, trying to put her thoughts together as the rats scurried underneath her bed. Raya picked something inedible from her teeth and gazed at it on her finger like a doctor studying a virus under a microscope before flicking it onto the back of an unsuspecting guard.

'You'll start a fight with your ugly friend from the other night?'

Emma peered around the room for likely candidates. 'Who it is doesn't matter, but it'll have to be somebody who won't try to kill me. Do you have any suggestions?'

Raya raised her face to the ceiling as her mouth turned into an odd shape.

'You were small fry before, but now everybody will have their beady eyes fixed on you – half will fear you while the other half will want to beat you down.'

'Fifty-fifty; there are no waverers on either side?' Emma asked.

Raya laughed, opening up her face to a smile that made the scars on her skin disappear, if only for a brief while.

'The waverers will all be on the scared side.'

'What about you?' Emma pulled a pained expression, which had nothing to do with what they were talking about and more to do with the terrible food she swallowed. Raya kept smiling, and Emma was glad to see something positive in that miserable place.

'Oh, I want to beat you down, have since I first saw you – you're far too pretty for your own good.'

They laughed in unison, drawing stares from the rest of the room, but she didn't care about the others. This small piece of happiness with Raya made her forget where she was.

'I think you'd probably get the better of me anyway,' she said, finding it impossible to keep the smirk from her face.

Raya finished her meal with a flourish. 'Yeah, you're right.'

It fascinated her how the other girl could quickly devour such unpleasantness. 'You must have a cast iron stomach.'

Emma played with her food, which was supposed to be carrots, but she was sure they were thick weeds pulled from the ground at the back of the prison. Raya took hold of her last piece of tattered cardboard masquerading as bread and wiped the whole plate clean.

'You should've tasted the grub I had in the previous place. This is Gordon Blair cooking compared to that.'

Emma was puzzled, squinting her eyes and pursing her lips in confusion until she realised she meant *cordon bleu*. However, she didn't correct her friend, and they laughed until Raya finished her meal. Emma left hers to stew on the plate.

'There's one thing puzzling me, though,' Raya said.

Emma glanced around the room, noticing the mice under the tables. 'What's that?'

'You never said how the coppers knew it was your DNA at the crime scene. How come they had a record of it?'

'It was via my father's DNA,' she said. 'It's stored on a military database, so God knows how the police accessed it.'

'What happened to your dad?' Raya asked.

His glorious smile flashed across Emma's vision. 'He died serving his country.'

Raya touched her hand. 'I'm sorry, Emma.'

Emma was glad of the warmth on her skin. 'It was a few years ago. I'm over it.'

They sat silently for a few minutes before Raya grinned.

'Hey, maybe it was your sister's DNA at the museum.'

Emma's laugh hurt her chest. 'Jane? She stresses out if she goes one mile over the speed limit.' The image of her sister as a criminal amused her. 'And you forget that the coppers found the jewellery at my flat.'

'Yeah, that is strange.'

They stood and left the dining area, moving down the corridor and stepping outside. Emma entered the yard first, checking who was there and where the guards were. The promise of violence followed them everywhere. The sky was grim, with a chill in the air. Being outdoors in any weather was preferable to being inside, which was why inmates were using most of the exercise equipment. She smelt the city above her, smoke and pollution drifting over from the other side of the river.

'One of the prisoners got locked out here last month,' Raya said.

They found a place against the far wall and leaned against the cold grey concrete that resembled ancient rhinoceros skin.

'What happened?' Emma asked.

'A new girl was exercising alone when the doors were locked behind her. She banged on the door, but nobody heard her – or so they said. It pissed down all night, and when they found her later, she was soaked and shivering. She wasn't a popular girl, so there was talk somebody did it on purpose to punish her for something.'

'The guards must have done it, then?' Emma wondered.

'Oh, the guards are always involved with the prisoners somehow – swapping favours for money, drugs, or sex. You'll see if you stay in here long enough.'

Emma's mind returned to thoughts of her mother. 'I need to leave here as soon as possible.'

'I'm sure your sister will get you out,' Raya said.

'Jane's very good at her job, but she'll need some luck to get me out.'

'Luck won't help you now, new meat.' A growl came from nowhere, settling over them like a great grey cloud. The Bride appeared, throwing bits of food on the ground like confetti and trailing half a dozen bruising bridesmaids behind her. If a female rugby team was in prison, they were ogling Emma like she was the ball they wanted to kick. 'But it must be my lucky day.' There was a slight tremor in the Bride's voice, which her acolytes didn't hear but was evident to Emma: she recognised the fear.

Emma's eyes darted everywhere, searching for a weapon as she spoke to Raya. 'Get behind me; it's me she wants.'

The Bride laughed. 'Don't worry, girl, we'll find something for her as well.' The guards had all disappeared.

Raya grinned. 'I didn't think I'd be getting any exercise today.'

There was assertiveness in Raya's voice, which surprised Emma. If that was unexpected, what came next was astonishing. Raya sprang forward and kicked the Bride in her right knee, sending her to the ground in a heap. She knelt and wrapped her skinny arms around that thick neck as the Bride twisted in the dust. Raya ignored her captive and stared at the six dumbstruck devotees looking gormless behind their stricken leader.

'You know I was transferred here because I killed someone in my last prison, right?'

Nobody replied. Emma was as shocked as they were, every muscle in her body frozen.

'Walk away now, and I'll only leave a little love scratch on her neck. Otherwise ...'

Then, a guard conveniently stumbled from the shadows

and headed towards them. Raya pushed the Bride from her and walked back to Emma.

'Well, that was unexpected,' Emma said. 'I guess you could beat me down after all.' She tried to sound serious, but couldn't keep the laughter from her voice.

'You better believe it,' Raya replied. 'Now all we have to do is get you out of here.'

Emma grabbed her friend. 'Is it true what you said? Did you kill somebody?'

Raya laughed. 'What do you think?'

As they joined the rest of the inmates, the guard strode towards Emma.

'Crowley, you're being moved tomorrow.' Emma stopped in surprise. 'Your lawyer's got you transferred to an open prison.'

She stared at the woman in a daze. Only Raya's excited arms around her waist brought her back to reality. Jane had done it.

'I'm going to miss you,' Raya said as Emma contained her tears.

As they returned to their cell, a group of rats slinked from the shadows and through a small hole in the wall. They scampered back into the free world as Emma considered her change in good fortune.

Chapter 22

Crowley: Doolittle

Chirpy clung to Crowley as if the comfort of his fur would protect her from the surrounding strangeness. 'What shall we do?'

'I mean you no harm,' Wells said to the perplexed animals.

He stared at the professor as the human brushed his long, dark hair away from his face. 'What do you want from us?'

His eyes darted around the room, lips shrinking inwards as he searched for an escape but came up with nothing. A ringing erupted from the professor's pocket. He removed his mobile and peered at it, ignoring the call. Five seconds later, Crowley recognised the ping of a text.

Wells held the phone so Crowley could see the screen. 'I need your assistance in escaping from her.'

Crowley read the message. 'Turn the cameras back on.' It was from somebody called Pandora.

'She'll be coming here soon. I'll fob her off to get rid of her. Then I need your help.'

He scrutinised the human, still amazed that Wells could understand him. 'What help?'

The professor puffed out his cheeks. 'Please follow her and find out where she goes. I'd do it myself, but my life won't be worth living if she spots me. However, she'd never suspect a cat was spying on her, would she?'

Crowley had no interest in this strange human's mad plans, but he'd agree to anything to leave the house. 'Okay.'

Wells shook his head. 'I know what you're thinking, my little feline friend – just say yes to get out of here, but if you do as I ask, I'll give you a sample of this.' He held a phial of the serum in front of him. 'They, the Project, are unaware of what this can do or about my fortunate breakthrough, and I cannot allow them to possess it. Even though the five previous versions had disastrous effects on the subjects they tested it on, creating various levels of damage in the human brain, they still pressurised me to continue with the experiments.'

'And it changed you so you can understand me and other animals?' Crowley asked.

Wells nodded. 'Apparently so. Unless it fried my brain like it did with the others, I'm in a coma, and this is only a hallucination.'

Crowley considered the offer the man had made. He could get what Darkstar and the Bullfather required, and all he had to do was follow some woman. The rest of the craziness meant nothing to him. How could the human understand what he and Chirpy were saying and why Darkstar wanted the serum? All he desired was to return to his own life.

And give Emma her freedom back.

'Why did you try it on yourself?' Crowley said.

The professor's face changed from happiness to

sadness, his eyes narrowing, his lips turning upside down, and depression invading his voice.

'I'd had enough of this life, had enough of her. I wanted to end it all, and what better way to do it than with my creation? I tweaked it a little first, thought I was strengthening it; I didn't want to end up a vegetable like the others. I sought a quick death. Instead, I have this, talking to you, hearing you.' The spring returned to his voice. 'It's a gift from the gods. So, what do you say: favour for a favour? The serum is easy to duplicate. It doesn't dilute in other liquids and infects every fluid it's dropped into, acting as a virus. Once I change the colour, you can hide it in water.'

Then the doorbell rang. Crowley gazed at the phial. 'Is that her?'

Wells was in pain as he spoke. 'She doesn't break in anymore.'

'I need you to let Chirpy out of the house to do something for me,' Crowley said as he formulated a plan.

'Of course; I'll do it when I let Pandora in. If you go behind those papers, you can listen to what she says, then follow her and see where she goes.'

'Did she drive here?' Crowley didn't fancy hiding in a backseat again.

'No. I've watched her when she leaves. She gets the bus around the corner, opposite the old cinema.'

There was banging on the door, and his phone started ringing. Crowley turned to Chirpy and whispered something into her ear.

'Okay,' the cat thief said.

He slipped into the hiding place while Wells and the little dog scampered down the stairs. The professor let her in, and Crowley heard the anger in her voice. He hoped Chirpy would have enough time to do what he'd told her.

'Did you try to kill yourself with your serum, Wyatt?'

She entered the room before he did: a tall woman with long red hair, dressed in black, sporting a tight jacket and tighter trousers. It always amazed him how humans could move around in some of the clothes they wore. Wells came in behind her, glancing at where Crowley hid.

'You've been spying on me again?' Wells said.

'You didn't die, so what happened?' She didn't ask why he'd taken such drastic action. There was a coldness in her voice, which reminded him of Darkstar.

'Your concern for my welfare is touching, Pandora. Nothing happened; maybe fate was looking down on me.' Wells tried his best to be assertive, but he was fooling neither animal nor human in the room.

She glared at him. 'Yet it's left all our test subjects jabbering mental wrecks, but you...'

'That's why I turned the cameras off. I wouldn't have a record of my death in the vaults of the Project.'

'Well, now you can turn them back on, post haste. How are you getting on with the latest batch, and why didn't it mangle your brain?'

She took a cigarette and a lighter from inside her jacket, ignoring Wyatt's look of disgust. Crowley stared at Pandora, guessing she trusted nothing Wells told her, this tale of the miraculous survival of a serum that had melted the brains of all the other subjects.

'I haven't worked on it since I recovered. I had other things occupying my mind.' He pulled a bin from behind his chair and pushed it near where her fingers were hanging, ash ready to fall onto his pristine floor.

'Has your dog been in here? There's a smell of animals.'

Her gaze darted around the room quicker than he could reply. Crowley scrutinised her as she studied her surroundings, noticing how her head jerked as her eyes examined everything. He shrank a little against his hiding place. She stopped when she got close to the refrigerator and the stack of papers concealing his quivering body. He sensed her presence only a few feet away and smelt the smoke from her cigarette drifting over his head.

Wyatt panicked and leapt in front of the fridge, trying to get between her and where Crowley cowered. 'Do you have any pets?'

'I hate all animals,' she said, her eyes constantly moving around the room. There was ice in her voice, and Crowley appreciated why Wells feared her so much. Pandora's gaze rested upon the array of magnets Wyatt had used to adorn the cold storage for his experiments.

She scowled at the range of cartoon characters and poor jokes sticking to the white plastic. 'I do like the utilitarianism of this room, Wyatt; apart from all these papers and books here – they appear so out of place.'

She was heading to the stack as she spoke. Before Wells could do anything, she lowered her face and stared into the space between the papers and the wall. The professor gripped his chest. When she lifted her head, there was a look of concern on her face as she blew smoke towards the ashen-faced man.

'I'm untidy sometimes,' he said.

'You've been keeping things from me, Wyatt. What did I tell you about having no more secrets?' Pandora's voice was coated in gravel, husky to the point her throat could be lined with nicotine.

'Whhhh ...,' he stuttered.

Pandora took a long drag, blowing smoke at him. 'Do you know you have mouse shit down there?'

'I have no idea how they find their way inside,' he said, sitting in the chair.

'They get everywhere; more dirty animals.' She went to him. 'You'll get back to work tomorrow.' It was a command, not a question.

'Yes, of course, Pandora.'

'And turn those cameras on,' she demanded, heading for the door without a glance at him. 'I'll let myself out.'

Crowley heard her voice as he slipped outside, having seen his chance to escape while the woman was flicking ash into the bin, moving down the street and towards the bus stop. It was strange that somebody working for a secret organisation would use public transport, but he had to trust Wells was right with his information. He also hoped Chirpy had found his contact.

Then, a voice told him the little dog had done her task perfectly.

'What's the job, dude?' The wings fluttering over Crowley brought a smile to his face. The pigeon landed in front of him.

'Thanks for coming, Doodle. I need you to follow some-body for me, find out where they go, see if they meet anybody. Can you do that?'

'Piece of pish, matey.'

The blurred look in the bird's eyes worried him. 'Are you high?'

'Well, I was when I flew here.'

Crowley sighed. There wasn't enough time for a different plan; Pandora was already on the way.

'That woman coming towards us, with the long red hair – she's the one. She'll catch a bus here. I'll try to keep up, but I need your help if I can't. You got that?'

'Aye, aye, captain.' Doodle raised a wing to his face and gave Crowley a mock salute.

The cat slipped into the shadows and waited for the woman to approach. She'd timed things to precision, the bus pulling up as she reached the stop. Pandora threw her cigarette so close to his head that he panicked for a second, assuming she'd seen him crouching there.

But so what? It's not like she's going to suspect a cat.

She got on and headed towards the middle. Crowley took a deep breath and prayed he wouldn't have too far to run.

Chapter 23

Pandora: Money

Pandora left Wyatt's place, knowing he was keeping something from her. The way his eyes squinted together and the flickering nervous tick of his mouth gave it away.

His lies lingered with her as she got on the bus, slumping into a seat. She dug her nails into the fabric, ripped the cheap material, and pulled out the foam. It was exactly what she wanted to do with her life: remove the things hindering her progress and move towards something new and thrilling: abandon the Project, disregard the professor and live her life on her terms. However, the thirst for revenge against those shadows in her head distracted her.

'If I don't do something about this soon, I'll join you in a tight-fitting white jacket, Mama,' she said. She could have walked back to her flat, but the bus journey from Wyatt's place was a routine she enjoyed.

The vehicle lurched forward, and she grabbed the seat in front of her. What Wyatt told her wouldn't go down well when she reported to the Director. The Project had invested a lot into Professor Wells, and they wouldn't be pleased if they didn't get a return on it soon.

The last client she'd handled who failed to deliver lost the use of her legs when the Project didn't get what they wanted. Pandora remembered standing in the woman's living room as two muscular agents held the crying woman down. At the same time, a third injected her limbs with a tissue-destroying drug developed by another client. It was a test and punishment in one.

They'll do worse to me if Director Adam discovers my plans.

The drunks at the back of the bus distracted her. It added to her impatience, a sharp pain riding down her neck and spine. They screamed and shouted obscenities. She blocked out the racket to focus on the decisions she had to make, not just with Wells but with the Project. Luckily, contingency plans were a skill she excelled at. No, it wasn't luck. A talent for planning was something she'd inherited from her father.

And she hated herself for being even a tiny bit like him.

She removed the phone from her pocket and searched for the file containing her financial details. As part of her fake profile for the Project, experts had taught her everything there was to know about high-end banking and the world of financial services, including their many illegal activities: knowledge which allowed her to build up quite a cache of ill-gotten bank accounts.

If the Project discovered she'd been stealing from them, Pandora would be the one screaming on the floor. She found the file as the bus turned a corner, only for the vehicle to get stuck in a traffic jam. She swore at the added frustration. The drunks behind her laughed at the obscenities she spewed. She clenched her fists and wondered what she could hit, glaring at the digital screen instead.

Her phone was triple encrypted, and then the files had two more levels of security. Anyone who got their hands on it would need to be a high-level hacker to break her safety protocols. Pandora opened the file containing the details of cash syphoned from the Project and then laundered through the shell companies she'd purchased. Money laundering was not something the Project deemed worthy of its attention – it was far too low-end for them to care and had too many associations with organised crime, which she thought was ironic considering they were an organisation involved in numerous crimes. Nevertheless, her bosses had instructed her in money laundering, which was another thing to thank them for.

A seven-figure number grinned at her, and she smiled back. She had enough to do whatever she wanted once she disappeared from their clutches but still desired more. She pulled up a browser window on her phone and found Wyatt's bank account, using the password she stole from him to access the money the Project deposited there. She transferred two thousand into her untraceable account: it was a routine she'd followed for the last six months. He asked her once why so much went from his monthly payment.

'It's for your rent,' she told him. 'We have to make it look legitimate in case the police come sniffing around.'

Wyatt had no choice but to believe her as she was his only contact at the Project. The first time she stole money from what the Project provided to their clients, she did it as more of a test than out of greed to see if they were paying attention and what they would do if they were. When nothing happened, she continued, waiting for the right opportunities while being as careful as possible. That initial dabble was over a year ago, and nobody from the Project had approached her.

The next bit she hadn't done before, but it was time to make her move. The Project wouldn't invest much more effort in Professor Wells if he didn't deliver something useful soon. She exited his standard account and found where he stored all his ill-gotten criminal gains. Pandora gazed at the two million in his statement, wondering why he hadn't fled by now since he had this to fall back on. She transferred all of it to her bank and then closed everything.

As the bus idled, she forgot about her wealth and stared out the window at the high-rise concrete blocks guarding everything like a decaying guard of honour. The city was a strange mixture of the prosperous and the run-down cohabiting next to each other. The good and bad parts existed side-by-side, with barely a gap separating them.

The drunks at the back kept on shouting. Pandora considered getting off and walking the rest of the way. The kid crying and the waft of burning flesh attracted her attention. As she turned, a large blob smelling like week-old vegetables dumped himself on the seat behind her.

'Whatcha doin, luv?'

It was as if a corpse had brushed its teeth with blue cheese and emptied its breath all over her neck. As he grinned at her, the kid screamed again, the boy's tearful eyes catching Pandora's gaze as the adult with him continued to torture the child. She gazed at the boy as years of submerged memories threatened to overwhelm her.

As the bus staggered forward, the drunk behind her attempted to grab Pandora, but she flicked his clumsy attempt to the side and slammed his fat face into the window. His front teeth shattered over the seat as she got up and strode down the other end.

There were four of them at the back, including the one hurting the kid. They all slurped from bottles of booze, too wasted to see her coming. Pandora grabbed the torturer by the neck, dug her fingers into his flesh, and threw him behind her. He hit the seats on the other side. She needed this, not some tedious babysitting job with a bloke who would never deliver. People required punishment, and she didn't care who they were.

An annoying wail attracted her gaze. Pandora stared at the kid. He couldn't have been more than eight or nine years old, his face a river of tears. Her eyes sank into his, and all she thought about was being stuck in that box again as the animals crawled over her shivering body. Those claws dug into her once more, ragged feline breath pouring down her cheeks in huge waves.

'What the fu...,' were the garbled words which brought Pandora out of her trance. She dodged the bottle aimed at her head. It smashed into the window behind her as she stuck her fingers into the right eye of the drunk, the force flinging him backwards and into the other two with him.

'If you stay down, I won't cripple you.'

Pandora's voice cut like a knife through the air, but it made no difference. The biggest bloke pushed his screaming, one-eyed friend off him and lunged at her. She shimmied to the side like a ballet dancer, bringing her knee into his groin and her hand across the nape of his neck. He didn't move. The last drunk stayed down, where he pissed himself and added another level of stink to the bus. The vehicle lurched forward, the driver oblivious to what was happening. She stared at the kid and wondered what to do.

'Where are your parents?' she asked the boy. He wiped

tears from his face with one hand while using the other to point towards the bloke sobbing and clutching at the hole where his eye used to be.

'Shame,' she said as she scanned the bus for prying electronic eyes, thankful there were no cameras. Her employers wouldn't be happy if her actions were plastered all over the internet.

The bus stopped. She turned from the kid and headed for the exit.

Pandora stepped into the cold night, seeing the boy grinning at the destruction she'd left behind as the bus disappeared from view. She marched across the road, striding towards the side street and the corner flat. Each building was decorated with extra attachments, sticking out of them like wild branches on haunted trees – satellite dishes, aerials, basketball hoops, weird statues and bits of metal and plastic, which appeared to have no discernible use. She walked the short distance to her flat, hunger pangs springing to life inside her. She forgot about the kid, her thoughts returning to Wyatt once more.

Maybe I should help him with his suicidal ambitions.

She put the key in the lock and entered. She was still thinking about the possible imminent death of Professor Wyatt Wells as she turned the television on and searched for the wrestling channel.

Somewhere deep in her mind, a kid cried, and she tasted the stink of animal shit.

Chapter 24

Crowley: Food for Thought

Crowley was pleased to see her leave the bus, only three stops from where she got on. The delay in the traffic was helpful, especially as it allowed him to observe what she was so good at. He stood by the side of the road when Pandora threw the man into the window and flinched as he hit the glass and slithered to the floor. He was mesmerised as she blinded another human before decking one more. The level of violence she was capable of worried him to the point he thought about turning around and leaving.

Then he remembered that Darkstar and the Bullfather were no strangers to such viciousness, and he kept moving forward. Doodle sat on top of a roof; a broad grin peeked over his beak as he waved his feathers at him.

'She's gone inside,' he said, stating the bleeding obvious.

'Check the back,' Crowley shouted at him.

He could return to Wells and give him the woman's address, but he wanted to learn more about her. However, he had to be careful. The redheaded woman claimed she hated animals, and he believed it; the venom in her voice was impossible to miss.

After two minutes, Doodle returned and landed with tiny bits of white powder stuck to his lips. 'She's in the flat, making something to eat. A big plate of raw fish she was cooking made my belly rumble it did, the smell of it.'

'Smell?' Crowley asked.

'There was a window open,' the bird replied.

A dangerous thought crossed his mind. 'Thanks, Doodle, I owe you one.'

'That you do, young Crowley, that you do.'

He laughed at the young jibe as the pigeon got high in more ways than one. Doodle flew away as Crowley crept around the side of the building and jumped onto the wall, thankful there was no barbed wire or broken glass; he'd been caught out like that before. He saw the window Doodle had described and smelt the aroma of grilled fish. It was difficult to recall the last time he'd eaten, amazed it was still the same day of the AA meeting.

The scent of the food swept everything else from his head. However, he wasn't the only one to have noticed its magnetic attraction. Two other cats got to the backyard before him. He threw caution to the wind and jumped next to them.

'Go away,' the dirty brown moggie with only one eye snarled at him.

'We were here first,' the cat with the speckled fur and missing teeth hissed at him.

Feral cats. That's all he needed.

'If you don't leave, we'll eat you instead.'

They would try. Feral cats didn't recognise the authority of the AA. They lived outside the civilised animal world, if you could call it living.

'You're not welcome here, Thief.'

It appeared everyone he met was aware of his reputation.

'Unless you're going to steal the food for us and bring it here,' the Cyclops cat said between laughter sounding like nails dragged across a board.

'He's not to be trusted,' the other one added.

There was desperation in their eyes, and he guessed they hadn't eaten for days. They wouldn't be subtle if they went inside the flat; that was beyond their capabilities. Maybe he could use that to his benefit.

'I have no desire for the food, but I'm coming in with you.'

'No,' they snarled together. 'We don't trust you.'

Tension coursed through them, coiled springs ready to snap. He had one last card to play.

'Darkstar sent me here.'

Fear replaced their hunger and threats of violence. They may not have respected the authority of the AA, but they cringed at the thought of the ebony cat. They stared at each other, silent communication weighing up their choices.

'We agree, but no food for you.'

'Knock yourself out, lads,' he said, jumping onto the ledge and stepping through the window.

Fish skin and bones lay discarded near the sink. He sniffed the remains from where he was, the aroma forcing a jab of pain into his stomach. He wanted to feast on the left-overs but knew he couldn't touch them; the bits on the plate would keep the ferals busy until their hunger forced them to search for what the woman took for herself.

He ignored the sounds behind him as they ate and searched for her. He slunk out of the kitchen, his body fuelled by stealth and guile, peering into the living room, noticing human feet dangling over the end of a bright red sofa. His eyes darted everywhere, seeing the large television on the wall. It was on, but with the sound off. Some semi-naked humans threw clumsy punches at each other while others cheered them on.

To his right was a set of stairs leading upwards. Years of thievery had taught him many skills at avoiding detection, as his brain calculated if he could get up there without her seeing him. If she focused on the screen, he could sneak around the back of the sofa and pass her. Crowley observed her as she pushed a can of beer to her lips and screamed at the TV.

'Smash the bastard!' she shouted as liquid dribbled onto the floor. She was glued to the TV. It was his chance to get upstairs, creeping over the thick carpet, trying to stick to the shadows. He was halfway there when a noise from the kitchen distracted the woman. She turned quicker than he expected, nearly seeing him as he rolled into the gap underneath the sofa.

'Damn!' she said. 'I shouldn't have left the window open.'

She dragged herself from her seat, touching the floor and only a few inches from Crowley. His heart beat like a drum inside his skull as the breath drifted from his mouth and landed on her exposed skin. She flinched as the dampness touched her fingers, pulling back as she stood.

Crowley had nowhere to go. He was doomed if she peered down or stuck her hand underneath the sofa. His throat shrank so he couldn't breathe, watching her feet as she went to the kitchen, fascinated by her painted purple toenails.

As she left, he grasped his opportunity, crawled out and raced upstairs. There were only two rooms: a bathroom, which he avoided, and a bedroom he crept into. He'd been inside many human rooms, and there was nothing unusual in that one. There was no sign that its owner worked for a secret organisation.

He glanced under the bed, found zilch, stared at the walls, books, and shelves, and discovered nothing useful about the strange redhead.

Crowley jumped onto the bed, inhaling the intoxicating aroma of her perfume. It reminded him of Emma, and sadness overwhelmed him. He forgot about the redheaded woman, Wells, and Darkstar and his mission; all he thought about was getting Emma out of prison.

The sound of breaking glass downstairs snapped him from his trance. He leapt off the bed, dashed from the bedroom, and towards the sounds of violence. The sight that greeted him at the bottom was not a cheerful one. The speckled cat was unmoving on the floor, a steak knife sticking out of his stomach; pure hate stamped all over the woman's face as she pointed a fork at the Cyclops she held around the neck. There were fresh scratch marks on her cheek, bits of blood dropping off her and onto the uneaten fish at her feet. Cyclops squeezed a few words out of his mangled mouth.

'Help me, Crowley.'

Time froze like one of those terrible slow-motion action movies Emma used to watch. The feral cat on the ground was surely dead. The crazed woman didn't know he was there; it would be easy for him to slip out unnoticed.

'Help me, Crowley,' Cyclops pleaded.

The crimson blaze in her eyes matched the colour of her hair. 'Crying won't save you now, you ugly piece of shit. I'm going to take out your other eye.'

She raised the fork to the feral cat's face. Crowley

jumped onto the sofa and launched himself at her. He sunk his teeth into her as hard as he could. He bit as she shouted, her grip loosening around Cyclops and dropping him. She took her free hand and grabbed hold of Crowley. He tried to scramble away, but she grasped his fur, digging her nails into him. His side burnt as she glared into his eyes.

'Did you bite me to save your friend?'

Blood dripped from her fingers, staining the floor as he squirmed in her grasp, staring down as Cyclops ran off. The watch around Crowley's neck trembled as his life ticked away.

'Should I kill you quick or slowly?'

Her face was a manic grin. Shards of electric agony swept through him when the TV changed behind him, and music blared through the room. The noises triggered his mind to other nights in a different flat, watching Emma dance and sing. The memory of her sent adrenalin surging through him, supplying the strength to squirm out of her hand and leap onto her chest. The shock knocked her backwards, falling and catching her head on the furniture.

He dug his claws into her ribs, and they gazed into each other's eyes. Her pain shimmered inside her pupils, and he knew it wasn't from him digging his nails into her.

Then Crowley let go and jumped off her. He sprinted through the kitchen and out the window, leapt up and over the wall, landing in the alley next to where Cyclops stood, panting. They ran together to the front of the house, across the road, and over a fence and dived into the bushes.

'Why are we stopping?' Cyclops croaked.

'You're welcome,' he said.

'That bitch killed my brother,' Cyclops said, anger rising in his voice.

'How did she get the scratches on her face?' Crowley

stared at the door, ensuring she hadn't followed them. The other cat was agitated, walking in circles and spitting.

A fire burned behind Cyclops's one good eye. 'What difference does it make?'

'It matters because if you attacked her for that fish, she'd defend herself.'

He checked the watch around his neck – it had been two minutes, and there was no sign of her. He decided it was safe to return to Wells.

'Where are you going?' Cyclops said.

'Home,' Crowley lied. 'I suggest you do the same,' knowing full well that feral cats had no homes. He took the longest route to the professor's house, staying in the shadows and bushes just in case she was on the street looking for him.

All the way back, the only thing he thought about was her skin underneath his claws.

And that pain burning behind her eyes.

Chapter 25

Crowley: Cat Night Evening

'Wells!' Crowley shouted from outside the house. He trembled from his encounter with the woman as the mist drifted in from the chemical plant. A toxic aroma wafted around him on the wind, making him wonder about the human and his experiments. 'Wells!' he yelled again.

The professor opened the door and let him in. 'I thought you wouldn't come back.'

'About time,' Crowley said, striding towards the fire to get warm. His fur tingled with the cold while his flesh burnt from the redhead's unloving caress. Her icy voice threatened him in his head. Crowley pushed her promise of violence from his mind and stared at Wells. 'Did you turn the cameras back on?'

He didn't want the redheaded woman to see him on any recordings at the house. He shivered from his confrontation with her, pain in his stomach where her nails cut into him.

'Don't worry; they're only in the lab upstairs. What did you discover?' The professor couldn't hide his excitement, seemingly more interested in Pandora's secrets than conversing with a talking cat.

Crowley stalked around the room in agitation, peering into the shadows to see if any of Darkstar's spies hid there. 'She only lives about a mile from you, 64 Regent Street.' He still saw the look on her face as he scratched her arm, the hate that poured from her eyes when she threatened to kill him.

'She lives nearby? That seems a lucky coincidence,' Wells said.

'Are you sure there's such a thing as the Project? I discovered no evidence at her place indicating she was anything but a normal human.' The heat from the fire ran through his fur, reminding him of her savagery as she dangled him in the air. There was nothing ordinary about her.

The professor looked surprised. 'You went into her home?'

'Of course. I did as you asked. Now it's your turn to uphold your promise.' It would have all been for nothing if he didn't get the serum and had to devise another plan to steal it.

Wells crouched near Crowley. 'I always keep my word.'

He moved back a bit, still not trusting the human. 'Give me it, then.'

Wells offered the phial to him. 'Here you go.'

Crowley held out his right paw and took the Doolittle. The professor grinned at the sight. 'You didn't think I could hold things, did you?'

'After seeing you trying to open the door upstairs, nothing would surprise me regarding what you're capable of, my new friend.'

Crowley stared at the serum, wondering why Darkstar wanted it. 'Just drop a bit into any liquid, is that it?'

'It's very potent, so be careful how you use it. One small sample could infect a river.'

'How does that work?' Crowley asked.

Wells smiled. 'It replicates at rapid speed once it bonds with another liquid.' He seemed proud of what he'd created. 'It's quite remarkable if I say so myself.'

'Have you only tested this version on yourself?'

Wyatt Wells sat cross-legged and stared at him. 'No. Once I survived my dose and grasped what was happening with your compatriots, I had to try it on others.'

His grin made Crowley uneasy. 'You weren't concerned it would kill or cause brain damage?' Crowley thought the professor might be as unhinged as the redhead.

'Of course. I selected my patient carefully and the mouse.'

'Mouse?' Crowley asked.

'I needed an animal they could hear, so I bought a mouse from a pet shop.'

Crowley couldn't decide if Wells was clever or devious. 'Who was the patient?'

'You have to understand that once I appreciated what it had done to me, I recognised the serum could cure many conditions which affect the brain, such as dementia and Alzheimer's.'

'What did you do?'

'I took a talking mouse to visit my dad.'

The glare of the fire reflected vibrant light off the clear liquid Crowley held. Was this indeed the Doolittle or just water in the glass?

'Your father?'

'There's no real love between Dad and me, never has been,

but to see him eaten up by dementia for the last five years has been cruel.' Crowley stared at the human as the insincerity poured out of him. 'I had to do what any dutiful child would do for their father and make their life as happy as possible.'

'Or maybe you wanted to cure him to prove you were the better man?' Crowley didn't like the human opposite him.

Wells laughed. 'You know me too well, little cat, much better than I know you.' He relaxed in the seat. 'The reasons aren't important; all you need to know is it worked.'

'You cured him?' Crowley still didn't understand why Darkstar and the Bullfather wanted this miraculous serum. Did they want to cure the humans who were ill with these brain conditions?

'Yes, and the old man now has a talking mouse he can listen to in that dreadful care home I put him in.' The smile on his face made Crowley sick. Wells stood and went to peer through the curtains. 'Though now he's better, he won't need to stay in that place anymore.' He slapped his forehead. 'Damn, I never thought of that. The old bastard will try to come and live with me.'

'How do you know this Project exists?' Crowley asked.

'I don't,' the professor replied. 'I only have Pandora's word on it. And the clips she sent about experiments one to five.'

'Show me these videos.' Crowley didn't want to watch a clip of a brain-damaged human, but he was formulating a theory about the redhead.

Wells got the laptop from the table. He searched for something before returning to show Crowley the computer.

'Here you go,' he said, starting the clip.

Crowley held his breath as a young woman, maybe in

her late twenties, walked into the room. She sat in a chair, and a person off-screen handed her a glass of red liquid.

'Subject is taking a sample of Serum Point Five,' a distorted voice said.

The woman drank it in one go, still staring into the camera. Her arms shook in under thirty seconds, moving up and down as if controlled by a demented marionette. Her mouth moved uncontrollably, saliva dripping from her lips and onto her chin. She tried to speak, but nothing came out except strangled attempts at language. Her fingers pressed against her face, clutching at her skin until she tore the flesh away and blood rushed into her hands. The screen went black as she let out a piercing scream.

Crowley shuddered, bile rising from his stomach in volcanic proportions. He lunged into the corner and emptied what little was inside his guts. 'What was that?'

'They're all like that: men and women, different ages, all the same results.' His voice had no sympathy, no concern that his work had caused such horror.

Crowley used his paw to wipe his fur clean. 'That could have been your fate.'

He found it hard to believe Wells would take such a risk with his own life. The professor's expression was a blanket of sadness and despair, his eyes shrinking to near pinholes, mouth downcast.

'When you think you have nothing to live for, no action is too extreme.' His tone was calm; his body slumped in his chair.

'You must have been desperate.'

'Do animals dream of suicide?' Wells replied.

'We're too busy struggling to stay out of harm's way to even think about such a thing.' Crowley's mind returned to the video. 'There isn't a good view of the drug before the patients get it.'

'No, you don't see that; just each of them drinking from the glass of red liquid. It looks like my serum, the earlier versions of it.'

'Then how do you know they took your serum?'

'Pandora told me.'

Crowley stared at him and wondered how somebody so bright could also be so stupid. 'She might have faked all of this, got some actors for those clips.' He didn't know what she could do, but it worried him.

'Why would she create such an intricate façade?' the professor said.

Crowley tied the phial into his watch chain and approached the front door. 'Don't ask me, professor; I've never understood how the human brain works.'

'I still need your help,' Wells shouted as Crowley left, never intending to set foot in the place again. He felt the Doolittle against his fur, not caring what Darkstar and the Bullfather wanted it for. He had his plans to follow, starting with getting Emma out of prison.

Chapter 26

Crowley: The Masterplan

Crowley spent a sleepless night wrapped in thoughts about two different young women as he devised a hasty plan involving a flock of seagulls, a bunch of psychotic mice, two poetic Labradors and an alcoholic duck.

The fact they were moving Emma to an open prison was pure good luck on everyone's part. He only discovered her fate when the police arrived at her flat and searched it. They didn't give him a second thought as he sat on the fridge and watched them turn the place upside down. When they found the jewels he'd stolen from the museum and spoke about discovering Emma's DNA at the crime scene, he realised she was in trouble.

And it was all his fault.

So, the day before the AA meeting, he gathered a motley crew of rats and mice who owed him favours. Their job was to monitor Emma in the detention centre and report everything to him. He didn't know how to get her out of that terrible place, but knew he had to try. Darkstar's demands put his timetable back a little, but he couldn't do anything for Emma until he received updates on her situation.

When he took the Doolittle to the abandoned building he lived in, Jonathan, the gulls' leader, waited with the latest news. Crowley was distraught to hear about the dangers Emma faced, but more pleasing was learning about the move to the open prison. The mice informed him the van transporting her would arrive at ten in the morning. He got everybody together as soon as he grasped what was happening.

He'd rested for two hours since leaving the professor's house, but adrenaline kept him awake. 'This is how we'll get her out,' he told the others.

They gazed at him in silence until Bukowski, the inebriated duck, spoke.

'What if something goes wrong? Do you have a Plan B?'

He had sympathy for the poor bird from the first time they met. Bukowski had a complicated childhood, abandoned by his father, with six older siblings who harassed him at every opportunity. He damaged his feet at birth, and the only thing that eased the pain was alcohol. As Crowley stared at him, the duck repeated his question.

'What if something goes wrong?'

Crowley paced across the top of the table, laying out the action plan. The seagulls sat in the rafters of the abandoned office, cooing every time he explained something to the group. Tim and Tom, the poetic Labradors, snuggled in the corner while the psychotic mice appeared grumpy and bored at the other end of the room. Chirpy was asleep under the table, having no nervous energy to expand. She didn't seem too unhappy to have left the home of Professor Wyatt Wells.

'Nothing will go wrong,' Crowley said with a determination he didn't possess.

He had to get Emma out of prison before he took the Doolittle to Darkstar. He still didn't trust the ebony cat, and his debt to Emma increased daily, especially when his spies told him what had happened to her in that terrible place.

'Did you leave the message in Emma's cell?' he asked the leader of the psychotic mice, Starkweather.

The mouse didn't reply, turning his nose up and snarling. Crowley would owe him and his followers for this. Some of his new gang were there for adventure, but for the others, he promised to steal anything they wanted.

'Of course we did,' one of the other mice said. 'We left a beautiful handwritten piece which was dazzling to the eye.'

The psychotic mice were all proud of their calligraphy skills. Starkweather and the others scampered into the corner. Chirpy snored under the table, a low, rumbling snooze reminiscent of a child's train trundling along a track. The little pooch had begged for inclusion, and Crowley couldn't refuse those wide-open puppy dog eyes. As Chirpy woke, Crowley reviewed the plan with them all one last time.

Then, they set off to rescue Emma.

'Is everyone in position?' Crowley was impressed with what the seagulls had achieved, handing everybody tiny earpieces and a communication system supplied by Jonathan. They were secure in the bushes across from the entrance of the open prison.

'The van is five minutes away.'

The gulls flew overhead, tracking Emma's journey. Crowley checked the watch around his neck. He was pleased to see everything was running on time. Tim and Tom stood ready to do their part; they would go in first.

'Where's Bukowski?' he asked no one in particular. The duck was missing. 'Everything's falling apart,' he mumbled under his breath. His heart rate increased to thumping inside his skull as the hands ticked on his watch.

'What's wrong?' Chirpy said.

Crowley groaned. 'If Bukowski isn't here to lead Emma from the grounds.' He shook his head. 'We'll be stuck.'

He could do it himself, but what if she froze when he appeared? There would be no time for hesitation.

'I'll do it,' Chirpy chirped up. The little dog bounced higher than the bushes. She was going to give their position away.

'Okay,' he said to calm the pooch down. 'Where's the sign for your back?' That blasted duck had left him with no choice. He gave Chirpy a sidelong glance. This was a bad idea. If the dog couldn't control herself, it would ruin everything.

'Some animals never go crazy, what ghastly lives they must lead.'

Crowley jumped at the sound of Bukowski's voice behind him. Bukowski staggered out of the bushes, a small bottle of tequila swinging from side to side around his neck, saliva and other marks staining his feathers.

'Stick that paper on my back; I'm ready.'

He stared at the sloshed bird, his ginger fur springing to attention.

'You're quackers!' the psychotic mice shouted at Bukowski, seeming not to notice the irony in their words, while the duck wobbled on his feet. At least his speech had been calm and measured. All he had to do was walk inside and out again.

Surely he could do that?

'One minute,' a seagull said as Crowley placed the communicator in the duck's ear and attached the sign to his back.

Then he wondered how Emma would feel when she saw him.

Chapter 27

Pandora: Girls Don't Cry

Pandora tasted blood at the back of her throat. It wasn't unpleasant, not as annoying as the scars on her face left by the attack of the ginger cat. She peered at her reflection in the bathroom mirror, the water cold on her skin as she washed away her crimson life.

The metallic tang in her mouth was familiar, almost comforting. She traced a finger over the raised pink lines across her cheek, the wounds rough under her fingertips. Pandora blinked against the harsh fluorescent lights, squinting to see her face more clearly. The dripping faucet was deafening in the silence. She shivered as she splashed more chilled water over the scratches, trying vainly to soothe the burning pain.

Exhaustion dragged at her limbs, her eyelids heavy and strained. But sleep was the last thing on her mind, knowing it would only bring fitful dreams haunted by flashing claws and sharp teeth – not from the feral cats that invaded her flat, but from her troubled childhood. She sighed, breath fogging the mirror. Drying her skin, she felt utterly and completely alone.

Pandora longed to wash away more than just the blood and grime - she wanted to rinse off this life altogether. To begin anew, far from the dangers lurking around every corner. A new name, city, job - a clean slate spread out before her, empty and full of potential. She pictured leaving everything else behind without a glance back.

Everything's ready to go. I have the money to start afresh.

The future called to her, bright and unmarred, as if she could escape the shadows of her past. Somewhere she could breathe deep, stand tall, and rewrite her story page by page. This weary world held nothing for her except the chance to begin again.

Pandora retreated to the living room, glancing at the blood and cold fish on the floor. The dead cat was rotting in a box in the back, the aroma disguised by the copious amounts of lemon air freshener she'd sprayed over the body. She peered at the silent TV, watching the country going to shit on the news, confused by the strange feeling sweeping through her.

Guilt. For the things she did to the cat.

Pandora couldn't understand it. She'd done worse things before – to people, not animals – and had never given any thought to them. So why were her guts churning now?

Perhaps I should give up any dreams of escape and continue being the Project's little helper. Once I've finished with Wyatt, I'm sure the Director will hand me more interesting jobs. And I'll work with Lulu again – get back to normal.

She'd avoided speaking to her partner since the Shoeless Joe incident, but hadn't missed her.

Maybe I am incapable of forming close relationships with anyone.

Pain rippled through her cheek, but she ignored the

temptation of drugs to ease her agony. Instead, she grabbed the beer near her feet and took a long swig from it. The stale taste of the booze splashed against her throat as she watched a group of protesters battling with the police on the news.

She waved the booze at the TV as if addressing the nation.

People feel alienated and disempowered because the world has alienated and disempowered them. They distrust authority because authority has shown itself to be untrust-worthy. And I can't trust the Project.

Pandora slumped on the sofa, flicking through the channels until she found one screening the director's cut of *Aliens*. Blood trickled down her cheek and chin as she thought about those cats in her flat.

The ginger one had a watch around its neck. Didn't I see that somewhere before?

She dug into her recent memories but struggled to find what she wanted. Then older images returned, haunting pictures she never wanted to revisit.

So, she kept on drinking, desperate to erase her past.

However, no amount of alcohol could do that for her.

Pandora finished the beer and grabbed her running shoes. The only thing that might clear her mind was pushing her body to the extreme.

She left the house and ran, jogging through a field of grey and silver. It wasn't crops, grass, or even weeds but stone and rubble, the debris and detritus of abandoned lives. Her heart rate increased, running past broken TVs, discarded fridges, music centres, and DVD players. There were piles of rusty knives and forks, cracked plates, and dirty pots and pans. The further she went, the bigger the rubbish became, seeing decapitated chairs, disembowelled sofas, and distressed beds until she stopped at the park of burnt-out cars.

Her feet crunched and scraped against the debris-strewn field as she jogged, the discordant rattling setting her teeth on edge. Her breath came in short bursts, sweat beading on her forehead as the exertion raised her body temperature. The pungent stench of charred plastic and rusted metal assaulted her nostrils with each inhale.

She glanced across the wasteland, taking in the twisted frames of appliances and furniture. The moonlight glinted off shards of broken glass and chrome trim, forcing her to squint against the glare. A row of vehicles sat blackened and gutted ahead, the stench of charred upholstery mingling with the metallic odour of scorched paint and rubber. She wrinkled her nose at the noxious stink and tangled her fingers in her damp hair, pushing back the sticky strands clinging to her neck. Her legs and lungs burned with fatigue, but she pressed on through the ruined husks of suburbia, stopping before the last house remaining on that street.

Pandora removed her top, tying it around her waist. The sweat dribbled down her arms, glistening over the freckles covering her skin.

'They're the Devil's tears burnt into your flesh, child,' her mother told her when Pandora was little. 'For the sins of your past and the ones to come.'

She didn't know what her mother meant at the time, but she did now.

Pandora gazed at the house. The government had bulldozed all the rest to make way for a high-speed train line they never built. All that stood there was a giant Victorian building built by four brothers who split the construction into quarters so they could live together with their respective families. By the time she arrived there, just before her tenth birthday, a commune owned the place.

'Father Lazarus will protect us from the cruelty of the outside world,' her mother claimed.

It was a lie, just like her mother calling those people a commune was a lie. They were a cult.

'I wouldn't go in there, missus. That house is haunted.'

Pandora turned to the child next to her, a girl only ten years old.

'Haunted?'

The kid shivered, and Pandora wondered why she was alone at night.

'The ghosts of dead kids live in there. That's what my mama told me.'

Parents lie, she should have told the child, but didn't.

'There's nothing in there now,' Pandora said. 'All the monsters left a long time ago.'

She watched the girl skip away as the confusion slipped from Pandora's mind. She touched the scar on her cheek and knew what to do.

Chapter 28

Emma: The Note

Emma thought of only one thing on the morning of her transfer: who had placed the note in her cell? *'Be ready when you get out of the van.'*

It was beautifully written, reminding her of a spectacular cursive script she'd seen on a school outing to a monastery.

'Did you see anything?' she asked Raya.

Raya shook her head. 'All I saw were those mice scurrying around in the shadows again. I've reported them to the guards, but they won't do nowt. It's a disgrace how much of a dump this place is. I bet you can't wait to get moved.'

There was disappointment in Raya's voice. Emma sat beside her, placing her arms on the other girl's shoulder and holding her close. They hadn't known each other long, but their bond was strong.

'You'll be okay. I'll make sure we see each other again,' she said as she smiled at her friend. Even though she was leaving that terrible place, there would be things she'd miss. They held each other for a few minutes, not speaking and enjoying the silence. Then she returned to her bed to reread the strange note.

'Be ready when you get out of the van.'

The message piqued Emma's curiosity, wondering who would be prepared to break her out of prison. She was ready to do anything to escape and see her mother, but caution made her fingers stiffen with tension.

Is this the Bride messing with me?

Emma slipped the message into her pocket and went for her last meal inside that dump. Her breakfast was short and unedifying, her mind unable to focus on the taste, looking around the room to find the Bride. She wasn't there, and anticipation of what would come washed over her; could her freedom be so close?

She said goodbye to Raya in the cell, holding her until two guards arrived to escort her to the van. The fresh air struck her, sweeping away the stink of imprisonment and reintroducing Emma to the free world.

The guards pushed her forward and bundled her into the back. Emma's shoulder hit the side of the van with a bang, a ripple of discomfort irritating her bones as her eyes adjusted to the gloom in the cramped space. As her vision returned, she noticed two female forms skulking in the shadows at the back.

'Fate loves me after all,' the Bride said, not attempting to hide the pleasure in her voice. Emma recognised the skinny girl next to the beast and wondered if she'd get to her prison break after all.

She gripped her seat. 'Why are you here?'

The Bride laughed. 'What a dumb bunny you are. Aren't you glad to see me?'

The van bounced along the road at death-defying speed. Emma swayed from side to side, fingers clutching at her seat. She never looked away from the others, waiting for one of them to pounce. She wouldn't have much chance of fending off the Bride in that confined spot, never mind them both.

'Yeah, I'm as happy as a pig in shit. And you're the shit.'

The Bride grinned. 'I know what you're thinking; how will I survive in such a small space?'

Emma was sure she could deal with the skinny girl. However, if the Bride pinned her down or against the side, she'd have no chance to defend herself. She had to talk her way out of trouble.

'If anything happens to me here, you'll return to the secure facility. Why would you want to risk that?'

The Bride shrugged. 'Maybe I hate you so much for being so damned pretty.'

A smile crawled across the Bride's face, leaving behind a slug-like trail of spit creeping from her big mouth. The skinny girl giggled, the laugh turning into a cackle, the blood in her eyes matching the red of her prison uniform. The Bride clenched her fingers and puffed out her cheeks.

'You're bluffing,' Emma said. She was confident even this terrible excuse for a human wouldn't be stupid enough to risk her cushy life in the new place. The Bride kept grinning while her little sidekick cackled like the Wicked Witch of the West.

'Clever and pretty. No wonder so many other girls like you.' Her smirk was unnerving. 'There's no need to do anything now; there'll be plenty of chances where we're going. An open prison means less security, so I can go wherever and do whatever I want.' The smile covered the whole of her extra-large head.

'You want me to put you down again to embarrass you in front of everybody else?'

There was steel in Emma's voice. She wouldn't let anything stand in the way of returning to her mother. A strange thought worried her: what if the Bride had left the message? Outside of the guards, she would have been one of the few people with access to the cell. And she knew the Bride was nasty enough to devise a twisted plan like that.

'Were you in my cell last night?'

The Bride laughed. 'Only in your dreams, sweetie; only in your dreams.'

The van stopped as Emma tried to shut out the other girl's laughter. The doors swung open, blinding her.

Then the Bride lunged for her.

Chapter 29

Crowley: Borstal Breakout

Crowley watched the van slow as it approached the prison gates. The gulls hovered above before flying behind the walls.

'About a dozen guards are waiting inside,' Jonathan said into their communicators.

The news crushed Crowley. The intel he'd received was there would be only a couple. This made things a lot harder. His stomach dropped as the van rolled to a stop. He exchanged a grim look with Chirpy, his jaw clenching. This was not part of the plan.

'Get ready, everybody.'

He glanced at Tim and Tom and their fetching jumpers. How had they got into such colourful attire? The doors of the prison swung open, and he gave the signal for Bukowski and the dogs to make their move. The psychotic mice were inside, ready to cause the maximum distraction.

Tim and Tom sprinted behind the van as it moved through the gates, moving so fast that their rainbow-hued jumpers became a blur. They shimmered like flickering lights, merging with the blazing sunlight to hurt his eyes, but he hoped it had the same effect on the guards.

Those vibrant sweaters flashed in Crowley's peripheral vision as the hounds raced alongside the van. Their rapid, synchronised footfalls kicked up plumes of dust in their wake. Crowley squinted against the prismatic glare, blinking away images burned into his retinas.

I hope I haven't put anybody in danger.

Then he watched the duck, surprised at how fast Bukowski was. He may have staggered when he walked, but he was the Usain Bolt of the bird world when he ran, sprinting like an express train behind the rainbow jumpers.

I shouldn't have doubted him. This might work.

The dogs and duck were inside before the gates could close. The gulls joined them from the sky, swooping to peck at the guards. The humans were confused, leaving the gates open so Crowley could follow the others.

Chaos greeted him when he got there.

The psychotic mice stabbed at the human's ankles with their tiny swords. The guards tried to swat their attackers away, failing as they shouted in confusion. He might have laughed at what he saw if the situation hadn't been so serious.

An avian cacophony filled the air, gulls diving and cawing as they harassed the humans. Underfoot, a writhing sea of mice swarmed the men, jabbing viciously with needle-like rapiers. Then there were the dogs.

'He walks in beauty through the day, waiting for the stars to say,' Tim sang to Tom while snapping at the first guard running towards them.

'And all that's best of you and I remind me of the starry sky,' Tom sang to Tim as he danced around the lumbering men, their rainbow attire a beacon of hope in the mayhem.

Crowley positioned himself just beyond the entrance. His heart thundered, his hair stood on end, and his breath came out in short gasps as Jonathan led his flock in dive after dive. The birds sent the startled humans scampering backwards as Crowley peered between the dancing dogs to find Emma.

But he only saw a bull-faced female human grinning like a manic baboon. Her face was tormented in rage as she screamed, yet he couldn't hear what she said above the noise surrounding him.

'I gave you the sun, wrapped in my heart,' Tim sang to Tom, his sweet, lyrical canine voice heard only by the animals.

'I gave you the moon, wrapped in my soul,' Tom replied to Tim, the smile on his face shining brighter than any celestial body.

Crawley took a deep breath and searched for Emma.

But she wasn't there.

Was he too late?

Chapter 30

Emma: Dreaming

Emma dodged the Bride, blinking against the harsh glare of the sun as she tumbled from the vehicle, disoriented by the sudden burst of sunlight. It took a moment for her eyes to adjust after the dimness of the van's interior. When they did, she found herself in the middle of complete pandemonium as two large dogs wearing rainbow-coloured jumpers ran past her.

Was she dreaming?

Emma blinked a few times, wondering if the bright sun was playing tricks on her. But no, the chaos before her was real. Enormous canines in extravagant attire menaced the guards, nipping at their ankles, while a flock of seagulls were diving and screeching overhead, aiming directly for the guards' faces.

'The world's gone crazy. Or I have.'

And there - yes! - a group of mice was dashing between the melee, tiny rapiers glinting in their paws. One mouse paused by Emma's foot, doffing his plumed hat courteously before scampering off to join the others. The guards yelled and swung their batons at the bizarre assailants, but the animals moved with astonishing speed and agility.

As she watched, the rainbow-hued dogs herded the men into a corner while the gulls continued their aerial assault. The mice scurried up the guards' legs, brandishing their weapons, and jabbed mercilessly at any exposed skin. Emma laughed at the absurdity of it all.

Did somebody slip drugs in my food at the prison, and I'm still there, hallucinating all this?

A seagull wearing a small earpiece flew close to her head, the breeze telling her she was awake and it was all real.

'Damn!' she said as one of the barking dogs knocked over a guard. The hounds in their extravagant jumpers and the mice with their tiny daggers were the strangest things Emma had ever seen. That was until the duck staggered towards her with a small bottle of alcohol around its neck.

'God, I hope it's bringing that booze for me. I need a drink.'

There was chaos everywhere, the strangeness of it freezing her to the spot when she could have made her escape.

'What is this shit?'

That was the unmistakable croak of the Bride. Emma turned to see the girl standing behind her but was distracted by the skinny teenager giggling like crazy as she ran through the carnage. She headed straight out of the open gates and to the freedom outside. Emma thought her life couldn't get any weirder until the duck warbled up to her.

'Quack,' it said before turning its back to her. Emma's eyes grew wider than the horizon as she saw a note sticking to the mallard's feathers.

'*Follow me, Emma,*' it said on the paper.

She gasped. It was written in the same extravagant calligraphy used on the message left in her cell. Before she could do anything, something punched her in the neck, and she fell, hitting the concrete hard with her shoulder. Pain swept through her as she rolled onto her back and stared at the Bride towering over her.

'I don't know what this shit is, Emma, but it's the perfect time for me to smash your face in.'

The duck quacked as the Bride's fist headed straight for Emma's head.

Chapter 31

Crowley: The Escape

Crowley watched his team do their stuff, seeing the plan work to perfection even though there were more guards than expected.

But where was Emma?

Was the information about her transfer to the open prison wrong? Was she still at the detention centre?

'Love is not love when I'm away from you,' Tom sang as he knocked a startled man to the ground.

'Your beauty is all I see when surrounded by life's great tragedy,' Tim sang before he snatched a baton from another guard.

More guards poured from the prison, batons raised as they waded into the fray. His team could only distract the security for so long. They needed to act fast.

As if on cue, the air filled with the thunderous flap of wings. An enormous murder of crows descended from above, swarming the new wave of guards with raucous caws. The men shouted in alarm, swatting futilely at the barrage of inky feathers.

'What?' Crowley said.

'I called in some reinforcements,' Jonathan replied in Crowley's earpiece.

Crows! And I thought they hated me.

He watched as the dark birds flapped above the guards, using their ebony wings to strike at human heads while the mice continued to poke and prod any exposed flesh. Tim and Tom snapped and barked, corralling the startled men into a spot away from the gates. Only they weren't barking, but singing.

'Your voice lifts my spirit, your laughter, my bliss. My life would be lonely without you in it, missing your sweet kiss,' Tom and Tim sang to each other as they herded the terrified humans back towards the building. 'Our stars are aligned, our hearts beat as one. Through darkness and light, our love will run.'

Crowley was impressed with how all the animals worked together, but he still couldn't see Emma.

Then he spotted her as she fell out of the vehicle. She wore a strange uniform, and the sunlight fizzled in her long white hair, but he knew it was her. His heart skipped a beat, searching for Bukowski so the duck could get the message to her. Without that, she wouldn't know what to do.

'Where's the messenger?' he said into the communication device, panicking until Bukowski appeared from behind Tom and Tim, wobbling towards Emma.

The impossible is unfolding, and everything is going according to plan.

For once, something was going right in his life. His strategy was working, and even the crows helped him.

Then he saw the big girl punch Emma in the head.

Crowley cried in despair as the bull of a woman attacked his Emma. He paused briefly before springing into action, running between Tom's legs as the dog pulled on a guard's arm. He reached Bukowski as the duck finished the last of the tequila he'd been carrying.

'You have to die a few times before you can live,' sang the drunken duck.

Crowley froze as the other female human thrust her chubby fingers around the back of Emma's neck and squeezed.

Chapter 32

Emma: The Bride

The pain in Emma's skull was immense, her body flat on the ground, eyes glazing over. In the distance, it appeared as if a cat was sprinting towards her. Then her vision faded, and she fell into the shadows of her mind.

The pounding in her head made it hard to focus, but when her eyesight cleared, she saw the zoo's bars and cages. People were laughing and pointing at the animals, but all Emma felt was sadness seeing the pain around her: the chimpanzees in their small enclosure, pacing back and forth endlessly, the lone polar bear swimming loops in his pitiful pool, and the birds with their wings clipped so they couldn't fly away. She stared at them all with a knot in her stomach, imagining what living in one of those pens would be like.

As her eyes closed against the pain, she felt something soft brush her hand. Her eyelids flickered open to another terrible sight. The Bride knelt beside her and dug those vampire-like fingernails deep into her flesh.

'I don't know what's happening here, my lovely Emma, but it seems too good a chance to waste.'

Warm blood swam down Emma's skin. The life slipped from her, heart pumping faster as her mind shut down. The Bride squeezed the breath from her lungs as she pictured her mother all alone.

I let her down again.

She waited for her existence to flash before her eyes, to witness all those moments when she disappointed her parents for the last time.

Then a tiny mouse jumped onto the Bride's ugly mug, thrusting a small sword deep into her left cheek. The Bride screamed as she tumbled off Emma, clawing at her face as the seagulls squawked above and the dogs barked around her. Emma regained her composure as the mouse that attacked the Bride – had defended Emma – stood on its hind legs and thrust its weapon into the air while the other girl rolled on the ground howling.

As she twisted her aching head, a cat sprinted forward to jump as high as he could. He landed full on the Bride's face and sank his claws deep into her flesh. As the dreadful girl screamed, the cat turned to Emma. She could only stare as it meowed at her.

That's my cat.

'What a bizarre day,' she said as the crazed-looking duck approached her, turning its back so she saw the note again.

Follow me.

'I'll kill you for this,' the Bride cried through her mangled face.

Cat jumped off the angry girl and stood next to the duck. Her cat smiled at Emma and winked. It was enough to spur her into motion as she picked herself up and followed the duck out the prison gates.

Maybe this is because I've been so kind to animals.

It was the only way her mind processed what was

happening. Nearby, ferocious seagulls attacked two of the guards. She had to move quickly, running into the road, so distracted she didn't see the car speeding towards her. The high-pitched cat's wail made her turn in time to stumble, the front wheel missing her by a hair's breadth, the ferocity of the wind adding to her movement as she staggered forward.

She fell into the trees lining the edge, a low-hanging branch cutting her across the forehead as she hit the ground. Her shoulder took most of the brunt, the thick mud sending an electric ache through her arm, stretching into her finger-tips. She rolled onto her back and stared into the leaves dangling above her.

Then the branches parted, and the shadows came for her.

Chapter 33

Crowley: Reunited

'Time to leave, everybody,' Crowley said into his communicator as he followed Emma outside. He hoped she'd stay with Bukowski down to the river and the boat waiting for them. He tried not to get his hopes up, but everything seemed to go according to plan.

'Find what you love and let it engulf you. Find what you love and let it consume you,' the dogs sang behind them as the road approached.

'We're keeping them busy here, Crowley; nobody's coming after you,' Jonathan's voice yelped through the communicator.

This is it. Now for the last part.

Then he saw the car racing for Emma as she stood in the middle of the road.

'Move, Emma!' he shouted as tyres screeched towards her. It swerved, missing her by inches as she stumbled head-first into the bushes.

As she fell, Crowley raced over, dodging more traffic and jumping into the trees. She lay on her back, with blood on her head and unmoving. Her eyes were closed, her breathing slow and laboured.

'Hurry up,' Bukowski said ahead of them.

'The guards are through the gates, heading for you,' Jonathan said in the earpiece.

Emma was so still, he worried she might be injured and unable to move.

Don't let this all be for nothing. We're so close now.

'Come on!' Bukowski shouted.

Crowley could think of only one thing to do: he licked Emma's face. Her skin tasted of fresh lemon, and he ignored the blood on her forehead. A vivid memory slammed into him of them playing with ingredients for a cake as she baked in the flat. He remembered the early days of their relationship when he first crept through her window one night, desperate to escape from Darkstar's reach. He didn't know what to expect when she discovered him there, thinking she might be one of those humans who hated animals since there seemed to be more of them every time he ventured into their communities.

However, she welcomed him into her home, cleaned his wounds, fed and watered him, taking care of him and asking nothing in return. She left the window permanently open so he could come and go as he pleased. He owed her so much, and then his mistake had led to her present condition, locked in that prison and now hurting by the side of the road. He had to get her away from there.

He licked her face again, tasting more memories and inhaling the aroma of burnt sugar. Then Bukowski called to them from the river.

'We have to go! Now!' the duck shouted.

Crowley pushed his nose up against Emma's. His lips

sprang upwards when her chest rose and fell, and her eyes flickered open.

'I love you as well, cat,' she said as she staggered to her feet. She looked exhausted, her eyes all bleary and wet.

'Follow me, Emma!' he shouted, hoping she understood his meaning. He smelt the river just ahead of them, rushing through the grass and hearing her behind him.

They were so close now.

Chapter 34

Emma: The Boat

Emma slowly opened her eyes as something soft and furry brushed against her cheek. The cat's ginger face hovered over her, his yellow eyes filled with concern. His wet nose nudged hers while his sandpaper tongue rasped over her fingers in affection. She smiled weakly and reached up to scratch the cat behind his ears, eliciting a rumbling purr.

The hard ground pressed cold and unyielding against her back as she lay there, grounded by the feel of his fur under her trembling hand. The smell of the trees and grass mingled with the cat's familiar musky scent. Emma's head throbbed, a relentless pounding echoing through her skull. Her mouth was dry and cottony. The cat gazed at her, and she felt the love seeping out of him as he purred and then meowed.

'I love you as well, cat,' she said as she stood.

Emma recognised the urgency in the cat's meow, struggling to move with the pain surging through her. She trailed behind him through the dense vegetation, the river ebbing and flowing nearby. She was amazed to see a boat moored there and the duck from earlier sitting in it.

Her cat leapt inside, and she followed him without a second thought as if all her life had been leading up to that moment. All those times her father took them out fishing, letting her and Jane steer the boat across those great northern lakes, was a preparation for that precise instant.

'I don't know what's happening, Cat, but anything is better than being in that prison.'

I have to get to Mother.

But she was a fugitive and knew the authorities would look for her.

She thought she heard a bird squawking from the cat's head, shaking at the craziness she'd witnessed. It didn't matter how it happened; she was out now.

Emma scrambled for the motor, turned it on, and steered it away from the reeds. She'd missed the outside world, missed the water and earth around her. The aroma of nature filled her lungs, a fragrance of berries and cherry blossoms sedating her weary bones. Her head ached, the not-so-gentle caress of the branch leaving its after-effects inside her mind. A small dog snuggled at the bottom of her legs, and she grinned, believing she was a child once more and this was one of her fantasies.

As the boat moved down the river - with no time to wonder where she would go or for the realisation she was a fugitive to sink in - the tension drifted from Emma, and fatigue took over. She slumped beside the motor and turned to watch the bank receding in the distance. She waited for the guards to appear and call her to stop, but nobody followed them.

There was a bottle of water at her feet, and, without thinking, Emma picked it up and drained half of it in one go, desperate to get the dryness from her mouth. Her cat and the duck sat at the opposite end of the boat, staring at her.

'Maybe I'll wake up in a minute,' she said as her eyelids got heavier and heavier.

They closed, and the ache slipped from her body as her hand dipped into the water.

Chapter 35

Crowley: The River

'Y ou put the serum in the bottle?' Bukowski said.

'A partial dose,' Crowley replied, hoping beyond hope he hadn't scrambled her brain.

'How long before it works?' the duck asked as Emma closed her eyes.

'I don't know,' Crowley replied. His heart thumped fast enough to sprint up through his chest and out of his mouth, concerned she'd fallen asleep with one hand on the rudder and the other in the water. The bottle lay at her feet.

Bukowski sighed. 'If it works.'

'Can you drive this boat?' Crowley asked the duck, only then noticing Chirpy slumped near Emma's legs. The poor little dog had finally found something to tire her out.

'I'm a duck, of course I can, and you pilot this thing; it's not a car.' Bukowski scowled at Crowley as he stretched his webbed feet over the sleeping pooch and placed one wing firmly onto the rudder.

Crowley scanned their surroundings, still waiting for the humans to follow them. 'You need to get us away from here.'

'We'll be okay as long as you don't want to stop,' the duck said.

Crowley's eyes widened at the thought of it. Bukowski laughed as the boat continued onwards. The river cut through the city, splitting it down the middle and separating its citizens into those who lived on the rich side and those who struggled on the other.

The water was blue in most parts, darker in the shadows and paler in the light, as he peered into its depths, always remembering how much he hated it. He jerked his head upwards towards the conversations of the birds. Somewhere above them, hidden by the marshmallow clouds, they talked about escaping to a different place. He wondered if he was doing the same thing.

Have I only made things worse for Emma?

He stared at her sleeping body and watched her breath as the wind caressed her snow-white hair. The rhythm of her sleep mirrored the movement of the water underneath them as they continued along its smooth, seductive curves, his mind racing ahead to think about the future. His plan to get her out of prison had succeeded; what came next was a mystery.

Where do we go from here?

'At least you didn't kill her,' Bukowski said as the boat lurched to the side. The sudden movement turned Crowley's stomach into a jumble of irritation with a promise of erupting bile soon.

It also shook Chirpy awake. 'Who's dead?'

'All of us if we get caught,' Crowley answered.

'You did a pretty number on that ugly human's face,' Bukowski said.

He smelt the girl's flesh between his claws. It was years

since he'd attacked a human, and now he'd done it twice in quick succession. 'I was desperate.'

'At least you couldn't make her look any worse,' the duck said.

Crowley's fur rippled with tension, worried by Bukowski's agitated movements and piercing stare. They'd need to get him something to drink soon.

'What will we do when she wakes up?' Chirpy asked.

'If she wakes up,' Bukowski replied, his wings shaking on the rudder.

Crowley slunk over to where Emma lay, watching her eyelids flutter. If she were dreaming, then maybe she was okay. Guessing she'd drink from it, he'd taken a massive risk of putting the serum in the bottle. But if it worked for Wells, why wouldn't it work for her?

Unless Wells lied to me.

'She's a fugitive from the other humans now,' Bukowski said.

That was why Crowley had taken such a terrible risk. Once they broke her out of prison, she would always have to flee from so-called human justice, maybe for the rest of her life. He appreciated what it was like as an outsider from your community, so he convinced himself that giving her the gift of understanding the animal world was the best thing he could do for her.

Or did I do it for my selfish reasons? I could've killed her.

That was if she lived and wasn't brain-damaged. Behind his eyes was the constant flow of images from the video Wells had shown him of the poor woman and her complete mental collapse after drinking the previous version of the Doolittle. He remembered her shaking and drooling and heard her cries as her mind melted. Is that what he'd condemned Emma to?

He tried not to think about it and concentrated on where they were going. The boat travelled on, past the warehouses on the industrial side of the river, floating by the luxury apartments on the opposite side. The weather turned hotter, the sun sinking closer to them as his fur sizzled. It was a similar tingle of heat to when sitting so close to Wells's fire. There were no mountains or hills on either side of them, just the constructs and constraints of humanity, nothing but the river bank of reeds, green bushes, the red-hued trees, and the sky resting on the tops of the green.

'Am I going home soon?' Chirpy asked.

She sounded desperate, and it was another question he didn't know the answer to. He couldn't take what he had left of the serum to Darkstar and the Bullfather. He didn't understand why they wanted it, but was sure it wouldn't be for anything good. And that meant he'd be a fugitive as much as Emma was. Darkstar would use the AA's resources to pursue the cat who'd defied him again.

'Do you want to return home?' he asked the little dog.

Chirpy wagged her tail so fast he thought she'd smash a hole in the boat. That would be all he needed: fighting against the water while trying to save Emma from drowning.

'Will we be having more adventures? I like our adventures.' The kid got more excited by the second.

'I would guess so,' he said, finding it impossible to keep the weariness from his voice.

'Then I'll stay with you longer, my friend.' She smiled at him as if she'd planned a wedding.

The cat marries a dog.

He laughed. He was living in a strange new world, so anything was possible. He stared at Bukowski as the duck mastered the art of piloting the boat, noticing the pained look on the bird's face, wondering how long he could keep himself under control without a drink. Emma mumbled something, and it swept the thought from his brain. She was waking up.

'Here's the moment of truth,' Bukowski said.

Crowley sat up as large as he could, nerves gripping his body as she opened her eyes and stared straight at her cat.

'Who's moment of truth?' she asked.

'Are you okay, Emma?' he said.

'Who said that?' she replied, twisting her head in search of the speaker.

'Are you blind?' Bukowski replied.

Emma's eyes grew in amazement.

'At least I didn't kill her,' Crowley whispered.

Chapter 36

Emma: Speaking in Tongues

Emma noticed a duck sitting next to her that appeared to be controlling the boat. And it had just spoken to her. She jerked her hand from the river and blinked as everything moved a thousand times slower than usual. She gripped the side of the boat, every beat of her heart pounding against her chest as if it was trying to claw its way out of her body. Blood throbbed in her veins as her legs shook.

She was scared, holding her breath, daring not to make a sound, waiting for the impossible to happen.

'Do you remember what transpired at the prison, Emma?'

It happened again; the cat spoke. She closed her eyes, the breeze caressing her face, hearing the sounds of the river as the water flowed nearby. She let her mind drift back to the last thing she recollected before waking.

'The courtyard at the prison,' she said. 'Birds were attacking the guards, and two dogs were jumping around.' She remembered the large Labradors in their colourful tops.

Then there were the mice. 'There were mice with tiny swords stabbing the ankles of the guards.'

It was all real. She opened her eyes again.

'Are you okay?' Crowley asked.

She gazed at the talking cat. Her talking cat. 'You saved me from the Bride, jumping on her face before she could attack me.'

'Was that the beefy ugly girl?' the duck said.

'Yes,' she replied without thinking how ridiculous it all was. 'Am I dreaming?' she asked none of the animals in particular.

'No, Emma, this is all real,' her cat replied. 'It's a long story, and I promise to tell you everything, but we must get you somewhere safe; the humans will look for you.'

She relaxed, accepting her bizarre situation. She leant forward and stroked her cat across his head.

'I've missed you, Cat,' she said, smiling at him, beaming brighter than the sun. The little dog moved away from Emma's legs, its nose pointing towards the clouds.

'What's that noise behind us?' the pup asked.

'I hear nothing,' her cat replied.

'I have excellent hearing,' the dog said. 'There's something behind us in the distance, in the sky.'

She turned, seeing a speck in the air getting larger by the second.

'A helicopter,' the duck said. 'It's probably the coppers searching for us.'

Emma didn't know if any of it was real or all a dream. She placed her hand over the side and ran her fingers through the water. It was cool to the touch and felt real. All she knew was that she was free, and people were likely already looking for her. She had to get somewhere safe. She needed to reach her mother.

'Okay, let's get this boat inland, then. You can tell me the whole of this amazing story on the journey north,' she said.

'North?' the cat, duck and dog all said simultaneously.

'Yes. I must see my mother before we do anything else.' Emma peered into the calming waters of the river and pondered a world of talking animals. If such a thing was possible, it gave Emma hope she could save her mother.

All she had to do was steal a car.

Chapter 37

The Bullfather: The Rising Sun

The Bullfather recalled his first meeting with the Guardian. 'Why should we trust you?'

The great bull awed the other animals. Darkstar sat in the corner, the flickering lamplight illuminating his ebony shape. The smell of human sweat mixed with the menagerie of animal aromas swirling around the room.

He was ready to rush forward at any second and kill the human if needed. Thinking of it sent ripples of excitement scurrying through his hide. The human, Stoker, rose from the sofa, making sure not to stand on any piglets squirming at his feet. There was trepidation and fear etched on his face, stretching his flesh so it was an unnatural yellow under the firelight.

'I owe you and all animals a debt I can never repay.'

He scrutinised Stoker. 'What do you mean?'

Stoker placed his hands on the bottom of his shirt, pulling it over his head, revealing the experiences of his life. Every animal in the room, except the Bullfather, gasped when they saw the dozens of thick scars littering his chest and back.

'This is a joyous moment for me.' Stoker's weather-beaten lips stretched across his cheeks. 'I work with a group who'll help you and ensure all animals are safe. They're called the Rising Sun - animal rights activists.'

The Bullfather peered at the man with suspicion and mistrust, glancing towards the dark cat who had convinced him to come to the farm.

'The Rising Sun?' the large bull asked.

'They liberate animals from places of suffering, pain and death, removing them from laboratories and farms, destroying facilities, arranging safe houses and veterinary care, and operating sanctuaries where animals can live safely. This is one such place.' There was pride in Stoker's voice, his scarred chest puffed out, his breathing returning to normal.

'I know of this farm,' the Bullfather said. 'Many animals have suffered here. Many animals have died here.'

Stoker's face darkened. 'I know, and I'm sorry. That was before when my father ran this place. I'm in charge now, and, with the help of the Rising Sun, we'll turn this into a sanctuary for everyone in this room and all the animals that come here.'

'Farms exist to make money from animal suffering and death. How will you survive without that?' The Bullfather had learnt a lot from his time on the other farm. Humans were driven by money, selfishness, and greed. The idea of one or any of them helping animals was hard for him to accept.

'I sold some of the land, so we have enough money to last for a long time,' Stoker replied.

Darkstar shifted from the shadows and moved towards the centre, next to the Bullfather. Then he spoke to Stoker.

'Tell everybody what happened to your father.'

The great bull peered at the dark cat, unsure what Darkstar had dragged him into, but certain anywhere was better than where he'd been only a short time ago. If what Darkstar and the human said was correct, they'd have a place of safety and a group of guardians for the rest of their lives. He stared as the bare-chested man and his scars slumped back into his seat, the piglets scrambling away from him.

'I killed him,' Stoker replied.

His voice had no emotion, just ice dripping from every word. The piglets pulled little pink faces of shock. The dogs bared their teeth, anticipating a tale of violence and brutality. The foxes grinned at the news of a farmer's death. Both cats in the room were unmoving, as was the Bullfather, who spoke next.

'Is he the one who gave you the scars you wear like a uniform?'

'He was,' Stoker replied. 'But that's not why I killed him.' His voice now had emotion – not sadness or regret, but pride and joy.

'Go on,' Darkstar said.

Stoker continued. 'People from the Rising Sun broke into the barn one night to free the cows locked inside. They were to be transported to a slaughterhouse the next day, so the group came to liberate them.'

The Bullfather had detected the history of death in the place as soon as he'd stepped from the river. He would never forget that unmistakable stench of torture and murder.

Stoker continued. 'Father caught them inside the barn. He had a shotgun in one hand and an axe in another.'

'He would kill other humans?' the Bullfather said in surprise.

'He'd been waiting all his life for that moment, to murder somebody. What he'd done to me was only part of his training. When they broke in, it gave him the perfect excuse to kill them and get away with it.'

All the animals in the room gazed at Stoker as he spoke, his face fluctuating between pleasure and agony as he continued his tale.

'I followed him inside when I heard the cows crying, hoping to find the courage to stop him. That was when I saw the other people in the barn. I was shocked to see them, terrified as I observed his joy. Something was clawing against my insides when my father shouted at the two trembling young women before him. He forced them onto the ground with the gun barrel, tears streaming down their faces as I suppressed mine.'

'You discovered your courage that night,' Darkstar said.

Stoker nodded. 'He pointed the shotgun at one of the women, moving up to her head until he was close to pushing it into her mouth. He laughed at their fear. I saw the bliss on his face and recognised the suffering he caused them. I couldn't take it anymore, and my terror left me. I called out his name, and he turned to me.'

'What did you do?' the Bullfather asked.

'He smirked in my face and told me to leave. Then he lifted his hand towards me, the axe in the air, ready to drop steel death on my head. But I knew he wouldn't kill me. He enjoyed torturing me too much for that.'

Stoker caught his breath. The room was silent apart from the rapid beating of hearts. All eyes were on him.

'He hesitated, allowing me to grab the axe from his hand as he lowered it to his side. He laughed at me again. I ignored it, feeling the weight of the wood and steel in my grip, understanding how it made me powerful. My father saw it in my eyes, and he hated it.'

'You killed your mother, and now it's my turn, is it, mother killer?'

'He repeated that as he edged closer to me. I snapped, striking him on the side of the head with the axe. He fell, shocked eyes peering at me, struggling to find the words in the back of his throat. Before he did, I hit him again and continued hitting until those terrible eyes could stare at me no more.'

Gasps and sighs drifted around the room.

Stoker touched the mutilations on his chest. 'I swore a pact that night with the two women I saved, with the Rising Sun. They have factions worldwide, and this is just one of the places they use as an animal sanctuary.'

'What did you do with the body?' asked the Bullfather.

Stoker's fingers lingered over his tattoos. 'I took the axe and chopped him into bits. Then I fed him to the pigs.'

The dogs and the foxes laughed a raucous cackle, a mixture of dying star and newborn scream. The piglets squealed and wriggled away from him. Darkstar and the Bullfather looked at each other and knew they'd found the right human. They had their Guardian.

Back in the present, the Bullfather strode towards Stoker as he finished talking to the piglets. Now was the time to put the final touches on their grand plan.

Soon, the sun would rise on their brand-new day.

Chapter 38

Pandora: Private Investigations

'You can't smoke here,' the Governor said.

Pandora surveyed the scene in the prison courtyard, quite happy to ignore his advice.

'Do you have video surveillance?' She took a long drag on the cigarette and blew it in his face. She disliked most people, but obnoxious older men were particularly repulsive. She resisted the temptation to stab the fag on his greasy cheek.

'No, I'm afraid we do not.' Irritation ripped through his voice.

Beyond the smoke, she saw his annoyance at her visit to his private empire. Pandora stared into his piggish eyes and wondered if he'd seen through her fake government ID. It was a perfect forgery, but there was something of the criminal about him, and criminals were always good at spotting their compatriot's work. She put her concern to one side and continued with the investigation.

'Just the ones somebody leaked to the media?'

Without it, she wouldn't have known about the extraordinary prison break. His frustration was substantial, the fumes drifting from his ears mixing with the cigarette smoke she blew at him. She enjoyed annoying people, especially petty little bureaucrats like him.

'Whoever did that will be reprimanded.' His skin was an unattractive shade of red when she arrived at the prison. Her constant stream of awkward questions made him glow a vibrant hue of ruby.

'There were only two guards in the courtyard that morning?' she asked. She'd read the reports but wanted to look into his eyes when he lied.

'Yes, as I've told you. Both are on compassionate leave because of the trauma of the attack.' He was a practised liar, but so was she. The released video clips only showed two guards assaulted by animals, but she guessed there would have been more.

'One teenage girl, armed with a table knife, overcame your experienced security and escaped through the gates conveniently left open?' Pandora didn't hide her sarcasm.

'It's all in the reports. She smuggled a blade into the van from the other centre. She surprised my men when they opened the vehicle doors, and the facility gates had a major electrical malfunction.'

'Why only two guards when the transport arrived here?' She threw her first cigarette onto the floor and lit another one.

'We are an open prison; things are different here. Only three teenage girls were in the van, not exactly hardened criminals.'

'I'm glad you mentioned the prisoners. Tell me about them.' It was a command, not a request.

'The youngest of them, Brie Webber, ran outside before the violence started.'

He tried to sound professional and detached, but

Pandora observed the tiny bits of sweat on his wrinkled temples. She couldn't understand why blokes like him always combed hair over their spreading bald patches. It only made them look more ridiculous than they already were.

'What happened to her?'

'We recaptured her not long after. The girl isn't the brightest.'

Pandora could tell he was proud of himself for whatever he did with the teenagers under his control. She stared at the grey buildings and the grey man in front of her, contemplating how a slip of fate had probably kept her out of such a place. Only it wasn't destiny but her abilities and survival instinct. A year of dodging predators and the police when she lived on the streets had saved her from places like this and people like him.

'Who participated in the violence?'

'Emma Crowley attacked Elsa Sullivan with the knife, leaving her with serious wounds to her face. They were involved in another violent attack at their former prison. I guess the Crowley girl was carrying a grudge and ran for it once she appreciated the damage she did to Sullivan and saw the open gates.'

Pandora had to admit he was a terrific liar, just not good enough. However, she couldn't understand why he was covering up what happened.

'Elsa Sullivan is still here, correct? You have her in your infirmary.' She ignored his pleading, pushed past him, and headed towards the building.

He followed her. 'Yes, but she's not ready for visitors. Her injuries are quite serious; she needs sedation most of the time. She's in no state to speak to you or anybody.'

He'd regained some of his assertiveness, but it meant

nothing to her. 'I don't need to talk to her. I only want to see her.'

Over in the far corner, a group of inmates stood staring at the sky, unmoving, as they gazed into the blue and white above them. The guards wandered around as if it were just a regular pedestrian high street.

'What are they doing there?' Pandora asked about the women gazing upwards.

'New in today; they've been locked up for so long they've forgotten what the sun looks like, so they stand there and stare until they have to go back inside.'

She entered the building and waited for him to take her to see Elsa Sullivan.

'How many prisoners do you have?' She took a more conciliatory tone with the exasperated little man, his eyes trying to crawl through the massive bottle-top glasses he wore. Contact lenses or stylish frames were beyond his imagination.

'It fluctuates between three hundred and three hundred and fifty, depending on how overcrowded the general prison population gets.' They walked through an empty corridor, with no sign of anybody apart from the guard walking behind them like a wife trailing in the wake of her husband in some ancient patriarchal society.

'Only women and girls, that's correct?'

He nodded. 'We hold an assortment of prisoners; some serve a few weeks or months and long-termers on anything from two years to life.' He made it sound like a selection box of sweets, with a mixture of soft centres and hard candy. 'We aim to provide a place for the system's less severe inhabitants to serve their time while gradually introducing the long-term prisoners into the outside world again. We put a lot of trust in our inmates.' There was pride in his voice, full of bravado and conceit.

'You must be pretty disappointed in Emma Crowley, then?'

They passed through the corridor into a large open space populated by inmates. There were only a couple of guards standing by the windows.

'Of course; not only did she leave a mark on our reputation,' by which he meant his own, 'she also ruined her chances of spending time in an institution like this.' He peered around the room. 'When we catch her, she'll return to a real prison. There will be no easy life for the rest of her sentence, which will be extended.'

'She was inside for theft?'

'Yes,' he replied. 'She stole jewellery from the City Museum. She tried to hide it in her cat box.'

That wasn't in the notes - the bit about the cat box - and it made Pandora halt as he continued walking. 'A cat box?'

'I suppose it's funny, considering the ridiculous item on the news,' he said. It may have been ridiculous to him, but Pandora wouldn't be on her way to see the injured prisoner without it.

'Ridiculous?' she asked.

He puffed out his cheeks. 'Yes, that stupid clip on the TV, the one somebody faked with the animals attacking my guards.'

She scrutinised his devious eyes. 'Why would anybody do that?'

He shrugged. 'Who knows? People with too much time on their hands are always doing crap like this, making fake videos and spreading conspiracy theories. The government should reintroduce conscription. A spot in the army would sort them out.' He gazed at her. 'Why are you so interested in Emma Crowley?'

They strode into the infirmary together.

'I can't tell you that.'

The little man shook his big head. 'I'll never get used to you government people and your secrets.' He laughed as he pulled the curtains back and unveiled the injured Elsa Sullivan. Pandora walked up to the bed and leaned in close for a better look at the girl's face and those wounds.

'That's not pretty.'

'Some of that was there before the attack, but you can see the knife marks on her cheek.'

She couldn't miss them, but they weren't blade cuts. Pandora raised her hand to the plaster on her cheek. 'It looks painful.'

'Were you injured in the line of duty?' he asked her.

'Something like that,' she replied, turning away from him and striding back the way she came. A group of teenage girls giggled as she walked past them.

Pandora wanted to watch the video again but controlled her anticipation until she got outside, going through the courtyard and towards the gates left open that day but locked now. She didn't look at the guards as they let her out, walking to the river in front of the prison. She strode through the bushes and down to the water, examining where Emma Crowley escaped.

There was a bench half-hidden in the trees, and she plopped herself on it. She reached into her jacket and retrieved her phone, finding the video. It was only by acci-dent she'd seen it, switching the TV channel over in search of something to distract from the pain in her face. Pandora caught the end of the news and the traditional humorous story to make the viewers forget about the previous twenty minutes of death and misery.

She didn't understand what she was watching at first: a teenage girl escaping from an open prison, which in itself wouldn't have been newsworthy in any shape or form until you noticed it appeared she was being led across the road and down to the river by a duck and a cat.

And it was a cat with a watch around its neck. The sight of the feline made her skin burn; she would never forget that night. The wounds on the girl in the infirmary were like the ones that adorned Pandora's face.

'That's got to be the same moggie.'

What happened in that prison, and why are they covering it up?

She sat on the bench, inhaling the sweet smell of the flowers behind her, an aroma of honey and apple blossom. Pandora viewed the video again, this time in slow motion, freezing every frame to look at it in more detail.

The side of her face throbbed as if her cheek was planted onto the live rail of a train track, and she was waiting for the oncoming carriage to roll over her. Then she saw it, the pain helping her focus more on what she watched on the screen. In the shadows, as the cat and duck approached the grass verge down to the river, Pandora saw the shape of a small dog: a Chihuahua she'd seen many times before.

It wasn't pills she needed to ease her agony, but a visit to Wyatt Wells.

Chapter 39

Emma: In the Country

Emma kept the speed under control in the stolen car. They'd been lucky the helicopter had continued down the river when they scrambled up the bank and found the perfect vehicle waiting for them. It didn't take her long to get into it with Crowley's help and bundle the animals inside. They'd introduced themselves to her as she broke into the vehicle.

The cat sat beside Emma, his ginger fur standing up and tingling with excitement. 'Where are we going?'

'To my mum's, about thirty miles outside the city. It should take less than an hour. It's in the countryside, and the isolation will be perfect for us.'

She stared at the road ahead, her mind a swirl of emotions. Emma's thoughts flipped between concern for her mother, the realisation she'd escaped from jail, and the fact animals were talking to her. Or at least she heard them for the first time in her life.

Or maybe I banged my head in that prison, and now I'm in a coma, and this is all a hallucination.

'Tell me everything,' she said. Chirpy and Bukowski

were asleep in the back of the car, snuggled up to each other like an old married couple.

'About what?' Cat asked.

Crowley, that's his name. Because of me?

Emma's eyes wandered away from him and to the world outside. It was the same world she'd stared at thousands of times before, but also a brave new one for all of them.

'The realm of talking animals; how long has it been going on?' Emma peered at her cat and deliberated if she should have strapped him into a seatbelt. Then she questioned if he was still *her* cat. She'd never given him a name because she had always been opposed to humanising animals, to turn them into pets.

'Animals have spoken to each other longer than humans have walked on the planet, Emma; you just haven't been paying attention.'

She kept one eye on the road but could have sworn he smiled at her. His feline voice had a smooth tone, making her grin every time he spoke. This strange experience was new to her; a gloom hanging over her at the realisation humanity had been denied the beauty of hearing animal voices for all this time.

The night whistled in her ears as she drove, the ocean blue Ford Focus speeding up the road, travelling north. At sixty miles per hour, the engine purred, the temptation in her foot to push the pedal even harder in the knowledge it wouldn't be long before they were on the narrow country roads that wound their way to her mother's house like a snake crawling across the sand.

The little dog had talked to her at a hundred miles an hour before falling asleep, and Emma only grasped about a third of what she said. The duck was calmer, but reminded her of a drug addict going through withdrawal. It had been a bizarre introduction to her new reality.

'The bottle of water I drank had the serum in it? This is why I can understand you and the others?'

Crowley nodded. 'That's correct.'

'Should I ask where you got it from?'

'Does it matter?' he replied.

'In the grand scheme of things, I would say yes, but it's not our current priority. I want to hear more about you and the animal world.' She noticed the sign ahead, which would lead them off the main road; the thought of her mother was never far away from her mind. Emma continued to drive and stare at him in anticipation. He used his paw to wipe something from his lips and then spoke.

'I've never been one for history lessons, but here are the basics: all animals live by a code drawn up by the AA - Anthropomorphic Anonymous. It hasn't always been this way, but around fifty years ago, a group of important animals in the Western world decided it was time for a new approach. The code allows all species to coexist peacefully without trying to eat each other. It works well most of the time - as long as you're not in the wild. Then it's everyone for themselves.'

'It's like a system of government?' Emma asked with her eyes focused on the darkness outside, the night lit only by the white lines on the ground and the occasional illumination around them.

'Not as you know it. It's more of a loose form of rules and regulations, modified and maintained by local councils of different groups.'

'It sounds ideal,' she said, thinking about the appalling state of politics and government in her country for most of her life, considering the dire circumstances that had been prevalent worldwide for a long time.

She sighed loud enough to disturb the sleepers in the back, Bukowski snorting through his nostrils, Chirpy's little legs vibrating to the car's speed underneath her slumbering body, running after something only she saw.

'Like any system of rule, it has both good and bad points; you'll always get some who want to exploit it for their benefit,' Crowley told her.

'You sound like you're talking from experience.'

She slowed the car to a crawl, navigating the sharp curves in the gloom with expert skill. The darkness pushed in against them, its ebony lips kissing the windscreen and leaving moisture dribbling outside the glass. Weariness wormed its way through her. She had to get to her mother first, see she was okay, and then deal with this new world of talking animals.

'It's my fault you were in prison; that's why I had to get you out,' Crowley said.

She laughed at his words, the sounds jumping from her throat like water cascading over a cliff. Her mind had nearly adjusted to talking animals, but she couldn't think of any scenario where her cat was guilty for her going to prison.

'How?'

'I'm sorry, Emma, but it's true.'

They were about fifteen minutes away from her mother's house. 'It can't be.'

'I told you about the AA, how they keep a sense of order through the animal world, and how some will always want to exploit it for their own selfish reasons.'

She nodded as she drove. 'Yes.'

'Well, some of those who live only for themselves forced me to steal the jewellery – that's how it got in your flat.'

Tears were in his eyes as he spoke, and she thought how unusual it was to see a cat cry and hear the sadness in his voice.

'My DNA ended up in the museum from your lips?'

He nodded. 'I'm sorry.'

She couldn't control her laughter, wondering if Jane could use it as part of her defence for her case. There was a clearing up ahead, and she drove towards it, the brakes screaming into the night by the shock of her action. It had been such a long time since she'd driven that her foot slid off the pedal, and the car twisted one way, nearly ending on its side in a ditch until she steadied the wheel and turned the engine off. Crowley fell into the door, on his back, with legs in the air. Emma leant over and scooped him into her arms, the seatbelt preventing her from falling to the floor. She hugged him with all her love, ensuring she didn't squeeze the life from his fragile frame.

'Oh, my poor cat. None of this is your fault.'

Tears were in their eyes as she kissed him on the head. She held him for a long time, sobbing between happiness and sadness, her fatigue adding one last nightcap to her trembling body.

'I'm glad you're free, Emma,' he whispered.

'Just be careful with my kisses in the future.' She laughed, and he smiled.

'Are we there yet?' Bukowski asked from the back, waking from his stupor and sticking his beak into his sleeping companion's stomach. Right on cue, the little dog farted.

'Sorry,' Chirpy said as her eyes adjusted to the darkness.

Emma laughed even louder, winding down the window as she released Crowley and returned to the wheel.

'Why do they call you Crowley?' she asked him as she restarted the engine.

'In honour of you, Emma,' he replied, smiling as she pulled into the driveway.

All four of them fell out of the car and into the night. Emma stared at the cottage, relegating the memories to the past and concentrating on the future. She had to see her mother again.

And she had to introduce her family to the talking animals.

Chapter 40

Pandora: Smells like Teen Spirit

'Detective Sergeant Snow to see Jane Crowley,' Pandora said as she held the fake ID up to the camera, assuming the lawyer would open the door for a police officer. There was a long pause while she cracked her knuckles and considered how violent she'd need to be to find this missing sister and the excitable dog and vicious cat. She ran her fingers across the scars on her face as the entrance opened.

'Come on up,' a voice said as Pandora strode into the corridor. She entered the building, noticing the smell first: body odour mingled with the stink of human faeces, puke and stale sweat. Something was unsettling about it beyond its unmistakable stench, a familiarity that returned her to childhood memories as unpleasant as the aroma leaking from the carpet. She placed her fingers over her nose sprinting up the stairs, pushing the lawyer's door open without knocking. Pandora nearly puked as she scratched at her throat.

Jane Crowley sat behind a desk. 'Sorry about the smell.

It was like that when I moved in, and no amount of cleaning will get rid of it.'

Pandora controlled her emotions and scanned the room. It was compact and tidy, precisely like the woman she stared at. Family photos littered the desk. She grinned at the NO SMOKING signs on the wall.

'You're Jane Crowley?'

'What can I help you with?' Jane said.

Pandora dragged a chair from the corner and placed it opposite the lawyer, sitting and letting out a gigantic sneeze. Instead of answering Jane's question, she slipped a cigarette from her jacket.

'I need to speak to you about your sister.' She put a notebook on the desk. As she did, she made a mental note of who was in those family photos.

'Can I see your ID again?' Jane said.

Pandora blew dirty smoke into the air, breathing in its poison as it destroyed the horrendous perfume that had invaded her lungs while climbing those stairs. She took the fake ID from her jacket and handed it to the lawyer, hoping its quality would fool her.

She thinks I'm too young to be a copper.

'Has your sister been in contact with you?'

'You mean after she escaped from the prison? No, I haven't heard from her.'

Pandora noticed her fidget in the chair. 'Do you know where she might go?'

'No.' She returned the ID to Pandora, who glanced at the papers on the table.

'Your sister stole jewellery from the museum.'

'That is what the police claim,' Jane replied.

'You have evidence to the contrary?' She enjoyed the

taste of nicotine in her mouth, the yellow glue wrapping a warm blanket around her lungs.

'You know I can't tell you that.'

The lawyer tried not to stare at a photo on her desk, but Pandora observed her eyes flickering towards one specific frame. There was a large cage nearby filled with straw. It stank of fur and piss. She was glad it was empty.

'Do you think somebody planted the jewellery in her flat?'

'It's possible.'

'And they left her DNA at the crime scene?' She smiled through the smoke, enjoying the role she was playing.

'Why are you asking me all these questions, Sergeant?' The lawyer fiddled with her fingers on the desk, eyes flicking away from Pandora, skimming over that photo again and peering into the space behind Pandora's head.

She's hiding something.

'If somebody framed your sister in such an elaborate plot, then she may have escaped to try to get revenge against those who put her in prison.'

'Emma's DNA could've been transferred from a girl she kissed.'

'A girl?' She stubbed her cigarette on the corner of the lawyer's desk, just behind the photograph Jane didn't want her to see.

'Don't be so surprised, Sergeant; it's been happening for a long time.'

She considered a witty reply when something moved inside the cage near her arm. A small shape rose from underneath what Pandora believed was a clump of sawdust. Then, sharp teeth were gnashing away at empty air, followed by pointed hair and watery eyes.

The hamster's fragrance floated over her and mixed

with what was there from the corridor. She glared at the cage and the creature inside it. Its furry face and claws were near enough to hear its breathing, its chest moving up and down, and inhale the aroma of rodents wafting from it. The images behind her eyes were not of the present but the past, all of her senses trampled by things beyond her self-control.

'Do you have a pet?' she asked the lawyer in an attempt to focus her attention.

'I'm looking after it while I work on Emma's case.'

Pandora struggled to contain herself as her father's voice erupted inside her head. 'We've brought you some new pets to play with.'

Darkness slipped before her eyes, and sharp claws dropped onto her chest.

'You've been naughty, but we still love you,' her mother said.

'Are you okay, Sergeant?' the lawyer asked.

Pandora watched the other woman's lips move, hearing the hamster's teeth jumping up and down. The smell from the stairs, that fragrance of dried sweat and human shit, came flooding back into her nostrils, and she tasted the bile pushing up inside her throat like volcanic lava on the cusp of erupting.

Something horrible slithered inside her guts. She jumped from the chair and stumbled back into the world, nausea rippling through her. Pandora kept swallowing, but the vomit continued rising as she fell, hands clutching the office bin, and her head submerged inside it as spew exploded out of her in a great wave. It was dark at the bottom of the bin, and she was back in that box with rats, mice, and feral cats all over her.

I had this under control.

One hamster in a cage shouldn't have made her like this.

It's because you let all the others get away with what they did.

'Are you okay?' Jane asked with genuine concern, touching Pandora's back. She threw up again, wishing to delete her memories quickly. She wiped her fingers across her mouth and stood.

'Something I ate mixed in with stink from your stairs.'

She turned away from the animal on the table, trying to erase those images from inside the box: from inside all those many boxes. She pushed her fingernails deep into the palms of her hands, every fibre of her wanting to rip the hamster from its cage and tear the tiny head from its neck. She pictured her father's abandoned grave, grabbed control of her breathing and remembered where she was, remembering what she was doing there.

'I'm sorry,' was all Jane could say.

'Thanks for your help,' Pandora said as she struggled up. 'Do you know why all those animals helped Emma escape that open prison?'

Jane Crowley handed Pandora a fresh bottle of water. 'I thought that was a fake video? That's what the authorities said.'

'It was real.'

The lawyer laughed. 'Excuse my laughter, Sergeant, but you think those creatures helped Emma break out? They're animals.'

She took the bottle and drank from it greedily, with that awful taste disappearing from her mouth as the memories slunk back into the shadows.

'That's what it looks like on that clip. Maybe they were trained for that.'

The lawyer seemed flabbergasted by the suggestion.

'Well, I don't know about the others, but if the clip is

real, that was definitely Emma's cat in the video. Every time I saw it at her flat, it was half-asleep or chasing its tail. I don't think it could be trained to do anything useful.'

'Why does it have that watch around its neck?'

Jane laughed again. 'Emma said it was an homage to some rap music she likes. I've known my sister all her life, Sergeant, and I've still no idea what goes on inside her head.'

Pandora nodded. There was nothing else of use for her there. She smiled and headed for the door. 'I'll contact you when we get more information about your sister.'

'Here,' Jane said to her, 'let me give you this before you go back down the stairs.' She opened her desk drawer and removed a perfume bottle, spraying some of it onto the scarf she was wearing. 'Hold this to your face,' she said, handing the scarf to Pandora.

Pandora steadied herself against the wall, staring at Jane, before lighting another cigarette and grabbing the scarf. She smiled at the lawyer, eyes scanning the room one last time and that photo frame she kept trying not to look at.

'Thanks,' Pandora said while holding the scarf to her face and pushing the door open.

She removed the phone from her pocket and took the steps two at a time, searching for Emma Crowley's prison file and her mother's address.

Then she tied the scarf around her neck, pleased she didn't have to hurt the lawyer.

Maybe I'm ill.

Chapter 41

Darkstar: A Forest

Darkstar sat in the field alone, waiting for the sun to rise and his spies to return. Sometimes, they were birds, but many animals worked as his ears and eyes in the world; today, he waited for his little mice.

Fat slices of orange light cut through the blue above him, throwing gentle kisses at the white balls rolling around the sky. The trees stood tall in his vision, their branches extended towards him, leaves shimmering in the morning wind like green fingers offering him his wildest desires. He lifted his paw, letting the soft glow of the sunrise pour through him and onto his upturned face.

How will the world look once we've changed it beyond recognition?

And all because of some mice and a cat he hated more than anything. He focussed on Crowley and their shared history as the sun revealed its majesty. Their first meeting was so long ago it was like it happened to somebody else, the memories flicking past his eyes like those books human children used to flip still images into moving pictures. It was on a day not too dissimilar; the sun hanging heavy in the sky,

Darkstar holding court with the other cats deep in the forest where they lived and survived.

The occasional forage into the nearby village was the only time they encountered the humans. War had devastated most of the country – human war – and the food was at a premium. The humans had grown desperate and were eating any animal they could find, even those they once called pets, so he led all the cats he could to the safety of the woodland. Crowley drifted into their group a few weeks after Darkstar gathered them together; only he wasn't called Crowley then.

Their food supplies ran low, just the occasional rodent or bird they could catch, their emaciated feline bodies growing weaker by the day. Desperation was sinking in.

'We should leave here, find somewhere the war hasn't touched,' Crowley told them.

'The war is everywhere; this is what the humans do – they destroy everything, even themselves.' When Darkstar spoke, all the others listened.

'And what will we do if we stay here? There is no more food for us in this place,' Crowley said.

The crumpled fragments of branches and leaves that had fallen in the recent high winds were about their feet, ready to engulf them into nature's blanket when their fragile bodies succumbed to the inevitable.

He knew it was a challenge to his authority, but it wasn't that which gave him an instant dislike for the other cat: there was something behind Crowley's eyes he feared.

'Some of us should go into the village, the ones who are strong enough, and find one of the weaker humans, maybe a child if any are left.'

'And then what?' Crowley asked. All the other cats waited for the answer.

'We kill it,' Darkstar replied. 'And we will feast on human flesh.'

A gasp went around the forest.

Crowley spoke the words all cats had known for thousands of years. 'We do not eat human flesh.'

'We have no choice,' Darkstar said, steel in his voice, violence never far from his mind.

'We do,' Crowley replied. 'We leave here and find somewhere else. The whole country can't be like this.'

'And how long would that take? How many will die on the journey?'

'It's better than what you're suggesting,' Crowley answered.

'No, it isn't,' Darkstar said as he leapt at the smaller cat.

Crowley was quick, dropping to one side, so the massive claws only caught the edge of his ear, ripping a slice of ginger from its owner, which fell to the ground covered in blood. The other cats gasped, their tired and undernourished bodies shaking at the violence next to them. Crowley crept around the dark cat, his back hunched as he bled. Darkstar smelt the skin amongst the leaves and watched the others eye it hungrily. At that moment, no matter what happened, he knew Crowley had lost most of the others. He saw it in the desperation possessing their faces.

He turned away from Crowley and faced the group. 'Come with me and live, or go with him and die. The choice is yours.'

He strode through the scattered leaves towards the village on the other side of the forest. He never looked back. It would be a few more years before he met Crowley again, but that first time set the mood for what followed.

The memories faded from the shadowy parts of his mind as sunlight bathed his face. In the distance, he saw the faint outline of the birds, looking as if they'd been sketched into the sky and then partially erased, so the light was shining through the middle of their bodies, flickering through the gaps in their feathers. They were a flock of sparrows, the lookouts on the farm, always keeping their eyes searching for animal and human intruders. One of them swooped down to sit at his feet.

'The mice are on their way,' the tiny one said, its heart beating heavily underneath its greyish-brown plumage.

'Thank you, Amy,' Darkstar replied, smiling at the little bird. 'Is there any other movement on the farm?'

There had been incursions across the river from the other farm the last few days, the one where he'd rescued the Bullfather from, and Stoker was their only human protection. A group from the Rising Sun had stayed with them recently, but they'd left to put Darkstar's plan into motion. To them, it was Stoker's plan they were following, Stoker who convinced them non-violent action was not working anymore. They couldn't hear the world's truth, but the Guardian did.

'There are more foxes around the edges of the perimeter, ones I don't recognise,' the little bird said.

He smiled at the news. He'd sent word out that the Bullfather was recruiting, and the rewards would be bountiful: only he and a few trusted others knew what those rewards would be.

'That's okay, Amy. I've been expecting them. You've done another excellent job, you and your family. You should get your feed from the Guardian now. Thank you again.'

The little bird floated into the sky and joined her brethren, leading them towards the barn where Stoker waited.

He watched the mice approaching him, their brown fur

contrasting with the vivid green of the field they scampered across. Their molten red eyes were alert, whiskers twitching in the wind. Their combined aroma of rubbish bins, fresh garbage, and pungent sewers assaulted his senses. But he didn't mind; these little mice had told him of the Wells serum and what it could do. Everything had started from that moment. Until then, they'd been living comfortably on the land, under Stoker's protection and with the Rising Sun bringing new animals every few weeks.

But it wasn't enough for him. He wanted to achieve more, constantly aware their peaceful existence could only be short-lived. Stoker promised they'd have money for a long time, but Darkstar knew he was lying and had seen his accounts scattered over the table one night. So, they forced Crowley to steal from the museum. The jewels would help fund their survival for a while longer. But the stupid thief had left the gems where he lived with his human. The thought of the other cat made his anger rise again.

'Welcome, my friends,' he said as the mice sat before him. 'The Guardian has your food and water ready for you; all well deserved.' His smile was genuine, watching their excited eyes darting everywhere. 'What news do you bring?' he asked their leader, Gerald.

Gerald was larger than the rest, his teeth longer, and his personality more ferocious. He rose onto his hind legs, towering above the other mice behind him. He had a small scar below his right eye, a present from the cat they both hated.

'We followed the Thief to the scientist's house and waited while he was inside with the dog. After a while, he left on his own.'

'Did he have the Doolittle?' Darkstar's anticipation of

this news was palpable. For once, illumination shimmered in the ebony cat's eye.

'I'm unsure,' the mouse replied.

Darkstar considered his options. 'The foxes waiting at his home should have him by now.' He saw all his plans coming together, loving how it would be Crowley as the final catalyst for everything to come.

'He didn't go home,' Gerald replied. Darkstar said nothing. 'He went to another human dwelling near the Wells place. Two feral cats joined him there, and they attacked the human inside, a redheaded woman.'

He was stunned by the news, his eyes moving as if they were not his own, being controlled by somebody else, flicking from side to side in search of his sanity.

'He assaulted a human?' Darkstar found the idea of it too incredible to comprehend.

'Yes. He did it to save the feral cat; the human was about to kill him.'

He struggled to digest the information. 'What happened then?'

'He returned to the Wells house. Not long after, he left again, with something tied around his neck, on the strap of his watch, which could have been what you seek.'

'And then?' His mind was a whirl of conflicting emotions. The mouse was sheepish, his eyes dropping to the floor, sticking there and refusing to look Darkstar in the face.

'I'm afraid we lost him, sir. I'm sorry.' His voice was anxious. 'But I do have something else which might interest you. Our cousins were asked to do a job this morning, strictly off the books at a human prison.'

'Not AA approved?'

Gerald nodded. 'We've been told other animals were

involved. We don't know who organised it or where, but a cat and a little dog participated.' He stepped back from Darkstar's impressive bulk.

'Thank you, Gerald; you can get your food now.'

Darkstar turned away and walked towards the house. He wasn't surprised Crowley had betrayed him. He'd expected that, but to attack a woman and then organise some action at a human prison was barely believable. Either the other cat had finally gone mad, or he had planned to jeopardise everything Darkstar wanted.

And that wouldn't do at all.

Chapter 42

Pandora: Light My Fire

The house was in shadow apart from the flickering light from the living room window. Pandora parked the scooter next to the upturned rubbish bin.

She turned her nose up at the stink and pushed the front door open. Inside, her feet squelched through the liquid swimming over the wooden floor. The smell of gasoline was overpowering. She stopped halfway into the room, thinking she would spew, and peered at Wells. He was slumped in the seat, eyes glued to the television.

Pandora coughed out the bad taste in her throat, but he ignored her. Wells watched the cartoon cat chasing the cartoon mouse. He smiled like he'd returned to his childhood. He held a drink and the TV remote. He sipped at the drink, muted the sound, and gazed at her. She stared at the screen as the cat stumbled into a wall and bricks fell onto him. A memory of a younger version of herself crept out of the shadows and giggled inside her head.

'Don't drop your fag, Pan.'

'What have you done, Wyatt?'

She searched through the gloom, finding a stack of petrol cans in the far corner. The cigarette was steady in her hand. Facing potential death was nothing new to her, and the rewards offered were too much for her to retreat from a bit of danger.

'I've prepared for my dramatic exit; yours too, if you want.'

She sighed. 'Don't be stupid.'

He turned from the screen and peered at her. He wasn't drunk, but he was happy. She didn't begrudge him a small indulgence with the alcohol, understanding how it could turn the grimmest moments into manageable memories.

Wyatt frowned when he saw her scars. 'What happened to your face?'

'A cat attacked me.'

He tried to hide his emotions, but they were as evident in his expression as what was happening on the TV as the mouse jumped up and down on the head of its mortal enemy. Wyatt laughed, spitting booze over his lap. Pandora dangled ash onto the floor, watching the sparks sizzle around her feet.

'I didn't realise we lived so close to each other. 64 Regent Street; we're practically neighbours. You could have invited me round for tea and biscuits.' The smile never left his face, his fingers caressing the top of the cigarette lighter.

His newfound courage impressed her. 'Have you been stalking me, Wyatt?' She focussed on him, on that lighter, but still scanned the room for any sign of those animals.

'I checked the house online, rented to one Pandora Halcyon,' he continued. 'I love your name. I hope it's real.'

She'd never seen him like this. It was more than the booze providing him with his courage. Something else about him had changed, and she struggled to identify what it was.

She flicked more ash towards him, smiling when he flinched, enjoying his sudden realisation she wasn't scared of the trap he'd prepared.

'Is this an extension of your death wish, Wyatt?' She noticed his eyes flickering at a hundred miles an hour, wondering whether she could get to him before he flicked the flame into existence.

'In a way, I suppose.' His smile vanished, replaced with sad contemplation. 'The death of my old life to prepare for the new, something I should have done a long time ago – if only I hadn't been hampered by forces beyond my control.' His hands trembled as he played with the lighter. 'Still, a chain is only as strong as its weakest link.'

'You shouldn't let your parent's expectations ruin you, Wyatt.' She flicked the dead stub over his head at the TV, so it landed in a bowl on the table at the back of the room.

'How...how do you know about that?'

She reached into her jacket and pulled out the thing closest to her heart. She lit another cigarette and puffed a massive chunk of smoke into the air. Only then, staring at the dark shadows on Wyatt's face and the sadness filling his large eyes, did Pandora realise she hated smoking. Her father had forced the foul poison into her mouth when she was still in primary school. It was only one of his many attempts at making her dependent upon him.

'I know everything about you, Wyatt. How you were bullied and sobbing in front of all the other kids. Your teachers told me about you wetting yourself in class. Your mother gave me a long explanation about why you didn't make any friends and how she knew you'd find nobody to love you as they did. I didn't even have to show her my fake ID as a psychiatrist from social services to get her to talk;

she couldn't wait to blab about her dear little boy who'd let her down so much.'

He wiped at his face and stared at her. 'What happened to you when you were younger to make you like this? My childhood was bad, but yours was worse, right?'

'Childhood isn't important, Wyatt; all that matters is what we have now. And I don't believe you want to burn this place to the ground, do you?'

His laugh was light and unnatural. 'I'll be a phoenix from the flames, appropriately enough.' He grinned at her. 'I've destroyed all the serum before you ask.'

'The Project will be most disappointed by this, Wyatt, just as I am.'

He laughed louder, like a burst water pipe spewing a river of liquid into the air. 'Do they exist, Pandora? All I've seen these last six months is you. As pleasant as that is, I'm having doubts your employers are real, and this has all been some twisted game of yours.'

She ignored his question and asked one of her own. 'Where's your dog, Wyatt?'

His eyes shrank, his lips pursed, fingers caressing the cold metal of the lighter.

'Chirpy – I gave her the night off.'

The scene on the television changed from the animated animals to a crazy black-and-white tale of three brothers from the last century, a clock on the wall striking ten, pretty dancing girls scattering rose petals and kneeling in homage to the important person they waited for.

'I'm here risking my sanity for you, and all I can think of is what a sucker I've been all this time,' he continued.

She inched closer to him. 'What did the serum do to you, Wyatt?'

'It transformed me into a new man, a better one. It was

the first stage of my metamorphosis, and tonight, I will complete it. It all depends on you, Pandora.'

'How so?'

'If you let me go, release me from the Project's grip, everything will be fine. If you don't, we know they'll make me work for them forever.'

'And why would I do that?'

'I'll tell you what happened to me, what the serum does,' he said. 'And you can stop creeping towards me, please.'

'You didn't destroy it all, did you?'

He let her see the phial of clear liquid he was gripping as if it was his lifeblood.

'What is one little lie amongst friends?'

His smile grew more crooked, his mouth moving in slow motion. As he slumped into his chair, she strode to the seat opposite him and sat. The television was to the right of her, its neon hum singing a lullaby around the room.

'If I promise to leave you alone, you'll tell me everything?'

'More than that, Pandora; I'll give you this serum, and you can do what you want with it. I must warn you, though; it's such an incredible story you might not believe it.'

They smiled at each other as he told her a tale more fantastic than any fiction.

Chapter 43

Emma: Of Mice and Women

Emma took a deep breath, watching as the animals waited for her like nervous recruits in the army. She didn't think about how to explain it to her mother; she just needed to see her again.

'Aren't you worried the police might be here?' Crowley said.

'I doubt the coppers have me high on their list of priorities. It's not like I'm an axe murderer or serial killer. We won't be here long; I only want to make sure my mum is okay.' Where they'd go after that, she didn't know.

The cottage crouched low inside the grassy embankment as if it had been transported from the Shire in *Lord of the Rings*, hiding amongst the overgrown bushes surrounding it. Through the dimness, she approached the wrinkled grey stones. The only flash of colour was the yellow door. She remembered her father complaining when her mother took a brush to the wood and painted over its drab greyness.

'Dark on the outside, dark on the inside,' she told them, ensuring her daughters dressed in lively colours. Emma and

Jane would only wear black when they sneaked away from their parents to pursue those secret lives young kids desired. She stared at the animals again and wondered what to do with them when she spoke to her mother.

'We'll wait out here,' Crowley said.

She nodded, slipping into that role where she treated them like humans. Her nerves jangled as she knocked on the door, the back of her neck shivering not just from the chill in the air. It had been a while since she had a key to the place, knocking lightly to not disturb her mother before realising how ridiculous it was if she needed to get into the house.

'Are you sure she's here?' Bukowski said, standing behind her with his legs shaking. Chirpy had regained her boundless energy and wandered around the bushes, searching for something only she knew.

'Maybe we should go somewhere else, Crowley,' the duck told the cat.

Emma knocked on the door again, louder and harder. The bird had asked a good question, strange as she thought that was. Not the actual question, but the fact a duck said it, one with the smell of booze wafting through its feathers. Something small sped over her foot, and she pulled away as it ran up to the cat.

'There's nobody home,' the harvest mouse said. 'She left a few days ago.'

She knelt to stare into the tiny rodent's face. 'Do you know where?'

The startled creature scampered to safety behind Crowley's legs.

'It's okay, my friend; she won't hurt you.' Crowley said.

'She can understand me?' the terrified mouse replied. 'I have no idea where she went,' he added.

Emma stood and turned towards the garden, hoping the spare key was still under the cracked statue of the miserable-looking gnome sitting in the waterless pond in the garden. She pushed the stone man over, breaking his brittle head on the ground, and scooped up the rusted key. All thoughts of talking animals disappeared from her mind as she opened the door and shouted for her mother, every ounce of her caution thrown to the wind. The silence that greeted her was worrying.

The two-story cottage where she was born opened into the living room; the large chimney and fireplace were the centrepiece, a faint, musty aroma drifting from them. Firewood and old newspaper sat stacked on the side of it. Emma stepped inside, leaving the door open in case her new friends wanted to follow, all thoughts of hiding them from her mother vanishing in the distance. She sprinted up the stairs in the dark, heading for her parent's bedroom, pushing the door open without thinking of what she'd find. The room was as cold as the rest of the house, the bed unused. As she stared at the patterned curtains protecting the window, she acknowledged that the little mouse had been correct and her mother was not home.

'I must call Jane.'

But we all have to take a break first.

She left the bedroom door ajar, walking back downstairs to find all four creatures waiting for her.

'Can you get this fire going?' the duck asked, his body shivering in the thin sliver of moonlight creeping in through the window.

'Yes,' she replied. 'It is cold.'

'I'm freezing,' he said as Emma recognised it wasn't the cold affecting him. She grabbed kindling for the fire, threw a couple of logs on top of it, and then screwed up some of the newspapers to stack around the edges of the wood.

'I'll grab some matches from the kitchen,' she said, turning the light on in the living room and smiling at the four animals lined up in a row, smallest to largest, watching her every move. The house phone was on her left, making her think about calling Jane before dismissing the idea. Paranoia took over - she didn't want to get her sister involved in this new craziness engulfing her. She found the box of matches in the cutlery drawer; her mind focused on Jane so much she didn't hear the cat behind her.

'I need a favour from you, Emma.' Crowley said.

She turned, head tilted to one side as she looked at him. 'I never provided you with a name, did I?'

It had been Emma's way of not getting too close to the animals. The lesson she learned from watching Bambi's mother die was always with her.

'It doesn't matter, Emma; I've had too many. They gave it to me as punishment, to shame me, but I'm proud to have it.'

She thought what a beautiful thing it was to see a cat smile.

'Was it those you told me about, the ones who forced you to steal?'

'They're part of it. The animal world is as devious as the human one.'

She resisted the urge to grab him, trying not to think of him as her pet and seeing him as an equal. 'What's the favour you want?'

'Is there any alcohol here? Bukowski's in dire need of a refuel.'

'The duck?' she asked.

'Yes.'

'Sure,' she said, throwing the box of matches at him and being impressed when he caught them in his paw with little effort.

'You light the fire, and I'll find the booze. I also want a drink.'

She went to the sink and opened the cupboard underneath as he entered the living room. Emma returned there carrying a bottle of tequila and two glasses, one containing a large yellow straw. Chirpy whispered something to the little mouse while Bukowski stood shivering.

'What's your name?' Crowley asked the mouse, removing a match from the box and striking it on the side. He tossed it onto the kindling and the newspaper; the flames didn't take long to get going.

'The other mice call me Ben.'

'Tell me when to stop,' Emma said to Bukowski as she poured the alcohol into the glass containing the straw.

'Stop,' he said when it was full. 'And thanks for the straw. That was very thoughtful of you.'

His beak was over the top of the straw before he finished talking. She sat near him, crossed her legs, and leant into the fire to catch some of its heat. It warmed her on the outside, while the tequila warmed her everywhere else.

'Where are the rest of the mice, Ben?' Crowley said.

The little mouse had enormous eyes and panted, his ginger hair and white belly incandescent as the flames blazed behind him. His tail, nearly as long as his body, was draped over Chirpy's legs as the dog was unusually quiet.

'Everyone got called away; big job happening. I was too ill to go,' Ben replied.

'Called away?' Crowley's eyes sank. 'That could only mean one thing.'

'A pigeon arrived with a message from the AA yesterday. I don't know what it was about, but all the other mice left immediately,' Ben added.

'What does it mean?' Emma asked Crowley. Before he answered, the little mouse jumped into the air like a jack-in-a-box, his eyes about to burst from his head.

'Somebody else is here!' he shouted in a high-pitched voice.

'That tiny mouse has the strangest of voices,' the redheaded woman said just before she punched Emma in the face, her glass dropping to the floor and tequila spilling all over Bukowski's feathers.

'Don't worry,' the duck said, slurring his words as only a bird could. 'It won't go to waste.'

Chapter 44

Crowley: House of Fun

Pandora had the bag over his head before Crowley could react, the light vanishing from his vision as the air crept from his lungs. When he awoke, he was behind bars, locked inside a small cage just big enough for him to stand.

'I found that out back.' She sat with her back to the window, unlit cigarette in hand, legs crossed. He observed Bukowski sleeping in front of the fire, Emma with her feet tied up next to him, and Chirpy staring at her with all the energy syphoned out of her. Ben was nowhere to be seen.

Crowley shivered. 'What have you done?'

'Don't worry, my feline friend, the duck is slumbering, and the petite mouse scurried off as soon as he saw me. Can't think what would've scared him so much unless it was these lovely lines.' She ran the fingers of the cigarette-less hand across the scars on her face. 'Or the kiss you gave me.'

He noticed the teeth marks gouged into her flesh. 'Wells gave you the serum?'

Or she took it from him. Crowley would be astonished if the professor had given it to her freely.

'It was a mutual exchange of gifts between colleagues.' Pandora got out of the chair, avoided the slumbering duck and knelt near his prison. But not so close that he could reach through the bars and attack her. 'I still owe you a gift for what you gave me.' The fire behind her eyes sent a spasm through him.

'No, Wells wouldn't have given it to you willingly.'

She smiled at him. 'I suppose this cage could be my present to you.'

'What did you do to him?'

She ignored Crowley's question and returned to the chair.

'It's freezing for this time of year. When I left Wyatt, he was warming himself by the fire, as we are now.'

'His serum could have killed you or mushed your brain like everyone you experimented on.'

All he could do was keep her talking while he tried to think of a way out. She removed a lighter from her jacket, Crowley noticing the initials WW on the outside.

Pandora stretched out her arm and pointed the lighter at Emma, whose head hung towards the floor. 'It could've killed her, but you let her drink it.'

'It was a risk worth taking,' he said, knowing the risk was all Emma's.

'And that's exactly how I felt once Wyatt explained its remarkable properties. Shame it's all gone now.' She moved the lighter between her fingers. 'You can lift your head, Emma. I know you're awake.'

She lit the cigarette as Emma spoke. 'Who are you, and what do you want?'

Pandora inhaled and sprinkled the ash onto the floor, observing the dead embers flicker briefly and then burn away. Crowley watched as if every one of them was a moment of his life.

'My name is Pandora, and I need what the cat has and maybe the chance to start a new life. That seems to be going around right now.'

'You appear to have a pretty good life,' Crowley said.

Smoke emerged from her nose and swirled up towards her vibrant red hair. It seemed to him as if she was the human incarnation of a dragon. He stared at their captor, seeing a woman who moved her head and eyes at the proper moment but unsure if she was striving to express joy, woe, anger, or satisfaction. She dipped the cigarette between those lips and spoke through the haze.

'"Never judge a book by its cover," my father would say, a horrible man that he was.'

'What do you want?' he said.

She sighed. 'Sometimes you grow tired of carrying the bulk of your past with you. The memories are like thick suitcases you've pushed under the bed, luggage full of stuff from your life you need to throw away. They weigh so much they affect the way you walk, the way you stand, the way you sit. Your shoulders sag, your spine buckles under the pain, all the muscles in your body aching because of things never forgotten.'

'Why are you telling us this?' he asked.

'If I can't unburden my soul on a group of animals and a teenage fugitive from justice, then I never will. You need to listen to this; it's important for me.'

He put his paws on the bars, willing them to snap so he could find a way of getting himself and his friends away from the disturbed woman. Pandora settled into her chair with an attentive audience, no matter how unwilling they were. The cigarette in her hand drooped languidly, dripping grey ash all over the cottage floor.

'Well,' Emma said, 'you've made us a captive audience.'

Pandora laughed. 'This is a nice place you have here, Emma. It must've been idyllic for you and your sister to spend your childhood in such lovely surroundings.' She gazed at the photos in the room, images of the Crowley daughters laughing and smiling with their parents in several spots worldwide. 'It looks like you travelled quite a lot.' There was a wistful tone in her voice.

'We were just like any other family; we had good and bad times,' Emma said.

'I'd guess your bad times were good compared to mine.' Pandora's grin was so wide Crowley imagined she wanted to eat them whole instead of talking to them.

'If you're going to give us your life story, I need another drink first.' Bukowski woke from his slumber and wobbled to where Pandora sat.

Pandora's smile increased. 'Why can't all animals be as funny as you?' She got up to get the half-full bottle of tequila in front of Emma's trussed-up feet. 'Open your beak then,' she told the duck, waving the booze before his face.

'Don't be a savage,' he replied. 'Use the glass with the straw and fill it up.' His eyes never left hers. She did as directed before taking her drink straight from the bottle.

'Don't I get some?' Emma said.

Pandora returned to the chair. 'I had my first alcoholic drink when I was seven years old. My parents gave it to me. To prepare me, they said. Then they put me in a large wooden box and closed the lid. I thought they were playing a game, but I was still scared of the dark.'

Crowley stared at the redheaded woman, recognising the mental scars.

'I waited in the blackness, not sure what for. Then I heard the patter of little feet inside the box with me, then crawling over me. They started with mice, then moved on to rats, and finally feral cats. Not all at once. They built up the agony over several days.'

'Your parents did this to you?' Emma asked.

Pandora nodded. 'That and more. I don't know how many animals they dumped in the coffin, but they ran all over me for hours. Across my chest, nibbling at my skin, getting tangled in my hair. I screamed until my lungs were about to explode, but nobody came to rescue me.' The room was quiet but for her words. 'It would be the last time I'd scream or cry, even though my life was about to get so much worse.'

'Why did they do that?' Emma asked, blood dripping from her mouth as she spoke.

'As I said, Emma, not everybody has a wonderful childhood. My family lived in the belly of a community without hope. He was a workshy skiver; she was a cleaner getting the bare minimum wage. But they were also part of another community that existed secretly within respectability, a cult, as it was.' She took a long drag on the cigarette. 'One that enjoyed torturing children. You may wonder why people do such things, but you can never understand why.'

Pandora gulped more of the tequila. Bukowski continued to slurp through his straw. Crowley recognised why she was telling them this; if you leave the darkness inside you for too long, it will eventually consume you whole.

'It started in the backs of cars. The group would meet somewhere remote – maybe an abandoned industrial estate or some isolated part of the countryside, but never in their own homes – and they would swap the kids around as if we were toys to be played with. After a while, I was glad of the booze and desperate to get back into that coffin.'

Silence engulfed the room. Crowley had experienced pain in his lifetime, but he was still shocked and saddened by what she said, guilt trickling through him about the scars he'd inflicted on her. Bukowski persisted in drowning everything out with more alcohol.

Emma seemed startled, her face a whiter shade of pale. 'I'm sorry.'

Pandora continued. 'I ran away from home at fourteen, living on the streets until my rescue, given a new life by people who recognised my potential. So maybe your bad family times were quite different to mine.'

'I'm sorry for what happened to you. But why are you doing this to us?' Emma asked.

Pandora touched the scarf around her neck. 'I nearly told all of this to your sister. She was kind to me, something I'm not used to.'

Emma's lips trembled. 'Did you hurt Jane?'

Pandora started her second stick of poison. 'Your sister's fine, don't worry.' She blew smoke into the air. 'It must be nice to have your life.'

As they spoke, Crowley noticed the little mouse's teeth nibbling away at the constraints on Emma's hands, admiring his bravery as he neared the fire. Ben had loosened the lock on Crowley's cage as the redhead had told her tale of misery and despair. He'd also bitten through the rope tying Emma's feet together, unseen by Pandora, while she focussed on spinning her web of woe.

Emma snapped the strings binding her, standing up

while the shock ran across Pandora's face. 'Always be careful what you wish for.'

She leapt at the woman in the chair, landing on top of her before she could get her hands up for protection.

'She could've waited until the redhead poured me another drink,' Bukowski said before belching loud enough to be heard in the city.

Chapter 45

Crowley: Fight Club

Crowley forced the cage open as the women rolled around the floor, trying to get a grip on each other. As soon as Emma had landed on Pandora, the chair had given way under their combined weight, snapping the legs and discarding them onto the carpet.

'This should be good,' Bukowski said before belching again, the smell of stale tequila invading the room. The duck dropped onto his backside while Ben scampered over, emerging from the shadows with tiny bits of rope sticking to his teeth.

Pandora held Emma down, the two women staring into each other's eyes. Crowley watched them, wondering how to help Emma before the redhead knocked her out again.

I'll jump on her head like before.

He was about to fling himself at her when she stopped, leaned into Emma's face and forced their lips together. It was an eternal kiss which lasted seconds, weakening Emma's resistance as she flopped in Pandora's arms.

The redhead released her. 'Isn't this exciting?'

'We should leave while we can,' the little mouse said.

'I don't like it here,' Chirpy chipped in.

'I'm not leaving Emma,' Crowley replied.

Emma wiped her mouth and leapt at Pandora. Her fist connected with Pandora's jaw, splitting her lip. Pandora reeled back, shock and rage flashing in her eyes. She recovered quickly, hitting Emma with her palm and then dragging her nails over Emma's cheek, drawing blood.

She tackled Pandora around the waist, both crashing to the ground. They rolled across the floor, landing punches wherever they could. Pandora grabbed a chunk of Emma's hair, wrenching her back. Emma screamed but continued struggling, kicking and scratching like a wildcat. She smashed Pandora's nose with an audible crunch. Blood gushed down Pandora's face. Emma put her head down and charged at the redhead, knocking her into the wall. She slumped onto the carpet and swore.

Emma turned towards Crowley. 'We have to get to the car,' she shouted.

Before he could warn her, Pandora kicked the back of Emma's legs, sending her tumbling to the floor once more. This time, the redhead didn't return to the fray. She moved to the window, glancing into the fading gloom outside.

'There's no need for this, Emma; neither of us is in the Fight Club now.'

Pandora's breathing sounded like a locomotive speeding down the track. Emma's back was stuck to the wall behind her, sweat running down her face in a torrent.

'You attacked me first, forced Crowley into a cage, so forgive me for not trusting you.'

Pandora snorted a laugh through her chest. 'Your cat has your name?'

Emma lifted herself from the floor, keeping her eyes on the other woman. 'Is there something wrong with you?'

Pandora grinned. 'Ah yes, when someone inquires as to my emotional state, the appropriate response is to say I'm great regardless of whether I spent the previous night inflicting pain on people. Great is the word I utter through gritted teeth while fighting the urge to peel off my outer layer of social pretence and expose the howling void within. But needs must - great it is! Chin up, shoulders back, stiff upper lip. I wouldn't want to trouble anyone with the inconvenient truth that I'm bloody miserable. Much better to swallow it and carry on with a false air of British fortitude. GREAT. Everything's just great. Now if you'll bugger off, I have a sudden urge to stab you in the face. But before I do, let me reassure you, should you ask - I'm great! Tickety-boo, old chap.'

Crowley thought she was insane. 'Leave now, and we'll forget any of this happened.'

The wounds he'd given Pandora's face leaked blood again. Pandora removed her jacket and placed it on the window ledge behind her, flexing her fingers as if she were getting ready for the next round.

'Sure, pesky cat; just give me the rest of the serum.'

'Why do you want it?' he asked.

'Isn't it obvious? Think of how the world would be better if everybody drank it.' She wiped the blood from her face. 'Wyatt told me you call it the Doolittle, little cat. Is that right? Will you give it to me?'

'I don't have it with me,' he said.

She shook her head. 'I don't believe you, Crowley.'

'I'm sorry for what happened to you when you were a kid, what your parents and the others did, but this path won't help you come to terms with your past.'

He spoke to her while she stared at him blankly. It wasn't so much a cold stare, but a vacant one. It was as if she'd taken an out-of-body experience and left only a husk behind, her mind trapped between those terrible childhood memories.

'They're coming,' Ben squeaked loudly, running up to Crowley, anxiety daubed onto his face and twisting it into a facsimile of a Picasso painting.

'Who's coming?' Emma and Pandora said together.

'Can we go now?' Chirpy asked with desperation in her voice.

He went to his friend and placed a paw on the little dog's shoulders as tears welled up in her. 'Soon.'

'They're coming,' the mouse repeated.

'Who's coming?' Crowley said.

'The police?' Emma said, keeping her eyes on Pandora, who moved to the window and gazed outside.

'There's nobody out there,' Pandora said.

'It's Darkstar and his beasts,' the terrified rodent cried. The tears ran down Chirpy's face, and Bukowski spat the last of the booze from his mouth.

'Who?' Emma said as Ben ran into Crowley's furry leg.

'Trouble,' Crowley said.

'They're here.' The little mouse's lips quivered, moisture glistening in the firelight's glow.

'Who's here?' Emma asked.

Crowley stared at her, his ginger fur standing on end as he glanced at Bukowski.

'We need to leave.'

'Nothing can get at us in here,' Pandora said. 'I made sure the place was secure after I broke in through the back.'

Her smirk caused the purple of her lips to shimmer as she took another drag on her cigarette. When she blew the smoke high above their heads, Emma heard the scurrying noises coming from the bottom of the walls. They all listened to the same thing: the sounds of claws scratching away at the plaster.

'What is that?' Emma said as Crowley strode towards her.

'Invaders,' he replied as the first signs of intrusion into the room appeared across from him: burning neon yellow orbs next to Emma's hand.

'Invaders?' she repeated.

'Emma!' he shouted as the rat pounced on her leg, teeth like scythes inches away from thrusting into her flesh. Her reflexes responded before anybody else did, her right arm swinging around in an arc until her fingers caught the rodent in its mangled, grey-furred body. The creature shrieked as it hit the window, just missing Pandora's head. It fell behind a chair and never reappeared.

'Damn!' Pandora said as she pushed a stray hair from her eye, courtesy of the wind generated by the flying rat.

'There'll be more,' Crowley added. 'It was only a scout.'

Emma moved from the wall as the sounds returned. Bukowski clutched the bottle in his wing. Chirpy rose as tall as she could while Crowley flexed his paws.

Pandora sank further into her seat, the cigarette in her mouth clinging to her bottom lip. 'Surely a cat and a dog, small as you are, can deal with a few rats?'

'They're Darkstar's soldiers; there'll be more than a few of them,' Crowley said. Right on cue, the noises grew louder, like miniature axes chopping away at the cottage's foundations.

'We need to get upstairs,' Emma said, still shaking after the incident with the rat. Before any of them could respond, tiny lights flickered around the floorboards. They reminded Crowley of small red and yellow Christmas illuminations.

But he knew they didn't bring joy with them.

'An army of rats,' he said as instinct kicked in, and he backed into the middle of the room. He needed a plan, but there was no time. He stared at the others, guilt overwhelming him for dragging them into this.

Apart from the redheaded woman, he didn't care what happened to her. He glanced over to where she was as the rats moved in for the kill, saliva dripping from their sharp teeth as the taste of fear lay thick in the room. He was shocked to see that Pandora had gone, disappearing while he focussed on the vermin approaching them.

Crowley forgot about her, concentrating on the thirty or so vermin getting closer by the second.

Maybe if we give them the Doolittle, we'll be safe?

They were so close he smelt the stink of dried cabbage wafting off them. Two of the biggest peeled away from the group and ran towards him. He tensed his muscles, ready to act, when human legs barged past him to stand in the centre of the room.

'I hope you beasts like to smoke?'

His startled eyes fixed on the redhead, her hands outstretched with an aerosol can clutched between each set of fingers. A burning cigarette hung from her bottom lip. She dropped it from her mouth, following it down to the floor in one motion. She swung both arms towards the flame, pressing down at the top of the cans and ejecting something highly flammable, turning each can into a flamethrower. The rats were running when the fire exploded, the redheaded woman twisting her body around in an exaggerated arc, so the flames consumed every rodent.

'Shit!' Emma cried as the aroma of scorching fur and flesh filled the room.

Some rats tried to escape into the walls, the sounds of death continuing beyond the plaster.

Pandora dropped her weapons. 'I love the smell of burning rodents in the morning.' She strode around the room, kicking smoking rats against the walls like a professional footballer.

'Are you okay?' Crowley asked Emma, the image of the rat baring its teeth at her legs still in his head. She didn't reply, her eyes fixed on the shrinking fire behind them. He wondered if she was in shock before seeing feathers floating down into the fire's last embers.

'More birds!' he shouted as the screeching followed the feathers into the room.

Chapter 46

Emma: Diamond Dogs

'I told Father we should've closed the chimney off years ago,' Emma said as a cascade of white fell in a clump and birdsong erupted from the flute. It wasn't a melody or a lullaby but the banshee's shriek from a flock of gulls spluttering out in a rush, dive-bombing everything in sight.

Pandora didn't flinch, lifting the cushion above her and swatting the birds away. Emma used her arms to cover her face, manic wings beating away at her head. Chirpy jumped up at her attackers, gnashing her teeth at anything in her orbit. Bukowski swung his bottle at the intruders. Crowley was unmoving until a giant seagull flew straight towards him. He ducked underneath its attack, rolling to one side and ending at Bukowski's feet. He pushed himself upwards as Emma strode past him. She grabbed the gold-coloured standing lamp her parents had bought for their anniversary. The bulb was exposed, so she unscrewed it before switching on the light. The birds soared above them in coordination, peering down before diving again.

The heat of the electricity ebbed from the socket as she

shoved the lamp into the air toward the nearest seagull, tiny sparks of blue exploding from its stomach. The bird fell screaming as Emma leapt towards the one attacking Chirpy. Its beak was around the little dog's ear when she stuffed the open connection into its head. It screamed as it burned, tumbling away from Chirpy and twisting like something from *The Exorcist*. The remaining birds darted to the fireplace and up the chimney.

Emma ran to the stack of wood piled at the side. 'We need to get this blazing to stop them from returning. Is everybody okay?' She threw wood into the fireplace as she spoke.

'They won't be back,' Crowley said. 'That was Darkstar testing our defences.'

She added the kindling to the pile. 'What will he do next?'

'Now he'll want to talk. Check the windows and see what's outside.'

Before anyone moved, the howling started, and everyone in that room, human and animal, froze. Then Crowley jumped onto the ledge and peered out the window. Emma joined him, seeing nothing but the morning light flowing over the countryside. The branches on the trees wobbled in the breeze, casting shadows across the front of the cottage and Emma's car.

Then the shadows moved, large dark bodies striding into the light. Six Great Danes, each with a glittering stud in their right ear, caught the illumination from the sun as they marched towards the house.

'It's the Diamond Dogs,' Crowley said.

Emma gasped. 'The what?'

'A human owner added the jewellery to their heads

before Darkstar liberated them into the Bullfather's empire,' Crowley added.

Emma wiped the sweat from her head. 'Why are they here?'

'Is the back door locked?' he asked in a shaking voice.

She sprinted into the kitchen, rushing past pots and pans that hadn't been used in weeks, her brain running through memories of better times: baking cakes with her mother, licking sticky wet chocolate from a spoon with her sister. The sweet aroma of sugar and flour invaded her senses and made her stomach rumble until she recognised the sounds weren't coming from inside her but from the back garden.

She checked the door before peering out the window, inspecting the overgrown lawn and the vast sweep of nature behind it. There was nothing there but more memories from her childhood, of Jane digging a hole to bury Emma's new toys, kicking a ball and bragging about who was the best and how much better they were than the boys in their school.

Emma heard the noises again, a low grumbling turning into a snarl. She noticed their eyes first, red and yellow orbs burning brighter than a shooting star, emerging from the trees as if floating in the air. About a dozen pairs glared at her, forcing her to step back for safety, even though the cottage walls were there for protection. She returned to the living room to tell the others.

'Foxes,' she said, 'a dozen of them, at least.' She noticed Pandora had made herself comfortable on the sofa, lounging at the far end as if it was the first day of her summer holidays.

'This is Darkstar's doing,' Crowley said. 'Foxes don't form an attack group unless they have the Bullfather's blessing, and that doesn't happen unless the dark cat approves.'

If things weren't bad enough, the sounds of feet landing on the roof, hundreds of them, attacked Emma's ears.

'You're popular today,' Pandora joked as she lit another cigarette.

'Birds?' Emma asked.

Pandora seemed to be enjoying herself. 'Just like that Hitchcock movie.'

Bukowski had sobered up. 'We're surrounded.'

Emma returned to the living room window, seeing the Diamond Dogs lined up in a perfect formation to stop anyone from leaving.

Pandora draped her legs over the end of the sofa. 'Dogs to the left of me, foxes on the right, and birds stomping their feet above me. How fitting, but they're only animals. Why should I worry?'

'Because they're here for the same thing you are, and they're more vicious,' Crowley said.

'I'll take that as a challenge,' the redhead replied before blowing smoke towards him.

'Who's Darkstar?' Emma asked as she moved towards the fire while keeping her gaze on Pandora.

'A cat who hates me, and he would be quite happy to see me dead.' Crowley continued looking through the glass at those ferocious Great Danes. 'Darkstar will be here some-where – he wouldn't miss the chance to witness my demise.'

Pandora smiled. 'That sounds like an animal I'd enjoy meeting.'

Emma regained her composure, realising the danger to them was outside, not inside, the room. 'Why does he want this serum?'

'I don't know,' Crowley answered, 'but it won't be for good: he hates humanity.'

Beyond the front window, the dogs stood motionless like

dark statues with one glint of light shimmering on their heads.

'Bukowski, can you watch the foxes at the back?' Crowley said.

'Aye, aye, captain,' the duck replied before staggering into the other room.

'I better check the windows upstairs,' Emma shouted, racing through the three bedrooms and bathroom, checking her mother's bedroom last, noticing again how nobody had been in the house for weeks.

She sat on the bed, giving herself a minute from what was happening downstairs and outside, staring at the patterned wallpaper and the framed photograph of her parents taken on their fifteenth anniversary, looking at that image and knowing they wouldn't have another.

Until Emma's arrest, her father's death was the worst time in her life, and she still hadn't gotten over it. Then she considered what Pandora had revealed about her childhood, pondering how fate could unleash good onto some while inflicting pain on others.

As that thought crossed her mind, a rhythmic tapping on the glass came from the other side of the curtains. Emma had forgotten to check if the windows were locked, caught up in memories of what her life used to be. She crawled off the bed and pulled the heavy material away from the window to see small brown sparrows lined up on the ledge.

'Let us in, they cried,' like a choir of tiny souls demanding salvation.

'Let us in,' they sang again. It reminded Emma of a horror film she'd watched when she was younger, of a child vampire pressed against the glass and pleading to be let into the human world. She ignored their words, replaced the curtains, and headed downstairs.

She stared at Crowley without speaking, standing near the fireplace and watching Pandora, who'd discarded the guts of two cigarettes onto the floor while Emma was upstairs.

'I've never known Wyatt's mutt to be this quiet,' Pandora said. Crowley went to the little dog and pushed his head against hers. She used her phone to take a photo. 'That'll be on the internet later.'

She smiled as Crowley scowled at her.

He returned his focus to the pooch. 'Don't worry; we'll be out of here soon.'

Pandora waved her mobile in Crowley's direction. 'I can call my employers; they'll have somebody here in twenty minutes.'

'The Project?' he said.

'Wyatt must've taken a shine to you to confide so much in a cat.' The disdain in her voice was apparent to all.

'Enough to tell me he didn't believe they existed, and you'd invented the whole thing.'

She was on her third cigarette. 'Why would I do that? And let's not mention the large amounts of money supplied to him regularly. Where do you think that came from?'

'I don't know,' Crowley replied. 'You're a complicated woman.'

Pandora snorted laughter like two pigs kissing before being dragged to the slaughterhouse. 'You got that right, little cat. If you hadn't cut me so badly, I could like you.'

Emma stepped forward. 'What is the Project?' In her mind, the sparrows pleaded with her to let them inside.

Pandora lost her frivolity. 'They saved me, gave me a purpose in life.' She touched her cheek. 'I thought they might be one of those secret government agencies you always hear about in ludicrous conspiracy theories, but I believe a multinational corporation runs them. Their aim is profit, not world domination.'

'What do you do for them?' Emma was curious to find out as much as possible about the mysterious redhead.

Pandora paused before responding. 'I collect things.'

'So, you don't want the serum for yourself?' Crowley said.

'Well, I didn't say that.' The crooked smile returned to Pandora's face.

'My Lord Darkstar demands entrance,' a voice hissed from the floor, making Emma flinch and Crowley grimace.

'What's he the Lord of?' Crowley asked the snake, which had slithered into the cottage unnoticed.

'All of you,' the snake said as he moved out of the shadows.

'Do you have a name, Mr Snake?' Pandora asked from the comfort of her seat, nearly flicking her ash over the reptile.

It turned to her, surprise written all over its scaly face. 'You can call me Jor,' he hissed at her.

'Well, Jor,' Pandora said while dragging her legs off the sofa and placing them near the snake's head. 'Tell your Lord he has no dominion over me.'

The snake dismissed her and switched his attention to Crowley.

'No harm will come to you; he is only here to talk.'

'Is that why he attacked us and brought the dogs and foxes with him?'

'We live in dangerous times, Crowley. You should know that. They're for protection only.' The snake stared at both humans in the room. 'What is your answer?'

'Tell Darkstar he can come in alone.'

Something resembling a smile crept onto the snake's face as it slithered into the shadows and disappeared.

Pandora watched it go, dropping ash over the trail it left. 'You should check the foundations of this place, Emma; all kinds of vermin could get in.'

Emma pressed her back into the wall, still waiting to wake up in her prison cell.

Chapter 47

Crowley: The Proposition

Emma opened the door, and Crowley peered outside. The sun sat in the sky like a massive piece of fruit as the Great Danes stared in their direction and growled.

The fluttering of wings above them joined the noise of canine hearts running at one hundred miles an hour, forcing him to look upwards to see the gulls drifting down. The birds landed and settled into two lines leading up to the cottage, forming a guard of honour for what was to come. A large bulk emerged from the trees, and he watched his old enemy approach them.

'Thank you, Ms Crowley,' Darkstar said to Emma as he stepped past her and into the building. His voice was deep and forceful, radiating power from each word. Every gull bowed their heads as the dark cat walked past them.

Darkstar addressed the little mouse first. 'Your family have returned, Ben; they wait for you outside.'

Ben didn't waste any time, running into the kitchen and disappearing into the wall gap.

Pandora laughed. 'You need to get this house seen to, Emma. There's holes all over the place.'

Emma closed the door, gazing at the enormous feline that had entered the room. He jumped onto the other end of the sofa, staring at the redhead through obsidian eyes.

He spoke to Crowley. 'Is it your competitive nature which drove you to have two special humans to my one?'

'I don't know who they are,' he replied.

A peculiar feline laugh crept over Darkstar's lips as he addressed Pandora. 'Your face looks painful, my dear. Did my good friend Crowley do that to you?'

A dead cigarette was in her hands, and a look of contemplation on her face as she gazed into the darkness opposite her. 'He told us you hated him.'

'We've had our fair share of disagreements, this is true, but I think hate is too strong a word to describe how I feel about him.'

'You tried to kill me last year,' Crowley said. 'And it wasn't the first time.'

'A simple misunderstanding, I'm sure,' Darkstar replied. 'I can't even remember what it was about.'

He walked towards the sofa, staring at the bigger cat, their eyes meeting like comets colliding into each other high above the Earth's atmosphere.

'Then I'll remind you, old friend: I had to stop you from putting your claws into the eye of a human child. I still have the scars under my chin as a constant reminder.'

The ebony cat's face turned even darker. 'Ah yes, the little boy who was in the process of drowning some kittens he stuffed into a bag. Your love of humans over your own kind is legendary, Crowley, but I see from this one you've inflicted some of your pain onto a select few.'

'You can call me Pandora, and I'll call you fat cat. How

does that sound?' She spoke as she smoked, using her lips to push dead fumes towards Darkstar.

'Your words are meaningless to me, human. You may be able to hear what the animal world is saying, but you don't understand us. I'm not here for you. If a small cat can do that to your face, imagine what I could do to you.' The menace in his voice was as dark as his fur.

Pandora laughed at the threat. 'From your admission, you couldn't kill the little cat, so excuse me for not being terrified. You may be a big thing in the animal world, fat cat, but we humans are made of sterner stuff.'

'You think you can fight through the dogs outside?' he said.

Crowley observed Darkstar. 'What do you want?'

'Exactly what we told you to get for us: the Doolittle. If you give it to me, you'll leave here unharmed, humans included. Otherwise, the consequences will be dire for everybody.'

Chirpy, who'd sat emotionless since Darkstar had arrived, shook uncontrollably. Bukowski was in the kitchen doorway, peering into the other room. Emma said nothing, while Pandora had a permanent smile, which only changed when she took a drag from the cigarette.

'Why do you want the serum?' Pandora asked. 'Why do you want something intended for humans?'

Darkstar peered at her. 'You've taken it obviously; you know the benefits it can bring to your kind. Imagine how much better it would be for all animals if more humans could understand us. Humanity might treat animals more kindly if you could communicate with us. Humans might stop eating us and wearing our skins as fashion accessories, don't you think?'

'Is your plan to starve everybody into submission?'

Emma asked. She loved animals, but she didn't like this big cat.

'We could, but that would take far too long. Instead, I'll send dozens of gulls to fly into the window behind me until it's smashed into oblivion. Then the Diamond Dogs will jump in here, killing you one at a time until Crowley gives me what I want.'

'You can't kill humans.' Chirpy found her voice at last.

'Of course I can, as the ginger cat knows all too well.' He jumped off the sofa and strode towards the exit. 'If you don't mind, Emma,' he said, standing before the doorway.

She opened the door for him.

'Bye,' Pandora said.

'I'll give you ten minutes to think about it,' Darkstar said as he vanished into the shadows.

Crowley watched him leave before turning to the others. 'We need an escape plan.'

Emma rushed into the kitchen, startling Bukowski. She yanked open the cupboard under the sink, dragged everything out, and dumped it onto the floor.

Pandora unglued herself from the sofa and followed Emma. 'Is this what fear does to you?'

Crowley joined them. 'What are you doing, Emma?'

'Getting us a way out,' she replied.

Pandora finished her cigarette and twirled her finger next to her head. 'The serum has frazzled her mind. Or maybe she was always like this.'

'There's an old smuggler's tunnel behind this panel, which leads to the garage at the back of the house,' Emma said while emptying the space.

'Smugglers? We're miles from the sea,' Pandora didn't hide the disbelief in her voice.

'About five miles,' Emma replied. 'The tunnel is four

hundred years old. My father told me they used it to move contraband anytime officials from the Crown turned up at the door. A small drop in this wall and then a narrow tunnel which runs for around five hundred yards and coming up in the garage.'

'And once we get to the garage?' Pandora asked.

'My father's car is there. We could be out and away before they even know it.'

She cleared the cupboard and knocked on the back, revealing the hollow space behind. She twisted her legs into it and kicked the wall. It only took a couple of thrusts before the wood collapsed. She removed her phone, found the app for the torch, and moved forward.

'Follow me,' she said as a massive thump erupted from the other room.

Crowley watched her disappear into the space but ran into the living room, shocked by what he saw: dozens of birds sacrificing themselves as they flew into the glass, which was already cracking and covered in blood. Seeing it sickened him as Pandora joined him.

She grabbed a broken chair leg. 'The fat cat lied; it hasn't been four minutes.'

'You can't trust Darkstar with anything,' Crowley said as the next wave of birds got ready to fly into the window, which didn't have long to last.

'We need to leave,' Emma shouted from the kitchen.

Pandora rolled the wood around in her hands. 'You bugger off, little cat. I'll keep them busy while you get to the car.'

He stared at her in shock. 'Why would you do that for us?'

'What can I say, little cat? You've grown on me. Now go.'

She went to the sofa and picked up one of the large, fluffy cushions as Crowley turned away. Emma, Bukowski, and Chirpy were inside the tunnel when he got to the kitchen. The light flickered from Emma's torch ahead of him.

As he jumped into the open space, he heard the window finally crack. The war cry of the dogs followed him down the gloomy passage.

Chapter 48

Emma: Rat Trap

Emma led them through the tunnel, guided by the flickering light from the phone. Bits of water leaked onto her from the roof as a puff of dampness pushed into her nose.

'Nearly there,' she shouted, assuming everyone else was following. The steps were ahead, the rusted metal sighing as the wind found a way in and swirled through the tunnel like a ghost desperate to find a passage to the next life. Something scuttled above her, but she couldn't see anything. She chalked it down to anxiety and an over-active imagination.

She put her hands on the first rung, holding her mobile, the cold and wet eating into her skin. Emma pulled herself up and hoped the hatch into the garage was unlocked, imagining her grand plan shrivelling away. She returned the phone to her pocket and gave the wood above an almighty heave. The muscles strained in her shoulders, and the fresh bruises gained from her struggle with Pandora sent pain through her. Dust dropped into her face, and she coughed through the smile that greeted the light emerging overhead.

Emma turned to peer at the little dog below. She leant down and picked her up in one arm, her hand underneath Chirpy's beating belly as she lifted the dog's slobbering face to her.

'Here you go, pooch,' she said as she dropped her onto the cold floor of the garage. Then she grabbed Bukowski and dropped him next to Chirpy. Emma smiled, forgetting what a dangerous position they were in.

'Crowley!' she shouted, realising how strange it was to call for a cat with her name.

'I'm here,' he said from the darkness below.

'Can you jump into my arm?' she asked.

He didn't reply and just did it, landing with a thump against her chest, both breathing like asthmatic coal miners. She used her one free hand to crawl up the last few rungs of the ladder and roll into the garage.

Sunlight beamed through the window, burning through the accumulation of dust and cobwebs. She stared into the garage for the first time in years. Visions of her father drifted through the building, ghosts of a past they once shared, adding to the clouds in her eyes. Emma shook her head, searching for what they needed to escape.

Propped against the far wall were the remains of a burgundy sofa she remembered falling off when she saw a Dalek on TV. She loved the comfort of that couch when she was younger, but now its insides were spilling out like a washing machine vomiting dirty soap all over the floor. She wiped those memories from her mind and peered beyond the furniture for why they'd gone there: the weather-beaten car used for all their family holidays.

'What a rust bucket,' Bukowski said, eyeing the mustard-coloured vehicle.

'It'll get us out of here,' Emma said, hoping there was

petrol in it and the spare keys were still hidden in the exhaust pipe. She crouched at the back of the car, pushed her fingers inside the pipe and found nothing.

She sighed, her body sinking closer to the ground as her escape plan came apart at the seams. Her knees hit the floor, and the concrete cut through the flimsy fabric of her jeans and drew blood from her flesh. The fresh pain forced her hands forward into the pipe as an automatic reaction. The tips of her fingers found the cold metal before grabbing the keys and dragging them out.

She smiled at her animal friends but quickly lost that happiness when she noticed they were staring at the enormous rat on their escape car.

'I knew you'd come here, Thief. Your silent steps creeping along, the sound of your little paws stolen away. Do you know why?' The words hissed from the rat's mouth. Emma stared at its pinched red eyes, teeth sharpened to the point they could puncture solid steel, its ebony fur standing to attention.

'No,' Crowley said.

'Because you're a dead cat walking,' the rodent said as it leapt at Crowley's head. Its claws missed by inches as he twisted to the side, the rat slipping on the floor and hitting the wall. Emma shuddered and moved to help her cat.

'Get in the car!' Crowley shouted. 'I'll handle this.'

The rat regained its balance as Emma got the door open. Bukowski and Chirpy followed her into the vehicle before the rodent attacked again.

'I'll rip out your throat and feast on your guts,' the rat said to Crowley.

'So many poorly chosen words in one sentence,' he replied.

Emma put the keys in the ignition, relieved that the

petrol tank was half-full, before realising they were missing somebody.

'Where's Pandora?'

Bukowski and Chirpy shook their heads. She scowled and got out of the car. No matter how she felt about Pandora, she couldn't abandon her if she was under attack.

'Are you okay, Crowley?' the rat was bigger than her cat, but she was confident he could defend himself.

He glared at the rodent. 'No problem. Where are you going?'

'I can't leave Pandora at the mercy of those other animals.'

She was surprised at how quickly her feelings for the redhead had changed. They may have gotten off on the wrong foot when Pandora punched her in the head, but she wouldn't just leave her.

'No – she chose to stay so we could escape,' Crowley said.

As he spoke, the rat sprang at him. He ducked underneath its claws and reached up with his own, catching the fat rodent across the face and drawing blood from its right eye. It fell to the ground and shrieked.

Emma watched the attack as she got the garage door open, making sure there were no other obstacles in their way. As she returned to the car, Crowley jumped into the driver's side and slid into the passenger seat.

'My money was always on you,' Bukowski said.

'Let's get out of here,' Chirpy added.

Emma thought of Pandora but knew they had to leave, starting the engine and flooring the accelerator. The mustard-coloured car sped towards the horizon, the open road and an animal-free zone on either side of them.

She glanced at the house, picturing Pandora and the dark cat together.

I should go back for her.

As she considered that, something landed on the roof with a thump.

'Gulls!' Crowley shouted.

One slid down onto the windscreen and glared at her through the glass. It was huge, with manic determination bulging from its yellow eyes. Before she could react, the bird attacked in a frenzy, slamming its beak into the glass at a hundred miles an hour.

'Shit,' Emma said, hitting the button for the wipers. The blades swept the gull off the car and onto the side of the road. As scared as she was, she hoped the bird would be okay.

'Another one will come along soon enough,' Crowley said.

She slammed on the accelerator. The tyres screeched and burnt rubber into the ground. A large group of gulls slid from the roof and scattered around them. Her foot pushed down as she swerved to avoid loose birds, speeding down the road.

'How fast can gulls fly?' Emma asked.

Crowley and Chirpy turned to Bukowski for an answer.

'Don't be birdist – we're not all the same,' he said. 'They won't be able to travel as quickly as this car, that's for sure.'

Emma relaxed a little, focused on the road, wondering what had happened to Pandora. 'Why would she do that, stay behind for us?'

'I liked her, that strange redheaded woman,' Bukowski said, his voice sounding as dry as sandpaper in the desert.

'I think I did as well,' Emma said as she touched the bruise on her head.

'It doesn't matter now,' Crowley said.

'Where do we go?' she asked, desperate to get on a phone and speak to her sister. She remained clueless about her mother's location.

'Close to here,' Crowley replied. 'There's a place on the coast where we might be able to hide out. Do you know where the caves are, near the skeleton of the old pier?'

She nodded. 'Sure. We used to go there as kids. It's only five miles or so away. What will we find there?'

The part of her mind that still dreamed of mermaids and sea creatures imagined they would head to an undersea kingdom run by dolphins and other aquatic life. She never thought about how she'd breathe in such a place.

Everything's possible now.

'The Pig Underground,' Crowley replied.

Emma drove faster, her nerves refusing to stop jangling as she wondered what she might find in a Pig Underground.

Chapter 49

Emma: Going Underground

They drove down the narrow track that led to the coast. Emma gripped the wheel, worried the car might slip off the edge at any minute. As they reached the bottom, she gazed at the expanse of orange leading into the oncoming spray and pale blue horizon.

'Go onto the sand, turn left, and keep going until you see the entrance to the caves,' Crowley said.

She didn't argue, looking at the sea as the waves drifted in and out onto the beach. It wasn't exactly a beach, as thousands of tiny pebbles covered the sand.

Emma drove for about half a mile, feeling the tyres bouncing off the stones and hoping they didn't get a puncture. She stopped when she saw the front of the caves ahead.

'What's the Pig Underground?' she said as they exited the car.

'A group of pigs who live underground,' Bukowski snorted, doing his best impersonation of a hog.

Chirpy ran past her, shouting something she couldn't hear. She tried to forget what had happened at the cottage, grinning at the little dog's exuberance. The rest of them followed Chirpy inside the large gap carved into the cliffs as if a giant had taken a knife and hacked away at nature.

She looked at her phone and flicked the torch on as they stepped into the cavern. As they entered the hollow, shadows surrounded them. The dearth of light meant the absence of its warmth as well. Emma's skin tingled in the temperature drop, and a shiver ran through her. The loose stones shifted underfoot, twisting her ankle to the right and shooting pain up her leg. She ignored it and continued forwards. Crowley led the way, his eyes accustomed to the gloom.

'Have you been here before?' Emma asked him.

'Yes,' he answered. 'It's just ahead of us now.'

He stepped through a large hole in the wall and down a set of natural steps. Inside the caves, darkness was an eternity, crushing Emma's optimism and squeezing the breath from her. She wasn't claustrophobic, but her world had shrunk rapidly, the dark playing tricks on her mind as a vision of Pandora thrusting her mouth onto Emma flashed before her eyes.

She descended the staircase by touch alone, fearing she might fall any second. She was surprised at the smooth walls – it was as if someone had spent hours sanding them clean.

Emma followed Crowley down the steps, welcoming the appearance of the candles and lamps illuminating the way. She held her breath as the light grew stronger, and she realised what was on the surrounding levels. Ominous looming shadows transformed into the faces of the pigs staring at her, their long snouts dispensing brief spurts of air in her direction.

My world gets stranger by the second.

Every one of them eyed her with suspicion. Around their feet were several piglets; their tiny upturned faces much happier, more trusting, teeth and eyes shining together at the unexpected guests.

The dog and the duck followed her down the steps until they reached the only flat piece of ground Emma could see, a place overlooking a vast cavern filled with crystal blue light reflected from a pool of water at the side.

'Who's in charge?' Crowley asked the pig with the bulbous head and eyes.

'We're all in charge.'

The voice was dry and raspy, drifting through the cavernous underground and echoing above their heads. Emma couldn't see everything, but it seemed like more than a hundred pigs were there. She saw one who fascinated her on the next level down, looking like a withered old man. Its skin was grey rather than pink, lines scattered across it like craters on the moon.

'We are a commune run by all,' the grey pig said as it gazed at Emma. 'I'm the oldest here – you can call me Major.'

Splintered illumination from broken lamps ambled up the walls behind him, casting awkward shadows on either side of his wrinkled head. On his right stood an old battery-operated compact disc player, covered in scratches but with a small green neon light flashing on and off.

'You listen to CDs?' she asked.

'Music is one of the few things we appreciate from the world of humans. There's an extensive collection of discs at the bottom of this cavern. You can pick one later if you like, but why don't we all sit together and discuss why you're here?'

They sat opposite him. 'Thank you,' Crowley said.

'We know who you are, Thief, but what do you want here?' His ancient eyes were like antique telescopes.

'We're looking for temporary sanctuary,' Crowley replied.

'You're on the run from Darkstar and the Bullfather.' It was an observation, not a question from Major.

'How do you know?' Crowley asked.

'The news has been on the grapevine for a few days, even reaching us here. You're welcome to stay, but I must warn you, not everyone will be happy to see you.'

As she listened, Emma shifted to get a better position to see Major. 'What is this place?'

He smiled at her, the lines on his face growing larger as his cheekbones extended ever wider. 'You have to excuse me for grinning. I'm not used to having conversations with humans.' He glanced at Crowley. 'I'd heard about the one at Bullfather's farm, of course, but to witness such a thing in the flesh is quite remarkable.' He returned his gaze to her. 'But to answer your question – we are a community created by those who escaped human farms.'

'This is a pig commune?' she said.

Major grimaced. 'This is a commune, but we don't use the other word as our name. We prefer to be called Suidae. We share everything we have, though our community is split between two different ideas about handling external affairs. That is why I said some here will not be happy with your presence.'

'Why won't they be happy?' Emma asked.

'We're only affiliated with the AA, not run by them. Some here believe we should be more militant in our deal-ings with the outside world. Others are happy to avoid any contact with humanity. There is constant discussion about how our community will continue. Everyone here knows how things may change in the outside world now that Bull-father has his empire on the farm.'

'And which group do you belong to?' Emma said.

He rolled his watery eyes at her and let out a great snort. 'I'm always impartial, my dear lady. It's what comes from being so ancient.'

'What do you know of the Bullfather's plans?' Crowley asked.

Major whistled through his crooked teeth, sounding like an empty old kettle somebody had switched to boil. 'The man who owns the farm has taken the animals under his protection. Like the young lady here, this is the one who can understand what we're saying. He's connected to a group of humans who call themselves animal activists and go under the fancy name of the House of the Rising Sun. They take animals they've rescued from human places of torture and death to the farm.'

Major paused. All around him, the smaller Suidae – Suidaelets – were gazing up at him with evident admiration. Emma resisted the urge to hug him, distracted by the approaching sounds of heavy breathing. Inside the cave, the noise echoed through their heads like a portentous warning of impending danger.

From the shadows, large shapes emerged and trotted towards them, mean-looking hogs with humongous eyes and even larger teeth. As he spoke, an aroma of pungent cabbage escaped from the bigger one's mouth.

'You're not welcome here. The human and the Thief must leave. The other two can stay if they swear loyalty to our cause.' Its voice was like the low rumble of thunder.

'And what cause is that?' Emma asked.

'The overthrow of all humans,' both hogs said.

'Do you have an army here?' Crowley wondered.

'We have enough. And we have brothers and sisters scattered throughout the land above,' the smaller hog said through chewed teeth.

Crowley nodded. 'The ones waiting for the slaughterhouse.'

The biggest hog lunged towards him but flinched as the old pig stepped between them. Major lifted his head as he spoke, his authority obvious to all.

'You know the rules, Gregor; no harm shall come to any of our guests.'

'You may be the Elder, but you're not the Leader.'

'Would that be you?' Major asked him.

The smaller hog sidled up to his brother in a show of support. 'There are no leaders here, old timer, you know that.'

'We have alliances outside of here. The war is coming,' Gregor said.

'Alliances? You mean with the Bullfather,' Crowley asked.

Gregor snorted laughter. 'The glorious revolution will be here soon, and you won't be part of it, Thief. Centuries of suffering under human hands shall be avenged.'

It was a threat and promise in one. Emma stood and stepped forward, her snow-white hair shimmering in the candlelight, trembling with sorrow and guilt.

'I wish the rest of my fellow humans stopped eating animals and started treating you with the respect you deserve, but I don't see how any animal uprising could succeed in a war against humanity. There are too many of us, and we are far too vicious.'

After observing a lifetime of animal misery, Emma's heart was heavy.

Gregor snorted again, stomping his hooves and pushing his impressive chest out.

'It makes no difference now, human child. The future is written, and your kind will have no part in it.'

Emma sensed many eyes on her as she readied herself for a discussion on peaceful cohabitation with this belligerent warthog. Before she could start, Crowley stepped forward.

'Thank you for your hospitality, Major; we won't take up your time any longer.'

The two hogs continued to glare at them.

'Where will you go next?' Major asked.

'Home,' Emma said.

Major lifted his wizened backside from the floor. 'Come, I shall escort you to the outside world.' He glanced at the hogs as he left.

Emma gave Crowley a knowing look before they followed him. They strode up the steps, and she felt the hot breath of the hogs on her neck.

'Why can't we stay here longer?' The words tumbled from her mouth as her body ached. She needed rest, but didn't know when she'd get it.

I'm in danger everywhere we go. We all are.

Crowley also sounded tired as he answered her. 'It's not just the hogs who are dangerous. Have you noticed how some of those pink eyes stare at us as if we're the next course on the menu? I don't trust Gregor and his group. If they're talking about a war against humans, Darkstar and the Bull-father must be involved. Darkstar would find us here soon enough. We need to get to somewhere beyond his reach.'

'Does such a place exist?' Emma asked.

She heard the first bars of "Shake It Off" by Taylor Swift rising from below as she reached the top. The sun's nimble orange fingers caressed her eyes as they moved outside. She watched as all the little pigs scattered out of the way and scampered back inside the underground.

Major spoke to Crowley. 'You need to get to the Menagerie. Do you know of it?'

'Yes,' Crowley replied.

'You'll be safe there from Darkstar and the Bullfather.'

Major returned to the cave, and Emma saw the tide approaching them. She was tired, thirsty, and hungry. Looking at the others, she assumed they all felt the same.

She knelt and stroked Crowley's head. 'What's the Menagerie?'

He purred under her touch. 'It's the Atlas mansion, holding the biggest private zoo in the world. We'll be safe from humans and animals in there. If we can get inside.'

Emma stood, her weary mind overwhelmed with one thought.

I have to go to a zoo.

Chapter 50

Emma: The Atlas Zoo

Once inside the city, Emma parked where she hoped nobody would see them, desperate for sleep. 'We'll rest awhile before heading to the Atlas mansion.'

'We can't leave the car,' Crowley said. 'Darkstar will have spies everywhere.'

Chirpy's stomach rumbled. 'I'm hungry.'

Emma rubbed the little dog's fur. 'We all are. I'll find us something once I've rested.'

She pushed her head back and closed her eyes, pain rippling through her limbs and her mouth drier than sand. Sleep came almost instantaneously, as did her dreams. She ran through the Pig Underground in one as the Diamond Dogs barked at her heels. Then it faded, and she was in the hospital, next to Jane, standing over her mother as she slipped away.

Emma jerked awake, finding Chirpy in her lap and the others whispering in the back seat. She rubbed at her aching neck. 'What did I miss?'

Crowley yawned. 'Not much. I'm still confused about why Darkstar and the Bullfather want the Doolittle.'

She tried to shake the fuzziness from her brain. 'Maybe it's because they want all humans to be able to understand what animals are saying.'

Crowley shook his head. 'I'm not sure, but even if that was true, do you believe people would treat us better?'

Bukowski burped. 'Yeah, they might stop eating us if they had to talk to us first.'

'I reckon it would change many people's minds,' Emma said. 'Not everybody, but enough to usher in a new era in human and animal relationships. It would change the world.'

'There's something else it can do, Emma,' Crowley said.

She stroked his chin. 'What?'

'Wyatt Wells told me it cured his father's dementia.'

Emma jumped forward, sending Chirpy into the passenger seat. 'What?'

'Wells might have been lying, but I don't think so.'

There were two bruises on Emma's head throbbing in constant motion inside her skull: the one from where she cut herself stumbling into the trees outside the prison and the other more painful one from where Pandora had punched her at the cottage. All that pain disappeared when she heard the news about what the Doolittle could do for memory loss. And then she broke down in tears when she remembered she'd had the last of it.

'I could've cured Mum if I hadn't drunk that water.'

She smashed her fists against the seats, wailing against the windscreen and scaring the animals. Crowley sat as she wept. When she finished, he smiled at her, and she wondered why he was so happy.

'You didn't drink it all, Emma,' he said. 'I still have half of it hidden away. You can give that to your mother.'

She scooped the little cat up, squeezing him tightly and getting ginger fur all over her chest and arms. Emma brought his face close to hers and kissed him on his already wet nose, her thoughts spinning in all directions. She twisted her neck, trying to devise a plan.

'How much danger are we in from Darkstar?'

What had happened at the cottage was fresh in her mind, but she found it hard to believe the dark cat could throw an army of vicious animals against them in the city. Then she remembered the kamikaze birds, the venomous rats and those frightening dogs. And Crowley had said that was only a small portion of what the dark cat controlled.

'I wouldn't trust any animal outside us three,' Crowley said.

She looked at Bukowski and Chirpy as they both nodded.

'I need to get in touch with Jane to see where Mum is, but I don't know if the police will be watching her or tapping her phone.'

Would they do that for a teenage fugitive? Emma didn't know, but knew how scared the others were about Darkstar and his animal thugs. The few hours' sleep had helped her, but she needed more rest and food. And she guessed they did as well.

'Do you want to go to your sister?' Crowley asked.

'No, not yet, but I could call her.' She reached for her mobile and cursed. 'The battery is dead.'

'The coppers could trace you through that,' Bukowski said.

He was right. 'I need access to a phone; we all require food and drink. And we have to get somewhere safe from

Darkstar and his spies.' She glanced out of the window at the birds hovering above. 'Does that only leave us with the Atlas mansion?'

'I think so,' Crowley replied. 'Darkstar has no influence there, and Zachary Atlas is notoriously opposed to all forms of authority. It would give us refuge while you contact your sister.'

Emma sighed. 'I hate zoos.'

And the Atlas Zoo was the most notorious one in the country. Run as a private playground by its owner, Zachary Atlas, it was built inside his vast mansion. She'd always dreamt of razing it to the ground and liberating the animals imprisoned there. Her stomach twisted in anger at the thought of going there for help.

'We won't be there long,' Crowley said.

She turned the key in the ignition. 'How would we get in?'

Emma's cat grinned at her. 'I have a plan.'

Forty minutes later, they reached the Atlas Zoo on the city's outskirts. Giant trees surrounded the building like great armies defending a castle, large branches protruding towards any unwanted visitors. She was surprised by the gates opening for them automatically, driving down a path enveloped by ornate statues of exotic animals standing guard over the track to the mansion.

Then they reached another set of gates, and a security guard demanded to know why they were there. Emma stared in the mirror to make sure the last of the sleep had disappeared from her eyes.

'Look in the back,' she said to the man, noticing the large handgun in his possession.

Another security guard studied her while the unhappy one peered into the rear seat. He gasped in amazement at what was there: a cat and duck playing poker while a small dog danced.

'Shit!' he said.

Emma laughed. 'I think your boss might be interested in these three.'

The only way to get in was if they convinced Atlas that Emma had something worthwhile for him to look at.

'And what do we do when we're inside?' Crowley had asked.

'One thing at a time,' she replied. 'Let's just get to safety first, and then we can devise a plan.'

Enlisting one of the country's wealthiest men could be part of that, she thought. She stared at the startled security guard as he spoke into his radio and waited for a reply. He dismissed them with his eyes, but waved them forward. She parked the car outside the main door. They climbed the steps, and Emma knocked.

One of the hired help opened up. The servant brought them into the mansion in silence. They marched down a draughty corridor over a weathered carpet that had seen better days and into a room large enough to fit Emma's flat ten times over.

The place was nearly as tall as it was wide, with a lavishly ornate beamed ceiling housing a magnificent chandelier. The walls were adorned with oriental silks and other exotic fabrics, while the floor was plush, with a thick mahogany-coloured carpet. Looking at it made Emma want to throw off her shoes and let her feet melt into its warm embrace.

Bukowski said, 'This is the nicest thing I've ever walked across.'

Crowley nodded in agreement. Some two and three-seated sofas were scattered around the place, with the spaces in between inhabited by cushions of differing colours. At one end of the room stood a thick black working desk, on which a phoenix statue rose from the fiery flames. From behind it strode an imposing figure of a man over six feet tall with a physique from a heavyweight boxing ring.

'My name is Zachary Atlas. Welcome to my home.'

Emma couldn't say which was the most impressive – the luxury or the enormous beard covering most of Atlas's face. It was as if nature had taken hold of all the space on his head that wasn't his eyes, nose and lips and covered it with thick, dark vegetation.

'Thanks,' she said.

'Please, have a seat.'

She was glad of the chance to rest her legs while the animals stood on the side and stared at the elegantly dressed man before them. He was twice Emma's age, attractive enough to turn heads when he entered a room, wearing an elaborate ruby red suit with a waistcoat and shiny green tie.

'It's an impressive place,' Emma said.

He sat opposite her, close enough for her to smell his musky cologne. His eyes were bright and full, continually observing everything.

'I'm guessing you didn't come for a private tour.'

'We need your help,' she replied, her gaze drifting around the room and settling on the works of art only the rich could own.

'We?' Atlas stared at the animals with barely concealed amusement. Crowley, Bukowski and Chirpy stood next to each other in a line like soldiers on parade.

Emma told him the story they concocted. 'For reasons I'd rather not go into, I need somewhere to stay for a few days. In return, I can train some of your animals as I've trained these three.'

'You're an animal trainer?' His emotionless eyes peered right through her.

She turned away from him and looked at her cat. 'Crowley, do a handstand.'

This was what they'd practised earlier. He stood on his hind legs, body fully extended, then placed his front paws on the floor and pushed the rest of his torso and legs into the air. For good measure, he gave them a delicate twirl.

Emma grinned, but Atlas was unmoving, hands clasped together as if he was feeling the cold. She didn't let it deter her, removed the pack of cards from her jacket, and put them face down on the floor.

'Chirpy, find me the ace of spades.'

'I wanted to stand on my paws,' the little dog said grumpily. Then she tipped the cards, looking for the right one. When she did, she moved it near Atlas's shoes.

The rich man looked unimpressed. Emma frowned, digging her nails into the seat, worried it wasn't going as planned. If he didn't take them in, they would be at the mercy of Darkstar and his army sooner rather than later. Even if she gave herself to the police, the others would be in danger.

It was up to the duck.

Emma looked around the room, glancing high above the paintings to find what she needed, settling on the bookcase towering behind Atlas.

'What's your favourite novel?' she asked him.

He scrutinised her face. 'The first book I ever read, given to me by my mother, *Alice in Wonderland*.'

'Bukowski, can you fetch Mr Atlas's favourite book, please? And take Chirpy with you.'

The little duck puffed out his cheeks and waved his feathers before Chirpy climbed onto his back. They lifted off the ground and over Atlas towards the bookcase's top shelf. Bukowski hovered above them for a few seconds before finding what he wanted, forcing his beak over the novel's faded edges and grabbing it tightly. He glided back towards the humans and dropped the book into Atlas's lap. Chirpy fell onto the floor and skipped around the room. Emma smiled at Atlas, hoping her friends had done enough to win over the enigmatic man sitting opposite.

'The cat acrobat was cute, but I've seen much better than that. There could have been dog food on the card to attract the Chihuahua. The duck was impressive. How did you do that?'

'I'll tell you everything if we can stay here.' Emma's tone was firm.

Zachary Atlas stood, still holding the Lewis Carrol novel. He grinned at the three animals before staring at her.

'Of course, Ms Crowley; any fugitive from a corrupt justice system is welcome in my home.' He bent onto one knee, looking like a man ready to propose, and stroked Chirpy on the head.

Emma stared at him and wondered how he knew her name.

Chapter 51

Emma: The Menagerie

Atlas stared at Crowley as if he was the cat and Crowley was the mouse.

'Come; I'll show you my menagerie,' he said, leading them out a different way than they'd entered. Emma didn't know how to reply to the revelation that he knew who she was, steering the conversation in any direction apart from that one as they strode down the extensive, winding corridor.

'How long have you lived here?'

'My family has owned this house for generations.'

He used the term house as if it was a semi-detached two-bedroomed terrace standing in one of the less wholesome parts of the city and not the embodiment of decadent luxury.

'It's remarkable,' she said.

'I've made significant changes to it over the years, which you'll soon see.'

His pace was brisk, as if he wanted to squeeze every moment from a fleeting existence. The animals struggled to keep up, so Emma slowed and glanced at Crowley.

'What's the new plan?' he asked her.

She shrugged and rolled her eyes upwards, seeing the extravagant chandeliers. Their perfect crystals winked at her as she caught up with Atlas outside another entrance.

'I assumed you'd have more security here,' Emma said.

He put his arm on the door and got ready to push. 'Why would I do that?'

'Many people dislike zoos; some might want to liberate the animals.' She'd thought about it enough times.

He appeared insulted by the very idea of it. 'Ah yes, animal activists. Rest assured, Ms Crowley, we are well protected here.'

She grimaced as he used her name again. Maybe the police had issued a national alert for her after all. Her stomach churned at the idea of it. All it would do was make finding her mother even harder.

'I need a drink,' Bukowski stated.

Atlas flung the door open like a ringmaster at a carnival. 'Feast your eyes on the Menagerie, the greatest collection of animals in the world.'

'Apart from the ones in their natural habitats,' Crowley said.

He ignored the cat's meow and took them to his grand playground.

'We share something in common, Emma; can I call you Emma?' He continued without waiting for permission. 'We both discovered our love of animals when we were children.'

My love doesn't reveal itself by locking them in cages, was what she craved to say but didn't. 'How so?'

'My father, like most fathers, had no interest in what his only child wanted, but my mother would do anything for me. Which is how all this started.'

He stopped talking and allowed Emma to gaze upon his wondrous world. She noticed the horde of exotic birds imprisoned on her left. The metal bars reached the roof, but it was still a cage of many colours. Bukowski placed his head against the gaps and spoke to its inhabitants – peacocks, puffins, macaws, parrots, and even a bird of paradise.

'We hate it here,' they said together.

'Can you get us out?' The bird with the brightest feathers pleaded to them.

Atlas came over and stood next to the little duck. 'I've had these the longest. They aren't the oldest residents, but they are the noisiest.' He laughed while the birds screamed. 'I thought about letting them out to fly around in here.'

'And?' Emma said.

He shrugged. 'Too much trouble.' He gazed at her and then the birds, staring right through them and never seeing them.

They moved to the next enclosure, made of a rigid wooden fence surrounding the animals. The tiniest horses Emma had ever seen were inside - not much bigger than the dark cat who'd threatened them at the cottage.

Crowley shivered. 'I don't like this, Emma.'

Atlas grinned at the cat, hearing nothing but a meow. 'My mother loved horses. I was never that keen, but these are the smallest in the world, so I had to have them.'

'Hello,' Emma said to the one at the front, holding her hand over the fence to touch its face. The unfortunate thing appeared tired, its long grey hair nearly reaching the lush grass it stood on.

'Hector is one of our senior citizens,' Atlas said as he handed the horse a sugar cube.

'I'd love to shove this down your throat,' Hector said before gobbling up the treat.

'Is it terrible in here?' Crowley asked as the horse ate the cube.

'I can't remember the last time the sun bathed me in its light. There is no way to run more than ten feet in a straight line, and every night is a cacophony of screams and nightmares.' Hector finished his sugar and glared at Atlas for more.

'They're always hungry,' Atlas said as he laughed again. 'It costs me a fortune.'

He threw a cube into the air. Emma watched as the tiny horse lifted its head and caught it between its teeth.

'And another thing,' the horse shouted as it crunched the sugar in half, and Atlas took his visitors to the next exhibit. 'My name is Fernando, not Hector.'

Atlas grinned like a school kid, lifting his eyebrows so far from his face Emma thought they would take flight.

'It gets more exciting as we go along. I'm always thrilled to show new people my collection. We had to close most of it to the public years ago; too many people were disruptive or tried to steal the exhibits.'

She couldn't contain it any longer, her anger rising through her lungs and threatening to blow steam from her eyes and mouth, a human volcano on the verge of exploding.

'Have you never thought keeping them imprisoned like this was cruel?' Her voice quaked with indignation.

He stopped dead in his tracks, frozen as if Emma were the Gorgon and glaring into his soul. 'They're animals, my dear; better to be here than in a slaughterhouse.' Patronising, condescending, arrogant, dismissive – he was all that and more. 'We'll have plenty of time for discussions later. Let's continue the tour; all the best bits await you.' He grinned at her. 'My Empire of the Sea is next.'

Emma had no choice but to stride past the caged creatures: a bear near a group of armadillos; an aardvark opposite a porcupine; pythons staring at swans; zebras,
platypuses, panthers, kangaroos, lizards, and so many
others. There didn't appear to be any rhyme or reason for
how they were arranged, placed on a whim wherever Atlas
would get the most pleasure from them. She had to shut her
ears to the harshness of the complaints which followed
them down the room.

But she still heard them.

Chapter 52

Emma: Empire of the Sea

They entered a giant aquarium. Emma's father had taken her to SeaWorld when she was younger, and she hated being so close to all those aquatic creatures confined inside tiny cages of water when they should have been swimming in the great oceans.

From the smallest exotic fish to the largest whales, they all appeared to be shedding watery tears to the young Emma. It had given her nightmares for months afterwards, and when her father brought a brightly coloured goldfish home in a bowl one day, all she could do was scream at him and run to her bedroom.

What she saw as she stepped into Atlas's Empire of the Sea was much worse than her childhood experience: numerous large see-through prisons housing creatures who shouldn't have been near dry land, let alone in deep underground captivity. The room was as big as an arena, running around the insides like a giant continuous inland waterway.

'This is one huge fishbowl.' Bukowski sounded impressed.

Emma stared in disgust at thousands of exotic fish

behind a piece of glass larger than the *Titanic*, her mind working overtime, considering what he must have done to the room to fit everything inside it.

'It's the world's biggest collection of sea creatures,' Atlas claimed proudly.

'Apart from what's in the sea,' Emma said near the massive school of fish.

Separated into their liquid enclosures, she walked past dolphins, sharks, squid, octopuses, whales and many strange and unusual others she didn't recognise. The glass was thick, and it was hard to understand what the creatures were saying, but she got the gist.

We want to go home.

She pushed her face against the cold glass, hoping to hide the tears she could feel coming, peering into the watery face of a baby whale, its pale skin making it appear malnourished and frail. Its eyes were large and wide, and she wanted to dive into them and tell the creature everything would be okay. But she knew it would be a lie.

'What's it like in the sea?' she heard it whisper.

'Isn't it marvellous we can breed them here?' Atlas said, oblivious to the pain and discomfort in every part of his underwater kingdom.

Emma needed to help those poor creatures but didn't know how. Her sadness cut through her in a great wave. She wanted to smash her head through the glass and liberate everyone, even though she knew how foolish that would be.

'It's horrendous,' she said.

'But I've saved the greatest part of my collection for last. You won't see anything like this anywhere in the world.'

Emma touched the barrier imprisoning the whales and whispered. 'I'm sorry.'

Then she faced Atlas, struggling to stop her head from exploding.

We're safe here.

'Do you have a couple of mermaids imprisoned as well?'

She hated herself for it, but she knew they were there for one specific reason, and she couldn't let her anger ruin it for the others.

His laugh was unconditional and wild, like a man not used to having other humans as company. 'No, something even better; look over here.'

Atlas strode to the far corner as Emma shook her head. There was a giant cage near the wall. It wasn't underwater, but a large, thick blanket covered it. Atlas skipped towards his secret possession, grinning like a court jester about to play his biggest practical joke. His eyes were wide and manic as he stared at Emma and ignored the others.

'Are you ready to meet the world's oldest living creature?'

He waited for Emma's response, but all she gave him was the angriest look she could muster, hoping the fire burning from her eyes would leave a permanent scar on his heart.

Atlas grabbed the cover and performed a mock flourish and bow before ripping it from the cage. Emma went to the metal prison and peered at the giant turtle through the bars. Its eyes were closed, and she wondered if it was even alive.

'I've had this fella for three decades, but I believe he could be more than one hundred and fifty years old, making him the oldest living creature on the planet.'

Atlas beamed, pride and joy shining out of him like the sun's rays. Inside Emma, it was as if an iceberg was sinking all of her hopes and dreams. She kept staring at the turtle, so motionless she thought he might be a waxwork. Then his wrinkled grey neck moved a little, and she saw life in his eyes.

'I'm sorry for what they've done to you.' She wanted to reach out and touch him, but stopped herself. She hated it when other people petted caged animals as if they were doing them a favour.

'Don't be,' he said. 'I'm safer here than in the outside world.'

His voice was like a grizzled old man who'd witnessed too much heartache. Crowley, Chirpy and Bukowski joined Emma in gazing at the great turtle in his cage.

'Why do you say that?' Crowley asked.

The turtle swivelled his legs inside his craggy shell, turning to face the new animals visiting him.

'There are too many people after my secrets out there, my friend.' His mouth appeared to move in slow motion, even though his words came out at normal speed. 'And you can call me Tommy.'

Atlas stood to one side, smirking at the sight of the cat meowing towards the turtle.

'This is the liveliest I've seen from him in years. You and your group must be having a positive influence on him.'

Emma ignored him as he walked across the room to answer his phone, returning to Tommy.

'What secrets?' she asked, her curiosity overcoming her natural hatred for the place.

'Well, if I told you, then they wouldn't be secrets anymore, would they?' The turtle chuckled as his head went backwards, his gaze falling on the cat opposite him. 'Maybe you should ask the Thief next to you what his secrets are.'

Crowley stared at the turtle while Emma glanced at the cat.

'Thief?' she said.

'I told you what I did, Emma, so don't look too surprised.'

'I thought you were joking.' She wanted to laugh, but standing inside the animal prison had sucked all the joy from her.

'All cats are thieves at heart. I'm just the best of them. This turtle is winding us up. He's been in captivity for years; he knows nothing about the outside world.'

Tommy laughed. '*Au contraire*, my little feline friend. I may know enough to save all your lives.'

Emma couldn't have imagined a turtle could look smug, but this one did. Then again, a few days ago, she wouldn't have believed anything she'd experienced since a group of talking animals broke her out of prison.

'I doubt it,' Crowley said.

'Are you the pet of this human?' Tommy chided him.

'I belong to nobody, neither human nor animal.'

'Does the ebony cat know that? Or the great bull?'

The turtle's smug countenance had transformed into a wide grin. Emma had witnessed similar expressions when arrogant people prepared to educate their audience.

'What?' Crowley said. 'How do you know of them?'

Tommy ignored his question. 'Are you aware that humans keeping pets is only a recent phenomenon? We're just commodities to them, possessions to make them happy, but when it comes down to it, they kill us as quickly as anything. Humans cherish their material belongings above all else. They would rather wear dead animal flesh on their bodies than let us roam free in the wild where we belong.'

Emma gazed at the turtle. 'How old are you?'

A smirk on his tiny face made him look like a pickled walnut about to combust. 'I'm much, much older than many realise. Centuries have passed since I was a small turtle scrambling for survival along the beach and into the sea.'

'What's the point of all this?' Emma lost her compassion for the turtle, which surprised and worried her.

'The point is, my dear human, the AA can't be trusted, and the Bullfather is ready to lead a glorious new rebellion.'

Crowley stared at Tommy. 'How do you know all this since you've been in captivity for so long?'

'Eyes and spies, my friend, eyes and spies. I've been imprisoned in one type of confinement for most of my exceedingly long lifetime, but I've obtained vast knowledge.'

'Such as?' Emma said.

'Did you know, in 1877, New York gathered nearly eight hundred stray dogs and drowned them in the East River? The humans shoved them into iron crates and used a crane to dump them into the water. You see, humans would rather kill animals than pay for them to be looked after while they go on holiday because it's cheaper to buy a new one when they return.' Hate flowed from the turtle's crumpled lips.

Emma listened to his rant, but wasn't convinced by it.

'I know we've committed terrible atrocities against animals over the years and still do today, but many of us think and act differently now. The number of vegetarians or vegans is growing every year. You talk about animals being pets for humans, but many people don't view animals like that – they're part of the family, loved and cared for, mourned for when they pass on.' She looked at the cat standing near her feet. 'You're part of my family,' she said. 'And I would forgive you anything.'

Crowley the cat stared at Crowley the human, and the tears flowed from them both.

'How touching,' said the turtle. 'Sentimental mush which will get you all killed.'

'Enjoy your imprisonment,' Crowley said. 'We're going back to the real world.'

They strode away from the grinning turtle and joined an equally happy Atlas. Emma looked at the sea life behind her, wondering how accurate the old turtle would be with his predictions.

Atlas's phone buzzed inside his jacket. 'Our meal is ready. Please follow me into the dining room.' He called it a dining room, but in reality, it was more like a medieval banqueting hall decorated with polished suits of armour. 'There's food and water for them at the far end if you want your animals to pop onto the table and tuck in.'

'You heard the man,' Emma said as she concentrated on what Atlas had provided. She pulled a face at the amount of dead flesh in front of her.

'Don't worry, Emma. I made sure there are plenty of vegetarian options.'

'You should eat something, Emma,' Crowley said between dipping his face into a food bowl. Bukowski drank all his water as if it were a stronger liquid while Chirpy scooped biscuits into her mouth like they were the greatest delicacy in the world.

Emma slipped into a seat close to where Atlas sat at the head of the table. She stared at the food, listening to the voice of hunger prompting her to go ahead, determined not to take anything from him.

'How do you know so much about me?'

He chewed on burnt flesh and talked with his mouth full. 'As soon as your car passed under the first arch on my property, the cameras captured images of you. My people ran them through a computer and discovered who you were before reaching the next arch. Once we had your name, we had your life, most of which – no offence – has been pretty uneventful until now.'

'You come from one of the richest families in the country, live in this sprawl of Victorian splendour and keep a collection of the world's most exotic animals and sea life imprisoned in your basement.' Emma stared at the food. 'I would think most other people's lives are uneventful to you.' She nibbled on roasted aubergines and glared at him.

'Hardly the basement,' he replied. 'And getting a group of animals to break you out of prison is beyond my reach and means.'

Emma gulped. 'What?'

He grinned at her while chewing on a chicken leg. 'Do you think your little friends will help you escape here?'

Chapter 53

Emma: Welcome to the Jungle

Emma stared at him, wondering if she'd swapped one cage for another. It was only supposed to be a temporary haven while they devised a plan to avoid Darkstar. Then, they could find her mother and give her the last of the Doolittle.

'I've seen some wonderful things in the animal world, but what was on the video with you at the prison was unique. You stirred my interest more than anything I can ever think of.'

'I'm glad to be of service.'

He laughed, and she forced a smile in return.

'You must think I'm a terrible person,' he said while carving a thin slice of flesh from the dead chicken on his plate.

She used a fork and scooped broccoli into her mouth. 'What else would I think when you imprison all these poor creatures?'

'Not everything I do is so terrible,' he said as he grabbed a small remote control device and aimed it at the large blank space on the wall. A huge screen descended from the ceiling. Atlas pushed another button on the remote, and the display came to life, the noise so loud it made Chirpy spit out a piece of biscuit and Emma throw both hands over her ears, grimacing as Atlas's digital voice spoke over the top of an image of a fabulous jungle setting.

'Shit!' she said.

'Sorry,' the flesh and blood Atlas said as he muted the sound. 'My hearing is going, and I forget how high the volume is. And I get so very few visitors here.' The sadness was thick in his voice, his smile finally disappearing.

Emma stared at the screen, guessing it was somewhere in Africa. A group of antelopes drank at a river, and a flock of exotic birds soared above the lush vegetation. Behind them and pushing their heads through the leaves of the trees, two giraffes walked into view, their glorious long bodies stretching to reach the sun and take a bite from it.

'Wow,' Emma said, wondering what those magnificent animals would discuss.

As soon as we leave here and my mother is well, I'll travel the world to talk to every animal I can.

'It is breathtaking,' Atlas said.

Emma's mind snapped back into the present, and she recalled where she was, remembered who she was with. Her appetite disappeared. She pushed the plate away and scowled at him.

'Is this one of the places you steal your animals from?' The food, which had tasted so sweet a few seconds ago, left a bitter taste in her mouth.

'Just keep watching,' he said.

She wanted to leave, regretting they'd come to such a terrible place. Instead, she turned from him and to the screen. The camera panned away, moving behind the trees as she saw something she'd only seen in books before.

'Wow,' she repeated.

Atlas grinned. 'I know, right?'

Emma gazed at a group of white rhinos strolling idly around as if they were chewing the fat. She was mute, stunned by what she saw.

Bukowski broke the silence. 'We need one of those to whip the Bullfather's ass.'

'It's a sanctuary funded for the next two centuries.'

What Atlas said was as surprising to her as what she saw. 'By you?'

He took a large fork brimming with venison and nibbled from the end. 'I told you not everything was terrible.'

'Why?' she put her surprised joy on hold and returned to distrusting him.

He pushed the fork onto his plate and removed a napkin from the top pocket of his jacket. Emma noticed it was monogrammed with his initials as he dabbed away a stray piece of dead meat sticking to the outside of his mouth. He stood as he cleaned himself and went to the television screen.

'I love my menagerie; it has provided me with many wonderful moments, but I've realised they're just fleeting instants in the life of a dying reality. The climate is crumbling, and humanity is only exacerbating the problem instead of fixing it.'

He was preparing to bombard her with his philosophical observations before Emma cut him off before he could get started.

'What's this got to do with your sanctuary? Is it an attempt to wipe away your guilt?' She couldn't accept that his one good deed would make up for everything else, no matter how magnificent.

He ignored her question and the tone of her voice, pressing another button on the remote control. Behind him, the screen changed, splitting into four equal shapes, and then again until there were eight, then sixteen – and it kept changing until there were too many to see or count.

'There isn't only one sanctuary, Emma; there are more than a hundred worldwide. I'm a very wealthy man and intend to do what I can for the environment and its creatures. How would you like to help me?'

She peered at the screen in a daze.

This could be a way out for all of us. I could even take my mother once she's drunk the serum.

Crowley was on the table, standing next to the plate she'd pushed away. 'It's an opportunity to escape the clutches of the police and Darkstar.'

Her mind buzzed with indecision. 'It is.'

'We could all go abroad, to one of these places. None of them would find us there,' Crowley added.

'You can even bring your mother with you. I guarantee the finest medical facilities and personnel to attend to her while you tend to my animals,' Atlas said.

Her fingers shook as she placed them on the table. Tears sprang from her eyes as she gazed at the white rhinos and thought of her mother. He was offering them sanctuary and a way out of the trouble she was in. And a place for her mother to recover once Emma gave her the last of the Doolittle.

'How do you know about my mother's illness?'

Her new animal friends and her cat peered at her in expectation.

Atlas wiped food from his lips, but not the annoying smile from his face. 'I told you, Emma, once my people informed me of your identity, your whole life was at my disposal.'

'Do you have a secure phone I can use?'

'Secure?'

'So nobody can track it here.' She needed to speak to Jane and find her mother. Would Jane believe what had happened to her in the last twenty-four hours?

Do I believe it myself?

Atlas gave her a knowing smile. 'Of course; you can use mine.' He handed her his mobile before returning to his seat to finish his meal.

She stared at Crowley and the others. 'Do you want to stay here?'

'Not particularly,' the cat said. 'But it's the best we can do until we have a plan. And if Atlas can reunite you with your mother, we'll give her the Doolittle and cure her.'

Emma rolled the phone around in her hand, using the conversation with Crowley as a distraction from calling her sister. She was fearful of what Jane would say about their mother. She would never forgive herself if things had gone so badly it was too late to use the Doolittle.

'You never told me where you put the serum,' she said as she watched Atlas scrutinising everything she did.

Crowley raised his nose while his tail swished. 'It's been frantic since the redheaded woman broke into the cottage, and we haven't had the chance to discuss it.'

The mention of Pandora caused Emma's heart to ache a little, unsure why she felt guilt at having left her behind to face those vicious animals.

'Of course,' she said.

'I had limited storage choice once Wells gave me the phial.' Emma gripped the phone and dialled Jane's mobile number. 'Can't you guess where it is?'

She looked at him as all hell broke loose inside the Atlas menagerie, and the loudest noise in the world smashed into her ears.

Chapter 54

Emma: Invasion

'This is why I drink.'

Bukowski's voice was the last thing she heard before the second, louder explosion battered her. A flashing, burning sun invaded the room, escorted by a thousand screaming banshees. Emma threw her hands over her ears as Chirpy ran around in a circle while Crowley scowled. Atlas sat there impassively as if the noise was a regular occurrence. He continued to shovel food into his face and grinned at her.

'What's happening?' she shouted at him.

He grabbed the remote control, pushed several buttons, and the alarm disappeared. Another button changed the scene on the display screen, the sanctuary transforming to outside the building. She stared at it, looking at the security team. They were agitated, talking into communicators and pointing at something out of view of the cameras.

Emma turned to Atlas, her puzzled expression radiating confusion as her ears vibrated. He kept on eating but pointed at the screen. She returned to the display in time to see the guards drop to the floor in one synchronised movement, swatted to the ground by some invisible enemy.

'We're under attack,' Atlas said, still emotionless.

'Is it the police?' It was Emma's first thought.

'No. This is far too violent for them.' He flicked through different channels, peering at the rest of his people, attempting to fend off a group of mask-wearing invaders.

'Then who?' she asked.

'Whoever it is, you must be quite important to them, Emma Crowley.' He turned from the screen and stared at her. 'Don't worry, they can't get into this room. But why do they want you so much to justify all this trouble?'

'Shouldn't you be calling the police?'

He shook his head. 'There are things here I wouldn't like them to see, and I assume you're in no rush to reacquaint yourself with the authorities.'

Emma concentrated on the screen, watching two intruders lead four security guards through the first floor of the Menagerie at gunpoint. They were masked and wore dark combat gear. She could just about make out a small badge or symbol on their jackets, but it was too tiny to identify.

Crowley stared at the same scene she did. 'They look like they could be military: maybe it's the Project here to exact revenge for what happened to the redheaded woman.'

'We don't know what happened to Pandora.'

Remorse returned to Emma, her fingers shaking with shame, still feeling guilty about leaving her behind. A faint smell of gunfire drifted into the room through the air vents as she stared at the digital numbers on her phone. She picked it up and went to the far corner, away from Atlas's prying ears, dodging Chirpy's hyperactive body. The little dog barked loudly, prompting Crowley to jump off the table and go to her.

'Are you okay, kid?' Chirpy's legs were going ten to the dozen, jumping up and down on the spot like one of those electronic drilling machines digging up the earth. Emma's teeth chattered, and she worried they might shatter in her nervous excitement.

Bukowski joined them at the foot of the table. 'We all need a drink.'

Chirpy stopped running in a circle, the tongue hanging from her mouth like a parachutist desperate to escape a plane. Her breath was long and difficult, her words struggling over the top of her wet lips.

'Popepper has come to rescue me.'

'Wells?' Crowley said.

Bukowski ran with the idea. 'This could be the people he worked for?'

'The Project?' Emma wasn't sure they existed and, if they did, who or what they were. But the invaders were professional and well-organised. Atlas had split the screen into multiple channels, Emma and the others watching the trespassers go through each part of the mansion, and a masked group approached the doors to the Menagerie.

'It's okay,' Atlas said. 'They can't get in there without fingerprint ID and a six-digit key code, which is changed every twelve hours. Or one of my palm prints. So I think we're safe.' He poured himself a large glass of wine and sipped it without hesitation. 'Reinforcements will arrive within thirty minutes.' He raised the glass to Emma and gave her a toast. 'Have you thought about my job offer?'

She ignored him, concentrating on the screen as the invaders dumped two security guards next to the door for the Menagerie. Blood poured from their faces. The first one shook his head as the intruders demanded something from him. Emma could guess what it was and admired his bravery. She turned away in disgust as the rifle slammed into his face and his jaw smashed into the floor.

'My people are fiercely loyal,' Atlas said as he finished his drink and refilled the glass.

Loathing welled inside her as they dragged the second guard towards the door. He hesitated before giving them what they wanted. The doors slid open, and they were a step closer to the banqueting hall. Atlas said nothing, his pupils turning redder than the wine he drank. He turned from the screen, his focus switching between Emma and the strange new animals in his midst.

'Don't worry; they still can't reach this room. Only I have the code for that.'

She returned to the phone as it could be her last chance to speak to Jane: to discover how her mother was. She ignored everything else and concentrated on the numbers. She pushed the final button and waited for the ringing tone on the other end. Part of her hoped Jane wouldn't pick up and give her the worst possible news; the other part needed her to. In her mind, it rang for an eternity; in reality, it was less than a minute.

'Who's this?' her sister asked.

Emma's throat throbbed as if she'd swallowed a bucket of ice cubes, the words frozen before she could get them out, knowing if she didn't, Jane would hang up.

'Jane, it's me.'

'Emma?' The relief slipped from her voice. 'Where are you?'

'No time for that. Tell me, how's Mum and where is she?' Fear and worry infused every word. Her sister paused, and she recognised it wouldn't be good news.

'It's gotten worse. I've moved her into my place.' Jane's breathing down the line filled Emma with dread. 'She's forgetting more and more things. The doctors say there's no hope now.'

Emma put one hand on her chest to calm her beating heart. 'God, no.'

She stared at Crowley, thinking about the serum and how it might be able to save her mother. She had to go to her.

Jane spoke again. 'I don't care what you've done or where you are, Emma, but if you can come and see her ...,' her voice trailed off.

Then the phone died. She stared at it as the large display screen snapped to black.

Atlas stood behind the three animals. 'They're blocking all communications.'

'For the phone as well?' she said.

He shrugged, still impassive about the attack on his home. 'I don't know how they're doing it, but they must have acquired some sophisticated equipment for you, Ms Crowley.' He stared at her as if ready to install her as the next attraction in his Menagerie.

Chirpy finally lost all her chirpiness. 'Is there another way out of here?'

'I could fly up to the roof, go through one of the vents and see what's happening outside,' Bukowski said.

'Maybe the three of you should find somewhere to hide.' Emma's mind was a dark cloud of fears, but this was the most imminent on her horizon.

Atlas crept even closer. 'You communicate with these creatures, and they talk back.' The realisation of what Emma could do was written all over his face. 'Think of what you might achieve if you worked for me. You could be in charge of all the sanctuaries.'

'Will you release every living thing you have in captivity in this house?'

Atlas grinned at her. 'When they speak to you, do they sound like children?'

'They're more grown-up than most humans I've met. All the creatures in your Menagerie hate it and cry for their freedom.'

He ignored her words. 'I can see why these people want you so much.' He got down on one knee as if ready to propose and gazed at Crowley.

'What do you think, little cat? Do you want to be part of my new community?'

'It would be easy to scratch his eyes out, Emma,' Crowley said.

'What did he say?' Atlas asked her.

'Is there somewhere for them to hide here?' They were her only concern now.

He returned to his feet, smiling like a manic clown, his face beaming as he turned to her. 'I told you before; this room is impenetrable.'

As he spoke, the wall exploded behind her. The force flung her forward, past Atlas and the others, and into a table. She collapsed as pain rippled through her chest. The sound of raised human voices drifted over her before disappearing into the billowing smoke filtering into the room. Jack-booted feet landed near Emma's head as Crowley's face disappeared.

Chapter 55

Emma: Red Storm

Emma's head was on the ground, blood pounding, ears ringing like Quasimodo on a bad day. Smoke and pain obscured her vision, no sight of the others anywhere. The insides of her skull were heavy with the stench of fire. An unknown chemical drifted down her throat and into her lungs. She coughed so hard it was as if all her guts were trying to scramble up and through her lips.

She was about to fall unconscious when someone glued their mouth to hers. Emma couldn't have fought back if she'd wanted to, so tired she was ready to slip under some warm, comforting covers. The taste of rose petals on her lips injected energy into her limbs and was delicious.

An arm went around her neck, gently lifting her head before a tongue was inside her mouth. She forgot where she was and pushed back, thrusting her tongue against the other one, remembering something from her recent past flooding all her senses. Emma wondered if it was all some exotic dream where pleasure and pain mixed with every fibre of her body. Strands of red hair shimmered above her face like vibrant ropes, ready to pull her to safety as they let go, and she breathed again.

'Don't worry, I made sure you weren't seriously injured before giving you the kiss of life,' Pandora said. 'How do you feel?'

Pandora's face hovered above her, smoke wafting behind her like fresh brushstrokes on a Rossetti painting. The redhead helped her to stand as Emma was unsteady on her feet, with her hand reaching out for something to stabilise her.

She wasn't sure if she was dreaming or not. 'Did you just kiss me?'

'Sorry, but it was a necessity.' Pandora's hair was a magical, ethereal entity behind her head.

'How is this possible?' Emma said.

Pandora had one arm around her waist, and Emma didn't try to push her away.

'Well, we placed a bit of explosive on the other side of this wall and then let it go bang. I'm sorry you got caught in the blast.'

Their hips squeezed together, Emma unsure if her feverish state was because of her injuries or this new intimacy. 'No, how are you here after the incident at the cottage?'

Pandora helped her through the gap and into the space beyond. There was a long corridor ahead of them. The muscles in Emma's legs strained as they advanced. Smoke continued to billow across their faces. Sounds of gunfire and shouting bounced off the walls.

'What happened at the cottage?' Pandora's face resembled a naughty child caught with their hand in the cookie jar as she threw the question back at Emma. They stumbled forward, her arm around Pandora, strength returning to her legs.

'You sacrificed yourself to save the rest of us.' Emma's lips brushed the redhead's cheek as they approached the exit. She was maddened and excited by what was happening, struggling to get her emotions under control.

'Well, it looks like it worked. Your pets are safe, in case you're worried about them. I'm not too keen on that cat, but I have a soft spot for the duck. The dog I can take or leave.'

She was close to the scars on Pandora's face, sensing the severity of the cuts even though they were healing. She wanted to run her fingers across the skin where it had been cut and massage it back into perfect health.

'This is twice you've saved my life; saved our lives,' she said.

Pandora grinned. 'Think nothing of it.'

The buzzing lessened inside Emma's head. 'How did you know we were here?'

'A little birdy told us.' She propped Emma against the wall. 'Are you strong enough to stand on your own?'

'Yeah, it's more shock than injury. You called your people for help?'

Pandora didn't reply as two of Atlas's armed security strode towards them.

Emma's heart rate increased. 'Do you have a gun?'

'Don't need it, love; my body is a weapon.' She popped Emma against the wall, arched her back and flexed the muscles in her arms, before turning towards the guards. Emma watched that flowing red hair sway from side to side as the two men rushed towards them. 'You boys should scarper before you get hurt.'

They ignored her and raised their weapons. She swerved to the left, pushing her arm into the torso of the closest guard and forced him hard against the wall. She smashed her palm into his chin as the other bloke brought the butt of his rifle into the top of her back.

The loud crack of the bone made Emma grimace as she thought Pandora would buckle. But she used the momentum to her advantage, dragging the first one down and cracking his head onto the floor. Then she moved to the side to avoid the weapon heading for her. Emma tried to shout, but nothing came from her throat apart from a surge of pain. She struggled to breathe as more smoke rushed into her lungs.

Pandora sprang forward, stepping away from the gun pointed at her. There was a second or less before he'd fire. 'You should think twice, mate.'

The guard ignored her advice and pulled the trigger. The bullet hit the wall as she twisted to the side, the slug missing her head by inches. As he went to shoot again, she grabbed him by the groin and squeezed. He screamed as he dropped the weapon.

'It's no pleasure for me either,' she said as she grabbed his neck, squeezing his throat as he writhed like a fish on a hook.

Emma's breath came in staggered bursts as she leaned against the wall. 'Shouldn't we go now?'

Pandora shoved him down and turned to her. 'We'll be free soon and get you into the van. Take hold of me.'

She was glad to feel Pandora's arms around her again. They stumbled forward and outside. 'Where are we going?'

'Soon be there,' Pandora said as she led them to the vehicle waiting and into a seat. Emma sank into it, more pain jumping through her legs as she hit the metal, and the van jerked away. Pandora put her arm around her waist, supporting her.

She sighed with relief. Pandora and her people had rescued them, and all she had to do now was get to Jane and her mother. She prayed there was still time for the Doolittle to work its magic. The whole of her ached, but she finally saw some light at the end of the tunnel. The darkness surrounding her with her mother's illness and the imprisonment drifted away from her.

She glanced around the van. Masked invaders filled the vehicle. She slumped into the seat before Pandora helped her up again, her body shifting into the redhead as they turned a corner. The bloke sitting opposite lurched close to her, and she got a proper look at the symbol on his clothes: an illustration of a house inside a flaming sun.

Pandora shook her head and grinned. 'I know it's a terrible design. I've said I'll create a new one for them.' She flexed her fingers. 'Art is my hobby.'

The van jumped forward, forcing her into Pandora's arms as exhaustion overwhelmed her, and somebody mentioned the House of the Rising Sun.

Chapter 56

Crowley: The Farm

The explosion smashed Crowley in the gut before the noise overwhelmed him. His ears trembled as the smoke and sounds flashed through the air. Emma flew past him and hit a table. Bukowski fell over and dropped to the floor with a crack, but he lost sight of Chirpy in the mayhem.

Something sharp struck him in the leg as he tried to get to Emma. He pulled up as the pain shot through him like an electrical current. Everything went dark as somebody thrust a bag over his head and down his body.

Instinct took over.

Crowley fought against the abduction, kicking backwards against his assailant but finding no strength to ward them off. He tried to shout, his voice muffled by the thick material pressed against his throat. Somebody scooped him up from the floor; human arms pushed into him, memories of his childhood returning as he stared into the dark, waiting for the water to engulf him again as those hands forced him into the river.

Then he was back in the present, squashed by someone

as they ran. His lungs shrivelled in his chest, hindering his ability to breathe. He hit an object hard, falling onto what he believed was the back seat of a car. He froze, his breathing coming in sharp bursts. Something dropped next to him.

'I've been thrown out of better places than this.'

'Bukowski? Is Chirpy with you?'

'I saw nothing between the explosion and the bag over my head.'

The duck sounded annoyed, and Crowley knew how he felt. The pain in his legs had him drifting in and out of sleep. When he woke, he was still trapped inside the sack but wasn't in the vehicle anymore as the cold concrete chilled his bones, and the aroma of ancient death filled his lungs.

He tried to stand, but before he could, the bag was lifted again, one hand underneath his belly while another untied the fastening at the top, tipping him out head first and towards the ground. He twisted in mid-air to land on his feet. Agony shot through his legs, and he grimaced as his eyes adjusted to the light.

'You could've saved yourself so much hurt.' The feline punch found his stomach before he finished hearing the words, knocking the wind from him. As his vision span, Darkstar circled him. 'All you had to do was what we asked of you.'

The dark paws hit him repeatedly like pneumatic drills. He lay there hunched in the gloom and the cold. The pain surged through him, starting from the injury to his leg and spreading through every sinew and muscle, shards of agony attacking him like sharp knives.

'Stop,' he whispered.

Darkstar ceased his attack. 'Just think of where you

could've sat in the new hierarchy we're bringing to this world. Even with our differences, I've always respected you, Crowley. You're the only other animal, never mind my species, to come close to what I am.'

'I'm nothing like you.' Crowley spat the words out, blood dripping from his lips.

'Of course not, but you might have been.'

The dark cat grabbed him by the ears, dragging him through the dirt and dumping him near a chair. Crowley strained to see what was around him before hearing a familiar voice.

'You'll pay for this, Darkstar.'

'Bukowski?' Crowley dragged his body beside the duck, who was tied to a pole. Next to him, secured to a chair, was Emma. He breathed a sigh of relief that she was alive. Darkstar stood to one side, and somebody else was in the room.

'I'm sorry, little cat. That was beyond my control.' Pandora knelt close to Crowley's head and stroked his coat. 'Your feline compatriot is a bit of a psychopath.'

Her voice was strangely soothing as the bruises formed across his stomach and back, seeing something in the redheaded woman's eyes that wasn't there in the cottage.

His jaw ached as he spoke. 'You survived, then?'

Pandora slipped her arms under his body and lifted him. 'I'll make sure they don't hurt you again.' She carried him to the corner of the room, laid him on fresh straw, and closed the cage door. 'You'll be okay here. Get some rest while I speak to Emma.'

Crowley was surprised at the genuine concern in her voice. She left him and went to sit opposite Emma, who appeared to be asleep.

'Your kindness surprises me,' Darkstar said to the redhead.

'I'm a complicated woman,' she said before turning her attention to Emma. 'You can open your eyes, sweetie. I know you're awake. We did this before in the cottage, remember?' She lit a cigarette, ignoring the scowl on the ebony cat's face.

'How did you know?' Emma said.

Pandora laughed between taking drags on the fag, the corners of her mouth curling upwards into a beguiling smile. 'I have many talents.'

Emma's lips trembled. 'Why are you doing this?'

'Saving your life? That's twice now – you're welcome.'

Crowley stared at the black cat sitting near Pandora and wondered which of them was in charge.

Emma glared at Darkstar. 'Saving it for what? To hand us over to him so he can beat the life out of Crowley.'

'I'm sorry it happened, but everything should be okay now,' Pandora said.

Crowley glanced around the room, seeing Bukowski tied next to Emma, but couldn't see the pooch. 'Where's Chirpy?' he shouted.

The redhead shrugged. 'The Chihuahua? I'm sorry, but we couldn't find her in the rubble.' She shook her head. 'Those Rising Sun boys and girls got too excited with their explosives.' She sighed. 'They were only supposed to blow the bloody doors off.'

He closed his eyes. Sorrow rushed through him as he stared at Emma's tear-stained face. 'Then Chirpy's death is on you. And for what, a serum you still haven't found?' He dragged as much resistance as he could and spat it at her.

'You mean this?'

Crowley's heart sank at her words. His vision adjusted to the light in the barn, leaning forward to peer at what she held. Something about it didn't look right. Then he recognised what it was: it was the wrong colour.

Darkstar didn't hide the joy in his voice. 'Yes, we don't need your serum anymore. We have an upgraded version.'

'You see, Emma,' Pandora said, 'what I have here is the original Doolittle. What you have is something different. What you have is a serum; this is a virus.' She let that sink in and winked at Crowley.

He grasped why the liquid was a different colour. 'It's part of Wells's original experiments?' It all made perfect sense to him now, apart from why they were there.

'Do you know why the mice called it Doolittle?' Darkstar was enjoying himself.

Emma shook her head. 'Amaze me.'

'Because it did nothing but fry the brain of any poor human who took it. It did little, you see.'

Crowley didn't and frowned. The ebony cat laughed, sounding like a freight train heading down the track at a hundred miles an hour, one just about to roll right over them all. 'What?'

The dark cat was amused. 'Mice - they lack any real imagination.'

'We gave it another name at the Project.' To Crowley's annoyance, Pandora and Darkstar worked as a double act. 'We called it Mush Juice; far more appropriate, don't you think?'

'You stole this from your employers?' Emma said.

'It's probably best to call them my former employers. I have new partners now.'

'Why?' Emma asked her.

Pandora finished her fag and dropped it into the straw at her feet. For one second, Crowley thought she'd done it on purpose to set the place aflame, the embers caressing the delicate yellow on the ground and threatening to spring to violent life before she squashed it stillborn with her shoe.

'I have no love for humanity, Emma. Well, most of it anyway.' She pulled her chair closer until her knees were touching Emma's. 'You know I've grown fond of you so quickly, but the rest of them are no concern of mine. If these animals want to mush a few million brains in this country, I won't stand in their way.'

Crowley glared at her, peering at the scars on her cheeks and wishing he'd done more to this woman in her home. 'You're mad.'

'I thought about doing something similar before I met any of you interesting creatures, but I never had an opportunity like this,' she said. 'Some people need punishing for what they did to me, but it will take far too long, even if I could find them all. This strange cat and stranger bull have the perfect distribution system to spread the virus nationwide. That's my revenge done in one fell swoop.' She smiled at Emma as she dragged on the cigarette. 'You'll be safe here while the troops drop it into the nation's water supply. Then they'll start using their contacts to ship it to the rest of the world.' There was no emotion in Pandora's voice.

Emma strained at her bonds with no success. 'You don't have enough of it for that.'

Pandora waved the phial at her. 'Didn't your little cat explain this to you? No matter how vast, you only need a small amount to infect any liquid. What I have here is more than enough, never mind that the Rising Sun has a sample to examine and then duplicate.' She grinned at Crowley. 'Thanks to my old mucker Wyatt Wells, this world will soon belong to the animal kingdom.'

Emma glared at her. 'You'd hurt millions of innocent

people for revenge? What about my sister and mother and those you worked with? You must have liked some of them?'

Pandora took another drag on the cigarette. 'The ends justify the means.'

Emma's head dropped to her chest.

Crowley spoke to Darkstar. 'Why are we here if you have what you need?'

'I have to punish you, old friend, and stop your human from disrupting our plans. You'd all be dead if it weren't for our new alliance. You can thank her for that.' Pandora gave a theatrical bow. 'And now we must be going,' he said as he went to Crowley's cage. 'If I see you again, the redheaded woman won't be able to save you.' The dark cat slipped into the shadows and disappeared.

Emma gazed at Pandora. 'You don't need to do this,' she said, her voice on the verge of cracking, her eyes pleading.

Pandora followed her animal partner. 'I'm sure we'll meet again, Emma, but one last thing: did you enjoy our kiss?' She didn't wait for a reply.

Crowley stared at them as they left, wondering how he'd got everything so wrong.

Chapter 57

Pandora: Deal of the Century

Pandora left the barn with her mind full of Emma: the grace of that white hair, the taste of peach on her lips as they kissed, and the aroma of sweat and excitement as she dragged her out of the Atlas mansion.

She shook her head, but it was no good. Emma Crowley fascinated her, and she wasn't sure why. She wasn't one for crushes. They were things that people had for her, not what she had for others. Brief dalliances were fine. But something which tugged at the heart?

She'd watched the video taken outside the prison dozens of times, stared at the data from the police files, and even hacked all of Emma's social media accounts. It was to understand the mindset of the woman she searched for, but all it did was create a fascination with Ms Emma Crowley. And she felt remorse for punching Emma in the head at the cottage.

It all came back to that cottage. Pandora had never unburdened her life like that before. Even when the shrinks at the Project asked her to, she only told them the slightest details: that her parents were horrible to her, never providing specific information. With Emma in the room, she couldn't help herself.

When the dark cat arrived with his beasts, she grasped the unexpected opportunity presented by the bizarre situation. She accepted it was impossible to punish those who had hurt her without assistance, and the fat cat and his vicious army of animals had fallen straight into her lap. All she had to do was convince him. Pandora had no doubt she could talk him around because she had a foolproof offer for him. And that partnership led to the farm.

'It's only a crush,' she said and lit a cigarette. There were many other things to deal with before she returned to her thoughts about Emma. 'Thank you, Wyatt, for allowing me to punish those who hurt me.' Her laugh hurt her ribs. 'And I can do it all in one fell swoop.'

She raised her hand, not thinking about the negative impact her alliance with Darkstar would have on many others. Her eyes scanned for the dark cat with no luck, realising he could be anywhere in the early morning gloom. Ever since Pandora had first encountered the cat, she'd wanted to tie a white cloth around his waist and had been on the verge of suggesting it on more than one occasion until seeing his scowl.

As she strode through the farm, her mind returned to the events at the cottage that had brought them together. Some birds flew into the room first; those left after their kamikaze compatriots had smashed the window into a thousand pieces. It impressed her when the two giant Alsatians followed, Darkstar sitting on a dog's back like a Valkyrie riding into Valhalla. She had to make sure the death symbolism wasn't taken to its logical conclusion.

That was when she made her deal.

'I can give you what you want, but you must let them go.'

Pandora sat at the end of the sofa, returning to her previous spot and a fresh cigarette. Both large hounds stared at her, teeth baring and saliva dripping. She knew they could smell fear, but none was on her. She ignored the aroma of wet dogs assaulting her senses.

The dark cat jumped from the dog and crept closer to her. 'And why should I do that?'

Pandora imagined stretching over, putting her arms around his neck and squeezing the life from his ebony body. The thought made her smile, but she couldn't defend herself from the mutts.

She studied the room, stared at all the Crowley family pictures, and wondered what it must have been like to have such an idyllic upbringing. She returned her gaze to the cat and the dangerous hounds.

'Nobody will have to die because you'll get what you want.' She recognised the lack of trust in his face and didn't blame him.

'Where are the others?' The dogs never took their eyes off her while the dark cat asked the question.

She had to play it right, or none of them would escape from the cottage unscathed. 'They're on their way to the garage at the back of the house. There's an old car there which they hope to use.'

'Follow the vehicle from a safe distance. Make sure you're not spotted, and don't lose them,' Darkstar instructed the gulls in the room. Pandora watched them fly through the broken window. 'Why are you betraying them like this?' he asked her.

She crossed her legs and took another drag on her cigarette to annoy the dark cat.

'I'm not betraying them. I'm their saviour; they just don't know it yet.'

'And what do I get in return?'

'You'll get a virus that will fry the brain of anybody who drinks it. It infects any liquid you put it in, and you only need a tiny drop to corrupt one large reservoir.'

The most unlikely of alliances were born at that point.

It was also how she found herself back at the Project, supposedly to deliver the report on the fire at Wyatt's house and hand in the last of his experiments. However, she'd kept that for herself. What she had for her former employers was a phial of tap water mixed with a sweet concoction of elements, including arsenic, radium, aluminium, copper, lead and mercury. She hoped it would fool the Project's experts long enough for her to get what she wanted. She also crushed a few painkillers into it, plus something illegal she acquired in a dodgy nightclub.

'It certainly looks different from the others.' Dr Athena Cross peered at the phial of clear liquid Pandora handed her deep inside the secure scientific unit of the Project.

'Wyatt told me it was his improved recipe.'

'Well, let's see what this is like by comparing it to the previous batch. Can you hand me one from the cabinet behind you, Pandora?'

She couldn't believe her luck at being handed such a stroke of fortune. She removed the first sample, placing her body between the view of the shelves and Cross. Then she pretended to move forward and close the door, using the opportunity to grab the second phial. When she closed the cabinet, she tried to slip one of the phials into the outside pocket of her jacket, but Cross shifted suddenly, knocking Pandora's arm. The serum headed to the floor. Pandora watched it fall and cursed inside her head.

Dr Cross moved like a gymnast, catching the phial between her fingers.

Pandora whistled and slipped the other one into her jacket. 'Well done, doc.'

'Years of playing volleyball have honed my reflexes to perfection,' Cross said as she placed the fifth version of Wyatt's serum into the chemical analysis pod. She took what was supposed to be version six and put it into the other analyser. 'I wonder if this is as potent as his earlier versions?' She gazed at the serum as it moved inside the machine. 'It's amazing how one small drop can replicate quickly within its liquid environment.'

'You're not bothered by the dangers?' Pandora asked.

The doctor shrugged. 'Science should always go where others fear to tread. This should take about twenty minutes. Do you want to stay around for the results?'

Pandora shook her head. She left the room and headed upstairs, using her key card to enter the security doors. Nobody spoke to her, and she avoided eye contact with everyone.

It was a journey up two flights of stairs and along three corridors, the jagged movement of the phial moving around in her pocket equal to the fluttering in her chest. Pandora allowed herself the luxury of thinking about the next part of her grand plan as she approached the exit.

Who should I warn not to drink the water?

She failed to notice the people approaching her.

'What are you doing, Pandora?'

The voice froze her to the spot. She turned to see the Director and the security guards on either side. The older woman was her usual unemotional self, her face a blank slate paler than a polar bear in a snowstorm.

However, the men were twitchy, hands by their sides moving far too much for Pandora's liking. She raced through the possibilities of who she'd have to take out first to escape. She grinned at the Director, flicking her red hair to the side as if possessed with a lifetime of insouciance when, in reality, she scanned the route to the exit and calculated her odds of getting out in one piece. They weren't promising.

'I've had nothing to eat all day,' she said as her stomach grumbled.

'Are you leaving before handing me your latest report?'

'I tried your office, but you weren't there,' she lied.

'That's because I was down here. Come, we can use an interview suite.'

Director Adam walked past her, and Pandora considered her chances of escape if she moved to the door and kept on running. She pondered the improbable scenarios for success while a hand rested on her arm. She was surprised to see the Director holding on to her.

'Do you have any sandwiches in your office?' she asked her boss.

'I've got something important to tell you,' Adam said while leading her through the door and into one of the Project's auxiliary rooms, populated by a single table surrounded by half a dozen chairs. It was spotlessly clean. Adam took the first chair and told her to sit.

'Good news?' she asked, not caring what it was but wanting to keep the other woman distracted as long as possible. Her right hand was on the phial like she was holding a hot coal.

The Director poured herself a glass of water and drank

half. Pandora imagined it was infected with the virus, picturing the Director's brain melting before her.

'Yes. I want to welcome you back to active duty. How do you feel about that?'

Pandora slipped into the chair opposite the Director and wondered if she'd escape the building before Dr Cross completed her analysis.

Chapter 58

Pandora: A Simple Plan

Pandora stared at the clock on the wall. Ten minutes had passed since Cross had started her analysis. She had ten minutes to get out of the room and the building. And the Director was not known for her brevity.

Pandora's tongue was like a carpet in the desert. 'Is this because you're happy with the job I've done with Wyatt?'

She shifted a little in the chair, wanting to stand but knowing it would look strange to the Director, that it would appear as if she were nervous. And Pandora Halcyon never got nervous. Her voice was calm, but the tension at the back of her throat sucked all the moisture from her body.

'Yes. Please let me know your news on Professor Wells. My latest report is there was a fire at his home.'

Pandora knew the Project would have access to the police reports, but she also trusted her ability to lie convincingly. 'His house was ablaze when I arrived. I retrieved the last of his experiments, but that was all I could rescue.' It wasn't a complete untruth.

'And what happened to Wells?'

She stared at the Director, trying to decipher what was

happening behind those dull brown eyes. 'I couldn't find any sign of life in the house. I searched for him, but because of the heat, it was impossible to check everywhere.'

She gripped the phial and twisted her hips in the chair. She'd never be free again if they discovered what really happened.

'It was courageous of you to go inside, Pandora. You've shown great dedication to our cause. The police report said the heat was so intense it melted everything in the building, probably because of the many exotic chemicals Wells had. It was a good job you rescued the last of his work. We can only hope he created something special with his final batch.'

'I was trying to save his life,' Pandora said to irritate the people she worked for. Director Adam wore the expression of a blank slab. She smiled at the thought of the virus working its magic on everyone in that building.

'I think it's time for you to return to more important duties than surveillance and collection. Lulu has missed you.'

I can't even warn Lulu.

Her heart fluttered, and it surprised her.

She's only a colleague.

Pandora's nails dug into her palms. 'Thank you, Director; I look forward to it.'

She was desperate to leave, pressure running through her legs as she waited for dismissal. The clock on the wall said it was less than five minutes before Cross would realise the phial was useless.

'Take a couple of days off, and I'll send you the details of your next assignment.'

Pandora smiled at the news as a trickle of blood stained her skin. She'd have no time to spare once they discovered what she'd done. However, she'd be heading for her rendezvous with the dark cat by then, and they wouldn't think of searching for her on that farm. She knew Darkstar didn't trust her, having noticed the birds following her to the Project since leaving the cottage, but the ebony cat had also provided her with an address where she could hide from the Project.

'Thank you, Director.' She stood to leave, deliberating if she'd forgotten anything, before closing the door on the woman who'd given her a new calling in life. She didn't look back and headed for the exit. There was less than a minute before Cross finished her work.

Outside, Pandora hurried to her scooter, breathing a sigh of relief into the afternoon wind. She got her mobile and turned on the GPS before entering the address Darkstar had given her. She attached the phone to the front of the bike, slipped her helmet on, and checked how long the journey would take - less than thirty minutes. She gave the Project one last look before setting off, thinking about how disappointed Director Adam would be when her staff delivered the bad news.

Then she pictured Adam's brain turning to mush.

The drive to the farm was uneventful. The birds overhead still followed her, but it didn't matter. Once through the main gates, other watchers, including rabbits, ran alongside as she rode down the path. There were cows and horses in the fields who observed her journey, and when she reached the front, a posse of fierce-looking dogs whom she was sure would eat her whole given half the chance.

Pandora got off the bike and strode to the door. It opened for her before she could even touch the faded wood.

Standing in the doorway was a man who looked as worn and tired as an old sofa.

'Darkstar said you'd be coming. My name is Stoker, and this is our farm.'

She watched him straighten his back as he pulled in his stomach and stuck out his chest. Pandora was used to men of all ages trying to impress her to no avail. However, she was sorry for this one, recognising in him a troubled childhood similar to hers; something burned behind his eyes that appeared all too familiar.

Where are all these disturbing emotions coming from?

'You must meet our leader, the Bullfather.'

Pandora smiled at Stoker and watched him melt before her. Whatever promises he'd made to these animals and their cause, she could get him to break as easily as taking candy from a baby.

She touched his arm as he showed her inside, feeling the tremors beneath his skin rippling through him. It was clear they had once used the place as the primary family room of the farmhouse. Still, she noticed somebody had removed or shoved the furniture to the side, so the biggest space had been set aside for piles of plush, comfortable carpets. Laid in the middle of them was the Bullfather. Then the great bull pushed his body to its full height. She gasped.

He stood nearly seven feet tall, his torso rippling with more muscles than an obsessive bodybuilder. She gazed at the impressive beast. If he fell on top of her, she wouldn't be getting back up in one piece — if at all.

The bull stared at her while Darkstar crept between its tree trunk legs and peered at her. She was about to speak when a raven flew in and landed on the Bullfather's head. Pandora stood there, dumbfounded for the first time in her life.

'Do you have what we want?'

Pandora continued to stare at the great bull's striking face, but the words didn't come from him, only from the raven. She produced the phial so they could all see it.

'You're sticking to that plan you told me at the cottage?'

Darkstar nodded. 'What do you know about breaking into a heavily secured building?'

She scanned the room for somewhere to sit, finding a tattered old sofa pushed into the far corner. She slipped into the middle seat and removed the box from her jacket. The dark cat, great bull and annoyed-looking raven glared at her as she pulled the last cigarette from its container.

'You've hit the jackpot, lads. Tell me where we're going, and I'll find the plans online and show you exactly how to get inside.'

She blew smoke into the air steadily over the next hour, occasionally winking at Stoker and looking forward to seeing Emma again.

Chapter 59

Crowley: Rescue Me

Crowley sat slumped in his prison, willing his body to recover from the beating Darkstar had given him. He watched them leave the barn, the redheaded woman and the ebony cat, separate but together, human and animal wrapped up in their special blanket of confidence. From the corner of his cage, he saw Emma in the chair, only the ropes around her hands and her back stopping her from falling forward. Next to her was Bukowski muttering something under his breath.

He was in constant pain, but his mind worked overtime. 'Emma, can you hear me?'

She'd been awake when Pandora spoke to her, but he was worried she might have succumbed to exhaustion.

'How are you feeling, Crowley?' Bukowski said.

'How's Emma?' he asked, more concerned about her than anything else.

'I think she's fallen asleep. I watched her when the redhead was talking, and she looked devastated. I've been trying to pull myself out of this rope, but it's too tight. Is there any chance of you getting out of that cage?'

'I've tried. The lock has a simple latch, but it's on my other side, and I can't reach around to get it. Our only shot is if Emma can get out of her bonds. Can you wake her?'

'I'll try,' Bukowski said. Within the confines of the rope which bound him, he stood up as tall as he could, pushing his back into the pole and flicking his wing out as far as possible, stretching his feathers to the limit until they pressed against Emma's leg. He kept fluttering them, increasing the speed, until he got a reaction from her.

'Are we alone?' Emma said.

'They left thirty minutes ago,' Crowley replied. 'It's just the three of us, with no way out.'

'Then what's that noise?'

He thought she was delirious and regretted asking Bukowski to wake her. Then he heard the sounds of tiny feet pattering along the ground near his cage.

The duck pulled his wing back. 'I hear it as well.'

'Can you see what it is?'

Crowley feared Darkstar might have left some animals behind to clear up loose ends. If it were a group from his rat army, they wouldn't last long in their current condition.

There was urgency in Emma's voice as she strained against the ropes. 'No, but it's near you.'

He wasn't worried about himself, but the others were defenceless. He would at least have a fighting chance since they'd have to open the cage to get to him.

There wasn't much room in his confinement, so he pushed his legs against the metal and readied to spring forward as soon as it opened. He wanted to call out to the others but resisted the urge as the door swung away from him, and he moved as fast as he could, aiming for the shadow outside the cage. He hit something warm and wet as he rolled with the intruder across the floor to land near Emma's feet.

'I missed you as well, my friend,' the little dog said. Chirpy was underneath Crowley, and the two friends were breathing hard.

'Are you a ghost, little dog?' Bukowski asked.

'You're alive,' Crowley said. He couldn't contain the joy of seeing her again, smiling despite the pain rippling through him. He stepped away from her, and she stood. 'But how are you here?'

'First, we have to release the others.

Chirpy ran to Bukowski, chewing through the ropes. Within a minute, the duck was free, and Chirpy set her sights on Emma's restraints.

'I still need a drink,' Bukowski said.

'You must lean backwards and down for me to get to them, Emma,' Chirpy said.

'No problem,' she replied.

The dog's tongue skimmed across her skin as her teeth ripped through the rope, canine saliva dripping onto her hands as the material weakened to where Emma snapped the last strands apart. Then she turned around and scooped the little dog into her arms, hugging the breath from her as she gave her thanks. She placed Chirpy on the floor before grabbing Crowley and Bukowski together.

'We're not free yet,' Crowley said.

Emma nodded. 'At least we're safe.' When she let him go, she asked Chirpy about her miraculous appearance in the barn. 'Do you remember what happened at the Atlas house?'

The pooch was the calmest Crowley had seen her since that first meeting at the AA gathering.

'I was next to you when something loud exploded in my

ears, and I fell. Pain rippled through me when I hit the floor. I couldn't see much because of the smoke. Then, human legs came towards me. I wanted to get up but couldn't because a chair had fallen on my feet. I tried to shout, but the words wouldn't come. Smoke was in my lungs, and I thought I was about to choke, pain hitting me as I struggled to breathe. Then someone picked me up, and I was out of the room and breathing again.'

'Did you see who it was?' Emma asked.

'No. They ran out through the corridor and dumped me into the boot of a car, never saying a word. I tried to shout but was dizzy, and everything went black.'

'And then?' Crowley asked.

'The next thing I know is I woke up underneath some straw in this barn. I saw what Darkstar did to you, my friend. I wanted to do something but was too scared.' She hung her head in shame, her voice trembling as she spoke.

'Don't be. You did the right thing by staying quiet. If you hadn't, all of us would be in captivity, and there would be no stopping Darkstar and the redheaded woman.'

'It must have been Pandora,' Emma said. 'She brought Chirpy here.'

'Why would she do that?' Crowley asked.

'So Chirpy would do what she's done – set us all free.'

He had his doubts. 'I find it hard to believe.'

Emma appeared confused as well by the turn of events. 'I don't know what she's up to, but she's the only one who would've rescued Chirpy and left her here.'

'Maybe she just wants to harm all the other humans.' Bukowski said what Crowley was thinking. 'Remember what she said at the cottage? What a terrible childhood her parents inflicted upon her – that must have messed her head up.'

'Of course it did,' Emma replied. 'But that doesn't mean she'd do something as dreadful as what Darkstar wants. I don't believe it.'

Crowley went to her. 'Let's face it, Emma. We know little about her. Everything she said could've been lies to manipulate us into doing what she wants.'

He didn't care what the redhead's motivations were. His primary intention was to thwart Darkstar. But he wondered about Emma.

She rubbed at her wrists. 'It couldn't have been anybody else but Pandora.'

'Do you want to find your mother?' Crowley said.

She nodded. 'I do, but there's no time. We have to stop them first.'

'But we don't know where they went,' Bukowski said.

'When they left, they spoke about heading to the nearest reservoir,' Chirpy mentioned.

Emma glanced around them. 'Okay, I know where that is. We must find a car and get out of here in one piece. Bukowski, if you slip outside, could you fly up for some reconnaissance?'

'I'm already on it.'

The duck ran towards the door, the others following behind. Emma got there first, placing her head against the wood to listen for any noises outside. After a few minutes, she pushed the door open enough for Bukowski to slip out and soar upwards.

'Make it quick and then return,' she said as he lifted into the air.

'What do we do when we find them?' Crowley asked.

'Whatever we can to stop them,' she replied while Bukowski flew over the farmhouse. 'We can't let that virus get into the water.'

He pictured the hundreds of thousands who would be infected. The reservoir wasn't far from the farm, but they were at least thirty minutes behind Darkstar. Pandora and the ebony cat could already be at the top of the structure.

As that thought ran through his head, Bukowski flew back. He landed at the front of the barn.

'The place is deserted. I don't know about the land beyond the farmhouse, but there are no humans or animals within five hundred yards of every side, and when I swooped down to look through the windows, it was the same inside.'

'They must've moved the Bullfather,' Crowley said. 'It can only mean they've taken him to the reservoir because he wants to witness his grand achievement.'

Emma was outside and scanning the area. 'Did you spot any vehicles?'

'There are a couple of cars around this corner. I flew close to them but couldn't see any keys inside.'

'Don't worry about that; we won't need them.' She ran around the corner, Crowley and the others following her, heading for the blue Volkswagen. The first bit of good fortune was finding it unlocked; the second was the keys in the glove compartment. 'Perhaps our luck is in, after all.'

They joined her, all three jumping into the back when she opened the door.

'Or maybe somebody left this for us as a gift,' Crowley said.

But were they already out of time?

Chapter 60

Emma: Sucker Punch

They completed the drive to the reservoir in silence. When they arrived, they stood by the side of the car, Emma staring across the expanse of pale blue water, knowing one drop in there and all the other reservoirs would see the start of Darkstar's attack against humanity.

She wrapped her scarf around her neck for protection as the winds sought her out and conspired to steal what little warmth she had left. The birds chatted to each other high in the sky, and she missed the days when those sounds would have been a mystery to her, now wondering if what they said was driven by the scheming of the dark cat.

'There it is,' Crowley said, nodding towards the back entrance to the reservoir. It was the largest in the country and an obvious place for Darkstar to drop the serum into the nation's water supply. They'd have to go down and then up to reach the pathway at the top.

'I don't see any guards.' Emma peered at the sweep of the dam as it cut into the flesh of nature surrounding it, human geometry forced into the environment. Grey brick upon grey brick reached up from the ground, enormous steps heading towards the gods. The trees had their green and brown arms down by their sides, like drunks loitering outside a brewery.

'Darkstar's army will be here somewhere,' Crowley said. 'So keep your eyes peeled.'

'There's movement on top of the reservoir,' Emma replied, taking her phone and turning on the camera. She adjusted the lens to zoom in on what was moving in the distance: two bodies and something smaller at their feet. They were blurred shapes on her digital screen, but she didn't doubt who they were. Emma's heart sank. 'It's Darkstar, Pandora and some bloke.'

'A human?' Crowley said.

'There's a path here that'll take us to where they are.' Emma had checked the area when they arrived, picking out the route they needed. 'There's a fence, but we can get over that.' There was no sign of anybody else apart from those on the reservoir wall.

'What shall we do?' Crowley asked.

Shadows crept over Emma's face. 'We can't get there in time to stop them. All they have to do is drop the serum in the water, and they've won.'

Once Darkstar saw them coming, any one of the three could throw the virus into the reservoir before they got there. She sank to the ground, her back resting against a stack of barrels. Bits of rough wood stabbed into her, but she welcomed the discomfort; it was a small price to pay for her utter failure. Maybe she should have gone to her mother after all.

I've failed her as well.

'We have to try,' Crowley said, pushing his face to hers.

He was right, but she couldn't shake the impending doom about to overwhelm her.

Bukowski waddled over to Emma and peered into her eyes. 'We can distract them while you make your way there.'

She stared at him, amazed at how brave these new friends of hers were. 'How?'

'I've talked to Chirpy about this, and we have a plan.'

The duck glanced at the dog, and the little Chihuahua jumped onto Bukowski's back. Bukowski tensed his legs, flapped his wings, and lifted them into the air. In this strangest of times, she could only marvel at the sight of the flying duck carrying the little dog into the cloudless sky.

'Be careful,' Crowley shouted.

Chirpy stared at him. 'You were right, my friend; sometimes it is good to be small.'

Crowley and Emma looked at each other in amazement. She lifted herself as the dog and duck fluttered away into the distance.

'Let's go,' Crowley said and sprinted down the path. She ran after the cat and hoped they'd get there in time.

Chapter 61

Pandora: Smoke

Pandora caressed the cigarette between her fingers, rolling it in every possible way before slipping it between her lips, wishing it was Emma's mouth she tasted again. With her other hand, she took the phial from her pocket and peered through its clear liquid to the dark cat on the other side.

They'd left the Bullfather and his guard of foxes down below in perfect position to see the glass when it smashed into the water. The raven had glared at her while she was with them, but the great bull ignored her as if she was something beneath him.

She noticed Stoker staring at her. She winked at him, amused as he blushed and turned away.

'Are you nervous, Chuck?' He flinched and stared at the ground. 'There's no reason to be. There's no one left to stop us, and even if there was, who would worry about two people and a cat up here?'

She had sympathy for Stoker. At their first meeting at his farmhouse, she recognised the pain he was trying to hide, identified in him a troubled childhood as painful as her own.

'I'm not worried,' he said.

She wondered if his motivations were the same as her own. 'You understand what's about to happen here?'

'Yes.' He found his voice. 'Everybody who drinks from this water will end up brain damaged.' His face was an unmoving picture.

'And you're okay with that?'

'Are you?' He'd also discovered his courage from some-where. She ignored his question and turned her attention to the cat.

'I suppose you want to do the honours.' She held the phial towards him, curious how he'd catch it.

'You think I can't hold it in my paw?' The irritation in his voice was no surprise to her. The ebony feline hadn't truly welcomed her into their activist group since they'd come to their arrangement in the Crowley cottage. She didn't care; it was a marriage of convenience that had already produced one colossal benefit: her disgust of animals bordering on phobia had withered away the longer she was around them. She even considered getting a pet once it was over.

That alcoholic duck was cute.

Pandora stared at Darkstar's annoyed face and threw the phial in his direction. Stoker gasped at seeing the flying glass, but the big cat pushed his body onto his hind legs and caught the liquid as if plucking fruit from a tree.

'I never doubted you,' she said as she exhaled a great fume of toxic smoke into the air, watching it swirl above her, transforming from ethereal wisps into a solid form resem-bling a twisted bird. Then she saw movement above them.

She grinned at the sight of the drunken duck flying

towards them and sitting on its back like a jockey was the tiny Chihuahua. Pandora's heart skipped a beat at the realisation Emma couldn't be too far away.

'What's that?' Stoker said.

Bukowski landed at Darkstar's feet, and Chirpy jumped off. The pooch slid across the ground like an ice skater, snatched the phial from the dark cat and ran past him.

'Come on!' Chirpy shouted at Bukowski, unaware that Stoker stood next to him. The Guardian scooped the little dog into his arms, and Darkstar smiled.

Pandora turned away from the drama behind her, peering across the water, waiting for Emma to appear.

Chapter 62

Emma: Running up that Hill

Emma and Crowley never stopped for breath as they motored down the path, watching Bukowski's shadow move across the grass before them. The muscles in her legs came alive as her feet bounced off the ground, her mind racing through their options when they reached the top of the reservoir. If the serum were in the water, there'd be nothing they could do but inform the authorities. That's if they'd believe her as they put her behind bars.

Crowley was at her side as they approached the barrier intended to keep the public out. 'Can you see what's happening up there?'

She was breathing hard. 'Bukowski and Chirpy landed, but I can't see where they went.' She grabbed her chest, hoping she hadn't endangered the dog and duck. She glanced at the fence. 'Do you want me to lift you over that once I get my breath back?'

He let out a feline laugh as he launched himself at the metal rings in the barrier. His claws caught the empty spaces halfway up and climbed over. Emma stared in amazement.

'Your turn,' he said.

She slipped her fingers into those same spaces and pulled herself up somewhat less gracefully than he had, scrambling over the top without stabbing herself in the gut. She rushed to the concrete path once she dropped to the other side.

Crowley jogged just behind her. 'What's the plan when we get there?'

Emma watched her feet as she ran. 'Get the serum to Bukowski so he can fly away from here.'

'And then?' he asked.

She stopped halfway up to catch her breath. 'Take the virus to the authorities and tell them everything after we get the Doolittle to my mother.' She still didn't know where he'd hidden the last of it, but there wasn't time to ask. 'Then I'll probably have to return to prison.'

'I'll admit I took the jewels from the museum,' he said.

She glanced ahead of her. 'Let's worry about that later. Come on.'

They ran up the makeshift path, striding next to each other, friends on the most important mission of their lives. She was glad no other animals were around them, expecting Darkstar's spies and helpers to be everywhere.

'How do you plan to handle the redhead?'

Emma didn't answer his question. 'What will you do about Darkstar?'

He never slowed for a second, his reply arriving as quickly as his little legs took him up that hill. 'The only thing I can do. Kill him.'

She shuddered at the thought.

As they got closer to the top, the unmistakable drawl of Pandora's voice drifted towards her. Emma couldn't decide whether to punch or kiss the other woman.

Maybe it was a bit of both.

Chapter 63

Pandora: Lovecats

'Throw the dog and the serum over the edge,' Darkstar told Stoker. The big man's eyes narrowed at the words. Pandora grinned at the ruthlessness of the dark cat. He would make a fine pet once this was over.

Stoker's voice trembled. 'We're supposed to protect animals.'

'We've talked about this, Charles – some will have to be sacrificed for the good of the many. You know how important this moment is to all of us.'

Darkstar's calmness impressed Pandora. The Guardian was the exact opposite.

'You made me follow Wells for months when he took this dog to the park at night, and I came to love this little girl. I can't throw her to certain death.' Chirpy had hold of the serum while Stoker stroked her head as if she'd been his pet all his life.

'Fine,' Darkstar replied. 'Give her to the redheaded woman, and she can do what you're incapable of.'

Pandora stared at Stoker. No matter how much he claimed to love the pup, he wanted her more: it was in his eyes.

'I'll be gentle,' she said as she blew smoke in his direction. But she made no move to take the dog from him, enjoying the uncomfortable look on his startled face.

'No more animals should die,' he said. 'I thought that's why we were doing this.'

She observed the drama as she drew the life from the cigarette, letting it simmer to its last embers and on the point of extinction. She wondered how this protest would play out and had forgotten about Emma.

'All we have planned will be for nothing if you don't do this now.'

There was barely concealed disdain in Darkstar's voice as he spoke. Not for the first time, Pandora marvelled at the sight of a human chastised by an animal. Stoker held the little dog as if it were his own beating heart plucked from his chest, his life dependent upon what was in his arms. She studied the mutt and wondered why it didn't just throw the glass to the ground and shatter Darkstar's plan into hundreds of tiny pieces.

I suppose it might not break.

'Do you serve the Bullfather?' the ebony feline asked the man. All he could do was nod in submission. 'Then you know what you should do. This is your chance to redeem yourself, not only to correct the wrongs of your family's farm, but to avenge thousands of years of humanity's cruelty to the animal world.'

There was power in his voice, natural leadership and the projection of complete and utter control. All mixed in with a modicum of fear, presenting a compelling cocktail.

He reminds me of Director Adam, only more ruthless.

She focused on the dark cat, speculating what Darkstar would have been like if he'd been born a human. She recognised herself in him, and she shivered. She switched her gaze from the feline machinations to Stoker, fascinated by the conflict in his eyes and the trembling on his lips. Pandora placed her hand on her heart and fought back her memories.

'Give me the dog, Charles. I promise I won't hurt her.'

She didn't believe her own words, pondering whether he would. Confused, he hesitated, split between protecting the pooch and doing what she asked. While he paused, Chirpy threw the phial to the sober duck.

'Fly away, Bukowski,' Chirpy shouted as Pandora laughed at the little duck and his reluctance to let the glass smash on the ground. Instead, he caught it in one feathered wing and sat there frozen in the headlights of Pandora's gaze.

She knelt and snatched the treasure from his grip. She winked at him as her mind went through all the potential scenarios for what would happen when Emma and her cat appeared. Then she had an awful thought that Emma was still tied up in the barn, and all that remained of the Crowley rebellion was this desperate bird and pitiful dog.

'You failed me, Charles.' Darkstar glared at Stoker. 'You failed the Bullfather; you failed us all. You're as bad as your father.' Disappointment punctured the dark cat's face. Anger sprang from that feline voice. Stoker dropped to his knees and sobbed. He was a broken man.

'Take my hand, Chuck,' Pandora said with as much sympathy as possible.

Before he replied, something landed on her back, and

she hit the ground like a weary boxer in the last round of a title fight, the glass phial stolen from her by a furry paw.

And all she pictured was being in that coffin as her parents threw the rats over her.

Chapter 64

Emma: Attack

As they crept to the top of the path, a thousand and one ideas swirled inside Emma's skull, none of which she found satisfying. A tightness gripped her heart as she pictured her dear mother, frail and weak, wondering where her daughter had gone.

That's if she still remembers me.

Exhaustion weighed heavily on her, but she resisted the urge to stop moving, knowing she had to stay alert. She longed to let her body and mind rest, if only for a little while.

She pressed against the cold concrete, her arms and legs like a praying mantis about to devour its quarry. Crowley was close to her, his fur standing upright as if an electric shock coursed through it. They paused in perfect unison, bodies tense and ready to pounce. Their eyes met in that moment of silence. Emma waited with every part of her crying out to spring forward and do something, do anything.

Emma's breath came in short, quiet gasps as her heart throbbed. Crowley let out the softest of growls, more felt than heard. She glanced at him, aware she should have told him to stay below and out of danger, knowing he would have refused.

She reached over to touch his face when she heard a familiar sound a few feet away.

'Take my hand, Chuck,' Pandora said.

Chuck had to be the bloke Emma saw from below, the one whose farm they were using to keep all the animals safe.

Pandora's voice melted Emma's limbs and liquefied her flesh, wondering how she could do something as terrible as poisoning the reservoir. The sounds from above washed over her.

She inched closer to Crowley and whispered to him. 'I'll go first, okay?'

He nodded. 'And do what? The redhead has the farmer with her. You can't overpower them both.'

Pain shifted through every sinew and bone as she fought against her doubts.

'I won't have to. I only need to distract them so you can help Bukowski get the serum and fly away.'

'And there's Darkstar to deal with,' he said.

'Yes. I'll leave him up to you. Are you up for handling him?

He smiled. 'I have before. If I'm lucky, I'll push him over the edge.'

Emma didn't like the dark cat, but was uncomfortable about killing him.

But what choice do we have? I might have to do the same to Pandora.

That grisly thought settled in her head as she realised it was now or never, looking at Crowley and signalling him to pounce.

They rushed forward together, human and cat, deter-mined to stop an atrocity. She saw Pandora first, then the tall man next to her. Pandora didn't appear shocked to see her, but she was taken aback when Crowley jumped up and snatched the phial from her hand.

In that frozen moment, Emma knocked the redhead to the ground. She straddled the other woman, expecting her to resist, but was surprised when she lay there unmoving.

'You've had this coming,' she said.

'I'm looking forward to it,' Pandora replied.

Chapter 65

Crowley: The Darkness

As Emma and Pandora gazed at each other, Crowley stared at the virus in his paw, his actions frozen, knowing all he had to do was to smash the glass, and all of this was over. Emma's hands moved towards the redheaded woman's face as he raised his paw high, smiling as he sensed a victory over the dark cat.

Then something hit his ginger fur, forcing him onto his side and the glass from his paw. Pain shot through him as he watched the phial roll away and land at the farmer's foot. The big man picked it up, and Crowley's spirits dropped as he stared into Darkstar's eyes.

'I think the humans have an expression for this – glutton for punishment, they call it.'

The ebony cat paced around him as he got back on his feet. 'It's not too late to stop this, Darkstar.'

'Of course it's too late, you fool. You came all this way for nothing, but I'll enjoy finally putting you out of your misery.'

He leapt at the dark cat's head, taking him by surprise and catching him on his right side with his claws. The ebony fur came away in a clump. When he landed, there was blood on his paw.

'You're right about one thing,' he said as the blood dripped from his fur. 'This will end here.'

Darkstar glared at him. 'Do you recall the first time we did this, old friend? We were deep in the forest all those years ago, and you refused to kill a human child, even though it was the only way for us to survive. All those who followed me survived. What happened to the ones who stayed with you?'

'What's the point of surviving just to become a monster?' Crowley said.

Darkstar's laughter echoed over the reservoir as the humans and the other animals watched the two cats. 'A monster? We live in a monstrous world, old friend. And whose fault is that?' He glanced at Emma. 'The humans, of course. They've had thousands of years to make this a better place, but all they do is kill each other and destroy everything around them. They're so ruthless they even obliterate the things that sustain them. They've had plenty of chances to do the right thing. Now it's our turn.'

'You're wrong,' Crowley said.

Darkstar shook his head. 'Keep the phial for me, Stoker. I'll have it from you once I finish with this mongrel.'

Crowley saw Emma behind him, but he couldn't see Bukowski. He had to get beyond the dark cat and retrieve the virus. Darkstar would try to overpower him with his weight; he'd learnt that lesson from their previous encounters. But it was Crowley's smaller size which gave him the advantage. If he didn't let the other cat take him by surprise, he'd use his superior speed to keep out of his reach.

'You won't succeed,' he said.

'This is it, my old friend,' Darkstar replied while

creeping towards him. 'After all that has passed between us over the years, one of us dies today.'

As Crowley prepared for the attack, Emma cried out behind him. He turned, losing sight of the dark cat. Then he heard enormous paws pounding towards him as Bukowski's shadow drifted over his head towards the humans.

Chapter 66

Emma: Reservoir Cats

Emma noticed a ginger-flecked torpedo launch itself into a black hole while she leaned down and touched Pandora's face. The tenderness of her skin glistened as she stared into her eyes. She forgot why they were there: the virus, her cat, the fate of humanity, and her sister. She even set aside thoughts about her mother. Pandora's hands were around her waist, and she didn't resist.

What am I doing?

'Well, this is great, but don't we have other things to do?' Pandora pushed her backwards and off her, forcing Emma to roll to one side. She hit something dark coming from the opposite direction.

'What?' she said.

'I ruined the moment, my sweet, but there's time for us to become more acquainted later. I want to see what that hunk of farm boy flesh will do when your lovely duck tries to take the phial from him.'

'You're infuriating,' she shouted, seeing Crowley fighting Darkstar and Bukowski landing on the man's head.

The human and bird became one giant joined-up beast while the cats leapt into the air as if struck by lightning.

'You're only saying it because it's true,' Pandora said, dashing past Emma and jumping over the two love cats to reach the bloke. The farmer dropped the phial, and it spun towards the ground. She watched it speed up, smiling as the glass was about to smash. That smile vanished as Pandora dived at the virus and caught it in one hand. Emma stared at her in horror. Pandora dangled her fingers over the side, and Emma couldn't stop her.

'No!' Emma shouted.

'I'd rather have your fingers in mine instead of this, Emma, but you should have recognised by now we have to let this little drama play out to the end.'

'You'll kill thousands,' Emma said.

Pandora shrugged. 'Yes, including all those people who hurt me. I think it's a fair trade-off. Don't you?'

'Of course not.' She held her hands out. 'I'll help you get justice for what happened to you, but not like this. This is savage, and you're nothing like that.'

'You don't know me, Emma. You've no idea who I am.'

She took a deep breath. 'There's something between us, Pandora. I can feel it, and I think you can as well. If you end this madness, we can get to know each other better.'

Pandora moved the phial between her fingers while touching the scars on her cheek.

'That is a tempting offer, Emma, very tempting indeed.'

Emma heard the cats fighting and hoped everything would be okay.

Then Pandora lifted her arm to toss the virus into the water.

Chapter 67

Crowley: The Enemy

Crowley stared at Darkstar. His bruises throbbed, and his muscles ached, thankful that Emma's fall had knocked the ebony cat to one side. He locked onto his enemy's gleaming eyes, their intensity burning through the pain in his battered body. He tasted blood, the air heavy with the aroma of the water hundreds of feet below them.

He jumped towards his enemy and punched him in the stomach. It was a repeat of the previous attack in the barn, only in reverse. Crowley's punch landed on Darkstar's abdomen with a solid thud, the sensation of the impact rippling through him.

The ebony cat tried to use his enormous bulk to smother Crowley, but the smaller cat danced around him, swerving and twisting to get in more punches. Everything passed in a blur, but he didn't stop until his paws ached, throwing rapid attacks like a pneumatic drill.

Darkstar was at the precipice of the reservoir, wheezing, his eyes burning with rage and pain. 'You'll have to kill me.'

Crowley took a step back, confident that Darkstar was spent, but didn't want to get too close to the edge. 'No need. Your plan has failed.'

'Are you sure? You should look behind you, old friend.'

That dark grin annoyed him. He turned to see Pandora with a cigarette in one hand and the phial in the other as she draped the virus over the edge. His heart sank as he gazed at Emma, glancing to see Darkstar's vast shape heading for him like an ebony shooting star.

He moved without thinking, throwing his body to the side and his paws up. His claws raked across the dark cat's face as they hit the ground together. Crowley rolled towards Emma while Darkstar twisted towards Pandora.

'You don't look good, partner.' Pandora blew smoke in the air as she stared at Darkstar. 'You appear to have lost an eye. Maybe I should call you Cyclops from now on?'

Crowley glared at his old enemy. His claws had left vicious marks as he'd dragged them across his face. That eye was nothing but blood and torn flesh.

'It doesn't matter,' Darkstar replied as he turned to Pandora. 'Give me the virus, and I'll end this.'

'No!' Emma shouted as Pandora dropped the phial into the one-eyed cat's right paw.

'Do what thou wilt shall be the whole of the Law,' Pandora said as Darkstar threw the virus over the edge.

Emma stared at in horror, Crowley in disbelief, but Bukowski acted, jumping over the side and diving towards the glass phial.

Crowley ran to the edge as the farmer grabbed the cat. 'It's over now,' Darkstar said.

'No!' Emma shouted.

Crowley's stomach churned, his heart ready to burst.

He watched Bukowski as he dived for the virus heading into the water.

Every human and animal eye was on the brave duck as he got closer and closer to the phial until he reached out with his beak.

And he missed.

Chapter 68

Emma: Endgame

Emma screamed as the glass smashed into the water. The pain in her head was intense, and she didn't realise Pandora had reached out to hold her hand. She wanted to pull away in disgust but could only turn and stare as Pandora grinned at her like a kid eating their first ice cream. Darkstar ran across the top of the reservoir.

'What news of the others, Stoker?'

The dark cat had a large red section on his face. The big man removed the phone from his pocket and checked something on the screen.

Emma glared at Pandora but didn't remove her hand. 'What have you done?'

'The little moggie and the strange bull wanted me to use the serum to make enough of a virus to infect every reservoir in the country. Then, I handed it to the good boys and girls in the House of the Rising Sun. The rest, as they say, is history.'

Emma gasped. 'You did what?'

'Just wait a minute,' Pandora said while squeezing Emma's fingers.

'There are no messages, and I can't get through to any of them,' Stoker said.

'And you won't,' Pandora replied. 'They'll have been rounded up by now.' She stepped away from the edge, pulling an unresisting Emma with her.

'What do you mean?' Darkstar asked as blood seeped from his face.

'Agents will have picked them up long ago. I gave them plenty of notice.'

The ebony cat's remaining eye burned red. 'You betrayed us?'

'Hardly,' she said. 'I wasn't with you in the first place.'

He crept towards her, his anger visible as dead flesh slithered down his face.

Bukowski returned and landed next to Chirpy. 'I failed.'

'No, you didn't,' Pandora replied.

Darkstar's eye had stopped bleeding, and a fine red puss was crusting over the socket. 'What was in that phial?'

'I changed my mind. It was ordinary water. I swapped it over, and the others, before we got here. Sorry, Chuck.' She stared at Stoker. Before she said anything else, Emma grabbed her waist and kissed her.

'Why didn't you tell me?' Emma said when she came up for air.

'A good agent never reveals their master plan until the end. And I wanted to tease you a bit.'

Darkstar glared at her. 'I'll have the Guardian kill you all.'

Pandora laughed at the dark cat's idle threat. 'No, you won't. He wouldn't hurt the dog for you earlier, so he won't do anything worse for you now. Plus, he's a little in love with me.' She smiled at Stoker as she spoke. 'Aren't you Chuck?'

The farmer blushed.

'It's over, Darkstar,' Crowley said.

'Chuck,' Pandora added, 'best you take Cyclops home before he loses more body parts.'

With no protest from Darkstar, he did as she instructed, picking him up before turning his back on the others.

'Shouldn't we do something about them?' Emma asked.

'There's nothing to do,' Pandora replied. 'We can't visit the police and tell them about a murderous cat and bull and their crime empire. They'll think we're mad.'

'What about your associates at the Project?'

'You mean my former colleagues? I sent agents to the other reservoirs with an anonymous message about domestic terrorists having samples of Wyatt's virus, and they were about to use it.'

'You killed Wells,' Emma said.

'Of course, I didn't.' Pandora frowned. 'We came to an arrangement, and I let him go, knowing the intense heat of the fire, with all the chemicals stored at his house, would be the perfect cover for no remains in the ashes. He's probably sitting on a beach somewhere talking to the fishes.'

'So where do we go from here?' Crowley joined them once Stoker carried Darkstar from the reservoir.

'I need to take the real Doolittle to my mother,' Emma said. 'It doesn't matter if the police are waiting for me. I'll return to prison as long as I can cure her.'

Pandora grabbed Emma and stared into her eyes. 'Do you trust me?'

Emma reflected on everything that had happened with the unusual redhead over the last few days: the violence, the apparent betrayal, and the suffering she'd put them through with switching the phials.

'Why did you switch sides? I thought you wanted revenge on humanity for what happened to you?'

Pandora shrugged. 'I'll punish those who hurt me, but not like this. I think there are some people I could like.'

'Then I do trust you,' Emma said.

Pandora grinned and reached into her jacket. 'This is untraceable,' she said, throwing the phone at Emma. 'Speak to your sister. Tell her a friend is going to return a scarf to her. Then I'll take the Doolittle to your mother.'

Emma was speechless, a great knot lifting from her chest. She didn't know what to say to Pandora and turned to Crowley instead.

'Do you still have it?' she asked him.

The darkest part of her mind imagined it had been damaged or lost on the reservoir. Crowley nodded to Bukowski, and the duck waddled over to Emma. He lifted his wing and revealed the glass phial taped there.

Emma laughed in relief. 'How long has that been there?'

'Since we were on the boat after your prison break,' Crowley answered.

Bukowski released it and gave it to Pandora. 'You were always my favourite,' she said as she took it from him.

Emma grinned. 'Lord, love a duck.'

'One more thing,' Pandora said before returning to the reservoir's edge. 'I don't need these anymore.'

She reached into her jacket, pulled out the packet of cigarettes, and threw them into the water rippling far below.

Emma and Pandora walked away, deep in conversation, with a cat thief, little dog and sober duck following behind them.

Chapter 69

Crowley

Crowley watched Emma walk away with Pandora, happy to see Emma's beaming smile. She still didn't trust the redheaded woman, but she'd helped them and saved the day.

Not just for us, but for humanity as well.

Plus, she'd deceived Darkstar. And anybody who did that would always be in his good books.

His body ached, and the dark cat's blood stained his claws. The grumbling sound bursting from his stomach was a reminder he hadn't eaten since the Atlas mansion.

Chirpy and Bukowski strode by his side away from the reservoir.

'What next for us?' Bukowski asked.

'I've got an idea of how to clear Emma's name with the police. Then we have to deal with Darkstar and the Bullfather.'

'Do you have a plan for that?' Chirpy said.

'I just might have,' Crowley answered. 'I just might have.'

Thank You!

Thank you, dear reader for purchasing this book.

Many thanks to my wonderful wife for all her support and patience.

Extra special thanks to Karina Gallagher for being a dedicated reader of my work.

Cover design by James, GoOnWrite.com

If you would like to join my mailing list and receive a free eBook then contact me at mail@andrewsfrench.com

Also by Andrew S. French

Science Fiction

The Time Traveller's Murder

The Mercy Sleep

Bodies

Another Girl, Another Planet

The Thief of Time Trilogy

The Queens of Heaven

The Queens of Time

The Queens of Space

The Arcane Supernatural Thriller Series

The Arcane

The Arcane Identity

The Arcane Quest

The Arcane Ultimatum

The Ella Finn Fantasy Series

Ella and the Elementals

Ella and the Multiverse

Ella and the Monsters

Ella and the Dreamers

Supernatural Short Stories

Dead Souls

Dead Souls II

The Shadow

Writing as A. S. French

Crime Fiction and Thrillers

The Astrid Snow series

Don't Fear the Reaper

The Killing Moon

Lost in America

Gone to Texas

The Final Girl

Snowstorm: An Astrid Snow Collection

The Ophelia Red series

Ophelia Red

The Detective Jen Flowers series

The Hashtag Killer

Serial Killer

Night Killer

The Killer Inside Them

The Frank Walker series

Where The Bodies Are Buried

Bodies of Evidence

The Teesside Crime series

No More Heroes

Crime Short Stories

Crime Stories: A Collection

Call Me: An Astrid Snow Short Story

Go to www.andrewsfrench.com for more information.

About the Author

Andrew French lives amongst faded seaside glamour on the North East coast of England. He likes gin and cats but not together, new music and old movies, curry and ice cream. Slow bike rides and long walks to the pub are his usual exercise, as well as flicking through the pages of good books and the memoirs of bad people.

Find out more at www.andrewsfrench.com

Facebook:

https://www.facebook.com/A-S-French-Author-150145625006018

Twitter:

www.twitter.com/andrewfrench100

Instagram:

www.instagram.com/andrewfrench100

And replies to all his email at asfrenchauthor@gmail.com

If you have the time, please leave a review at Amazon or Goodreads

Thank you!